BEST EUROPEAN FICTION 2010

EDITED AND WITH AN INTRODUCTION BY ALEKSANDAR HEMON

PREFACE BY ZADIE SMITH

BEST EUROPEAN FICTION 2010

DALKEY ARCHIVE PRESS

CHAMPAIGN AND LONDON

ISBN 978-1-56478-543-5

www.dalkeyarchive.com

Funded in part by grants from Arts Council England;
the Illinois Arts Council, a state agency; and with support
from the University of Illinois at Urbana-Champaign

Please see Acknowledgments on page 415 for additional
information on the support received for this volume

LOTTERY FUNDED

Designed and composed by Quemadura, printed
on permanent/durable acid-free, recycled paper,
and bound in the United States of America

Contents

Preface

Anthologies are ill-fitting things—one size does not fit all. It's no surprise to find the authors in this volume, collected under the broad banner "European," voicing a consistently ornery resistance (with variations): "Well, yes, I am European, Slovakian, actually, but I am also an individual, and what really matters to me is Nabokov, Diderot and J. G. Ballard."

Which is as it should be. Good writing cannot permit itself to be contained within checkpoints and borders. But still it's tempting for readers to seek a family resemblance and I'm not sure we're wrong to do so. It seems old fashioned to speak of a "Continental" or specifically "European" style, and yet if the title of this book were to be removed and switched with that of an anthology of the American short story, isn't it true that only a fool would be confused as to which was truly which?

It's more than the obvious matter of foreign names and places. It's hard not to notice, for example, a strong tendency towards the metafictional. Characters seem aware of their status as characters, stories complain about the direction they're heading in, and writers make literary characters of themselves—and of other writers and artists. When the real Christine Montalbetti (France) has breakfast with a notional Haruki Murakami in a Japanese hotel, the fantastic threatens to overwhelm them ("leaves were trembling behind the windowpanes, as if they were crouched, dying to pounce") and we know for sure we're not in Kansas anymore. Meanwhile Goce Smilevski of Macedonia wants us to believe Gustav Klimt's fourteen illegitimate sons were all called Gustav, and Jean-Philippe Toussaint—in one of my favourite pieces—boldly enters the soul of Zinedine Zidane to reveal the philosophical *Weltschmerz* hidden deep within that footballer-enigma.

What else? An epigraphic, disjointed structure. Many of these already short stories are cut into shorter, sub-titled sections, like verbal snapshots laid randomly on top of each other—and they end abruptly. They seem to come from a different family than those long anecdotes ending in epiphany, popularized by O. Henry. And their authors name different progenitors, too. Certainly no one mentions O. Henry. Or Hemingway. Laurels are offered instead to the likes of John Barth and Donald Barthelme. Meanwhile poor Dickens is dismissed in a single line by a young Icelandic experimentalist: "I weep with boredom over every single page he's written." More likely to be name-checked: Beckett, Bernhard, Sebald, Claude Simon and Kafka, who, "of course, is always there," as Josep M. Fonalleras (Catalonia) asserts, and he's right. Judging from this collection, Kafka is literary Europe's primary ghost and heaviest influence. He's there in Antonio Fian's (Austria) concretely expressed dream-stories, and in David Albahari's (Serbia) frustrating trip through Lyon, with its many obstructions and misdirections. And when this Kafkaesque respect for digression unites, in an author, with the headier brews of Laurence Sterne and Jorge Luis Borges, then we get baroque shaggy-dog tales like Julián Ríos's (Spain) "Revelation on the Boulevard of Crime," and Giedra Radvilavičiūtė's (Lithuania) "The Allure of the Text," both of which offer mazy structures in which readers may get blissfully lost.

Finally, in Europe the violent distortions of Dostoevsky seem to have trumped the cool ironies of Tolstoy. In this vein I particularly enjoyed Peter Terrin (Belgium), who revives the archetypal axe murderer in a banal and futuristic landscape, and Michał Witkowski's (Poland) "Didi," which brings notes from the underground of hungry hustlers. Of course, sometimes in Europe the reality outstrips all but the most garish literary fantasies and so a satirist in the Gogol-mode need only touch upon his subject very lightly. Thus the masterful Russian, Victor Pelevin, finds the perfect metaphor for the oligarch cash-grab of the 1990s, and the story seems to write itself.

For me this anthology and the series that is to follow represent a personal enrichment. Books-wise, I was educated in a largely Anglo-American library, and it is sometimes dull to stare at the same four walls all day. I was always refreshed to discover those windows that open out on to Kafka, Camus, Duras, Genet, Colette, Bely ... as I imagine some equivalent Russian schoolgirl marvelled at the vista through the Muriel Spark window, or the John Updike. There should be more of that sort of thing—so we're always saying—and now here are Aleksandar Hemon and Dalkey Archive Press to encourage it.

ZADIE SMITH

Introduction

Not so long ago, I read somewhere that only three to five percent of literary works published in the United States are translations. It stands to reason that a few of those translations are reworkings of the classics like Tolstoy and Mann. At the same time, many lesser-known foreign writers are published by struggling university presses with neither marketing budgets nor strong distribution networks. Thus the presence of translations in the American literary mainstream is uneasily divided between the couple of recent Nobel Prize winners, the odd successes that go down well in American book clubs, like Per Petterson's *Out Stealing Horses* or Muriel Barbery's *The Elegance of the Hedgehog*, and the confrontationally controversial European blockbusters, like Jonathan Littell's *The Kindly Ones* or Charlotte Roche's *Wetlands*, which tend to fail embarrassingly in the U.S. But if you are curious about the state of contemporary Polish literature or the lively writing scene in, say, Zurich, Switzerland or Lima, Peru, you'll be hard-pressed to find any stories or novels that would allow you to enter that particular field of knowledge. The American reader seems to be largely disengaged from literatures in other languages, which many see as yet another symptom of culturally catastrophic American isolationism. And all this before the deluge of recent recession, before the American publishing industry entered a full panic mode and started busying itself with deciding what not to publish.

Moreover, there appears to be a widespread consensus among the all-knowing publishing pundits that short fiction is, yet again, well on its way to oblivion, dying in the literary hospice room adjacent to the one in which the perpetually moribund novel is also expiring. Given that poetry is already dead and buried, soon the only things left for a committed, serious reader to read will be Facebook status updates, funny-text-message anthologies, and confessional memoirs. This time around, the short-story demise is due to the general vanishing of the printed word (good-bye newspapers, magazines, paper books!), the mass transference of readership to the Web, the volcanic rise of mindless entertainment as the main form of brain stimulation. Consequently, the reputation of the short story as a pinnacle of literary art, gloriously practiced by Chekhov, Joyce, O'Connor, Nabokov, Munro, has been steadily waning, to the point where many new writers have come to believe that writing short stories is merely a warm-up exercise for writing a novel. Thousands upon thousands of ambitious young writers enrolled in American writing programs are churning out half-dead short stories, creating suffocating hyperinflation, all in the hope that one day they'll be skillful enough to write a death-defying novel.

With all that in mind, we have decided to offer you a selection of short fiction from throughout Europe, some from writers working in English, but the majority translated from myriad languages. It includes a few select novel excerpts, but is primarily and unreservedly composed of short stories. Taking up a doubly lost cause could appear noble to some, but, frankly, we think that all that death and demise talk is nothing but a crock of crap.

For one thing, the short story is alive and well, thanks for asking. No further evidence ought to be necessary beyond the stories in this anthology, which is more interested in providing a detailed snapshot of the contemporary European literatures than establishing a fresh canon of instant classics. The short story, these nimble selections show, is marked by vitality and ingenuity that is not always easy to commit to in a novel, which is almost always an unwieldy undertaking. Working equally well in the hands of a witty experimenter (Finland's Juhani Brander) and an earnest storyteller (Wales's Penny Simpson), a scorching satirist (Ireland's Julian Gough), and a sharp realist (Latvia's Inga Ābele)—just to name a few—the short story is always capable of bridging the false gap between the avant-garde and the mainstream. The sheer diversity of narrative modes and strategies evidenced in the selections in this volume is mind-boggling. Rather than accepting the situation of perpetual death, the European short story, sparklingly capable of transformation, is eager to embark upon a new life.

This formal diversity is, naturally, directly related to the intellectual wealth, cultural richness, and historical conflict contained in a geographical space that is, by North American standards, fantastically, ridiculously small. European history is at the same time a history of fragmentation, caused by wars and political reconstitutions, and a history of transcending—by necessity—differences, borders, and distances. No country in Europe can be understood outside its historical relations with other European countries, no culture in Europe can be comprehended outside its interactions with other cultures. Europe is a fragmented space that always strives toward some form of integration. This has, I believe, always been the case, but the simultaneous processes of fragmentation, interaction, and integration have certainly been intensified with the formation of the European Union. In this context, European literatures have found themselves stretched between the reductive demands of national culture (the culture that is for us, by us, whoever we may be) and the transformative possibilities of transnational culture that can exist only in the situation of constant flow of identity and exchange of meaning—in the situation of ceaseless translation.

Hence the stories you will find in this volume (which have not been selected for any kind of thematic continuity) inescapably question and probe and sabotage various national myths, often featuring migrants and vagrants, unabashedly questioning the propriety of the old forms in the new set of historical and political circumstances. These stories not only cross and trespass all kinds of borders, they are, quite literally, generating translation in doing so.

At the heart of this project, which we hope to undertake annually, is a profound, non-negotiable need for communication with the world, wherever it may be. The same need is at the heart of the project of literature. That project is most obviously impossible without translation and if the communication is to be immediate and uninterrupted—which seems to be a self-evident need in today's world—the process of translation must be immediate and uninterrupted. We simply have to keep in continuous touch, translation has to be a ceaseless process. Not only do we have to provide a continuous flow of literary texts from other languages into English, we also have to be able to monitor in real time, as it were, the rapid developments in European literatures.

And there is no better gateway than the short story, which has retained, from the days when every decent newspaper or magazine printed short stories, the immediacy that comes with the daily engagement of the press with the world; the immediacy, I might add, that is currently flourishing on the Web. The short story still has the flavor of a report from the front lines of history and existence.

This anthology is, then, not putting up a fight in the battles that to many seem lost, it is indeed declaring a victory. As far as we are concerned, translation and the short story—essential means of communicating with and understanding this world of ours—have been restored to their rightful place. Now, start reading.

ALEKSANDAR HEMON

BEST EUROPEAN FICTION 2010

ORNELA VORPSI

FROM The Country Where
No One Ever Dies

*I would like to dedicate this book to the word "humility," which
does not exist in the Albanian lexicon. Its absence can give rise
to some rather curious phenomena in the destiny of a nation.*

1

THE ALBANIANS LIVE ON AND ON, AND NEVER DIE

Albania is a country where no one ever dies. Fortified by long hours at the
dinner table, irrigated by *raki* and disinfected by the hot peppers in our
plump, ever-present olives, our bodies are so strong that nothing can destroy them.

Our spines are made of iron. You can do whatever you want with them.
Even if one gets broken, it can be repaired. As for our hearts: they can be
saturated with fat, suffer necrosis, an infarct, thrombosis, or whatever, but
they'll still beat on heroically. We're in Albania—there can be no doubt
about it.

■

This country where no one ever dies is made of clay and dust. The sun scorches it until even the leaves on the grapevines look rusty, until our minds begin to melt. Living in this environment has one inevitable side effect: megalomania—a condition that sprouts everywhere, like a weed. Another consequence is fearlessness, although this might be caused by our people's flattened, malformed craniums—the seat of indifference—or a simple lack of conscience.

The word fear has no meaning here. Look an Albanian in the eye and you can tell right away that he's immortal. Death is something that has nothing to do with him.

Morning raises its head at five o'clock, in summer. At seven, the old people are already having their first coffee. The young sleep in until noon. God decreed that time in this country should be spent as agreeably as possible, like with a sip of strong espresso on the terrace of the café around the corner as you stare at the nice set of legs on a girl who'll never deign to look back.

The steaming coffee seeps slowly down your throat, warming your tongue, heart, and guts. Life, after all, isn't as bad as they say. You savor the bitter black liquid while the lady behind the bar, who's just had a fight with her husband, gives you a ferocious glare.

It's eleven thirty. Thank God you still have the whole day ahead of you, and lots of time to waste. There are all sorts of things you could do—thousands of them. Dusk is nowhere to be seen.

Suddenly, Xifo comes in, rubbing her chapped hands, going on and on for the umpteenth time about her ailing heart and liver, giving us the details as though they were part of some old fable that had nothing to do with her—something very important, but far away. Everything here seems exaggerated and distorted. And then, in a low, conspiratorial voice, she adds:

"Have you heard the news? Our neighbor, you know, Suzi's father, died in the shower last night. He came home from work, had dinner, took a shower, and kicked the bucket."

"You're kidding! He was so young, poor guy!"

"Well, what can you do? Life is full of surprises."

As you can see, it's only *other people* who die.

That's the way life goes in a country where everything is eternal (with the exception of whatever might happen to *other people*). But there are things even dearer to Albanians than death. It's no exaggeration to say that one of these things in particular is the quintessence of their existence.

I'm referring to fornication.

They take endless delight in the subject. Their hearts burn with it (though, really, Albanian hearts can ignite over just about anything). Everyone is completely absorbed, young and old, educated and illiterate, to the point where they can't even see straight.

Thus, certain maxims have arisen, quite naturally, in our nation's thought. They grow like leaves on a tree. These maxims derive from one universally held supposition: a good-looking girl is a whore, an ugly one—poor thing—is not.

In this country, a girl has to pay particular attention to her "immaculate flower." A man can wash with a bar of soap and be clean, but a girl can never be pure again, no matter how much water she uses—not even a whole ocean's worth.

Whenever a husband is away on business, or in prison, people tell his wife that it would be a good idea for her to sew up her slit, to convince him, when he gets back, that she's been waiting for him and only him—that his absence has shrunk the crack between her thighs—because she missed him so much (men have a highly developed sense of private property in this country).

Whenever a pretty girl passes by, muffled sighs rise from the terrace where the men are sitting around and enjoying the day, sighs that are steamier than their coffee:

"Look who it is!"

"She's not worth it! You know how many times she's had herself stitched and unstitched?"

But still they go on, wistfully:

"Oh, Ingrid, my Ingrid! Who was it that snapped the stitches between your sweet, hot thighs last night? Come on over here, my beauty. When we're finished with you, we promise we'll pay to have you stitched back up again . . ."

They stare so hard as you pass by, it's as though you're becoming transparent. As soon as you're penetrated by one of their stares, it transfixes you forever.

At home, it's the same story. "Don't worry about it," my aunt tells me, "we can always take you to the doctor to find out if you're a virgin or not."

She spits these words out from between clenched teeth, her menacing glare cutting into me, and though I'm only thirteen and haven't even seen whatever it is that men keep in their pants (a secret that I know has something to do with the fornication), I already have the feeling that I'm a perfect whore. My aunt's staring makes me blush.

Stiff with fear, I crawl into bed, thinking: "What if they *do* send me to the doctor and he finds out that I wasn't born a virgin? Like those children born blind, or deaf, or without hands, or—worse still—without an innate devotion to the Party?"

Sleep finally overwhelms me as I beg my aunt in the silence of my room to accept the tragic fate that's struck our family: "I swear, Auntie, I swear I haven't done anything wrong! It's the way I was born! Believe me! I swear it!"

In this country where no one ever dies, my aunt is no exception. She doesn't die either.

■

I used to have a recurrent dream (which I've never told anyone about). Before I fell asleep, with my eyes half open, I'd have a vision of her funeral.

I saw myself with a black scarf (a nice lace shawl would have suited me better) draped around my neck just like Madame Bovary or Anna Karenina would've worn it. Of course, I was pale and cried a lot because I really did love her, but my desire to escape her terrible temper—which was always directed at me—was simply too great not to wish her dead.

Since I'd grown up without a father and apparently wasn't bad looking, it wasn't long before I was confronted with the aforementioned subject of fornication.

"You're going to turn into a big whore, someday. Oh yes." My aunt's voice and my cousin's would always tremble when they said this, as if to tell me there was no point denying it: "Come on, we know all about you." They would shake their heads. "There's nothing we can do about it. We didn't choose to take you in. You just landed in our laps. And soon we'll have to swallow all the shame you bring home—just swallow it, like bread. What else can we do? One day, you're going to come home with a big, swollen belly."

My aunt and my cousin both made agonized faces, as though they were being forced to chew their shame sandwiches that very moment, while my grandfather silently rolled himself a cigarette.

The thought of my swollen belly was terrifying. Do you know Bosch's paintings? The anguish and madness on the faces, and the bodies of the fallen pressed together like souls in hell? Yes, I could see it clearly: a brownish and dark-red landscape brimming with scraps of organic refuse, with me as its container—all inside me. You can't hide a swollen belly, and you can't crawl out of your own skin. You're *marked*. A swollen belly means that you've been screwing around in the bushes (I'd learned from my aunt and cousin that fornication took place in the bushes—bushes were apparently the ideal venue for these unspecified activities). It means that you've been letting the worms of shame get fat off you—nourishing an embryo that will disfigure your body and make it obvious to everyone that you've been screwing around.

Even today, I have trouble keeping it out of my head—that a pregnant woman is someone who's been screwing around in the bushes.

What they wanted more than anything was a good tragedy. My whole wonderful country thirsted for them! It created tragedies out of nothing, just like God created us from a handful of dust.

Whenever I was sick, everyone would make a fuss over me. They would come into my room and whisper "my dear," and when they went back out, murmur "poor thing."

They would prepare delicious foods for me without ever considering the possibility that the illness might have robbed me of my appetite. I stared longingly at the pots of jam they'd left on the night table beside my bed. I exchanged loving glances with the meatballs, but the sight of these delicacies made me nauseous, and I had to look away.

Whenever I was sick, my mother, my grandmother, and my aunt suddenly turned into the most affectionate people on God's earth, and I was convinced that, with them at my side, and given their foresight concerning my future fornication, I would be able to be strong, I would never make them ashamed of me.

I had a great time whenever I was sick. I didn't get yelled at, didn't have to bake potatoes after school, and I could sleep in as long as I wanted. I didn't have to husk rice, grain by grain. There was no wood to be chopped and, for some reason, I was no longer a whore . . . until the day of my recovery—that unlucky day when I finally had to get out of bed, when the insults and imprecations would resume. I was a whore again, and the pots of jam vanished, finding their way to the bedsides of other sick children. You only get jam if you have one foot in the grave. Otherwise, forget it!

In our beloved country, where no one ever dies, where bodies are as heavy as lead, we have an old adage, a rather profound and popular saying: "Live that I may hate you, and die that I may mourn you."

This proverb is our country's lifeblood. When you die, no one says another bad word about you. I'd even go so far as to say that no one *thinks* badly of you. There's a real respect, here, for the institution of death.

(It's no mean feat to gain an Albanian's respect: it only rallies when you're on your deathbed—and when you breathe your last, you've finally won it.)

All of a sudden, after death, men become imbued with the noblest of qualities, and women become exceptionally virtuous. Everyone cries for them, lamenting the loss of such wonderful human beings. All anger evaporates.

And then sometimes I'd hear my aunt use another old saying that was popular in our country—her voice trembling like a sibyl's: "Your people (meaning blood relatives) may gobble up your flesh, but at least they'll save the bones."

My country has a way of stumbling over this kind of sublime truth.

And, indeed, my aunt's voice was thick with a sublime beauty.

"But Auntie," I said to her once, "if they gobble up my flesh, they might as well throw away the bones too, no? What good will they be?"

She threw me one of her withering glares, turning me to ash where I stood. It was her way of reminding me that I didn't share the distinguished pedigree of my mother's family—no, I'd been an unfortunate accident: I resembled *him*. Her stare was a rebuke: "Shut thy mouth, oh daughter of *that* man."

I shut my mouth and could hardly wait to get sick again.

2

When I was six or seven years old, I snuggled up close to my mother one night specifically because I'd discovered, to my horror, that she—the center of my universe—was powerless.

It began with an innocuous case of the flu, like children often get. I had to stay in bed and was leafing through some books. My cousin, who was two years older than me, had lent me a book on the anatomy of the human body. I was fascinated by it, with all the color illustrations of muscles, internal organs, bones, and long, bluish veins.

So this is what we were made of! There were all sorts of curious and colorful things inside us that weren't even under the control of our, or rather my, will.

Flesh and bones, you understand?

How was it possible, dear God? How could it be? And though I couldn't imagine any other way for it to be, did all those body parts really have to be so unreliable? Was there even a God around whom I could have petitioned in this regard? My mother, poor woman, could do nothing for me. She too was only made of flesh and bones.

I despaired at this thought as I nuzzled up against her and smelled the odors I knew so well. The idea that my mother, whom I loved and feared, could be so vulnerable, that all of us with flesh and bones were vulnerable, was profoundly unnerving.

"I'm scared," I said again and again. "I'm scared, Mommy, to be made of flesh and bones."

She put her arms around me, not understanding a word, and stroked my hair as mothers convinced they can successfully console their children always do. She kissed me and whispered tender words into my ear as we sat in the damp basement kitchen, covered in white tiles, where we lived.

■

On one of these tiles, next to our sofa, there was a blood-red stain the size of a pomegranate seed. It refused to be washed or rubbed away, try as I might to get rid of it. Every day, when I was cleaning, this little red stain insisted that I spend more time with it. It gave me the impression of being sad. Whenever I took a cloth to it, I would stroke it gently.

There was something painful about it. I was convinced that it was a bloodstain. I was convinced it was from her. It must have dripped onto the floor when Daddy beat her. He had thrown her down and whipped her with something. I could see it so clearly . . . and that was how the little stain was born.

It was a stubborn little bloodstain. It wouldn't budge.

I plucked up my courage one day and asked her, "Mommy, what's that red seed over there? Isn't it funny that there's a blood-red seed in the middle of a white tile?"

I looked into her face, stared into her big green eyes, watching her expression, trying to see whether she was finally going to tell me the truth: that *the bloodstain was hers*. But she only replied, "It's probably a production error, a little drop of red paint, that's all."

My mother was beautiful. She would spend hours taking care of herself, combing her hair back and outlining her lips with a black eyeliner pencil. She'd put on a tight-fitting dress and throw the colorful handbag that she'd sewn herself over her shoulder and then, after checking the mirror a few times, head out into the night, though not before telling me: "Be good, and don't leave the house. I'm going to visit Grandmother."

She went to visit Grandmother every evening, the eager eyes of our men and the jealous glances of our women following her every step down the road. I could see the envy in their eyes. There was something bitter in them, corrosive like an acid eating through their veins and intestines. One small dose would have been enough to destroy a castle, a whole town. They would have torn the flesh off her bones and eaten her alive or thrown her to the dogs, if they could have.

"Be careful, Mommy."

The real reason for her visits to Grandma was that she wanted to be seen and desired. The men would whisper: "How beautiful you are, Diella! I could almost eat you up, skin and bones and all. God, look at those legs of yours, Diella. They're perfection itself, like a bottle of champagne."

(We should note, at this juncture, that there's never been any champagne in this country. You can't imagine the terrible thirst this untasted beverage—which everyone said was so wonderful—provoked. It was nothing more than a dream, and it made them sick.)

So, Diella's legs were like champagne.

Or maybe they meant, like the champagne bottles.

She strolled down the boulevard, head held high, enjoying the compliments being whispered to her but pretending all the while to ignore them. She was still young, twenty-eight. The years passed with visits to Grandmother.

Her wedding photos sat abandoned on a shelf in the closet.

One of these pictures in particular used to fascinate me. It continued to attract my attention even after I'd studied every inch of it—the interplay of light and shade, the way the veil my mother wore was draped around her hair, the palpable excitement of the big day, which seemed to have made her lose her composure.

It's the custom in our country for a bride to cry a little at her wedding, to show how distraught she is at leaving her mother and father. This is the way we get married—screaming, as we did at birth.

Over time, a brown stain began to appear on the photo, covering my mother's face from her right eye to her temple, and, eventually, the rest of her as well. This was from the damp in the closet. It upset me, because it made Mother look sick and depressed. Every time I thought about it, I'd burst into tears, imagining the day her hair would go gray.

I rescued the photograph from the closet, hoping that the stain would go away if I took care of the picture and put it somewhere safe—in a nice photo album, for instance.

But the stain didn't go away. And one day, we moved.

I lost the photograph. It vanished at some point in my topsy-turvy life. But I still carry the stain. The stain infected me. I can still see it covering my mother's right eye and temple. She doesn't bother to hide her unhappiness, now. And the red seed is within me, and the visits to my grandmother's house have stopped.

TRANSLATED FROM GERMAN AND ITALIAN BY
ROBERT ELSIE AND JANICE MATHIE-HECK

ANTONIO FIAN

from While Sleeping

DOLPHIN

A cousin of mine had an aquarium built on her terrace, a rather imposing tank where strange, exotic sea creatures amused themselves in the company of all sorts of local specimen, destined to be eaten. She invited hundreds of guests to its grand unveiling, including E., the children, and myself. Everyone stood around the tank and stared at its colorful chaos. More than anything else, it was the young dolphin the crowd found most entertaining—its boldness and playfulness. Our view was constantly being interrupted, however, by cooks who politely but firmly asked us to make room for them. They stepped up to the edge of the tank, dipped into the water with nets, killed our meals-to-be with a little specialty hammer, one blow to each head, then disappeared again into their kitchen. Little by little, the guests too began to leave the terrace, filing into the dining room where various delicacies—consisting primarily of the newly killed, freshly prepared aquarium fish—were being offered. E. and I followed the others, and in the end only our children, both still in kindergarten—grade school at the most—were still out there by the tank. At once present and not present, observing, without the power to interfere, I was able to follow their conversation. They had been impressed by the cooks killing the fish. Our daughter suggested they try it themselves, and her brother, while skeptical, did nothing to hold her back. Since there was no net at hand, they decided to drop something heavy over the edge of the tank onto the head of one of the fish. They took a large amethyst out of the display case in which my cousin displayed her fine china and other valuables. The children approached the edge of the tank, managed to attract the most playful of the sea creatures, the dolphin, and let the stone fall on its head—killing it instantly. Upset—though more confused—by the effect of their actions, the children stared for some time at the floating dolphin corpse. Then our daughter began to cry, and her brother said accusingly: "You killed the pretty fish!"—a statement for which I, present again and taking part in the scene, shouted at him: "A dolphin is not a fish! A dolphin is a mammal." That upset him all the more: "A mammal!" he yelled and ran to the dining room. "My sister killed a mammal!" Everyone abandoned their half-eaten fish and thronged onto the terrace. Extreme agitation followed—shouts, screams, loud crying, "The dolphin! That sweet dolphin!" I moved to the edge of the tank to stand by the children and to protect our daughter from the anger of the hysterical guests, but now when I looked at the surface of the water I saw with horror that it wasn't the corpse of a dolphin there but of a girl, a girl about our daughter's age, exceptionally pretty, her long dark hair floating in the water, encircling her pale, dead face like a halo. No one else seemed to notice this girl, however. People were only talking about the dolphin, and, truth be told, when I looked again, I saw the dead dolphin after all—the child's corpse had disappeared. I must have been hallucinating. Meanwhile, the children cried and cried. Our son too: he felt responsible for the dolphin's death because he hadn't stopped his sister. E. was with me again now, and we were trying to pull our kids away from the enraged mob when my cousin appeared out of nowhere, clapped her hands, and everything calmed down. She said with a smile that we didn't have to look at it as such a tragedy, and anyway, we shouldn't be so hard on a couple of children who after all were still small and weren't conscious of the severity of their actions. Certainly it was a shame about the dolphin. After all, he'd been so cute and playful. But in a few weeks he would've grown too big for the tank anyway, and would've had to be killed. So, everything was only half as bad as it seemed. Besides, her guests shouldn't worry about being deprived of so unusual a sight next time they visited, my cousin continued. She would go to the exotic pet store first thing the next morning to order another fish. "Mammal!" I called, "the dolphin isn't a fish. It's a mammal!" My cousin gave a friendly nod, "Mammal, that's right."

BOXES

In the prison camp, where I was interred along with many others, including some acquaintances of mine, every prisoner received a piece of cardboard cut in such a way that it could very easily be folded and put together to make a box. Once this was done, according to our warden, we were to label our boxes with our names and keep them with us at all times. We'd just begun putting them together when word came that these boxes were actually urns in which, after we'd been killed and cremated, the ashes of each prisoner would be stored. Putting our boxes together was nothing less than digging our own graves. Chaos then. Most of us believed the rumor and asked to be excused from our work. Others, myself among them, feared the punishment that would surely follow such a demurral. In order to avoid this punishment, I attempted to bring as many members of the opposition to our side as possible. I convinced them that the boxes weren't themselves a danger but rather a concession of the administration to our own needs—the boxes were only containers meant to store the smaller objects we'd brought into the prison with us, so that they wouldn't get lost. Really, the boxes might even save our lives at some point, since, if the administrators really wanted to kill us, and the method had something to do with drowning, for example, the boxes could serve as life preservers, keeping us afloat.

TOKYO

Images of Tokyo on the TV news, a panorama at first, then the people in the streets. Although no snow could be seen on the houses, the people had cross-country skis strapped on and moved ahead side by side in unending, disciplined columns. Then the clip ended and the anchorman appeared on the screen and said that we'd have to get used to such images in the future. The garbage accumulating every day in Tokyo would from now on be compacted into a substance similar to snow and spread on certain streets, a different one every day. Trails would be laid out so that residents could practice cross-country skiing the whole year round. My father, watching TV with me, was disgusted by these developments, but I found them perfectly acceptable.

Not long after, I was in Tokyo myself. In a café in Ginza there was an exhibition taking place that attracted such an enormous crowd, I became curious too. The reason for the crowd was that the café was displaying the very latest in fashionable hair-clasps, which, despite their enormous price, drew so many young Japanese girls that the event gradually turned into an ongoing auction. The clasps were prisms about fifteen centimeters long with triangular bases and rectangular sides, each created from five to ten smaller prisms of the same design, consisting of an artificial resin into which a measure of dog shit had been mixed. Thus, color-wise, shades of brown predominated, some almost black; but then, in an especially expensive piece, which the auctioneer—who also happened to be the designer—

clearly considered a masterpiece, one of these prisms glowed brick red in the middle of the brown, and I immediately remembered some dog shit of exactly this color that I'd seen on the sidewalk in front of our house a few days earlier. I'd had to look away in order not to throw up. I began to imagine how awful and demeaning the construction of such a hair-clasp must have been, but I was quickly forced to the side by a swarm of young girls waving money and looking ready to fight each other for such an unusual piece.

BARBIE

I was looking for a present for our seven-year-old daughter in the toy store when I happened to notice a Barbie playset called *Barbie Kneels Naked in Front of Her Altar and Reads from the Bible*. I took it off the shelf in order to get a closer look (Barbie was kneeling naked in front of her altar, reading the Bible). A salesperson appeared behind me and congratulated me on my selection. He thought it a particularly lovely item, and said it would certainly be a collector's item someday. Still, he wanted to make it clear to me that I shouldn't give the set to my child. It was meant for people eighteen and older. I put the set back in its place and said it seemed absurd to me that there should be toys in a toy store not meant for minors. The salesperson said that that's just the way it was. After all, he didn't make the rules.

TRANSLATION RIGHTS

I'd already been writing to the publisher of the American musician Loudon Wainwright III for a long time now, asking for permission to translate some of his lyrics into the Viennese dialect, and had already nearly given up hope of receiving a response, when Wainwright called me up personally and explained that he intended to combine business and pleasure and spend a few days' vacation in Vienna. We could talk about everything then. He suggested I pick him up at the airport, so I took a rental car to our appointment, which—because I don't have my own license—I had my seventeen-year-old daughter drive (though it was strange for this to be allowed, considering the driving age in Vienna is eighteen). She drove slowly and carefully so that, undisturbed, I could prepare some friendly greetings in English, with which I hoped to win Wainwright over. This turned out to be superfluous, however. He spoke fluent German, and right after we'd shaken hands he told me he still didn't know where he'd be staying in town. Apparently he'd flown to Vienna on a whim and wanted to know if I could recommend a hotel, so I recommended the Hotel Praterstern on Mayer Street, as I'd done for many friends in similar situations in the past. Wainwright thought this sounded good; I leaned forward to my daughter and said, "To Mayer Street, you know, where Turrini stayed." She nodded and took a wrong turn a moment later as though following my directions, taking us further into the third district, farther away from the city instead of toward it. No matter how much I tried to direct her and get her back onto the right route, she always did the opposite of what I asked. The day continued, and we continued to get farther and farther from Mayer Street and the Hotel Praterstern. We were already in Simmering and nearing the edge of the city. I apologized to Wainwright, telling him my daughter was actually a first-rate driver, but she didn't really have her license yet, and was still learning how to navigate. I tried to joke with him: "*Women!*— am I right? Of course, no one knows that better than you! But it's not so bad. We just have to turn left at the next intersection, and then . . . left!" I yelled, but my daughter would let nothing deter her and turned right. We passed a sign that indicated we'd left Vienna. My desperation grew. I stammered more excuses, but Wainwright smiled at everything, calmly saying that it was no problem, really, that he had plenty of time—but I knew that he didn't. His politeness was fake. The translation rights were lost.

EXECUTION 1

Nazis ruled the land, but not historical Nazis, operatic Nazis, in colorful uniforms, dripping with medals. Still—they were dangerous. My mother and I were sentenced to death by crucifixion without even being given a reason and were led immediately by a former school friend who'd joined up with these Nazis and whose duty it was to guard us to the place of execution in Prater Park at the foot of Constantine Hill, not far from the children's choo-choo. While I discussed the possibility of a pardon with our guard, who—if you ignored his inclination to obey orders without question—was very nice, proper, even friendly in dealing with us, my mother was being killed, nailed like Christ to a cross. Meanwhile, the head executioner was getting the ropes ready to tie me to my cross—I'd only just noticed him, and was suddenly convinced that he was the man responsible for our being denounced. But this wasn't really the time to think about assigning blame. I wanted to save myself at least, so I shoved our guard to the side with the strength of someone who has nothing left to lose, running as fast as I could down the park's main path leading away from the city . . . but as is usually the case in such situations, I didn't come out ahead. My school friend and the other Nazis who had taken up the pursuit didn't even make the effort to run after me—they simply walked at a leisurely pace, smoking, carrying on pleasant conversations, even doubling over with laughter on occasion, all without losing ground.

EXECUTION 2

Again I was condemned to death, this time by the noose, and not *with* my mother but *by* her. True, the death penalty had been abolished, de jure, but just as one can still find traveling knife-grinders, we also had traveling hangmen who were tolerated by the authorities and went door to door taking on execution contracts and carrying them out for a moderate fee.

One came to S— once a year and set up his gallows in front of the train station. I'd known about my mother's condemning me for a long time now, but I'd never taken her threats seriously, reacting cynically and arrogantly whenever it was brought up. Now that it was clear to me she'd been serious, a great terror came over me. I searched my conscience, trying to figure out what wrong I could have done, but I couldn't think of a single thing— except perhaps one tiny, entirely meaningless act, not even an act, really, but an omission with regard to my mother, which I guess she'd never managed to forgive me for. I screamed, I begged. It wasn't like her to be so inhuman, but she didn't react, so my father—who admittedly had no say in the matter—tried to comfort me, and likewise tried by way of alluding to the much greater suffering that would befall my mother and indeed the entire family thanks to this unfortunate but nonetheless necessary event, tried to lead me to a serene and dignified acceptance of the inevitable. What was my death, really, compared to the suffering of those who had to condemn me, he asked. And even this suffering was nothing compared to the suffering of other townspeople, for instance the family of my old principal. He'd had to condemn all three of his children. All three must be lying in front of the train station already hanged. Their parents would now have to collect all three and bury them—what agony!

My struggling was useless; I was put in a car with my mother at the wheel. My father sat in the passenger seat. We took the short way to the train station. There was no way out. Nevertheless, I talked to them both, trying to show them how trivial my offense was—and it was—pointing out that no law or punishment existed for what I'd done, or, better, what I hadn't done, but neither reacted. So, as a last attempt, I screamed at the two: "If you really do this, if you really allow my execution, then you're both murderers, murderers!" Then my mother slowly turned toward me, without braking the car or deviating from our route, looking at me seriously, wordlessly, but with an expression on her face that seemed to say: "That is the most useless, the most laughable of all arguments, and you ought to know this better than anyone."

LOVER

I slept with a young, petite, black-haired woman I'd just met for the first time, but who I knew was friends with E., my wife, and I didn't really do a good job of it. It was awkward for me, doubly awkward: after all, what's the point of cheating on your wife in order to fail as a lover? Covering up my embarrassment, I apologized to my partner. I said I'd probably had too much to drink, had a bad day, etc. I asked only, trying to joke with her, that she not feel too bad on my account the next time she talked to E. To which she replied very seriously that this wouldn't be necessary. E. knew everything. She was E. Confused, I looked at her closely. No, she was lying. She wasn't E. She didn't bear the least resemblance to my wife. I told her that and she laughed and said it all made sense now. I really didn't know anything at all about women. Of course she wasn't E., but she, like every woman, was not only herself but simultaneously every other woman, and thus E. as well. "So, all the women in the world know about us?" I asked. And she nodded, as though at something entirely self-evident.

TRANSLATED FROM GERMAN BY DUSTIN LOVETT

PETER TERRIN

FROM *"The Murderer"*

WITH THANKS TO ALEXANDER VERBRUGGHE
FOR HIS SPECIAL "MEASURE"

Ferdinand found himself back in his neighbor's house. He held tight to his axe, a tool he'd used to chop kindling years and years ago. Of course, it had been ages since he'd last seen the thing. It had probably been stuck in the cellar sixteen years back when they'd still lived near the city. But now it rested naturally in his fist and even felt like an extension of his arm. This had allowed him to split his neighbor's head quite efficiently.

The young man, poorly dressed as always, lay at his feet. Blood still flowed from the wound that had parted the man's greasy hair. Ferdinand, brow wrinkled in disgust, stepped back when the dark liquid began to creep too near his leather shoes. The music was still pumping through the computer's speakers. Ferdinand walked to the corner of the living room and used the axe to hack the small machine to bits. The sudden absence of noise buzzed in his ears. He remembered how easy it had been to murder his neighbor. The only physical effort required had been prying the axe, which was still razor-sharp, out of the dead man's skull afterward. You always imagine things will be harder than they actually are, he thought. It's no different from slicing into a roast, as long as you use the right tool.

He tugged on the blinds and daylight flooded the lived-in room. Ferdinand glanced through the slats at the street. Could it be that no one else had noticed the sudden cessation of pounding noise? Now and then he'd heard someone besides himself yelling at the shit who used to live here. The police had bigger fish to fry, however, since the government had instituted the New Measures; little things like noise complaints didn't really concern them anymore. But none of the other neighbors were on the street, confused in the new silence. No one and nothing was showing any sign of relief that the music had finally stopped.

Ferdinand adjusted the blinds again so that the room was hidden from prying eyes, though not from the light. Everything in this house was a mess, and the new silence was like a fresh wind blowing through it. The young man who lived there had claimed to be an artist, the romantic type, Ferdinand remembered. The sort of person who'll never ever produce anything of value, who wallows in laziness and vanity, who thinks he's been chosen for important things and spends his life waiting for some divine stroke of inspiration. In the meantime, though, this particular artist had played his music at a deafening volume, the music of his idols—all of whom had died young, all of whom had probably had more raw vitality in their little fingers than this so-called artist ever dreamed of. Even a beautiful summer evening like this one couldn't change the facts. Ferdinand's neighbor had lacked the will to kill himself, and likewise the talent to make his own death even the least bit interesting.

In the beginning, Ferdinand had asked him politely to turn the volume down. The neighbor had simply looked down his nose and closed his door without a word. He didn't turn the volume down. Over the course of a few months, Ferdinand formed a clear resolution concerning the young man. He'd heard the house tremble as the artist descended his stairs to open the front door. The smell of old carpet had hit Ferdinand full in the face.

The house had been a gift from the artist's father, an entrepreneur who sold cheap plastics. Along with the house, the young man also received a monthly allowance enabling him to pursue his sublime insights from within an oasis of financial security. Thank God the artist always slept late. But as soon as he tumbled down those stairs in the early afternoon, the bass started up, along with those nonsensical lyrics—and the drums. For the rest of the day, through the evening and a good part of the night, the noise penetrated every corner of Ferdinand's house. He sat on his sofa and contemplated the walls centimeter by centimeter—the walls that were the boundaries of his home, walls that had been stolen from him by the arrogance of the nonentity next door. When Ferdinand opened his refrigerator, everything there—from the butter to the milk—seemed to have been curdled by the noise. He could never be alone in the bathroom. He could hardly bear the thought of his neighbor's repulsive appearance. Of course, thanks to his disinterest in personal hygiene, the artist usually had a terrible cough—but though Ferdinand listened hopefully to his every spasm, these attacks had never, sadly, proven fatal.

Now, however, at long last, the parasite was lying dead on the ground. No doubt about it. The blade had sliced deep into his skull. It hadn't taken much effort. Almost as though gravity alone would have done the job. No strength required. What an ally, thought Ferdinand, who had devoted his life to the natural sciences. The other neighbors were still staying out of sight, even though they'd all had to put up with the same provocation all these months. Perhaps they'd been watching as Ferdinand shouted at his neighbor from the latter's doorstep and—a miracle—had actually been heard. The artist had come down and opened his door, but still couldn't understand Ferdinand through all the noise, and so turned his back to head for his computer. Ferdinand followed him and, with stunning simplicity, put an end to the misery of the past few months.

This ongoing stretch of silence in the middle of the day astonished Ferdinand. He quickly shut the front door, which had been standing half open. It felt as though Ferdinand had been hiding here for an indeterminate length of time, waiting for something, something as yet unknown, but which he'd be sure to recognize whenever it occurred. The artist hadn't fallen on his face, as might be expected, but had stumbled backwards due to the awkward reactions of his nervous system. He lay there the way all dead people do, a position that can't be imitated by the living. The daily press was filled with photos, a whole illustrated inventory, of the victims of the New Measures: long columns of passport-like photos documenting the dead. Looking at those people, even when their faces were still intact, you could tell immediately that they were dead, just from the pictures. Death can't be imitated.

The floor plan of the artist's house was just like Ferdinand's. This model, however, showed obvious signs of neglect. The old-fashioned couch, covered with green velour, retained the unmistakable impression of its owner, and was littered with crumbs. On the mantel above the fireplace, Ferdinand saw a loose collection of figurines from the Far East. He imagined that long before the establishment of the Commonwealth some tourist must have bought them from some kid in front of a temple. Via the usual unfathomable routes, the objects had landed in this house. Unfathomable since the neighbor never went out and never had visitors. Ferdinand speculated that the fact that no one had ever wanted to hang out with the artist was probably the only reason he hadn't been killed sooner. The murderer is usually someone you know.

Ferdinand crept deeper into the grim house, instinctively crouching down. In the kitchen, the disorder was less obvious, though everything was dirty. The windowsill was covered in dead flies, as if someone had shaken them out of a sifter. Piles of trash littered the yard; when the trash was in garbage bags, these weren't tied up. Ferdinand hadn't pictured the house quite this way. But his conclusions remained the same.

Back in the living room, he parted the blinds with two fingers and peered out. A spotted cat, seemingly lost in thought, was crossing the street. The other neighbors were still out of sight. Perhaps they've all got bigger problems, Ferdinand thought. Perhaps they've put up with more than I have, and so take a wider view. Perhaps they just didn't consider the young man worth it. They probably wanted to save the two murders allotted them by the New Measures for better targets. They're probably afraid to waste their opportunities on little nuisances. But I'm old, thought Ferdinand. I don't have to save my murders for anyone else. My neighbor was the most important person in my life.

The dark, gleaming puddle around the artist's ruptured skull was no longer spreading. In fact, it now seemed to Ferdinand that the corpse was just another part of the décor, and that the real owner of the house was probably used to stepping over it on a daily basis. Ferdinand took a couple of careful steps across the living room and peered up the staircase. The next floor, lit in a particular way, stirred a faint memory in him, and Ferdinand suddenly had the feeling he'd been there before. He saw a young woman lying naked on a bare mattress, her dark pubic hair curling up toward her belly, her chest flat, her dull white tongue sticking far out of her mouth. Both legs of the panty hose around her neck were lying to the left, as if a fashion photographer had draped them just so. I didn't kill her, Ferdinand thought anxiously. I'm imagining things. It's impossible that I killed her, I have no idea who she is. I've only ever murdered my wife. I gave her poison. Because she was clumsy. And because she'd asked me to.

Nevertheless, since the New Measures were instituted, Ferdinand had been fantasizing about killing just about everyone he met. Before the New Measures, he thought, you'd see someone and wonder how they'd be in bed. Now you wondered what it would be like to kill them. And Ferdinand was haunted by these visions. He didn't know which were true. The only thing he knew with certainty was that no one else had gotten to him yet. "I'm seventy-three," he said aloud, as proof.

His words disturbed a balance. Now Ferdinand remembered that he'd only just entered the house, and specifically to kill his neighbor. He stood motionless in his leather shoes, caught, captive. The front door, his means of escape, was less than three meters away. It was unreachable. He couldn't move, not until the echo of his words died away. Again he saw the image of the girl. Her face was frozen in panic. I don't know her, he said to himself. I've never seen her before.

The axe began to weigh down his arm. He was racking his brain trying to assure himself that he'd never killed anyone aside from his wife. He also wondered what he should do with his axe. The New Measures required that you report your murder and hand in the weapon. After that, the state police made sure that the person who reported the murder was really the one who'd committed it. Shortly after the proclamation of the New Measures, there had been many cases of people offering to sell their allotment of murders to career criminals or to people for whom two murders just weren't enough. After it was proven without a doubt that you had committed your murder and that no robbery had occurred, they let you go. This was also the procedure with all sorts of other crimes. No one was punished right away.

The State hadn't wanted to impose limits on the number of children a couple could have. This seemed a terribly cruel means of population control. The official line was, if you do your fellow men no harm, no harm shall be done to you.

I have to hide the axe, Ferdinand thought. I have to put it back in my cellar, where no one's thought to look for sixteen years. I can't take any risks. I have to be on the alert. If you turn someone in who's overstepped the New Measures, you don't have to worry about that person anymore. He's eliminated. It happens several times a day. Naturalized murder. Ferdinand made his way to the door gingerly, distributing his weight as though walking on thin ice. He hid the axe under his clothes. He still couldn't see any neighbors outside. But through their glass doors or from behind their shrubs, he was certain that they were watching, that they were curious about the sudden silence. After he closed the neighbor's front door, he felt empty. All in all, it was a farewell: the end of an era.

He didn't know what the future held; he'd only planned as far as killing his neighbor. I'm too old for the unknown, he told himself. He made his way to his own house, dejected. But I'm still alive, he repeated. I'm seventy-three.

Ferdinand closed the door to his cellar. Back in his living room, he sank into the chair where he sat each day to read old books—books from before. Those were the only books he had. Now, however, he just watched the light cluster into patterns on the wall. Despite the silence, he felt no peace. He laid his arms on the armrests, head on the headrest, but he could still hear his heart beat, keeping him from relaxing. I can't stay here. I have to get away. He stood up, went to the kitchen, and opened the refrigerator. He bit into a tomato, tasted something strange, and spit the cold mess into the garbage can. He used his hand to wipe his mouth. Then he went into the bathroom. Standing on a stool, he removed the picture of his wife that had always hung on the wall. He looked her in the eye for a moment. Then he removed the photo from its frame, folded it, and stuck it in his pocket.

The street was about a hundred meters long. All sorts of people occupied the houses on both sides. They'd painted the trim around their windows, marking the small rosettes impressed into the plaster with bright colors. They heard me yell and saw the neighbor come out, he thought. How long before someone calls the police? As far as I know, I've never made anyone around here angry. Nevertheless, someone will make the call sooner or later. They'd rather see me dead than alive. They don't know what goes through my mind. They don't know if they play a role in my thoughts. It worries them.

He adjusted his collar and began to walk, abruptly turning left. Surely it wouldn't surprise anyone that he was walking in that direction. He took this same route to buy bread every day, around the same time. But today it felt like he was escaping, rushing to the end of his street, since that's where he could find a world whose inhabitants hardly knew him. He had to stop himself from running.

Ten meters in front of him a door slowly opened. The first thing out was a dog that was small and obscenely fat. It lost no time in shitting against a wall. Then Ferdinand saw the head of a shriveled old woman. Holding onto both sides of the door to maintain her balance, she made a huge effort and lifted her gaze from the ground to survey the rest of the street. I didn't know she lived here, Ferdinand thought. And yet I pass this house every day. Is it possible we've simply missed each other all these years? Was it just chance that led her to send her dog out when she saw me passing by her window? Maybe the animal just couldn't hold it anymore? Whatever the case, the sight of the old woman calmed him. She belonged to the generation before his. It was possible that, despite all the drastic changes taking place in the world, she was simply pursuing her normal life, same as ever. Yes, he remembered her now, as if he'd suddenly picked her out of a crowd. He gave her a friendly greeting as he passed her door. But though her toothless mouth had been working the entire time in a constant droning mutter, Ferdinand now clearly heard her say, "Murderer." The dog ran up to Ferdinand, sniffed him once, and then discovered something more interesting on the sidewalk. That doesn't mean anything, he thought. Everyone's become a murderer. Her words are completely meaningless. Finally, five or six houses further on, Ferdinand looked behind him. She was still watching him from her open door, her head straight, as though resting on an invisible cushion. She lives too far away from my house, he thought. There's no way she knows what happened. He listened closely, but he couldn't distinguish between any of the sirens sounding in the fog of city noises. The old lady didn't mean anything by it, he decided; she mutters nonsense like that all day long. Ferdinand had almost reached the end of the street when he saw the blood on his shoes. His neighbor's blood, which had dripped from his axe and stained his beautiful, calf-leather shoes.

I can't go back, he thought. I can't waste the time changing shoes. Then I'll really look suspicious. Rounding the corner, he leaned against a wall and lifted his foot. A cluster of drops, obviously blood. Those shoes had lasted him twenty-five years. They didn't make shoes like this anymore. Instead, shoes were mass-produced in factories—without real skin, real sickness, real manure. He licked his thumb and massaged the stain. He heard someone put his fingers to his mouth and whistle back on his street. Then this person cried a few words Ferdinand couldn't understand. Still, he realized that these sounds must be coming from a place about as far away as his own house. He didn't dare to look. Someone saw me hurrying away. He knows I'm around the corner and he's calling me back. I have to run. I have to reach the next street before he finds me standing here. If he sees me, he'll run after me and grab me by the collar. He's probably younger than me.

Twenty meters more and Ferdinand was out of breath. He pulled himself over a railing and hid himself on a porch. His lungs were expanding and contracting like two thin paper bags. He smothered his wheezing in his jacket. No one passed. He waited and waited and finally realized that if the other man were going to pass by, he would have seen him by now.

A small lantern dangled over his head. Its four sides were spotless. Perhaps there wasn't actually any glass in the thing. A stately door, decorated with gleaming copper, was set deep in a recess nearby. If only I lived here, thought Ferdinand. Everything would have been different if I lived here. He changed position. Maybe that stranger had been calling to someone else. Or else he'd given up. Ferdinand looked over the front door with its thick wood, perhaps fifty years old. The owners had taken such good care of it, however, that it looked brand new. Perhaps the woman of the house is standing nearby, Ferdinand thought. Perhaps she needs to run an errand

and is deciding on what coat to wear. He stood up. If the woman saw him crouching on the ground, she'd immediately start yelling.

He went back down into the street calmly, as though he himself were the owner of this property. Turning left, he followed the route he'd chosen earlier and tried to ignore the windows on either side of him. He resisted the urge to look back over his shoulder. He knew he had to disappear.

I don't know her, thought Ferdinand. A bare mattress, and a summer dress with puffy sleeves. The girl in his vision was clearly too old for that kind of outfit. The hose around her neck was a winter brown. Fashion designers sometimes come up with strange ideas like combining a bright summer dress with dark winter colors. Unless the hose didn't go with the dress at all—maybe it was found in the room, maybe taken out of a chest of drawers? He couldn't see any. Had the young woman dressed like a little girl for her lover? He looked at the slight body, its bones pressing against its skin. I didn't fuck her. That's just impossible. He wanted to shut her eyes. He wanted to push her tongue back in her mouth and close her lips. He wanted to cover her naked body.

Ferdinand found himself on a park bench. The shadows lengthened under the trees, and a light drizzle hung shimmering in the air over the grass. A man with a classic black umbrella, which could have been plucked out of virtually any picture of virtually any street, strolled down a nearby path. He heard the man talking on a phone. Or was he talking to himself? It was impossible to tell with all these new implants. The microphone extends inconspicuously to just below your lower lip, the speaker is embedded deep in your ear, the antenna hidden in the curve between your outer ear and skull. It was the newest in telecommunication technology. The computer controlling it was actually inside the microphone, which itself was no bigger than a pinhead. The whole system could be installed shortly after birth. The earlier the operation, the simpler it was. Besides, that way parents always knew how to locate their children, and they could hear and speak to their child wherever it happened to be. Most people paid for a lifetime subscription. The monthly cost was low.

The talking man strolled in Ferdinand's direction. Only his mouth and chin were visible. The rest of his face was hidden in the darkness under the umbrella, which he held upright. He was still chatting away unintelligibly. For safety's sake Ferdinand shoved his stained shoe farther under the bench. It was too late to get up and run. Flight encourages the hunting instinct in carnivores. On the other hand, no one could tell just by looking at him that Ferdinand might have killed anyone, or know how many times he'd done it. Yes, the names and addresses of perpetrators were printed next to the names of their victims in the daily news, but that meant nothing. There was no external evidence to point to Ferdinand. Many first-time murders were committed on a simple impulse. Because a dam had burst. Because too much had been bottled up.

The man was slowing down now, as if his conversation was taking up so much of his attention that he could barely put one foot in front of the other. Of course he'll stop next to my bench, thought Ferdinand. The man turned his back recklessly, absently. Now I can go, Ferdinand thought. Now I can get a little head start, maybe put enough distance between us to discourage the man from doing what he's planning. But the moment passed. Ferdinand saw the man's lips now, even heard a few words of what he was saying, figured there was a microphone hidden under his lip. This is how death comes to meet you—under a black umbrella in an empty park. Death comes out of nowhere. You watch him approach over a gravel path until he stops right in front of you. He's got nylon thread neatly rolled in his pocket. Any minute it will cut into your throat as easily as into a wheel of cheese.

The man no longer seemed to be carrying on a conversation so much as a monologue. He passed by the bench, but was still too close to Ferdinand for comfort. There were deep creases in the back of his overcoat. Perhaps he came to the park every day to pass some time on a bench. His voice was steady—as though in prayer. Perhaps he was one of those neurotics Ferdinand had read about in the paper—people who develop strange psychological conditions because of their implants. People who don't even hear what other people say to them anymore—they just go on talking regardless.

After the man had walked a few meters more, Ferdinand decided to stand up. His body was tense with anxiety; he felt a pain in his lower back. Nonetheless, he began walking down the path. After he'd put some distance between the bench and himself, taken a few turns, he looked back. He could just about make out the black umbrella—casting a shadow that swallowed the talking man whole.

I have to find shelter, thought Ferdinand. I don't want to be out walking around the city after dark. My jacket is wet—hunger I can stand, but I should get out of the rain. A man like me doesn't need to eat much to stay alive. This cheered him up, brought him a moment's peace. He'd always been that way. Hunger didn't worry him.

Now that Ferdinand was alone, the park regained its usual, recreational appearance. It was easy to imagine that this was the way it had always been: trees here, grass there. An oasis in a hostile environment. He moved slowly, taking on the pace of someone trying to comfort a tired and tearful baby, and who therefore can't stand still.

Ferdinand finally turned right at the baroque park gates. The streetlights were coming on, giving him a familiar feeling of coziness, a sense of community that nonetheless receded as the lights became brighter. He soon arrived in a desolate neighborhood. The houses had become impregnable blocks, with no windows or openings through which the least light could trickle. In the first weeks of the New Measures, districts like this one had erupted in violent protest. The occupants denounced the ambiguity of a state that called on people to be on their best behavior, but still assumed that these same people would run around killing each other. The official projection was that the New Measures would severely reduce the overpopulation problem in less than ten years. Another positive result would be that everyone would have to become extremely pleasant to one another. Of course, there were a high number of minority citizens attending these protests, since a report was leaked that the State had high expectations that the lower social classes would decimate themselves if given the chance. That way, society would cull itself until all that was left would be right-thinking, law-abiding citizens (who happened to have the largest taxable incomes). Still, a week after the declaration, a high-class banquet thrown to show support of the New Measures turned into a bloodbath. None of the survivors could explain what exactly had led to the ninety-three reported deaths. There was a rumor that it had something to do with a party-crasher's hand perhaps coming to rest on the ass of a waitress who was serving him pancakes—but a State inquiry was ruled to be unnecessary.

Ferdinand examined the houses, which were set far back from the street, their backyards hidden from view by high metal fences. He hurried on his way—he knew that some of these neighborhoods had curfew laws. He forced himself to look straight ahead as he walked. It felt as though he were moving down a long tunnel. He thought: bullets travel faster than the sound made by their being fired. I'll be listening for the sound and won't even know that I've already been shot.

TRANSLATED FROM DUTCH BY KERRI A. PIERCE

JEAN-PHILIPPE TOUSSAINT

Zidane's Melancholy

Zidane watched the Berlin sky, not thinking of anything, a white sky flecked with gray clouds lined with blue, one of those windy skies, immense and changing, of the Flemish painters. Zidane watched the Berlin sky over the Olympic stadium on the evening of the 9th of July 2006, and felt the sensation, with poignant intensity, of being there, simply there, in Berlin's Olympic Stadium, at this precise moment in time, on the evening of the World Cup final.

No doubt it came down to a question of form—form and melancholy, on the evening of this final. In the first case, pure form: the penalty converted in the seventh minute, an indolent *Panenka*[1] shot that hit the crossbar, passed over the line, and re-exited the goal, a billiard-ball trajectory that

---

1 Antonín Panenka, taking the last penalty for the Czech team in a penalty shoot-out during the final of the 1976 European Championship, fooled the German goalkeeper into diving for a save, before chipping the ball into the centre of the net. (Translators' note—henceforth TN. All other notes are the author's, consisting exclusively of citations of other works, although originally without bibliographical details or page numbers. We have provided full references to English translations where appropriate.)

flirted with Geoff Hurst's fabled shot at Wembley in 1966.[2] But this was still only a quotation, an inadvertent homage to a legendary World Cup moment. Zidane's true act on the evening of the final—a sudden gesture like an overflowing of black bile into the lonely night—will only occur later, and then will cause us to forget everything else, the end of the match and the extra time, the shots at the goal and the winners, a decisive, brutal, prosaic, novelistic act: a perfect moment of ambiguity under the Berlin sky, a few dizzying seconds of ambivalence, where beauty and blackness, violence and passion, came into contact and provoked the short-circuit of a wholly unscripted action.

Zidane's headbutt had the suddenness and suppleness of a calligrapher's stroke. Though it took only a few seconds to accomplish, such an act could only occur at the end of a slow process of maturation, a long, invisible, and secret genesis. Zidane's act has nothing to do with the aesthetic categories of the beautiful or the sublime; it is beyond the moral categories of good and evil; its value, its strength, and its substance stem from nothing other than its irreducible congruence with the precise moment in time at which it occurred. Two vast subterranean currents must have carried it there from afar. The first, from the depths, wide, silent, powerful, inexorable—as much a product of pure melancholy as of the painful perception of the passage of time—is linked to the sadness of the ordained end, the bitterness of a player competing in the last match of his career, a match he can't make up his mind to finish. Zidane has always had trouble with endings: he is familiar with false exits (against Greece) and missed exits (against South

2 Hurst scored his second goal of the 1966 World Cup final from inside the penalty box in extra time, striking the ball upwards with his right foot. The ball hit the crossbar and bounced down, and was only awarded when the linesman confirmed that the ball had crossed the line. (TN)

Korea)[3] both. It's always been impossible for him to bring his career to a close, least of all to do so beautifully, for to end beautifully is nonetheless to end, to seal one's legend: to raise the World Cup is to accept one's death, whereas ruining one's proper exit leaves prospects open, unknown, alive. The other current that carries his gesture, both parallel to and contradicting the first, fed by an excess of black bile and other saturnine influences, is the wish to be done with it all as quickly as possible, the wish, irrepressible, to leave the game at once and return to the locker room (*I left abruptly, without telling anybody*),[4] he feels such weariness, sudden and incommensurable tiredness, exhaustion, a bad shoulder, Zidane is unable to score, he can't bear his teammates any longer, can't bear his opponents, can't bear the world or himself. Zidane's melancholy is my melancholy, I know it, I've nourished it and I feel it. The world becomes opaque, one's limbs are heavy, *the hours seem leaden, longer, slower, interminable.*[5] Zidane feels broken and becomes vulnerable. *Something in us turns against us*[6]—and, in the intoxication of fatigue and nervous tension, Zidane can only complete an act of violence, channeling his intoxication, or else of flight, relieving it, unable otherwise to defuse the pressure weighing on him (this is the *final flight from the finished work*).[7] Since the beginning of extra time, Zidane,

3 Zidane retired from international football after France lost to Greece in the quarterfinals of the 2004 European Championship, but announced his comeback a year later. In 2006 he received a yellow card during France's group stage match against South Korea, and so missed France's next game against Togo, a match that, had it been lost, would have seen France eliminated from the tournament. (TN)

4 Jean-Philippe Toussaint, *The Bathroom*, trans. Nancy Amphoux and Paul De Angelis, Champaign, IL: Dalkey Archive Press, 2008, p. 37.

5 Ibid., p. 42 (translation modified—TN).

6 Jean Starobinski, "L'Encre de la mélancolie", *Nouvelle Revue Française* 11.1 (No. 123, March 1963), p. 411 (our translation—TN).

7 Sigmund Freud, *Leonardo da Vinci and a Memory of his Childhood*, *Penguin Freud Library* Vol. 14: *Art and Literature*, trans. James Strachey, Harmondsworth: Penguin, 1990, p. 155 (translation modified—TN).

unconsciously, has continually been expressing his weariness with his captain's armband, which keeps slipping down, this armband which keeps coming undone and which he keeps readjusting clumsily on his arm. Zidane thus signals, despite himself, that he wants to leave the game and return to the locker room. He no longer has the means, or the strength, the energy, the will, to pull off a last stunt, a final act of pure form; the header deflected by Buffon a few moments earlier, for all its beauty, will definitively open Zidane's eyes to his irreparable impotence. Form, at present, resists him—and this is unacceptable for an artist. We know the intimate ties that link art to melancholy. Unable to score a goal, Zidane will score minds.

Night has fallen now on Berlin, the light's intensity has lessened, Zidane has felt the sky darken palpably over his shoulders, leaving only flayed streaks of twilit clouds in the firmament, black and crimson. *Water mixed with night is an old remorse that will not sleep.*[8]

No one in the stadium understood what had happened. From my seat in the Olympic Stadium stands I saw the match resume—the Italians returning to the attack and the action moving away toward the opposite goal. One Italian player remained on the ground, the act had taken place, Zidane had been overtaken by the brutal gods of melancholy. The referee stopped the game and people started to run every which way on the grass, toward the prostrate player and in the direction of the assistant referee, whom some of the Italian players were now surrounding, I looked from left to right, then, through my binoculars, I instinctively singled out Zidane, one's eyes always find Zidane, the silhouette of Zidane in his white shirt standing in the night at the center of the field, his face in extreme close-

8 Gaston Bachelard, *Water and Dreams: An Essay on the Imagination of Matter*, trans. Edith R. Farrell, Dallas, Texas: Pegasus Foundation, 1983, p. 102.

up in my binocular sights, and then Buffon, the Italian goalkeeper, appears and starts to speak to him, to rub his head, massaging his scalp and the back of his neck, a surprising gesture, caressing, enveloping him, a gesture that anoints him, as one would a child, a newborn, to comfort it, to calm it. I didn't understand what was happening, no one in the stadium understood what was happening, the referee headed toward the small group of players where Zidane was standing and pulled a black card out of his pocket, a card he raised toward the Berlin sky, and I understood at once that it was addressed to Zidane, the black card of melancholy.

Zidane's act, invisible, incomprehensible, is all the more spectacular for not having taken place. If one limits oneself to the live observation of events in the stadium, and to the legitimate faith we can have in our senses, no one saw anything, neither the spectators nor the referees—it simply never happened. Not only did Zidane's act never take place, but even if it did, even if Zidane were to have had the mad intention, the fantasy, the desire to headbutt one of his opponents, Zidane's head would never have reached this opponent, since each time Zidane's head would have covered half the distance separating it from his opponent's chest, there would still have been another half to cover, and then another half, and then still another half, and so on eternally, such that Zidane's head, progressing continually toward its target but never reaching it, as in an immense slow-motion sequence infinitely looped, could not, no, never, because it is physically and mathematically impossible (this is Zidane's paradox, if not Zeno's), come into contact with his opponent's chest—never; the only thing visible, that all the spectators around the world could have seen, was the fleeting impulse crossing Zidane's mind.

TRANSLATED FROM FRENCH BY THANGAM
RAVINDRANATHAN AND TIMOTHY BEWES

IGOR ŠTIKS

At the Sarajevo Market

She took me to the Markale Market. Alma said that you could appreciate the true soul of Sarajevo here. And she wasn't talking about black-market food or the other quotidian products that were becoming more inaccessible to normal citizens by the day, but rather about the things that had until recently filled the apartments and houses of all Sarajevans. And indeed, here we found people trying to sell their precious possessions, or at least those with which they were ready to part. For now they're still selling books—I thought as I walked with Alma through the crowd, listened to her talk to people, greet them, ask questions, and continue on—paintings of little value, majolica, beautiful but unnecessary knickknacks, dominoes, pipes, antiques. But tomorrow they'll be bringing silver, gold, diamonds, and other rare items to the market, they'll sell collections amassed over many years, expensive china, the finest Persian rugs or family heirlooms, and they'll come to measure the worth of these relics of their past lives in sacks of rice, kilos of wheat, a couple of eggs or spoonfuls of oil. Simon is right, the noose is tightening. Soon they'll understand this, and then despair will set in. Maybe the looters, who profit from anarchy, who take things from abandoned apartments, already sense or know this. Wouldn't the old owners—refugees now somewhere outside Bosnia, or else on the enemy side—be shocked to see what low prices their stuff is selling for in today's wartime marketplace.

Alma told me that at first she had allowed herself to buy some rare books or little household objects and even some antique jewelry, but now she understood how crazy she had been to think that this would all be over soon and so only came here to allow herself to be amazed at all the objects the city had been keeping hidden away. She said she wouldn't be surprised to find the most incredible things here—great works of art that had once disappeared or been stolen might be brought to light from formerly sealed-up cellars, from underground sewer tunnels (some of which might even empty outside the ring of encirclement, far from the siege, who knows?), from old safes and chests; or else, conversely, someone might end up, sooner or later, wrapping a kilo of precious meat in a worthless Rembrandt self-portrait ...

Why not, I said. Cities inscribe their history on walls and in objects, not in the unreliable and corrupt memories of their citizens. That's the only way. Don't we ourselves write our lives into those objects, diaries, jewelry, the painstakingly dried flowers that illustrate best of all the fragility of our memories and sensations and in this way link our existence to the existence of the city and to other similar attempts to preserve some record of our passage over this earth? That's how nations and cities inscribe themselves, too, wherever they can, both the things they want us to know and think about them as well as their deepest secrets. It's possible that we wouldn't like what we'd find in those opened cellars, rusty safes, in the hidden pockets of grandpa's clothes. Maybe there are thousands of enormous rats in those sewer tunnels that would be quite happy to attack us if we disturb them, to cut off that escape route and thus make their contribution to the siege of the city.

Then we examined the books on offer. People were selling their personal libraries, especially retirees no longer receiving their pensions. Most of the books were printed in Cyrillic or concerned communism. Regarding the latter category, no one here believes that such books could possibly be useful to anyone anymore. Still, some of the sellers were trying to keep their prices up. It must have been hard to part with what were clearly the most beloved books on their shelves. They weren't even sure they wanted to sell to you in the first place. But these types were rare. In general, the market is pretty merciless. Some people were even selling books they'd found in other people's apartments. One man had pioneered a peculiar approach—all his books cost one Deutschmark. I'm not sure how long he'll be able to keep that up. To buy books instead of, say, noodles borders on insanity. Nevertheless, a lot of people had gathered round and they were looking, flipping through pages, putting books back, reaching for their wallets, but then hesitating . . . a pile of books in front of him, stacked haphazardly, clearly from all over his stall. Here and there I recognize the name of an author, sometimes a title. Spinoza, Hegel, Plato, Hobbes, Homer, Dostoyevsky, Cervantes, Stendhal, Nietzsche, Babel, Musil, Joyce . . . all my old friends. Now they're nothing but paper, stuff that has to be disposed of for at least some kind of profit, because soon it'll all be totally superfluous, except perhaps as fuel for fires. One mark! I have the feeling, I told Alma, that the Deutschmark has never been worth more.

We found some youngsters, fifteen- or sixteen-year-olds, selling some really old books. Perhaps they'd burgled a used bookstore or gathered up the books from an apartment that had been bombed along with someone's precious library. They had no idea what they were offering. I was beginning to believe Alma's claim that we would be amazed by all the treasures the city is hiding. I pulled out a dusty and moth-eaten volume of Diderot and D'Alembert's *Encyclopédie générale* . . . there were also dog-eared anthologies of classics for use in the turn-of-the-century schoolrooms of the long-dead monarchy; in the same pile I found and flipped through a technical-statistical study called *Das Bauwesen in Bosnien und der Hercegovina vom Beginn der Occupation durch die österr, ung. Monarchie bis in das Jahr 1887* . . . edited by one Mr. Edmund Stix; then the first Gallimard edition of Malraux's *La Condition humaine* from April 1933; I skipped over a couple of local titles; I saw Enzo Strecci's songbook, the first issue of *Das Fackel*, a velvet-jacketed edition of de Sade's *Justine*; last of all I dug out a German translation of Shakespeare's *Merchant of Venice* from 1935, in Gothic script and lacking Shylock's famous monologue from act three. I recited it to myself from memory: *Hath not a Jew eyes? Hath not a Jew hands . . . If you prick us, do we not bleed? If you tickle us, do we not laugh? If you poison us, do we not die? And if you wrong us, shall we not revenge?*

I asked one of them where the books came from and he just shrugged his shoulders. He asked me whether they were worth a lot. Depends to whom, I responded.

Alma called me over. She found something interesting at an antiques booth. She shows me a pocket watch on a chain. On the lid is an engraved picture of a girl next to a man in some bucolic spot, her head resting on his outstretched arm. She's wrapped in a diaphanous shawl and looks seductively at some faraway something. Opposite her is a soldier, his rifle on his lap; with deep melancholy, he looks from his guard post toward a distant field, which lies somewhere near his beloved. Alma opened the watch. Surprisingly, it still worked. On the inside of the lid it said, in German "Dear Rudi, with every second the war comes closer to its end, and we to each other. Your Teresa, Prague, 1914."

We asked ourselves what had happened to those star-crossed lovers from Prague and how the watch had ended up in Sarajevo. The seller had no idea. Teresa's prediction about when the war would end certainly turned out to be overoptimistic. We wondered whether Teresa had really waited for Rudi through the entire war. The cold Prague nights demand a little human contact, I figured, and besides, military desires need outlets too—perhaps Rudi had found relief in some mobile wartime brothel. Alma didn't like that version. But she was not so sentimental as to imagine that the lovers had managed to reunite again after the war, that they got married, and lived happily until, say, 1939. Had that been the case, it would be hard to explain how the watch had ended up in Sarajevo. Alma surmised that in this admittedly unlikely scenario some Bosnian regimental comrade had perhaps stolen the watch from the gawky Rudi. No. Alma was sure that after having endured all sorts of wartime horrors Rudi had decided to spend a leave in Sarajevo in the summer of 1918 at the invitation of a regimental friend, and met said pal's sister here. Love flared up and—despite the initial opposition of the Bosnian friend, who didn't want to see his sister marry his best wartime comrade (with whom he'd spent more than a little time hanging around the aforementioned brothels), and who was well aware of the precarious mental state of a battle-tested *K. und K.* soldier after almost four years of fighting, a soldier about whom one could at the very least say that he was somewhat *überspannt!*—it all ended with a wedding. Rudi sold off Teresa's present the day after his wedding, deserted his post, and awaited the entrance of the royal Serbian army into Sarajevo hidden in the attic of his cute little bride's house.

Just to put up a little resistance I insisted that things might have happened a bit differently. Rudi, it seems, hid the gift because he frequently recalled the good times he had shared with Teresa in the cellar of her father's tavern and remained sentimentally attached to his former life in Prague. And today it had gotten here just like most of the other stuff at the Markale Market in the summer of 1992. And Teresa? Alma asked. What happened to her? Teresa quit working in the tavern and, as early as 1915, ran off with the very first officer ranked higher than corporal who showed up in her life, having decided to live a nomadic existence with a regiment whose movements were dictated by fragile wartime fortune. It goes without saying that her father was hopelessly depressed by all this.

We laughed at the fates we had stitched together in our imaginations. In any case we had allowed our heroes to remain alive. That much was cause for celebration. We were in an excellent mood. I asked if she wanted the watch.

"Then you'd have to change the inscription," she said. "If you really did give me the watch, what would you put on the inside?"

"Dear Alma: I'm not sure I can wait for the end of the war. Your R., Sarajevo, summer 1992," I said quickly, as if I'd been waiting for the chance.

I stared at her, waiting for her answer. Surprised, she tried to guess from my expression just how much of what I'd just said was premeditated. Then she turned her head and continued on as if she hadn't heard me at all, as if the end of our conversation hadn't happened. She looked left and right, honestly fascinated by all the goods on offer, beginning short conversations with the sellers, asking about prices, and slowly moving away from me. I'll never forget how she walked through that crowded wartime market. There was no sign that she'd grasped any of what I'd said. I stood like a statue with the watch in my hand. Finally she turned around and waved me on. Nothing had happened. Our walk could continue. I understood the game. But somehow in the meantime the price of the watch had mysteriously risen from ten to twenty marks. Clearly the seller had been following our conversation. When he saw my surprise, he answered with a shrug of his shoulders: wartime economy, you shouldn't invest any emotion in things. I didn't buy it. In the end, only Teresa and Rudi could have understood that story about coming close and moving apart—in short, everything that love should be in time of war.

TRANSLATED FROM CROATIAN BY ANDREW WACHTEL

GEORGI GOSPODINOV

And All Turned Moon

Castor P. was going out to die. He had been living for seventy-nine years and three months and didn't see any point in going on. There was no tragedy or self-pity in his decision. His grandfather had died at seventy-nine, and his father too had departed life before turning eighty; Castor found this age respectable, a natural span for a human being who hadn't tampered with his genes.

He had to settle a few formalities. Death makes us get organized, he thought, as he walked towards the Central Office of Last Wishes, the Department for the Finalization of Earthly Existence. "Last Wishes" sounded like "Last call!," as in a bar. Once upon a time, people could just lie down and die, he thought with a touch of sadness. Now even death had been formalized. Another fifty-five years on Earth were due to him. His insurance was in order and it provided against death before his one hundred and twenty-fifth birthday. That was the official upper limit—though, off the record, there were plenty of rumors to the effect that VIPs and wealthy space bankers were buying themselves up to three hundred years or more.

Castor was entitled to renounce the remainder of years due to him; he only had to submit an application in person, confirm it a couple of months later, and then have the exact date of his death arranged.

It was now precisely three months since he had submitted his first application. The only request he had made to the Department was that they send a message to his son, letting him know about his decision. "Do you have other close relatives in our galaxy? We could send them messages as well. Your insurance covers it all." "No, I don't have any other relatives in . . . the galaxy," he had replied. Language is a dangerous thing. Everybody was talking in these cosmic terms. It made him feel queasy. It was one thing not to have anyone on Earth, and quite another to know you were alone in the entire galaxy.

He'd had to record the message himself. It took less than a minute. He thought up the words in advance and had even decided on the proper tone. And yet, his treacherous voice had risen right at the end: "I think it's time. Please come to say good-bye." There was no need for a long message. The girl in the Office helped him fill out the paperwork. The recipient's location was too distant even for the new means of communication: the sub-orbit of a planet whose coordinates Castor P. had never been able to memorize. "Out in the middle of nowhere," he said, in the idiom of the previous century, already unintelligible to the young girl. She smiled kindly and answered that the fastest transmission would reach the addressee in about two weeks. My father's letters used to arrive faster than that, Castor smiled—in just a week or so.

Actually, he had planned everything in advance. Two weeks for the telegram or whatever they called it to reach his son, a week for his son to be furious that his old man had apparently lost his mind. Another week during which his anger would subside and he'd start hesitating. Then the fifth week of decision. Two more weeks for him to request an emergency leave, sort things out before his trip, and then finally reach Earth—in almost a month and a half.

But the three months had passed, and there was no sign of his son yet. Castor P. had been checking with the Department daily over the past several days, but the amiable employee just went on shrugging her bony, girlish shoulders as sympathetically as ever.

Today was Castor P.'s last day. He had another few hours to roam the streets of the city. It should have been spring, according to the calendar. And indeed, the chestnut trees were topped like cream cakes. White acacias were swaying in the wind. Green flooded the streets. But it was nothing like the springtimes he remembered. Lavish though the blossoms were, they had no scent. Castor P. still remembered the way things used to smell—and he remembered too all his unsuccessful attempts to describe the scent of acacia to his son, born in a world without odors. There's no way, however, to describe a smell without comparing it to another. Yes, acacia smells like lilac, though it's more delicate—but lilacs don't have a smell anymore either. Nor were there any bees hovering around the blossoms. It had been a long time since biological bees had become extinct. They had started vanishing mysteriously forty years ago. Some people believed that cell phone transmissions had confused the bees' own means of communication; others said it was a new, aggressive virus. The extinction of the bees was yet another sign that things were going wrong. Technology was developing faster and faster, but it was still limited in the ways it could patch up the damage it had already caused. The attempts at a new global artificial pollination system, and, indeed, the gene modification of common houseflies in an attempt to turn them into a new species of bee, were already heading for total catastrophe—thus opening up new chinks in the chain.

Castor P. had spent a lifetime trying to fight against these insane projects. Early in his youth, at the beginning of the century, he had started work at the biggest European telescope of the time—forty-two meters in diameter. In distant 2011, he had even discovered the smallest black hole in the universe. Until recently, he had kept the newspaper clippings about his success, with all their sensational headlines. There was a certain irony about using the biggest telescope in the European Union to discover the smallest black hole. Then he decided the job was too uneventful and slow. He joined a radical group of "green" scientists. They were trying to prove that biofuels were not an alternative energy source. They were the first to issue warnings that the extinction of the bees would bring about a biocenotic apocalypse. Nobody took any notice of them.

He sat in the shade of a silicon acacia. Everything around him confirmed the series of failures that characterized his life. The world was developing in a direction contrary to all he had hoped for. He looked up: even the sky looked as though it had been ineptly sewn up after surgery. The enormous yellow spots came from unsuccessful attempts to patch up the holes in the ozone layer by means of injecting sulfur particles into the stratosphere. That was the last battle he had lost, his last effort to take up arms, proving that the ozone layer would get even thinner after this kind of treatment. Now he knew he had been right, and that made him even more miserable.

It was time. He only had another three hours remaining on Earth. If he was going to write any farewell letters, it had to be now. Of course, no one had been writing on paper for years. It had been smart of him to put aside a pencil and unused pad. He had purposely saved this job, or rather ritual, until the last minute. He still hoped his son might arrive.

He decided to start with a letter to his father. He was more than fifty years overdue to give his father a proper good-bye. Castor hesitated about the form of address, then simply wrote, "Dad."

The scratching of the hard graphite against the paper delighted him. And suddenly the words started flowing, as if they'd always been waiting for a pencil and some paper to let them out. He told his father how the world had developed and how happy he should be that he had managed to avoid seeing it all. His father had been one of the last true gardeners; he had loved talking to his trees. He'd had one tone of voice for the apple and cherry trees, another for the pear and walnut. He would go to his beehives without a mask, entirely calm, and talk to his bees as well. What was happening now would have been the end of his personal world. "Dad," Castor P. wrote, "I couldn't save the garden; the bees are gone, but the old walnut tree is still alive." At last he wrote that he had decided (here he groped for the right word for a long time) . . . to *go*. "Everything's okay, don't worry. My son even came back," wrote Castor P., "unlike me, who didn't manage to return for your final hours. Forgive me. Yours, Castor. P.S. Soon we'll be able to meet and talk as long as we like. Unless they've destroyed the hereafter too . . ."

Castor felt relieved: he realized that he'd spent longer writing this letter than he'd ever spent talking to his father while he was alive.

The letter to his son was more difficult to start. He tried again and again, tore up the page, then started over from the beginning. He didn't want any pain or grief in it. Eventually he settled on the following, surprising even himself: "Since I've failed in everything I've ever attempted, I took to fractals and chaos theory over the past few years. I observed the clouds and the rivers, trees and ferns, as long as there were any to see. Through the geometry of nature, I wanted to see how the little that has survived here on Earth might develop. You know that I, unlike yourself, have never quite believed in space, or its colonization. It feels draughty, dark, and cold. But then it's already the same here. What my grandfather and father grew in their gardens—what I'm trying to describe—is gone now. And the geometry of nature makes no sense without it. This might make you angry, but I still think that we were too reckless rushing into outer space. We weren't quite ready. Long ago, when the Bedouins were roaming the deserts, they used to take frequent rests, not only to rest their camels, but so that their souls would have time to catch up. The soul's speed is different, you see. Just think how many lost and late souls there are who've missed the caravan, still roaming through the desert of space. I can hear them weeping. I lie back at night and watch the moon—where I'll be in a couple of hours. Do you know what the basic substance of space is? What it's made of? It's made of loneliness. And loneliness is volatile—it expands to fill the area around it.

"My grandfather, your great-grandfather, lived in a house he built himself, worked in his garden, and the farthest he ever got was the forest near his village—so his loneliness was only as big as his house and his small garden. My father's loneliness was the size of the apartment and the city he moved to. My grandfather used to say that my dad had 'run away' to the city. Then I 'ran away' to another country, and now you yourself have run away to somewhere in space. I've been thinking tonight about what your loneliness is like: does it have the dimensions of the universe it-self? Is it lighter and more rarefied? What is its mass? How does gravity affect it?

"In the past, loneliness used to be more concentrated—smaller. You could tame it, pet it like a cat. Now I find it impossible to cope with its new, cosmic proportions. Now I'll never be able to finish my 'Treatise on the Fractal Geometry of Loneliness': I can't put it all into an equation, can't figure it out . . . Now that I've grown old, you know, I've started complain-ing, turning into my father and my grandfather. And it's time I went back to them. Don't hate yourself for having come too late; it will be enough for me to know that you are on your way.

"Oh, and before I forget—when you come to collect these letters from the Department, pay attention to the nice girl who'll deliver them to you. Talk to her; ask her out for a drink in my memory. We knew each other—she's a good, decent person."

Castor P. caressed the closely written sheet with his hand and folded it. He had said farewell to all the people he cared about in the universe. He walked to the Office to leave the letters. He was watching the people streaming in the opposite direction in the early evening—aloof. He walked past a few Angelina Jolies and Brad Pitts who had already started ageing, rapidly and irreparably. Cheap clones—probably pirate versions of cells from doubles, grown to indulge other people's whims. And now, all their lives, they were condemned to wear these bodies that had gone out of fash-ion years ago. Thank God, the girl at the Department simply looked like herself. Before going in, Castor P. stood outside a while—watching, from the corner of his eye, the discrete space capsule that would soon take him to the new cemetery on the Moon.

As she was taking his farewell letters, the girl suddenly embraced him for a second. That was certainly against the rules.

"He's definitely going to come, one of these days," said Castor P., trying not to burst into tears like a child, now that it was time.

"I know," said the girl.

Dusk was beginning to fall, and now the soft phosphorescent glow Castor P. had known so well ever since he was a child was getting closer and closer. And all turned moon.

TRANSLATED FROM BULGARIAN BY EVGENIA PANCHEVA

NEVEN UŠUMOVIĆ

Vereš

1.

After a certain length of time—or would it be better to say: uncertain?—I began wasting hours and hours on questions such as: "Budapester," "Budian," or "Pester"? That is, what's the correct name for these people around me, my temporary fellow citizens? This problem acquired undreamed-of dimensions when I set off from Déak Square (i.e., in Pest) to the other side of the Danube, to the Déli railway station. Because: which station is it where Pesters get out but Budians get in? Is it before or after crossing over/under the Danube?

What I mean is, George Soros's money had never been so pointlessly wasted! Yes, I completed all my course assignments enthusiastically, I perfected my English until it was intuitive; but when I went outside, into the street, when I plunged breathlessly into the murky depths of Hungarian babble, I shriveled up and shrank to the size of a question mark: Budian or Pester? *Pest is beautiful,* I wrote on the postcards I sent home. *The Danube is wide, and Gellért Hill is high.* After that I stopped sending postcards. I became a Pester. A Budason! Luckily, with the payments from my scholarship arriving regularly, and with my pre-secured accommodations, my only real existential concern was in choosing a cheap but decent-quality menu (as though everything advertised in the big city wasn't automatically both cheap and of decent quality!).

Of all the cafeteria-style restaurants in town, I quickly settled for and became most used to the Chinese ones. The question of whether I would go to the *Kínai fal*, the *Kínai nátha,* the *Shangai*, or the *Aranysárkány* was entirely a matter of my energy level and how much time I wanted to spend walking. The food tasted the same everywhere: the slight sweetness of the rice, the soy sauce, the mixed eggs and boiled carrots all went very well with the—to say the least, vague—taste of the tofu. Why, that's *me*, I would say to myself at my worst moments—an unbearably vapid sweetness.

Nevertheless, with time it was the *Aranysárkány* (The Golden Dragon) that came out on top. That is, one day as I waited my turn for my favorite meal of rice with eggs, tofu, and pickled bamboo shoots, I heard a familiar swear word, a curse in my own language. I turned and saw a young man whom I had thought till now to be one hundred percent Hungarian stringing together the most varied possible expletives in Croatian while staring unblinkingly at the ceiling! I supposed that this was his way of trying to alleviate some—to me invisible, but nonetheless concrete—pain.

"What's the problem, friend?" I called to him.

And, as though our Croatian in the middle of Pest was the most normal thing in the world, he replied, his gaze still fixed on the ceiling, "Oh, I've just poured boiling Szechuan soup over my shoes, that's all. Fuck, I might as well have stuck them in the oven!"

A door at the back of the restaurant opened, and the young man—his name was Vereš, as I would soon discover—disappeared into the darkness.

2.

I usually went to the *Aranysárkány* for lunch, around two o'clock. I didn't get in line immediately, but put my backpack with my notes and books on the first free table in the small back room, where there were four tables set with four chairs each. There would always be two employees taking turns working the counter: apart from one Chinese person, there was usually an Indian girl working there, or else our own Vereš.

Although the dishes on the menu changed day to day, the smell was always the same. At first it seemed as though something spicy and attractively sweet was hanging in the air, but then, when you sat down at your table, you would quickly find yourself overwhelmed by a sense of emptiness in the scent, a lack of essence, as though each of the foods here had passed through some Eastern European disinfecting laboratory on their journey from China to Hungary.

The actual cleanliness of the restaurant was another matter, however; it was a cleanliness that never shone, a cleanliness that seeped into the skin, steaming from the ceramic tiles, as in a bathroom, beading your forehead, beading the walls. A very low-level, institutional cleanliness: rational and merciless.

There was no music. The customers ate in silence. No smoking either, only the clouds of steam rising over the deep, square containers of food. No windows anywhere inside, except at the front. That was why some people sat exclusively on the uncomfortably high stools there, eating on a raised counter, looking out onto the street. I stuck to my corner, I was quite content to let the airily resonant Chinese voices there free me from the usual stifling cage of the Hungarian language, with its *Jó napot* ... *Tessék* ... *Ez nagyon finom, ez is, ez is, hogyne* ... *persze* ... *Jó étvágyok.*

Vereš would say a word or two as he rushed past. Nothing in his haste suggested that he worked with Chinese people. He hadn't adopted any of their indifferent pleasantness; on the contrary, he was like someone being compelled to search among the restaurant's customers for a mask he'd managed to lose without trace.

After combining my rice-tofu-egg-soy sauce in two or three ways, I sat vacantly pouring myself a green tea. The tea leaves as fat as caterpillars rose from the bottom of the pot and kept interrupting what was in any case a thin trickle. I drank, and every sip spread a flowery peace through my insides.

At such moments of tranquility, Vereš would often make some nonsensical remark:

"Well, well, my countryman. Dogs may bark, but you just sit there and droop!

"Make sure you don't fall in!

"Hey, keep both feet on the ground!"

And when he was in a particularly good mood, he would start to sing, right into my ear, the Hungarian children's song that goes *Hull a hó és hózik-zik-zik, Micimackó fázik-zik-zik*—about Winnie the Pooh freezing.

I had to have a real talk with this Vereš character, one day. One fiiine daaay! I smiled as I put on my backpack. *Szia* (bye, ciao!) *Vereš*!

3.

I stayed on a bit longer than usual in the Széchényi Library one afternoon. I didn't reach the *Aranysárkány* until around four P.M. Now I'll just get whatever they've got left over from the lunch rush, I thought, but no, everything was exactly as it always was, as though it were only just midday: full dishes of the usual Chinese specialties, the intoxicatingly sweetish, piquant steam in the air, the pleasant, stiff, masked Chinese faces . . . Only Vereš was absent. His shift must have ended.

As though they had figured out—it was only logical—that I was hungrier than usual, the servers piled my plates high with boiled rice and salad. I quickly sat down at my table and got to work.

When the first beads of sweat from the spicy sauce were breaking out on my face, my Vereš suddenly appeared, large as life, from some room I hadn't known about before—that is, some room I'd never noticed. He made his way over to me; without asking permission or even saying hello, he sat down at my table.

"We're lucky these Chinese guys exist," he said loudly, as though his employers could understand his Croatian. Then he went silent, waiting for me to finish eating and for his colleagues to bring us tea.

But Vereš's story began even before the tea had cooled in our cups:

"I ran away too, like every 'citizen of Serbia' who had half a brain! Which isn't to say I have half a brain myself . . . besides which, what little brains I do have these Hungarians will turn to mush soon enough."

"Wait a minute—you're one of them, Vereš is a Hungarian name, right? You're some kind of Vojvodina mutt, or else you're a pure . . ."

"A pure Croat, thank you—my name's spelled with a Š at the end, you know? Not the way the Hungarians write it, without the little squiggle. But, look," he added cynically, "when I'm here, I'm Hungarian, for everyone except you!"

The Vojvodina Hungarians saved their own skins as best they could. They ran from being inducted into the army reserves: they would have been treated like sacrificial lambs by the other, Serbian reservists. One of the best ways to get safe was to make an illegal run (the Serbian police probably already had files on us) across the border.

"I went through Kelebija, with Hungarian friends. They all had someone *over there*, someone who'd described the *procedure* for them. And it wasn't even a proper, daring escape, since everything happened under Kraus's direction. Mihajlo Kraus, the customs officer. He would wait for you in a precisely determined location. You met up and paid him for your crossing.

"That night, we spent hours making our way along these sandy trails through Kelebija Forest. We found Kraus at some faraway checkpoint. This Kraus, he was a bony scarecrow. It looked like the devil had splashed his face with acid. He had this enormous nose with yellow eyes crouching at its base.

"The most humiliating thing was waiting to be searched. He insisted on doing this in strict order—and he started squawking the instant any of us so much as twitched! The first thing he did, though, was take our money: a minimum of a thousand marks a head. If you could pay more, it might reduce the length of your search and increase Kraus's politeness, but that was all. So he stripped us bare, checking every document we'd brought with us, and then he threw every single thing we had onto a heap (of course, watches, gold chains, and that sort of thing all ended up, without discussion, on a special pile). He worked without much commentary, as placidly and precisely as a butcher. He was a smuggler, and we'd brought him a good haul for selling in Hungary. We were his pawns.

"Although we already knew what was coming next, we still let out a sob when, with the aid of two young soldiers, in a series of practiced movements, Kraus poured gasoline over that heap of our most personal possessions and set fire to it. Illuminated by that pyre, our angel of destruction cursed us all with a loud: *Now—pick up your clothes and get lost!*

"Luckily, near Tompa, the first Hungarian settlement on our route, we were hidden by plumes of fog and smoke. Dawn was breaking and it was only then that we finally felt the cold of that winter morning, as well as fatigue. Our steps faltered. We were being steadily choked by the smell of burning, overcome by a ghostly deafness in which we heard the echoes of stifled crying. We felt like a band of criminals, like Chetniks sniffing round a recently burned village. We were expecting shots, an ambush.

"The first signs of life were in the courtyard of a luxurious house that looked like it had been built pretty recently. Apparently the villagers of Tompa had laid down their hoes at some point and become traders— thanks to the embargo on Serbian stewing pots, the village had been transformed into a commercial mecca. István and I agreed to be the scouts for our band of refugees. We crept up to the fence and heard the hissing—we realized at once—of a pressurized-gas flamethrower. Several men in black rubber boots, and with fur hats on their heads, were wading through puddles of fresh blood. They had stretched out a huge dead sow, while a man in a grimy white coat burned off the animal's hair with his weapon. The smell of scorched pigskin, we realized, was what had settled on our stomachs and driven fear into our bones.

"'*Kocám, kocám*,' a little girl was crying behind her mother's back, '*szegény kocám, leölték most téged, leölték . . .*'

"By the evening, we'd all dispersed—this way and that—through Hungary. We steered clear of one another as though we were all accomplices in some bloody crime. In Tompa they'd given us food and drink: they didn't skimp on the freshly made sausage and black pudding. They directed us to addresses in Szeged, Kecskemét, Budapest—and that was that. We scattered.

"The following day, on a train, I looked forward to Pest with a sense of foreboding. Before this I'd only ever gone there to see concerts at the *Fekete lyuk* and *Tilos az Á* . . . but now I was a frozen, bloodless refugee. But for the Hungarians—whether we were Hungarians from Vojvodina, Serbs, or Croats—we all had blood on our hands. And they treated us like we were mounds of stinking carrion."

4.

One of Vereš's colleagues, a Chinese girl with a long, pale face, brought us a fresh round of green tea; as though there were a precise rule, a proper moment when this had to be done. She directed a meaningful smile at me at the corner of her eye: she knew what Vereš was like and how long his story was.

"Budapest was everything I could have wanted, at a moment when I didn't really want anything. Just to disappear into the city—though also, of course, NOT TO DIE! I kept cruising round the Oktogon, slipping down always-dark Dohány Street, walking endlessly beside the Danube, up and down. I circled the city for days, without any kind of refuge. At first I slept in the studio of a painter from Senta. He was called Zoltán; he'd been given the attic of an abandoned electric-motor factory. Everything in it was broken, the constant draft drove me crazy, and loneliness even crazier, because I soon found out that Zoltán's art consisted in doing absolutely nothing: he was a conceptualist—as he explained to me—and his particular concept amounted to a complete abstinence from creating, from leaving any kind of trace of himself in the world. What was essential to me was that he wouldn't let anyone find me, so on that score we had an understanding, but beyond that, every word was torture for him, because speaking is creating, isn't it? and let's not even mention going to the bathroom!

"Nonetheless, I still had to give my particulars to someone or other on several occasions. I concentrated on the Hungarian pronunciation of my surname:

" '*Vörös?*'

" '*Vörös!*'

" '*Magyar vagy Szerb?*'

" '*Magyar!*'

"Budapest was my harbor. The aroma of garlic and ground paprika, the indescribable noise of the busy streets filled with silent people. I staggered through the empty side streets, sniffed around dives, taking in the stench of alcohol and warm human flesh. Dull, colored glass hid miserable basements and vibrated with shrill Hungarian gypsy songs and the booming of hideous male bass voices. The wine was too sweet, it made me sick, just like the insane make-up of the whores and streetwalkers. 'No, no, my dear,' my too-young, now-dead friend Daca recited drunkenly behind a counter, 'you can't disappear between their legs . . . not even with ample use of Hungarian Easter eggs . . .'

"But still, I was lucky: one evening I ran into (or got into?) Anikó, a girl with red hair and white skin . . . I called her Anikó after a favorite cheese I'd eaten as a boy, kind of moist, but all rubbery and squeaky between your teeth. And the stuff was always painfully white, just like my little friend, the rubbery Anikó. She was the real embodiment of male fantasy: a little porcelain angel that any one of us—for a fairly low price—could tickle and dandle on his knee . . . But, above all, like I said, she was like rubber, invulnerable, unbreakable—and so uninterested in life that I was able to let her passivity rub off on me. I found the idea of a life without real physical pleasure very attractive; I wanted to join a pure, silent community of dulled existences."

5.

"Later that evening, after she'd opened the door of a truly isolated little room in her apartment, made up the bed, and quickly, at a run, gathered up all the cobwebs within reach, she explained, as we were getting comfortable, that from now on we would only be able to see each other back in town; the apartment she'd brought me to was the 'empire'—she stressed that word ironically—of her younger brothers, Árpád and Géza, *I mean, no, forget those names,* I remember her face darkening, *just call them 'Hartmann and Conen.' In any case, they've already seen you. They'll get in touch soon.*

"And they did. The next morning I found a piece of letterhead on the floor, with an ancient seal reading *Hartmann és Conen Rt.* On the paper, in rather poor Hungarian, they'd written a whole lot of nonsense, something about the rules of the house, emphasizing again—among other things— that the two brothers were *only to be addressed* as Hartmann and Conen, not in any other way, and absolutely not with some kind of *primitive* Hungarian first names! I remember that my head kept buzzing all day with the verb with which the brothers had 'politely' repeated their childish command: *méltóztassék, méltóztassék, méltóztassék* . . .

"I took a little walk round the neighborhood. A street or two, and I found myself at an enormous construction site; this area of ancient apartment buildings—*bérházak*—had evidently been taken over by the construction mafia. The building I'd just left was already in line to be knocked down. I walked back and looked it over. But first there'd be bloodshed, I thought, being a little theatrical. After all, what did I know about that kind of thing? Two dark little heads whistled past me:

"'*Szia Vörös*, Hi Vereš!' Only the echo of their greeting was left when they'd gone. *Hi Vereš!* One of the kids had called out in our language. It was a bit of a shock.

"I followed them. The building stank of cat piss; the large wooden door was lying broken by the steps in the garbage. The walls were scrawled with coal. If you can say that something is nicotine-colored, then that whole place was nicotine-colored.

"Everything was suffocating in that smoky tint. I continued my search for H&C, in the hope that they might lead me to some breakfast and a coffeepot full of that wonderful black liquid. *I'll give you a kran for a coffee!* I yelled up the stairs. *A kran for a coffee!*

"And, indeed, those two black faces appeared above me, on the next floor up. *Just follow us, Vereš, gyere ide*—up here, one of them called down in Hungarian. *Just keep following*, called the other in Croatian, as though he wanted some confirmation that I would reply. I followed them, listening for the clatter of their footsteps; they didn't stop until they reached the attic.

"When I got there, all sounds died out. It was pitch dark. *Hartmann, Conen*, I shouted and my voice spread through the attic in distorted echoes. Instead of the boys' voices, I heard something like a constrained, hampered flutter of wings. And then a hideous bird's cry cut through me. I stopped, petrified. And then I yelled, *Árpád, Géza, what on earth are you doing up here? Where are you?* I was really furious. I shouted all sorts of things, even that I'd beat the shit out of them.

"I heard laughter. *Come on Vereš, come here, what are you afraid of?* one of them asked, in Croatian again. I saw his silhouette in the meager light coming through the roof struts. *You've come at just the right moment, Vereš*, came the voice of the other, *maybe you can help us out* . . .

"At last I reached them. They didn't look round, they were too preoccupied with something else. They were kneeling over a creature that was lying bunched up on the floorboards, and I realized at once that the appalling shriek I'd heard could only have come from this creature. *In the air here, as you can see,* one of the kids went on mockingly, as much to himself as to me, *in the air here there are plenty of soft, sticky women, prettier and better than your goddamn Anikó, Vereš, Vereš!* ... I was about close enough to smack him when I finally got a good look at what they were crouching around, a bird, a fettered, bleeding bird. I asked them what it was. *An owl of course, can't you see?* they said at the same time. They were proud of it, proud to show it to me.

"'Is it yours?' I asked them, but the little idiots only laughed. *It's ours, ours, but it's going to die, Vereš, do something, we haven't got any food for it!*

I looked a little more closely at the owl. Someone had gouged out its eyes. *Only fresh meat,* I said, without thinking. I was so astounded that I'd lost control of the situation—then one of them hit me over the head with a metal bar, and I lost consciousness as well."

6.

We went out for a cigarette. There was no smoking in the *Aranysárkány*. Vereš made some jokes at his own expense, but I was only half listening. It was noisy and lively outside, already evening, car headlights crisscrossed the city streets with their bright beams. Women's fur coats left little clouds of perfume in their wake; I breathed these in absentmindedly together with the smoke from Vereš's cheap cigarettes.

Inside, a new round of tea was waiting for us. I looked affectionately for our Chinese waitress, but only found one of the cooks staring dully at me from behind the counter.

"I woke up the next morning, in another room, narrow and dark, tied to a bed, with an unbearable pain in my head and legs, and I saw that one of my legs was covered in blood. H&C came in soon after, in a great mood, and they threw their school bags into a far corner.

"*It wants it, the owl wants your flesh! You've saved us!*

"I probably cursed at them then, I don't know what else I could have done. Apparently they had sliced off part of my calf and given it to the owl. *Cool it, Vereš, relax, we've got drugs for you, it won't hurt at all next time! We've got to keep you going, fresh and healthy!*

"And that's how it was, they put me to sleep with a pillow soaked in some disgusting chemical—I always thought they were about to suffocate me. I was tied up and helpless. I always woke up in horrible pain—if you can call that druggy, groggy dream state being awake. I kept hearing a piano tune, over and over again, hundreds of times, as though some child was practicing Bartók's *Mikrokosmos*, or just playing that children's song: *Boci, boci, tarka, se füle, se farka* ... The sounds collided, rang out, as though a hundred cats had hurled themselves at the piano at the same time, yes, I could smell their stink, there must have been cats roaming around the apartment, around my corpse, waiting for their share, waiting for a moment of Hartmann's or Conen's mercy or inattention; I was staggering again down the sandy Kelebija Forest trails, through those dead vineyards, in the frozen darkness, no one could help me, there was no wine or wedding brandy buried in the sand, I rooted through it nevertheless, furiously, in a frenzy, but all I found were some disgusting insects, *mole-crickets*, they were used as bait for catfish and sterlet, but not for me; and then I saw I was surrounded by Chinese people. *You eat mole-crickets!* I yelled at them from my bed, *yes, I know it, you eat them both fried and boiled, you eat them with those little sticks of yours!*

"I don't know how long I was stuck in that room, but I think that the Chinese people had been there for a while already. When they first came in they took no notice of me at all, who knows what Hartmann and Conen had told them, no doubt the blanket they'd covered me with stank to high heaven by now, soaked with pus from my wounds. I guess the Chinese are used to anything. Someone had probably sold or rented them this apartment, because I knew enough to guess that this wasn't part of Anikó's place. Those two crooks must have hidden me here because the apartment was vacant at the time, but now, with the arrival of the Chinese tenants, H&C had vanished.

"When I realized that I had been left entirely at the mercy of the Chinese, my horror reached its peak. I could hear them opening their enormous suitcases and taking out shiny blades. Their snake-like eyes pulsed in the darkness like little sparks of fire. I knew that they seasoned their tasteless rice with little pieces of human flesh, I knew that they fed their snub-nosed yellow dogs with human bones, and I knew that soon after their dogs too went under the knife . . ."

"Oh, good evening, *Jó estét kívánok Vörös úr.*" We were interrupted by a tiny Chinese man who came up to our table, impeccably dressed and courteous. "*Jó barátja?*" He turned to me.

"Yes, a friend from Subotica," Vereš lied. I don't know why.

"Pleased to meet you." The Chinese man offered me his hand. "Do you speak Hungarian?"

"A bit," I said.

"Yes, we all speak just a bit," said the Chinese man seriously. "We ought to try harder. This is their country after all. But your friend Vereš is one of the best. I'm glad that we got him out of a jam and gave him a job. We Chinese work for two Hungarians, but you know," the Chinese man said with a broad smile, "Vereš works for two Chinese people! Two plus two equals four! Isn't that right?'

"That's right," we agreed. The Chinese man looked us over again, with a satisfied air, and then touched the brim of his hat.

"Have a pleasant evening!" he said, then quickly raised the lid of our teapot. "What, you're out of tea?" he asked, astonished. There followed an explosion of incomprehensible sounds intended for the staff, then he turned toward us once again, gave a small bow, and left without a word.

The tea arrived at once. We drank it in silence; now everything was perfectly clear.

TRANSLATED FROM CROATIAN BY CELIA HAWKESWORTH

NAJA MARIE AIDT

Bulbjerg

We suddenly found ourselves in an astonishing landscape: luminous, white-sand hills on all sides, wind-swept trees twisting beneath the blue, open sky. We gasped for breath, joyfully, as if coming up for air after being too long under water. We stopped and looked around us, blinking our eyes that had been focused for so long on the gravel road in the darkness of the plantation. Even the smell was different here, salty and fresh, the sea had to be very close now. But we had lost our bearings long ago. We were going in a circle. It was hot. We had a six-year old boy and a dog with us. The bikes were old and rusty, the danger of a puncture was imminent. We stood completely still and listened. The wind blew through the leaves with a faint rustle, birds were singing, one was screeching, hoarse and desperate, as if for dear life. Sebastian looked at me anxiously. "It's just a common buzzard. Nothing to worry about."

"Come over here, Seba. Would you like a biscuit?"

You called the boy over, a show of kindness, and I looked back, turning my head too suddenly, and too apprehensively. There was the forest we'd just come from, as black and still as a deep lake. The trail in front of us went through what appeared to be a birch grove and, after that, there was more of the dense coniferous forest, moss, heather, and fallen tree trunks, grayish-black, with broken branches sticking out like spikes.

"My legs are tired," Sebastian complained. Then he broke down; his dirty hands covered his face, his shoulders were shaking.

You put him on your lap.

Sitting in the grass, you rocked him gently back and forth while he cried. You looked at me with large, worried eyes. I stared back. "What?" I asked. "Nothing," you answered and stroked the boy's head, "it'll get dark in four or five hours."

"So what? What can I do about it?"

You sighed.

I lay down, arms behind my head.

Sebastian will be seven in two weeks. In August, he'll be in first grade. In a way, he's just the same as ever, the same as when he was a baby. The same worried look, the same little wrinkle on his forehead. It looks like his front teeth will stick out when he gets older. Then we'll have to go through all that stuff with braces and who knows what. I open my eyes and you're standing over me, looking at me with disgust. Perhaps you've been standing there for several minutes. "Should we get going?" you ask. I get up and notice how tired I am. My arms are limp, and a sense of weakness begins to overwhelm my entire body. The water bottle is empty. The dog pants with its tongue hanging out of its mouth. You put it in the cardboard box on your bike rack. Sebastian, keeping his chin up, gets his bike and rides ahead of us. His bell rings with every bump in the road, and the streamer attached to his rear mudguard—which he took such pride in when I put it on—suddenly looks cheap and shabby. We go on in silence. Every time we come to a crossroads, you look at me inquiringly, but, after all, I'm not the local here, and each time you end up saying something like: "So, I think we should go to the right here. I seem to remember that woodpile." Then, without another word, we turn right, until Sebastian throws himself on the ground, yelling and screaming. He's gone into complete hysterics now. He flails at us when we approach him. You try the gentle way; I do it rough.

In the end, I shake him hard and yell that he'd better relax now, and if not we'll just have to leave him there where he can bawl his eyes out until the buzzard comes and gets him. I regret it immediately and put him down. He cries and holds on to my legs. You're leaning against a stump of a tree. Some ants are crawling up Sebastian's chin, dangerously close to his mouth. "What the hell are you doing?" I shout at the boy. He hurls himself to the ground with a strident squeal. He spits and sobs and hits himself in the face. I have to take off all his clothes to brush off the ants. He kicks and flings his arms and legs. He's been bitten in several places. Snot's running from his nose. I lift up the naked boy and we stand like that for a while. Now he's just sobbing, nuzzling his face into my chest.

"If we're not riding in a circle here, we should reach Bulbjerg at some fucking point. And it's impossible to ride around in a circle here, for Christ's sake," I say, "it's impossible to get lost in a shitty little forest like this," I hiss, "Anne!" I shout. Finally, you've gotten to your feet, your face gray and streaked. You rub your eyes like a child.

"I know the guy who owns the take-out place over there," you say.

"What take-out place?" I ask, annoyed. "The take-out place outside Bulbjerg," you whisper.

Sebastian is breathing so close to my ear that it tickles me unbearably; I let him slide down to the ground. He wraps his arms around my hips.

"Seba will ride with me, now," I say, loud and furious.

I free myself from the child's grip and fling his yellow bike into the shrubbery. I think of how it's still lying there like evidence in the investigation of some appalling crime. Someone will stumble over it one day. They'll find my fingerprints on the crossbar and Sebastian's on the handlebars. Perhaps they'll find yours, too. Perhaps they'll think that we killed the boy. "We'll come back and get your bike another day," I assure Sebastian. He's sitting behind me, arms around my back, still naked, his legs are dangling, and my fear of getting his foot caught in the wheel annoys me—

like a mosquito waiting somewhere in the darkness when you're about to go to sleep.

We ride like this for almost an hour, it's muggy, it's about six o'clock, I guess, but none of us actually has a watch. We left home at nine in the morning. It was supposed to be about fifteen kilometres between the summerhouse and Bulbjerg. We'd wanted to look at the beautiful Ice Age landscape up there. I also wanted to show Sebastian the German bunker. We were supposed to have had a nice little talk about the Occupation.

When I woke up this morning, you were watching me. We were both lying on our sides, facing each other, and you were watching me. You smiled. The light fell oblique but bright on the white covers through the roof window. I felt like I was being spied on. Then Sebastian stood in the doorway. He said the dog had peed on the rug in the living room. A little later I heard you laughing and chatting in the kitchen. We used to do it on that rug. We were here in the autumn, it was cold, and we lit a fire in the evenings. I slowly stripped off her clothes, and she looked fabulous on the red Persian rug in the warm light from the fire. She spread her legs. She looked at me with dark, almost sorrowful eyes. Your sister's cunt is tighter than yours. I wonder whether girls are born that way, or if it's just because she's so young. Tine's only your half-sister. Sebastian is adopted.

"No one in this family is properly related!" your stepfather usually cries out at Christmas and Easter, when he's getting up to make a toast. "Assholes!" he yells a little later and collapses in a drunken heap, so your cousins have to carry him out.

Now it's usually on the rug at home that I love her. And she loves me. When you're out, when Tine is looking after Sebastian. When he's sleeping. I like to watch her, when she's lying there, exposed and vulnerable on the cold floor, but also protected by the soft weave of the rug. She's a little cold. She gives good head. The roof of her mouth is warm and hard, and she really concentrates, making it into a real performance. I miss her. I miss her thick, brown hair, her warm neck, her profile when she's lost in her thoughts, one hand under the chin, unaware that I'm watching her there in the darkness. I feel lust and hopelessness. That's the point I've gotten to. I thought that I could easily handle a couple of weeks on holiday up here. We do have a child together, after all.

We're riding down the hill at a high speed, and I have no clear recollection of how it actually happens, but a stick gets caught in your wheel, and I drive straight into your rear, our bikes tumble over, and both boy and dog are thrown clear; they land in a ditch, Sebastian knocks his head on a large stone, and the sound of him hitting the bloody stone makes my skin burn, my throat is dry; I'm afraid he's dead. You're already all over him, you call and cry, I push you away with great force, you gasp for breath and fall back and away. Sebastian is unconscious. He's white as a sheet, and his new, jagged front teeth have split his bottom lip open. He's bleeding.

"Seba," I whisper. My voice sounds far away, is resonating strangely. "Can you hear me, Sebastian? It's Dad."

You have crawled into a thicket. You look at me with bright, green eyes while you hold the dog by its collar. It bares its teeth and snarls, and for some reason it barks violently. "Quiet! He's not dead! Anne!" And it's as though my calling your name out makes you act. You tie the dog to a tree. You pick Sebastian up and stagger down the path with our big, limp child over your shoulder. I don't know why, but I don't relieve you of him, even though you seem about to sink under his weight. I just walk behind you and keep about five meters' distance, while the dog's bark turns into a pitiful whimper over our shoulders as it realizes that it's being abandoned.

I remember vividly the first time I heard Anne say her name. Almost like a whisper, and with downcast eyes. She blushed and smiled a little. And then she did something completely unexpected: she suddenly leaned over with great conviction and kissed me long and hard. She really impressed me. I was touched. I thought she was so cool. I let my hand run through her hair and pulled it gently, bringing her head back a little. She closed her eyes and grinned, almost vulgarly. "Anne?" I whispered. The smell of her skin was unbelievably strong, almost acidulous.

Five years later we were called to our first adoption interview.

"My name is Anne," she announced, loud and clear, and placed both hands on the back of her chair before she finally sat down in the small, stuffy office. No one had asked for her name. Her announcement seemed odd and pompous. As if her name was of vital importance as far as her suitability for motherhood. "There are no guarantees that you'll get a sweet little baby. You have to envisage getting a three-year-old with a harelip and severe brain damage. If you're ready for that, then you're ready to adopt," the caseworker said. At once, Anne replied that she was ready for it.

Much later, when we picked Sebastian up and were sitting on each side of the king-size bed in a hotel in Hanoi, him between us, throwing up, she suddenly said: "His name is Sebastian, and I won't budge."

Their names sit like two awls in my main artery: If you pull them out, I'll bleed to death immediately.

You push forward with Sebastian, at least five hundred more meters, and I can hear how breathless you are. You don't say anything. The foliage above us is dense, it's overcast now, dark and damp where we're walking, I smell resin and mold and wet grass. Then you suddenly turn away from the path and into the woods. You stagger a few meters in, almost tripping over a thick, gnarled branch, you squat and put the boy down gently. Sebastian's a deathly pale color against the dark-green moss. You swat away a fly from his face. I bend down to the child and feel his faint breath as small gusts of warm air on my face. I get up and place my hands on your shoulders, "Look at him," I say, "he'll recover. Really. We're leaving now. We're leaving, Anne, and before you know it we'll be in Bulbjerg, and then somebody will have a fucking car, and we'll be able to get him to the emergency room."

I pick Sebastian up and carry him like a bundle on my back. "Come on,"

I say. You follow me obediently. You stoop as you walk, exhausted, I guess, but you don't cry. I tell you we're already through the woods, and I'm sure we just need to cross one more hedgerow and one more rise before we'll see Bulbjerg and the whole fascinating landscape surrounding the cliff. Kittiwake breed out here. Fulmars, too, I believe. Strange name for a seabird.

"I'm having an affair," I say. You turn your head.

"I have a mistress," I say. You knit your brow and look blank.

"I'm fucking your sister. You understand?" You pick up your pace. "I'm fucking Tine, I can't get enough of her, she gives me head like she's paid for it, I can't get enough, I fuck her on the rug at home, I fuck her on the kitchen table, in the bathroom, I take her from behind, up the ass, in our bed . . ." I'm breathing hard and hissing, I notice. You stop.

"In our bed?" Anne says. "Up the ass?" she says.

I turn around and look at her. She grasps at her throat, she sways back and forth a bit. She looks at me for a long time, and I see her nostrils vibrate. She shakes her head. Fear and an almost celestial innocence shine from her wide-open eyes.

"You're sick," she whispers then.

But quickly her voice becomes loud and shrill. "You're crazy!" she cries and points at me, she's running backward away from me, she points with a stiff finger, "YOU SICK BASTARD!" she shouts, with more rage than I'd imagined, she's ugly and distorted, her motions are mechanical, clumsy, "You disgusting, sick BASTARD!" she shouts, that's the only thing she can get through her lips, sick bastard, disgusting, sick, filthy bastard. And she turns around and just runs, she sprints, as if the devil were on her heels, and I finally see Bulbjerg towering up ahead. My eyes follow the first, soft stretch of coast, then I look over the sea, down below, the great, fierce North Sea, which is a grayish-green today and almost completely calm. I close my eyes and open them again. It's windy out there. I want to lie down and give in to the white light, close my eyes to it, only feel the wind in the grass, hear the particular whispering sounds that the summer wind calls out of the grass, and the hum of bees, and the grasshoppers close by, very close.

But Sebastian groans at that moment, makes little whimpering noises. I take him down into my arms and hug him. The bump on his forehead is big and blue and red, and a deep gash cuts right through it. Fluid flows from the pink, naked flesh. His hand reaches up and cautiously touches some dried blood on his lip. His tongue runs over this wound, he furrows his brow, winces, and calls out for his mother.

"Mom ran ahead of us. We need to get a car, so we can take you to the hospital. The doctor just needs to take a look at your head. Are you nauseous?" He nods. I carry him like you'd carry an infant. His eyes slide shut while I walk with him. I try to keep him awake. I remember that you're not supposed to sleep when you've hit your head. I retell stories from his life, I ask if he remembers the time we played football with the big boys on the field in the park, when one of them gave him a cap? "And when we were at Tivoli Gardens with Mom and Granny and Auntie Tine, and you had three helpings of cotton candy, and we could see the tower of town hall from the rollercoaster, and you had an accident?" I speak loudly and make sure to laugh now and then, to startle him, I want to keep him awake at all costs. I run a little. Now I see Anne far ahead, on her way down the big hill. She's stooping and reeling in the middle of the road. The many different kinds of grass wave with the wind in every direction, it's very beautiful here. The ocean glints down below, the sky is wide and open. It feels good to be out of the woods, I feel light and at ease, I can breathe here. I begin to sing for Sebastian. I sing, and I walk down the hill, down the steep asphalt road, which is sticky and soft from the sun. I feel like running down; it's not only tempting but logical, you're supposed to run down a hill like that, hooting, exhilarated, but I don't. I walk and walk, toward land again, toward the main road with both Bulbjerg and the ocean behind me.

Little by little, Sebastian seems better and clearer-headed. I put him on my shoulders, so he can look at the landscape. When I look for Anne again, she's gone. A little later I see the sign clearly. Imagine opening a take-out place in such a desolate area. Imagine actually breaking even.

Sebastian spots a butterfly and flaps his arms like wings. He asks how long butterflies live. For a brief moment the sun penetrates the cloud cover and sends a jolt of warmth through me. My son is healthy and happy. I have a feeling that things will get increasingly simple, clear. But when we turn into the yard at the restaurant, the first thing I see is Anne. She's with a man, and they're sitting on a bench. The man has an arm around her, and she's burying her face in his chest; it looks like she's crying. I stop. Sebastian says, "Mom." She raises her head with trepidation and looks at us for a moment. Then she collapses again into the man's arms. He has dark, curly hair and is very tan. "Anne's not feeling well," he says. He speaks in the local dialect, slow and dull, the dialect that Anne and Tine dropped a long time ago.

"My son hit his head. I need an ambulance right now." The man shakes his head despondently. "A phone," I say. He gets up from the bench. "What kind of man are you?" he asks. Slowly, slowly he moves toward me. "I'll tell you what kind of man I am, I'm Anne's husband, and I need to use your phone." I go to the counter. A strong smell of burnt oil hits my face.

"A hell of a husband," he mutters. I reach over the counter and get hold of a cordless phone. But he must have crept up on me, because as I'm about to dial the number, he tears the phone out of my hand. He's so close, his eyes are slits, his upper lip curling back a little.

"You deserve a good beating, you," he hisses. Sebastian pulls my hair. "Just call," I say wearily. Out of nowhere, Anne cries out. I reach out for the phone again and try to wrench it out of the man's hand. He lets go of it, it tumbles down to the ground, he puts a big hand on my shoulder. "Give me the boy and get the hell out of here." I lose my balance and nearly drop Sebastian. He must have pushed me hard. "Dad?" Sebastian says. His voice is weak, polite, he's scared. I turn around and look at Anne.

"Who is this man?" I ask. She gives me a grim look.

"This is Sebastian," she says, and the boy, who's still on my shoulders, jumps. "Do as he says. Get out of here."

Sebastian, our son, takes hold of my head with both hands, I feel his warm breath all the way into my auditory canal. "I want to go home," he whispers.

"Come, Seba," Anne says, standing up. "Come." She draws closer with her arms stretched out. "Come and have an ice cream from Sebastian, he's the one you're named after." Her face twists and turns into a crazy grimace.

He looked like a monkey, standing there with his broad chest and hairy arms. He stepped forward and pointed at me, threateningly, with his short, fat finger. I moved backward and started to run. He didn't follow us. When I looked back a little later, I thought I saw him standing in the middle of the road, kissing Anne deeply and pulling her ponytail. I also thought I could hear her mooing, like a cow, but perhaps it was him, I don't know. We reached the main road. Sebastian was silent and stiff. I didn't say anything. Tine's white breasts and the small, dark nipples. The fat finger pointing to the soft spot between my eyes. I was sweating heavily and jumped at the sound of my own breath.

It was almost dark before a car finally picked us up. Sebastian was basically fine. The doctor examined him, the nurse tried to make him laugh. He didn't say a word. They bandaged his wound and sent us home. You were sitting in the dark by the window late that night when we returned to the summerhouse. You hadn't even picked up the dog.

TRANSLATED FROM DANISH BY ANNE METTE LUNDTOFTE

ELO VIIDING

Foreign Women

I remember numerous kind women translators and poets bringing me all sorts of knickknacks when I was a child—pencils, calendars, and erasers; and then, for my parents, creams, facemasks, and aftershave. During the Russian days we simply couldn't buy anything from the local shops. These women, generous and outspoken, were foreign women. Usually they'd managed to go straight from the airport to meet their bohemian friends at the local Artists' Club. These foreign women would stay at a hotel, and all sorts of interesting things were always happening to them there: for instance, at five-twenty in the morning, they would often be woken up by the clanking of some triumphant janitor's buckets as his shapeless body hauled these by their door; or else their sleepy eyes would find the crumpled corpse of a cockroach, pregnant with young, in their morning cup of coffee, the creature having been squashed by the blow of a spoon.

So, generally speaking, these foreign women seemed to be living the good life—they could risk taking things less seriously than their Soviet sisters: they would even demand the right to be treated with respect at customs, would demand to be allowed to leave with suitcases full of cosmetics and, of course, countless bottles of liqueur—they wouldn't allow the customs officers to rifle through their belongings just like that . . . or would have the guts to scream their heads off at the very least. They would allow themselves to make their presence known in the company of men, on the street, or even in bars, and sincerely believed that they were being treated seriously, and that men wanted to treat them as equals. The foreign women lived their noisy, bohemian lives to the full, without being much bothered by their conscience. Their husbands were back home taking care of all their practical concerns, after all, in their native lands—and if they weren't, well, it was relatively easy for a foreign woman to get divorced from a man who complained too much.

The foreign women hinted to my mother and other silent wives of male authors—about whom they often talked behind their backs—that they might perhaps be petit bourgeois crackpots, sucking their untalented and unlucky husbands dry in order to secure a better social position for themselves.

The women over here did not, unfortunately, learn anything from the foreign women, and one or two became completely convinced that their single duty in life was simply to keep their husbands alive.

The foreign women would never have believed, if anyone had told them, that writers in our occupied country only managed to stay alive thanks to the ministrations of their drab and patient wives. What our women saw, even loved, in the self-destructive lifestyles of their husbands remained inexplicable to the foreign women.

A clean, sharp, and expensive fragrance would always waft into the room when the foreign women came. I remember one of them would often be sitting on the leather sofa in my father's room, behaving in a relaxed, uninhibited way, her long hair falling loose; they would have brought photos of their fatherless little sons, or books that they themselves had written, or many other such treasures, all to present to my father as gifts. I also remember that for some reason or other, my mother never felt that she could disturb the foreign women's private conversations with my father, nor to criticize the length of time they spent alone with him—though I was pretty sure she didn't approve.

The non-poet wife of a productive poet living under such dismal political circumstances as ours was obliged, I understood, to be understanding and willing to make concessions to said poet, something that my mother hardly found easy. And yet, I thought that these heroic foreign women would never have stood for such treatment—they would have smoked any other women out of father's study in no time, or at the very least said something cutting or even openly offensive to their rivals. Or perhaps just threatened to leave their husbands. No, the foreign women would never have allowed themselves to be ordered around. They never would have sat by and watched their health and good looks be systematically destroyed over the course of their lives by any so-called intellectual of the male persuasion.

Not one contemporary foreign magazine, dedicated as they were to the enjoyment of life, ever dared demand that the foreign women subjugate or sacrifice themselves without recompense. They did, however, recommend that the foreign women walk with their hair uncovered in the Middle East; that they bathe in the blazing desert sun and talk about human rights; that they shave their bushy eyebrows and draw them in again with eyeliner; that they cut off their hair and try a wig for a change; that they sit cross-legged on their carpets for hours with their husbands and talk candidly about labor relations; that they believe shy men would cheat on them less often; that they always smell good while at the same time seek to combat the use of toxins in the production of cosmetics; that they seek psychotherapeutic help and sue their most recent ex-husband to cover the expense; that they find the Ur within themselves by having affairs with younger men; that they only wear jewelry from a Tibetan monastery, with whose cause they would of course empathize deeply; and, likewise, the foreign-women journalists did of course advise the foreign women to seek their animus inside every uncultured repairman. Clearly, the foreign women would never have been able to live with our brilliant male writers who, during one of their rare visits to a grocery store, were usually incapable of finding a bag of salt on the dry-goods shelves, and who, after one of these unsuccessful forays, began to act completely insufferable. The foreign women weren't interested in getting a more in-depth knowledge of the suffering of men, and although they were interested in the various paradoxes of modern life, and even in what our local male authors wrote, they could only really manage to be enthusiastic about their own lives and problems. Obviously, they also wouldn't have mothered their husbands or pretended to believe the muddled lies they told during their evening walks, but would have shot them down devastatingly and without hesitation. Presumably, the foreign women often wished—when they were between husbands—that their exes, irrespective of their social status or the relative size of their egos, had participated wholeheartedly in every element of their marriage, even the divorce process, even in helping their foreign women move away, or, at the very least, wished that their men had gone along to their lawyers' offices to finalize things in a spirit of equanimity and resignation.

Educated Soviet women would never, for the most part, have been able to make such demands of their husbands. And even when a local woman did manage to ask for some concession, she usually ended up falling back on the generally accepted rules for her gender almost immediately: apologizing, even feeling ashamed.

Soviet women, with their gaunt faces, exhausted on account of being deprived of spare time, loved to smile and chuckle over and noisily publicize the stories of the dishonorable declines that had, like lightning, followed the scandalous acts of any proud but treacherous members of their gender to have dared express some discontent with the status quo—the better to feel that they were secure in the unshakeable sanctuary of their own high social standings, which had been obtained only after terrible effort and anxiety in that male-dominated world.

This brand of treacherous female, refusing to acknowledge the sanctity of the male essence, refusing to live lives centered around some man's sense of self-importance, nor lives of twisted self-assertion, could easily end up being labeled vain and vulgar sluts, little wailing dykes, even half-witted, half-crazy whores. Impugning their sanity was especially offensive, since these women tended to be strong, pithy, sharp-minded, in-the-know, indomitable—all things that clearly disturbed our men.

Of course, it was usually the younger intellectuals who kept these insults alive, men who were always complaining about the latest beautiful but self-centered woman who'd disturbed their lives, men who used such barroom talk to engender a sense of community between themselves and their peers, a sense of equality; while older men, on the other hand, given the opportunity, would simply mutter something admonitory and reserved into their moustaches, strewn with breadcrumbs, glaring at the woman in question with their lustful but rigidly maintained, conservative stares.

A good woman, with whom a proper Soviet intellectual would want to live—working, eating, sharing their home, sleeping—was always bright, alert, effective, discreet, handy, and well-liked; she never whined, never drank or talked too much, knew when to make herself scarce, knew how to sacrifice her own needs when necessary; was simultaneously ladylike, childishly dependent, politely adult, and wise as an old sage. To expect such qualities in a man was a terrible crime against our societal norms, not to mention dangerous to a woman's equilibrium both psychologically and socially—such a woman could easily risk her reputation if she didn't quickly show herself, at least in front of other women, and in as demonstrative and emotional a manner as could be managed, to have realized the ridiculousness of such expectations.

With regard to sex, it wasn't the custom among our women, their hair falling out from giving birth so frequently—and especially not the custom among their humanist husbands—to bother spending money on those extremely uncomfortable, ridiculously priced condoms from Ukraine, which were in any case thought of as being inimical to life, since it was clear that they would speed the extinction of so small a nation as ours, and which were, regardless, rarely available in the shops. Polish anti-conception hormones, which give our women light dizzy spells and damaged their livers, were much more convenient, especially when working one's way through the Kama Sutra, and, according to the men, made their women far more permissive, made them much better in bed, almost as good as whores; and besides, a woman could always run to some doctor she knew to get an abortion if it was really necessary.

The foreign women thought all this was completely unhinged; as often as not, they would leave their middle-aged friends with the gentler sorts of sex toy available back in their countries, like those innocent pink furry handcuffs, which, according to the foreign women's instructions, were meant to be used by the stronger party, i.e., the woman, on the weaker, i.e., the man; or else bestselling sex manuals would emerge from the depths of their Burberry suitcases, adorned with pictures of married couples smiling frankly.

Of course, by giving such daring presents, they were risking some of the more patriarchal family fathers breaking off their friendships, but since these women represented the better, capitalist, free world, they were usually forgiven. Various pink Taiwanese sex toys were, in any case, often given to the children to play with, while the sex manuals, intended to enlighten and embolden, were usually used to light the stove.

I liked these foreign women, so meticulous, in their cheap-looking broad-brimmed hats, hiding their stark smokers' faces. Some of them were even poets themselves, or were members of the feminist movement. In my opinion, they were each proud and brave in their own way, and sometimes a little comical too, for instance when they couldn't understand why Estonian men were unwilling to empty their own ashtrays or take a dirty shirt even as far as the kitchen tap. The foreign women actually believed that our local women were joking when the latter hinted at the extent of the wearying but inescapable double burden of home and job, and laughed loudly at their stories, laughed with sympathy, heartily and in solidarity. However, some of the other foreign women, who, on account of their spiritual nature, weren't particularly bothered by stinking, overflowing ashtrays, and who might perhaps have harbored a certain resentment toward their Estonian gender-mates, and who might even have been in the habit of emptying ashtrays in their own families, merely shrugged their shoulders. In their opinion, focusing on such pseudo-problems was simply suffocating—no wonder Estonian women had no self-esteem. At least I can say that these minor frustrations were never a problem for them during their visits to our own home, since my mother was attentive enough to silently collect all the ashtrays from all corners of the apartment towards morning, fumbling and stumbling, half-asleep, between living room and kitchen, emptying them one after the other into the trash.

Our men, of course—even my father—wanted to be liked by these proud and independent-minded foreign women: they were drawn in by their superficiality, their easy laughter, their ability to live in the here and now, their open displays of animal sexuality and strength, and the foreign women enjoyed the boyish attention they were being paid, happily teasing our ranks of toy soldiers.

When the foreign women, now back in their homelands and reunited with their better halves, phoned us at night, tipsy, thanking us for our hospitality, they would always tell my mother to feed my father better, since he'd seemed exceptionally thin, or they would advise my mother to wear more colorful clothing—maybe a little more revealing too. On one occasion, my mother burst into tears when some especially candid woman— a literary type, a feminist—asked her in genuine bewilderment why she would ever wear such a horrid, featureless, and pointlessly modest dress.

Still, when the foreign women arrived at our place, my mother would always make them nice sandwiches to go with their vodka, or else oatcakes to go with their coffee, which the foreign women would eye with suspicion at first, then gulp down with delight, full of praise.

The foreign women talked and laughed a lot; it seemed they had little in common with Soviet women, who'd always had a certain tendency toward depression. Furthermore, the foreign women were never able to pay attention to anyone else's problems for more than a few minutes at a time. Not that this really mattered: no one in their right mind would risk confiding anything in them—with their big mouths, firm convictions, and sharp tongues; even their silence, when they were silent, seemed a ploy to make them all the more audible. Thus, they found my mother entirely too cautious and unapproachable—though my father's social skills compensated for my mother's shortcomings in this respect.

But it seemed that even the attentions of our local men would begin to bore the foreign women eventually: the more they drank vodka and walked around in the dust of the city, the more they tried to tell us—directly and selfishly—exactly what they thought of our men and our life. It seemed as though the foreign women couldn't stand having to respect anyone for too long: couldn't stand having to look them straight in the eye, mouths wide open, couldn't stand having to admire their intelligence. No doubt our men saw this as unpleasantly pragmatic.

But, then, our men soon began to tire of the foreign women too, wanting nothing more during the last days of their visits than simply to take a break from socializing and sit in silence at the table reading a newspaper in their cramped kitchens.

Having downed a portion of tepid solyanka at the Artists' Club and then drunk a stiff one for the road, the foreign women would rush off in their pre-hired, dirty-yellow taxis through our city full of posters of balding, senile-looking politicians to the airport, where they would be greeted by the turned-up collars, brown fur caps, and seemingly impassive faces of a phalanx of police informers, who'd already had more than enough of their antics, having been obliged to keep an eye on them for hours on end back in town.

When the long, drawn out visit by the foreign women had finally come to a close, when they'd finally departed, as Saturday moved towards sunset, my mother and father would fall, in the early evening, into a sleep so deep it almost seemed drug-induced, remaining silent in bed until dinnertime on Sunday. Once awake, they wandered pale and sleepy through the rooms of our apartment.

Father would try his new aftershave, light a good cigarette, leaf through *Conversations with Ionesco* or *Man: In a Changed World*. Mother would rustle the empty wrappers from liqueur-filled chocolates listlessly, having scooped the slivers of glass she found behind a window curtain into a dustpan, a small worn comb in her other hand. I would still be playing proudly with some doll or other, a doll brought by a foreign woman, pretending that this doll with her long hair, this doll that cost as much as a whole Estonian toy shop, was sitting on a plane on its way to Philadelphia, drinking sherry, with orange negligee in her suitcase, as well as an issue of the magazine *Naiste Tund*—"Women's House"—a book about magic, a wand, and a photo of some distant lover . . .

The foreign women would always leave countless essentials behind, accidentally: brightly colored scarves; sweetly scented bookmarks; stylish sunglasses; bottles of anti-hangover pills, with a lemon on the label; small flasks smelling of stale whisky; unsharpenable, environmentally safe pencils; letter-openers decorated with kangaroos or peacocks; flame-red, all-day lipstick—all of which they would no doubt promise to come and reclaim the following year.

TRANSLATED FROM ESTONIAN BY ERIC DICKENS

JUHANI BRANDER

FROM Extinction

FOES

Maire is from the southernmost corner of the province. Got into university on her second try to study cultural anthropology. Maire's parents spent the whole of this last July just bursting with pride. Her father bought her a new Nissan Almera, gave her a few plump stalks of advice for her new life, his daughter leaving the nest, and smacked his potato-farmer lips. Her mother was dumb, not from birth, but had dampered her vocal cords little by little over the years out of some void, some understanding of the dark side of her dreams. Maire's father called her mother a shoal so gloomy even the gulls avoided it.

Maire is still remembered in the village for her wild childhood, the satirist's black sense of humor that she vented on the Midsummer birches, the seigneurial droit's bastard kids, and the stolen landmines. Maire would wander through the village, gathering material, chatting with the widows, chortling like an idiot at the stories the winos told her. It's widely believed that this restlessness of hers, this tendency she had to act as if she were some kind of writer, was the result of an unfortunate incident in which she saw her first love Gabriel dancing under all the stars and angels without a stitch on, the northern lights licking his naked body. After that, nothing could be sacred.

In the city at a student party, Maire starts fucking Petrus, a great lonely lame mystic always in search of quality time with a bottle of red wine. Month after month he inserts his dirty fingers into the timid thicket between her legs, and soon an infection, having marinated in the dark, sprouts symptoms. The thicket itches and fizzles. Maire goes into a pharmacy, she just wants help, that's all, o saintly Gabriel, o beautiful prince, o first love already pushing up daisies. The checkout girl's hands tremble, unmarried, young, first day on the job, here she is ringing up some thicket medicine, all human dignity has been stripped away by the public display of a drug like that, she can't look Maire in the eyes, with this gesture like a tiny animal I give you the gift of self-respect. Behind Maire the line of the sick and the Samaritan now vanishes into the park-pounding autumn wind outside; here in the pharmacy is waged the eternal battle between good and evil, between the right and wrong man's potato blight. Here are weighed in the balance the sucking up of teachers' pets and the condemnation in advance of the rowdy back-row boys to jail or the docks; here are measured the buffalos' shrinking prairie and the slow extinction of the pike stock. Yes, there's no one left in the pharmacy now except two mortal foes, in one corner hard work and accomplishment, in the other humiliation and disappointment in the public soiling of a good name. The name on the checkout girl's shirt front, in that last demonic irony, that telling detail that always finds its way into a tall barroom tale, is also Maire. Seeing the name, Maire stops wrestling with her demons over that horror in her thicket and smiles broadly, the smile of a con-artist, a businessman, a dentist drilling teeth without cavities. Accepting her change, Maire grabs the checkout girl by the chin and subjects her for just a moment too long to the red eyes of a disgraced woman. The checkout girl wets herself. In a flash, she also grieves for the treachery of that thicket, the vulnerability of every thicket in the world to the fraud so often hiding behind the love of a fair prince, and the helpless victims then left in its wake. Maire laughs the pharmacy windows into the street; the glass shards slice into many a beautiful person, and the envious rejoice.

HAMLET WAS A SHIT

That's why they got fed up that Monday. Aki, cute as a bug, always had hysterical giggling fits before they committed one of their heinous crimes. Henna decided that this was no day to worry about being underpaid. They wanted to have two children: Luukas and Oinas, future merit scholars, CEOS, fox-hunters, rollers of eyes at vulgarity.

Aki and Henna chose the top of the hill. There was no crosswalk for two meters. The sky was cruel. It was trying to rain. It was the Monday of destiny, if business school students are allowed to wax poetic. The BMW generation trod their gas pedals furiously, and Aki and Henna ran, full of joy, bellowing like autumn calves. Not even slightly concerned now with making money or that dreamy Keijo who worked in the supermarket checkout line. In an instant it was over. His boyhood was not curtailed. They heard the squealing of brakes, those two business school students, the furious cursing from rolled-down windows. Henna looked at Aki. Total understanding sealed them off from the rest of the world. Pubescent defiance rose up in Aki. He ran back out to the middle of the street and glared at Henna like Hamlet, surrounded by scheming courtiers. A semi rushing to the nearby port, a miracle from the east, ended Aki and his business school dreams. They put him in an oaken box under a big rock.

Against her parents' wishes, Henna married the driver of the semi that killed Aki. The driver sang in a choir and talked in his sleep.

SAIGON

Pasi Aarnio needed freedom outside of work, so he spent his summers riding his motorcycle and wore moccasins when he helped out around the neighborhood. Pasi's biker name was "Saigon." Saigon had bested Roadkill, the former gang leader, on the scales. Roadkill weighed forty-seven grams more, so naturally he had to step down as gang leader. Roadkill was so depressed at this loss of status that he accepted an honorary consulship in a warm country, there becoming an alcoholic, refusing the call of the sea, and delighting the locals by growing his hair long.

Now Saigon pulled the gang's strings. Saigon decided where they would and would not drive on a Sunday afternoon. This aroused some opposition, even rebellion in the up-and-comers—the futures traders and nouveaux riches all ridiculed Saigon's cockiness, even though he was indisputably the cock of *their* walk, reliable, unyielding, a champion chanticleer if ever there was one.

The day came when Saigon and the garage gang were supposed to drive more than a hundred kilometers. Saigon was up all night before the ride, he hit his wife, called his only son a fag, and tore the kid's down comforter. The comforter was very warm, a shame to ruin it. Saigon didn't water the leaves on his withered money-tree, with a sardonic laugh he gathered dust from under the rug and sprinkled it on his salad. Saigon sent messages full of double entendres to his firm's angel-faced courier boy and told his wife all about it; she suffered from insomnia and the memory of her father's younger brother getting lost in the bulrushes and dying.

At dawn Saigon drove to the garage in plenty of time, circled a nearby church with his helmet off, burning rubber, wrong, wrong. The elderly flock leaving the house of the Lord trembled with fear at the sight of someone they'd read about in the paper carrying on like that. Saigon shouted gray war reparations at them. The gang was ready. Nine engines roared in satanic thunder.

It was a Sunday, traffic was light, a hundred kilometers slid beneath them without pain or perspiration. The garage gang was on edge, though, suspicious: is this all there is to it? Saigon sensed his gang's unease. Then he got it, by God he got it. Biker etiquette requires that you greet oncoming bikers. On the ride out the garage gang had greeted every biker they'd passed. Saigon decided that on the ride back there would be no greetings.

This radical notion boiled and burned in the group, but the gang members all got onboard with the decision. When the first biker passed them, they all turned their heads, but then instantly there was nervous laughter and growing regret. Saigon tried to stay strong at the head of the gang, but caved in at last. At the first intersection he turned, the gang faithfully following behind, and soon they chased down the biker they'd ignored, shouting "hi" to him. The biker nodded in reply. That made Saigon's gang smile.

At home Saigon apologized to his battered wife, took her to a private hospital, and hired his son a hooker. That should get him interested in women, the scrawny kid. Saigon ate his dusty salad with gusto and tried to write a short story. The next Saturday night when his wife returned from the hospital he tripped her in the front hall and went out into the yard to gather night crawlers. He began to feel free again and cast his bloodshot eyes over the handsome house where his loved ones were still safe.

MAKE A NOTE

His work day starts at seven. He showers, brushes his teeth, makes coffee, makes oatmeal, reads the paper, tsking a little at the strong emotions on display in the letters to the editor. He rubs good smells into his armpits and onto his chin and drives to work. This is a nicely set-up studio apartment just off the main street downtown. His first client is an insatiable heiress. She's sick of her new husband's incompetence between the sheets. Before she arrives he likes to recite the tenets of his faith and thank God for his well-earned work day, water his flowers, iron his favorite shirt, and meditate. In his eyes every moment in God's hands is a blessing. The heiress arrives on time. She gets tongue and penis. She gives him a hundred euros extra and he throws in a tickle or two for the erogenous zones on her breasts. She leaves satisfied and promises next Monday. I'll make a note of that, he says. After she leaves, he goes out for lunch. His next client isn't until the afternoon. For his appetizer he chooses a mushroom soup and radishes. For his main course he wants crane in sour cream with potatoes in Aura cheese, and for dessert the always-safe strawberry ice cream. He adds a little quality time with a French coffee and a cigarillo. After his filling lunch it's back to work with the human race. Two twentyish girls want a proper fucking. The girls leave satisfied and that makes him feel good. He has done his bit to alleviate frustration and contribute to public hygiene. It's four o'clock and he drives home. At home he rides his exercise bike for a moment, works his abs, then picks up his wife, with whom he goes to a prayer meeting at a nearby church. The female pastor winks at him. He is disgusted by overt desire. The pastor can't just do her job but has to whore it up before her entire flock like a lost sheep.

SWIMMERS

We modern romantics, what are we doing out here on the boat's hull, hugging? Uncle comes and demands an explanation, but we're adults, we decline to answer. We tell Uncle to hop in the water with his clothes on. He refuses, goes and gets the heavy drinkers from the village to join him in defiance. We listen, we lovers, dodging bottles and knives. We wonder why this would only happen in Finland, but our answer stands before us, the whole machismo thing, the negative capabilities of drink. We swim away across the lake to the island, where mad cows were kept through the summer. Uncle and the drunks from the village swim after us, only make it halfway, one by one their slack bodies go under. Love only laughs. We swim back to the humans' island, no floaters yet. We do our thing on the boat hull again, that thing that brings babies into the world. The constable takes our information and looks out over the lake longingly. He doesn't say it, but he's thinking about fish. We spend the night in my room, bury the other swimmers. We light our cigarettes and memorial candles, let them burn in secret.

ELVI A DEALER?

Elvi in the old folks' home called a wrong number. That's how it started. Osmo, in hock for his life to a drug dealer, saw the unfamiliar number and panicked. Osmo got an ulcer. Osmo imagined the Estonian thugs, their cruel fists-for-hire. Osmo, sweaty, called back, the individual's freedom forgotten now. Elvi in the old folks' home picked up on the fifth ring. Osmo said, someone at this number called me. Elvi heard the heavy breathing, got scared, grabbed at his chest. Elvi filled his voice with bailiffs, sheriffs, and his outlaw brother. This all gave Osmo another ulcer. Elvi hung up and told the guy in the room next door, Jurtta Kuusisto, that it had been a bad person on the phone. Jurtta said to Elvi, you and your stories, but in another dialect. Osmo coughed up his health, his soul, en route to a new diocese. The doorbell rang. Osmo saw himself on the reaper's shitlist. Osmo headed toward his fate, toward opening the door, two coins in hand for the ferryman, hoping he'd still take Finnmarks. His kidneys collapsed before he got there, and degradation soaked his pants. Osmo thought, nothing more to lose, opened the door, his teeth fell out, though no one had punched him. On the stoop two singing Jehovah's witnesses with all their promises: heavenly joys, fancy words. With his last ounce of strength Osmo closed the door and felt a fierce pain in his chest. Osmo believed in God's wrath and was certain he was heading for the dark. On the edge of consciousness Osmo heard the witnesses still singing and rose again for battle. Osmo had heard that natural yogurt is good for a bad stomach, had some in the fridge. Then the phone began to ring goddammit. That did it. Later, investigating the cause of death, police listened to a message on his answering machine saying that Mailis, the dealer, had given up drugs, forgiven the debt, found Jesus, and wanted to wish Osmo a pure life and God's love. A month later, Elvi died of old age and a childhood as a war refugee. The memorial service was held in the same chapel as Osmo's.

CREATION STORY

Markku aspired to metrosexuality. Markku had his behind liposuctioned and piles coins on his bookshelf as a total feng shui solution. Markku's better half, the healthily cynical and sharply conservative Janita, raked over her relationship with Markku in therapy. Markku often urged Janita to cheat on him with men and women. Markku drilled a hole in the wall so he could watch Janita writhe. Her therapist found nothing wrong in that, it was a new era, and anyway Janita didn't have to worry like her mother about getting pregnant or thrown in the poorhouse. Janita was annoyed by the therapist's reaction, she would have liked to get her full money's worth of support for every problem, a reason to hate Markku for this and that; she wanted to damn her mother to the lowest circle of hell and to steal her father to redeem her childhood. There was nothing for her to do but seek out Markku's parents, whom no one had seen in years. Markku's father groped everything in sight, even daughters-in-law-to-be, and Markku's mother considered it a daughter-in-law's duty to submit to the paterfamilias, even though Markku's father was a retired ferryman. Janita whined to her as if to a sister about Markku's new desires and the whole circus of compulsions Markku had developed. Markku's mother was delighted with the change in her shy son, while his father was too stupid to do anything but wolf down the pastries Janita had supposedly made by hand. They had blood and lipstick on them. Janita ended up alone, though she was open to life and wished nothing but the best for everyone around her. Markku squandered his advance inheritance on designer drugs and private coaches at the gym. He wasn't muscleman material, his genes and bad technique worked against him. Janita resigned herself to skiing and roaming the woods, occasionally she'd collect the odd dagger that had been used in some bloody revenge to place as a focal point in the interior décor of her brother's sailboat. Finally Janita took Markku in his business suit back to his roots in the woods, because she did not believe they had been born of a perch or the story about the rib in pieces and the wrath of some lizard. Janita burned Markku's military passport and gas card and ran naked around an alder. A bear padded out of the woods with Janita on his mind in terms of dinner. Markku woke up then and wrestled the bear. The bear won that round. It let Janita off easy and she escaped without much damage. At home Janita hung the suit back up in the closet and poked her finger into the hole through which Markku while alive had seen everything.

PLACES FOR EVERYBODY

Christ's brides are at the door, vulvas off limits. No confessions of sin here. Butts strain against tight skirts, pubic hairs glisten. The brides' bodies serve only Jesus. Birgitta would rather not remember losing her virginity, she despises that painful moment in the barn when the hired hand stole her maidenhead. Ripa is a midwife who found ten angels on her first day on the job, the mother and both twins dying in childbirth. Ripa and Birgitta found a better life in the sect, where nothing can bruise them, the world outside is all pollution, the devil's playground. The joyful ladies ring the doorbell ninety times. Arttu is certain that behind the door stands some eager writ-server, some broad-shouldered balding man who hides the street-fighting days of his youth from his loved ones. Arttu is supposed to go to court and perjure himself as a witness in the matter of the beating of a poet, honest your honor those guys didn't mean to turn the guy into a vegetable. Arttu has been avoiding the summons, fearing the long arm of the law. In his younger years he went to church and admitted many weaknesses to pulpit supply. Arttu feels repulsed by the world and justifies that feeling with the tribal rituals of the dispossessed. His father's moose rifle passed to Arttu when his father had himself passed violently in the public sauna. Arttu fetches it from under his bed, loads it with shiny bullets. Four sharp reports follow. The entire apartment building wakes up. Telephones begin to ring off the hook at the police station; domestic disturbances, the unhappy fingering of many a teenaged girl, and the eating of many a cheap liver casserole are all interrupted. The police arrive within allotted response-time parameters. They find two middle-aged women in unnatural positions with their skirts around their ears and their flesh torn by bullets. Arttu sits in the living room humming some hymn and reading the literature the two women had brought. The police join in the hymn. Arttu in the third year of his majority smiles, looks up to heaven, and is taken into custody.

SWAP

Jokke wanted to fall in love with a courtesan, but they don't exist any longer. Jokke found Helena, who'd been to all seven seas and whose eyes had given up. A seagull was their only witness on the windy rock where rings bought on credit were exchanged. Jokke claimed that it was the same day the Berlin Wall fell, though that was ten years before. Helena was eager to rub up against him, but not sexually, the movement was mechanical, and Jokke saw no future in it. Helena swapped her rags for a beer in the company of some dangerous men. Jokke closed his eyes and watched it all with sadness. Helena didn't want to go to work and Jokke knew that something had happened at sea. Even her mechanical rubbing died out in time and impossibility. Helena was going to swap Jokke for a couple of beers, but his jeans stank and his socks were dirty, and the ladies sunning on the lawn wanted nothing to do with him. Helena cared for Jokke and let the magpies take from the windy rock the rings they finally owned free and clear.

TEX WILLER

Lauri got really pissed off when Saara wanted to role-play Tex Willer. To
Lauri's mind she'd read the comic books so totally wrong. Saara called
Lauri a man without sleep. Lauri called Saara goiter-proud. Lauri felt
Saara's salmon had never developed, since Saara had given herself to the
rich rancher's son too early. Lauri had heard—since everyone considered
him a doctor's son—that penetration at too young an age prevented full female development. Saara denied it. Saara insisted that she was still pretty
as a virgin, and only looked at straying townspeople. Lauri asked Saara if
she'd ever given it to someone named Sir. Saara disdained to answer and
handed Lauri a cowboy hat. Saara whistled and out on the balcony Lauri
hollered at the neighborhood kids to shut up. The neighborhood always
hollered back, but by then the balcony door was closed. Lauri went along
with Saara's desires, it wasn't sex, just dressing in silence and living ordinary lives in different clothes. For a brief moment the prairie was a possibility for them, until their next-door neighbor Aaron asked if he could have
a beer. Lauri went to the front door out of habit. Aaron gulped and giggled
like the janitor who stole fire from a stevedore. That was the end of his career as a stand-up comic. It was a relief to his father figure, because Aaron
was an only son and that was reason enough for anything. For the rest of
their lives Lauri and Saara watched adult entertainment in sweaters, and
the neighborhood wept for its children.

TRANSLATED FROM FINNISH BY DOUG ROBINSON

CHRISTINE MONTALBETTI

Hotel Komaba Eminence
(with Haruki Murakami)

Murakami spoke to me, he was addressing me, but really, I felt as though none of his sentences had been composed especially for me. The things he said were well used, he was drawing from a stock of phrases that he must have tried out a thousand times before, as though we were still in his bar and he was playing a record for me, many records in fact, having decided to make me, me in particular, listen to them, naturally, but having chosen all the selections long before.

I was listening, his body was like a record player for me, his glottis was the needle, his vocal chords were the grooves in the vinyl. I liked the jazzy bits best. Yes, it was jazz, it was improvisation, but frozen in the imprint of a record, to be played in exactly the same way, over and over again.

There's nothing wrong with that. When it comes to slightly mundane situations, like the one we were in, we're all the disc jockeys of our own internal radio stations, pulling out tried and tested 45s as needed, one after the other, from our libraries. Still, I would have liked it if my presence had made Murakami say something new, had made him speak a new phrase that took even him by surprise. I was dreaming of, desperate for, what one might call "conversational gems"—those phrases that form unexpectedly in the presence of other people, and that we then offer to them, at once their muses and recipients. With this phrase in hand, our interlocutor departs, contented; he may now return home with his gift, a gift of which he was by no means undeserving, having caused the phrase to be formed in the first place, having been its mysterious inspiration. I would have liked it if such a sentence had left Murakami's lips, a sentence arising from our situation, the specific result of those immaculate net curtains having been released from their tiebacks, of the green mass of vegetation that could be made out through their transparent layers, of the layout of the tables, of the white cotton tablecloths decorated with magnificent, twisted patterns, and of both our presences, there, looking down on our white earthenware cups and bowls, now partially empty.

I imagined him jogging in the gardens before getting back to the Hotel Komaba Eminence. I imagined his stride, his breath, its acoustic intensity increasing on the garden paths, his body moving through that narrow scenery.

Because at this same hour of the day when I, for my part, was barely emerging from the vague fabric of my dreams—having forced myself to leave the tiny bed where I'd gone to sleep the night before, motionless like a guard in his sentry box, readying myself for dream journeys throughout which I would be forced to lead my body along, constrained, stiff as a board, floating there in that rigid posture (bigger beds, allowing us the comfort of free movement, of adopting lazy, hunched, crooked postures, open up paths to far more luxurious, voluptuous dreams, in my opinion)—the person I was speaking to, as was his habit, was already well into his day. Up at four in the morning to work at his desk, he would only leave it at nine to go running or even swimming, heading for some pool in Tokyo I knew nothing about.

I let my mind conjure up his body sitting at his desk, which I imagined was situated in front of a window, facing the Tokyo night, a lamp lit and reflected against the windowpane, where his silhouette, bent over his work, was also reflected—when he lifted his eyes, his self-portrait would be spread in the grain of the glass, superimposed onto the town.

At that same hour, confined to its thin mattress, my own body was nothing more than the screen onto which a short, incoherent, and sterile film was being projected.

To follow up on this metaphor, I could easily imagine Murakami and myself on parallel sides of a split-screen interlude: To the left of the frame the moment when, still lethargic after the summons of my alarm clock (it was nearly nine A.M.), and having undone my nightgown, I entered the confined space of the shower—almost the same size as my bed, though aligned vertically (keeping my balance as best I could, I rubbed my skin with the tiny soap I'd been provided, which gave off the same bland and slightly acidic scent of all hotel soaps); to the right, separated, say, by an opaque, coloured strip, the precisely concomitant moment when his body was displacing torrents of the chlorinated water enveloping him so sumptuously, the gently undulating surface ahead lapping against the plastic of his goggles.

Or should we have said it was armfuls of air being displaced, in the humid atmosphere of a park, his breath slipping between the various plant species there in little jerky wisps, a light cloud of dust being kicked up by his shoes behind him?

The disproportion between our two usages of the early morning gave me a strange feeling. It seemed to me that we were separated by a kind of schedule time-lag. It was as if this moment we were now sharing was happening to us both at a different point of the day: the middle of the day for him, since he'd already filled six hours in such active and productive ways; but only the beginning of the day for me. Our two bodies were operating according to entirely separate cycles. He represented a world in which the conscious portion of life begins at four in the morning, and I a world in which it only starts after nine. These two worlds bear no relation to one another. Thus, we were in the same space, but not governed by the same temporality. Witnesses to our two incompatible worlds, we faced one another from either side of the table as though we had found a neutral territory where our two presences could somehow, artificially, be brought into synchronization. The fabric of the white tablecloth and the deep folds of our fine, expensive napkins were absorbing the gravimetric stress such a meeting should rightly have generated. And we two ambassadors, representing our respective parallel universes, suddenly finding ourselves forced to coexist in the material city of Tokyo, soon were reduced to near-speechlessness beneath the weight of the fantastical burden that had fallen to us.

While we were both concentrating all our efforts to try and make our meeting possible, this meeting between two inhabitants of two such different worlds, something like a crack began to run through the beautiful veneer of our situation.

This crack was centred around the vegetation that rose up so luxuriantly in the area around the hotel, and whose mass I had noticed right away through the transparency of the net curtains. Its intense, almost obscure green, and yet a green endowed with such chromatic strength that it almost seemed to burn, had the effect of a kind of retinal massage—a sensation from which I found it more and more difficult to free myself. This optical fascination was so overwhelming that when my eyes left the dark and persistent sight of the foliage behind in order to return to my companion's body or to the white tablecloth on which our dishes were still arranged, its image, now evanescent and fluid, continued to appear to me as a ghostly superimposition. From then on it spread out over the whole situation like a veil—something colored and transparent, floating over everything.

I was also preoccupied with thinking through everything that was necessary for each gesture I made to be successfully accomplished, paying attention to the way I had to deal with the various objects spread out on the tablecloth, putting as much precision as I could into everything. I responded as best I could when Murakami spoke to me—not to the question he was asking me (he rarely had any), but to whatever could be perceived as interrogative in any assertion he made. I prolonged whatever he said, fitting discrete little comments between his words; I tried to give my own point of view on the subjects he brought up, even though my natural propensities still drove me to withhold my opinion when it came to certain things. Where it was honestly impossible for me to offer an opinion, I tried to express my indecision, at the very least—searching for the proper terms to account for my uncertainties as accurately as possible, in order to give a full picture of my ambivalent and hesitant state.

At last I determined that, as far as this level of our conversation went, and in terms of the small, practical manipulations demanded by the occasion of breakfast, I could not be faulted. But despite the close attention I was paying to the situation, I still found there was always some underlying, hidden element to which my thoughts continually strayed.

My breakfast companion had his back to the main picture window, and he could only see the lateral shadows cast by the two others in the room, which must have frayed his field of vision, though he didn't deign to pay these the least attention. He seemed much more engaged by the leaves of seaweed or the omelet he was savoring with an appetite worthy of one of his characters. Sometimes, a particular gesture he made—a folding movement of his arm—would cause the fabric of his sleeve to lift, revealing a waterproof watch with big red numerals, whose brand I didn't manage to make out.

He seemed unaffected by the vague hegemony of the vegetation outside, which crowded the windows—it was all you could see out of them—and my thoughts with an inexplicable insistence. As I said, the sight continued to be etched in my mind even when I'd managed to tear my eyes away from it; and yet, these same eyes still found themselves drawn back, again and again. The power it seemed to have over me was becoming more and more threatening, as though it were the vanguard of a greater physical threat. Its density, its scale, and the intensity of its color had put so much pressure on the room that I couldn't help but be alarmed. My suspicions, which had appeared without my recognizing them, a vague and sickly feeling that had crept up inside me, surreptitiously, along with the beginnings of my defiance, was growing now, all of a sudden; and in the terrible discourse of my suspicion, in my mind, I understood that we were, in essence, under siege by this vegetation, which was watching and waiting for us to show a moment's weakness, at which point it would launch its assault.

It was as though the leaves were trembling behind the windowpanes, as though they were crouched, dying to pounce. From where I sat, I felt the effects of the quivering that ran through them, those waves of dreadful elation at the thought of what they were preparing to do; those waves coming through the glass to disperse and die in the center of the room, like those horrible little ripples that reach past the usual tide line and persist in stretching a little further onto shore, stubborn and lifeless.

Haruki, indifferent to the imminence of this attack, which I, however, was increasingly positive was about to take place, continued to devote himself happily to his nori. We were sitting opposite one another, close enough that our knees could have touched, or perhaps our shins, beneath the cotton of the tablecloth concealing the sides of the table.

I didn't know whether his impassivity was a strategy, perhaps a method of averting threats by blatantly disregarding them, or indeed whether he was continuing to eat simply out of ignorance of the danger we were in, but in either case, it was less than encouraging, and I felt he'd left us both helpless. After all, what little of the vegetal pressure was reaching him from the sides must have had the blurred quality of some lacy décor faintly hemming his vision, a vague and diaphanous edging whose strange power he could hardly appreciate. To do so, he would have had to turn his head to either side and absorb himself in at least a semi-serious contemplation of the picture windows, taking in the sinister qualities of the overly powerful, overly verdant vegetation massing behind the panes of glass. But this was obviously a concession he wouldn't permit himself, restricting his vision to roaming the limited perimeter of his plate, occasionally alternating this with my face—or sometimes, how could he help it, toward the distant entrance, just to the side of my face from his perspective, watching the other customers coming into the room, or else following someone getting up behind me and making their way toward the buffet.

The heat of Murakami's body too almost radiated as far as my seat. And the distant, subtle fragrance of a mild soap he must have used after swimming to scrub away the smell of the chlorine (which persisted, however, beneath the flowery scent) battled with the heat now, attacking it with voluptuous waves of jasmine oil, which did not fully dissolve its recalcitrant bitterness.

In this new, olfactory struggle, smells were emanating from the woven fabric of his shirt and wafting gently over the table. It also happened that through some gesture the collar of his shirt would suddenly come away from his skin before pressing back against it again, allowing a more powerful whiff—a condensed cloud of these conflicting fragrances—to escape from the fleeting gap.

Something about these smells made my head spin. And yet, I knew all too well that the vegetation outside was continuing to exert its pressure on the windowpanes, gathering up all the strength of its sap, ready to charge as soon as it decided the time was right. It would then shatter the picture windows and begin to spread into the room, deploying its branches, which would have been badly damaged by all their bumping, bending, and twisting against the barriers of glass. And finally, who knows, emboldened by its new freedom, it would begin producing an endless series of fresh offshoots, which, once they collided with the inevitable obstacle of the interior walls, would begin to wind in various curls, in order to continue to grow, tangling up our poor bodies and immobilizing us in their ever-tightening grip.

All Murakami seemed to be doing to oppose this terrible havoc was to perpetuate the little war going on between the faint but nonetheless perceptible smells of chlorine and jasmine, which were themselves under siege now by the encroachment of a more effective odor—the fumes rising from his omelet, sausages, and slice of toast, which constituted serious rivals. These food odors cut across the other smells almost at right angles, hitting them where it hurt; they pierced them with their powerful arrows, given extra momentum by the heat, breaking up their molecules with tremendous force, silencing them in the air. Off-balance, dumbfounded, the majority of the weaker scents let themselves be absorbed, fading between us under the pressure of the merciless food smell, which acted like a pressurized water gun dispersing all competitors beneath my helpless nostrils.

I made the most of our physical proximity to get a better look at the author's face. I no longer wanted to take it in its entirety, as I'd been doing before, but in its details. And my eyes, making all sorts of excursions over the landscape in question (so to speak)—so much so that I could no longer think of its bumps and hollows as anything other than hills or basins—ended up focusing on that vein jutting out at his temple. A venous confluence, let's say, rather than a simple vein, formed there like a 'y' or a fork—the definite outline of a bifurcation.

Without the thought of the encroaching vegetation ever really leaving me, I lingered on the glyph drawn there and wondered almost compulsively what its possible meanings could be. It was as if there might be something encrypted there that could lead me to a better understanding of the situation he and I were in and the danger to which I had, despite myself, been exposed. For all my efforts, however, I found nothing there that could open my eyes to what might be awaiting me, nor what part Murakami was playing in all of this.

However: there really was something remarkable about that venous crossroads on the author's temple. Although incapable of telling me anything about the vegetal invasion I feared would occur at any moment, it could, if you think about it, stand as a good representation of the act of narration itself, which is, after all, nothing if not a process constantly beset by bifurcations, by possible choices (choices concerning the possible actions of one's characters, but also choices between available words, from which —mentally crossing out the various alternatives—one finally seizes one's preference). This is all the more true if one writes in a linear fashion, as Haruki had told me he did.

The stamp engraved on his temple was a symbol. Despite himself, our author bore a simple tattoo representing his occupation, as if his body itself had come to manifest, even in the layout of its vascular system, the act with which he was constantly confronted. He was marked: the pattern of those surfacing veins showed that his fate had long since been decided (given that it was Murakami Haruki, this only half surprised me).

It seemed that I could hear a knocking against the glass now. The supple leaves, assisted by a breath of wind, unfurling them in fits and starts, brushed the windowpane. It was as if they were cajoling it with insincere caresses; as if they were petting it. This stroking motion, which the window might even have been enjoying, nonetheless indicated the precise threat weighing on the glass: that of the inevitable crack, which the leaves themselves wouldn't make, of course, but which the branches would take care of the instant the order was given.

Yes, the gentle tremor of the soft green tissue against the glass was in fact a shudder of pleasure, a shudder running through those leafy veins at the thought of the imminent destruction. Their limbs licked the glass surface like tongues—hundreds, thousands of little mocking tongues. Had my breakfast companion really not noticed their murmuring? What part was he playing in this story, exactly? The muscular leaves stuck their papillae against the picture windows and increased the rhythm of their lingual caresses, throwing me into a panic. I felt now that these were no longer the simple intimidation tactics they'd begun with, but something like the beginning of a vicious cycle: the frenzy with which the leaves were lapping at the windows of the room, their insatiable little thuds, were only the first taste of the coming upsurge—which, once begun, would be unstoppable. No longer content to simply occupy my thoughts, in which the insidious things had long since taken over the room, the branches were at last marshalling themselves to physically invade the enclosed space in which Murakami and I were sitting. Tiring of their playful, irritating game, wasn't it obvious that they were about to start boring into the picture windows until their determination got the better of the poor sheets of glass? Soon these would be riddled with holes, through which the unscrupulous branches would then undermine the windows entirely, sending huge fragments crashing to the floor, with the consequences I've already mentioned.

I decided to risk everything, to stand up just like that, right in the middle of what one could no longer really call a conversation—to leave this situation, this meeting, which I myself had sought out, to leave it unfinished so as to escape the imminent disaster—either with him, if he wanted to fall in behind me, or else far, far away from him, if it turned out he was a party to what was being planned, and had been trying all along to keep me from escaping the trap that was already closing in on me. And yet, it was getting harder to deny that this was indeed his intention. Because at almost the same moment I was going to make my exit, hoping to escape the disaster whose terrible reality loomed larger and larger the longer I waited, at the very moment when I was, regrettably, about to leave my companion in the lurch, since apparently he thought it best to ignore the enemy, Murakami caught hold of me by the arm. He held on so tightly that I could feel the knitting of the wool I was wearing leave its imprint in my skin. Christine Montalbetti, he said to me, articulating slowly, forcing me to stay in the room despite the considerable risk we were both running. He seemed willing to take all the time in the world to say what he had to say to me, as though it wasn't urgent that we get up together and flee, as though it wasn't urgent that he perhaps show me the best way to escape through the corridors of the hotel—not the ones I knew, more or less, from having already taken them, but others, for staff only, by which we might have more chance of escaping. Christine Montalbetti, he said to me again, calmly, but without gentleness, no, without any apparent desire to reassure me about what was happening, maybe I was wrong about it all, not knowing the rules that governed these places, maybe I'd been panicked into inventing a fiction that bore no relation whatsoever to the actual situation. I knew this much: I couldn't move. And then I began to feel terrified, not only of being prevented from leaving the room by his vice-like grip, but also—if not more so—of yielding before his authority, of remaining paralyzed, motionless, incapable of making even the slightest response to the dangerous circumstances I'd found myself in, as inert as when, in a dream, confronted with danger, our bodies suddenly freeze, mesmerized, having forgotten to look for a way out. Unsteadily, I faced his dark, smooth, glazed face, in which it seemed to me that I should have been able to see my reflection. Believe me, I almost did: I almost saw my own silhouette reflected in his face, a figure stopped in its tracks like a runaway from Pompeii caught in mid-motion by lava. And I devoted what remained of my reason to wondering whether I could find a protector in him, whether I should give myself up to his firm gesture and rely on him to take care of things; he who had decided to speak to me, to treat me in this authoritarian manner, perhaps about to advise me as to how I could escape, by his side, from the agony which lay in wait; or else, if he was actually an accomplice to the plant invasion, maybe even its mastermind, wondering whether he would keep me here by force, prevent me from leaving the table so that all his terrible plans would be carried out as anticipated.

Christine Montalbetti, he said to me a third and last time, in a voice that suddenly seemed gentler, though still tinged with the same determination it had demonstrated in his two previous apostrophes, you know that we have never, never ever, had breakfast together.

What do you expect me to say to that?

TRANSLATED FROM FRENCH BY URSULA MEANY SCOTT

GEORGE KONRÁD

Jeremiah's Terrible Tale

In the ninety-ninth year of his life, approaching his one hundredth birthday, Jeremiah Kadron returned, after a long journey, to his native Budapest, to his own house on Leander Street, where he had been brought as a two-week-old straight from the maternity ward, and which remained his permanent residence, excepting his trips around the world, some of which were brief, others quite lengthy.

After he unpacked his few belongings in his room, he cast a terrified glance at the more or less ordered contents of his smoothly rolling desk drawers, and quickly pushing them back, stepped out on the pillared terrace. His eyes passed over the hillside, the city, the wind-ruffled green of the lake, and then he planted himself in his old wicker chair.

He saw a carriage of gleaming light descend from the sky and come to a halt between a walnut and a sour cherry tree. It was waiting for him. In case he changed his mind about this place, he could get on and go somewhere else. But Jeremiah, from his terrace chair, waved it away; the carriage took off empty.

Save for these interruptions, he lived in this house under the supervision of various transitory women, and lived rather well. First his mother and then his wives had ruled over him, to the extent that they could, and finally his daughter.

This last guardianship was probably the most peaceful; still, he felt an urge to travel around the world one last time. And were he to find a good place, he might just settle down. Jeremiah didn't feel like dying at home, and didn't want to upset his daughter. Let her get used to his being away; let Papa's death be nothing more than a news item. The practical details of the funeral would be arranged by others, elsewhere.

But now a message arrived, driving Jeremiah away from his home in Buda with irresistible force. According to this message—which Jeremiah had simply felt, somehow—the wagoner-angel was on his way again. Jeremiah would simply have to step down into the conveyance from his terrace stairs, and that chariot of light would start moving under him and whisk him away to a place whence there was no return.

Let the angel come, then, if he was coming for him. Jeremiah would clear out ahead of time; their rendezvous hadn't been prearranged. He knew how things worked in this world; celestial bureaucracy couldn't be all that different. When they don't find him at home, they'll forget about him, and stop keeping track of his whereabouts.

■　■　■

He left, and then waited here and there for death to come, but it didn't. The place where Jeremiah stayed longest was Safed, city of holy and mad sages, where in the afternoon he would sit for hours in the chair once occupied by the great, spiritually enlightened Rabbi Ariel, who in his time had sat in the chair of the equally great Rabbi Luria, and who happened to be Jeremiah's grandfather. At three o'clock in the afternoon, a shaft of light flooded in through the synagogue window, a light so intense that it practically pinned Jeremiah's head to the back of the chair, right to the hole made once by a bullet: he couldn't have pulled his head away if he wanted to. It was as though that powerful beam had burned its way through his eyes; he felt the warmth of it in his groin, the same warmth women praying to be fertile must also feel when sitting in that chair. The light and the tingling that accompanied it took hold of Jeremiah, moving upward through his body for minutes on end, renewing the old man.

He thanked the Heavenly Father that he could once again huddle in this miracle-working chair, and early in the morning he said an ancient prayer. He didn't have to read it, he knew it by heart: "I praise thee oh God, blessed be Thy name, Thy greatness is unknowable; each generation conveys to the next the awesomeness of Thy power. Eternal Father, patient and of abundant mercy, I put all my hope in Thee. O, hear my prayer, lend me Thy ear. I rejoice in Thy word as one who has received a great prize. Look, my legs stand straight. The Everlasting God supports those who are about to fall and straightens those bent with age or care. Thou art Mighty, o Lord, who frees the captives, makes the wind blow and the rain fall, nourishes the living with His grace, and preserves the faith even of those who sleep eternally inside the earth. Sound the great shofar to our liberation, lift the banner to gather Thy exiles from the four corners of the world. Rule over us with mercy and compassion. Thine gift to us is knowledge. Thou teachest man to use his reason. From Thee we receive our ideas and observations. Blessed be the Everlasting God, whose gift to us is understanding. Forgive us when we trespass, punish us within reason when we sin, and when we act wickedly, consider our miserable state, and free us quickly, for Thou art a strong redeemer. Evildoers and false accusers should vanish like a fleeting moment. Extend your mercy to the just, to the few who are truly learned, and to strangers with genuine faith. Make our own lot resemble theirs. And return to Thy city Jerusalem with mercy, and dwell there, as Thou hast promised. Rebuild it in our own day into an eternal edifice, and place in it the throne of David. If only Thou wouldst become fond of Thy people!"

Jeremiah murmured this morning prayer to himself in Hebrew, then voicelessly added commentaries to each sentence in his own way, not holding back the scandalous conclusions of some of these interpretations even from the One about whom he said: "Holy, Holy, Holy is the Eternal God!"

Jeremiah walked over to the Messiah's Stairs. Those arriving from infinity as well as those proceeding toward it must climb these steps, all three hundred and sixty of them, between walls and fences that press in close on both sides. There isn't much room on the narrow staircase, so the messiah will have to make it up all by himself. The long climb will certainly exhaust him.

This is why Lina sits waiting for the messiah on a stone bench in her garden, near a low stone parapet. She won't put a pillow on the bench, only a thin blanket. If the messiah is willing to endure such hardships, then she, Lina, should suffer a little too. Thus she waits for the mighty king, the christ of the Lord, with cakes and fruit on the two hundred and ninety-ninth step.

By the time the anointed made it up here, he would have to be tired and thirsty, and surely in need of some food. Besides, from this point on, not only would he have to climb the rest of the stairs, he'd also have to hold his own up there in the little square, where holy men were always walking up and down as though immersed in a dream, though in reality with eyes sharp and focused.

Reaching the holy men, the messiah would try to blend in and modestly follow them to the well. But they would recognize him, gather around, and keep him under close scrutiny. Though suspicious, they wouldn't want to question him openly; they would prefer to catch him unawares, figure out his secrets, wait for him to reveal all.

■ ■ ■

Lina had come to Safed from Oradea via Auschwitz. She and the messiah had very similar tastes in food. Whenever he passed through town, the messiah found it most stimulating to stop for some of Lina's cooking. He ate in the garden where children from the local kindergarten splashed around in a small wading pool. And in the afternoon, sitting in an old, red armchair, Jeremiah read under a bower of vine and figs.

Once here, the Chosen, who was expected to perform great deeds, would nod off after lunch. The woman rented one of her rooms to Jeremiah, and when it grew dark, she offered him some of the food she had prepared for the messiah.

It never occurred to her that the messiah might arrive at night, in the dark. He would have to arrive when it's light, when everyone is in the main square, when old people and youngsters stream out of the *yeshivoth* and fill the square under the afternoon sun. After eating the messiah's meal, Jeremiah withdrew, and from the large terrace next to his room, he looked out at the Sea of Galilee. This would be a suitable burial place. He had here what he had at home: a room, a terrace, and water.

The landlady was curious and a little crazy; but she wouldn't hurt a fly. She put his food in front of him, hung his ironed shirt in the cupboard, and asked if he'd like a cup of coffee.

The following morning, when his body was taking in its desired dose of the sun's rays, Jeremiah too waited a while for the Chosen One who hadn't yet appeared, the one anointed by an angel, the one who would trek up that very narrow, endless-seeming stairway, feeling increasingly weary and disheartened, but would still be anxious to reach the marketplace of the holy ones.

The messiah hadn't come yet; the old woman sat on a stone bench and looked down at the burial ground of the *tzadikim* and, still lower, at the lake, which lies well below sea level. There, on that water, the messiah's famous predecessor had once walked. What would that fellow's successor have to do? Not a thing, maybe, thought the old woman. We'll see. In the meantime, she told herself, go and greet the long-awaited one; let the old man have some food. Imagine, I'm past seventy, and that's already too much for me; he'll be a hundred this year, and for him it's still not enough.

■ ■ ■

"Come, come, Mr. Kadron," said Lina to Jeremiah, who just then appeared in a rocky alleyway—the Jeremiah who on his mother's side came from a long line of rabbis, and was the grandson of the famed Rabbi Ariel, spiritual leader of the Old Buda community, the strange man who at the age of fifteen had become head of his congregation, and at twenty-five looked into a well and decided that he must leave on pilgrimage to Jerusalem the very next day, and did indeed set out in the morning with his faithful assistant.

Ariel entertained crowds in the market squares along the way with tales and jokes. He parodied gendarmes, the town magistrate, a Turkish pasha, a general, a scholar. He could mimic anyone who passed by, and would say incredibly daring things in his screeching voice.

Of course, Ariel got into trouble for all his mimicking and screeching. He was caught and dragged by armed men in front of a stern group of officials, whose leader shouted him down and wouldn't give in to the temptation of laughing at his captive's jokes. But Ariel did receive permission to play something on his violin for the gentlemen, and with that he was able to appease them and continue his journey to Jerusalem.

He pushed on unrelentingly to the holy city—he believed, after all, that if he didn't set eyes on Jerusalem, his arm might as well wither away. He traveled through the Balkans, made dangerous by the Napoleonic Wars and the turmoil of the disintegrating Ottoman Empire. He kept himself afloat by playing the violin and performing card tricks, which also made life easier for his sidekick, Mendel, who never failed to belch with relish after consuming the large pieces of roast meat placed before him.

They continued their journey by boat from a Greek harbor to the port of Jaffa, and from there they walked the rest of the way, passing countless ramshackle huts, rusty iron hoops, huge tents, orange trees covered with fruit, and sandy plains with sparse, slender trees.

After arriving in the holy city, Ariel found himself smoking his pipe among the motley inhabitants of the alleyways: Armenians, Persians, Arabs, and Turks. He prayed little and exchanged stories instead. One morning, in the steam rising from his tea, and then in the smoke of his hookah, he saw the face of his wife. After the glowing morsels of Galilean hemp resin burned themselves out, he put his hand on Ahmed's and bade his friend and new-found partner in merrymaking farewell.

He went to look for Mendel, his assistant, who was usually hanging around the marketplace at this time of the day, or else in the garden of an Armenian, praising the earthenware pitcher that stood on a stone table, in which the wine made by Salesians was kept cool. Mendel got up in his usual lackadaisical way.

"Let's go, Ariel, if your story's ready. The Jews of Kandor can't wait to hear it. Without it, those damned Jews won't be too happy to see you."

They journeyed back to their city, where local Jews as well as ones who'd walked several days to see him all crowded around Ariel. But his story was not to their liking. One of his disciples actually spat on the master and said, "Oh, how I despise you." The community decided not to commit the story to writing and not to spread it by word of mouth. It would be best simply to forget it, they said. Everyone should put it out of their minds, as if they had never heard it. And from that day on, they wouldn't let their sons set foot in Ariel's courtyard. The master should look for another line of work. Let him harness his father's horses and become a hauler. After dark, however, the younger Jews showed up and listened to him, albeit more distractedly, taking their leave not long after.

What on earth could Ariel have told them?

TRANSLATED FROM HUNGARIAN BY IVAN SANDERS

George Konrád 113

STEINAR BRAGI

The Sky Over Thingvellir

We soar out of a clear, blue spring sky over Thingvellir and glide toward the mist rising over a waterfall and what will be, for a while, our destination, which begins along the scarp of the ravine. Two people, a boy and girl, are just settling down on a grassy patch near a waterfall. The boy, blond and unremarkable, but with a kind face, spreads a blanket out over the grass, and takes a wicker basket from the girl; then he says something to the girl and she responds, their mouths move but we can't hear what they're talking about yet. In order to get even closer to them—I see no reason for us to announce ourselves—we'll continue on to our destination, set down at the base of the cliff, land on a branch on one of the little scrub trees by the riverbank, and discover the scents of the waking shrubs, grasses, and a single flower. After pacing the branch for a while, we fly to our ultimate goal in this little patch of the world: the minds of the girl and the boy, by turns—as it suits our needs.

"... chill it," said the boy.

"It doesn't matter," said the girl. "Put it in the river and prop it up with a rock or something." It didn't matter to her if the wine was cold or not. She just wanted to drink it, firstly, enjoy it, secondly, and then do it all over again before bringing their trip to an end. "Or leave it in the bag and throw it into Drekkingarhyl," she said. "How about that? That water's so cold it could freeze your soul out."

The spot they chose was just above Drekkingarhyl, far from the roar of the waterfall, but near enough that they could still hear it. Occasionally the spray would blow over them; she found that refreshing.

She hadn't said much in the car on the way up, and he'd finally asked her if everything was all right, and the tone of his voice was so tender and full of concern that she wanted to smile. On the other hand, he got on her nerves whenever he wasn't like that, when he was like he usually was—happy and easygoing, always getting carried away by his little fantasies.

"I brought a cooler," he said, "but I forgot to bring any ice, what are they called . . . those bags . . ."

"Put it in the river," she said. He walked over to the riverbank, stepped carefully between the rocks, and placed the bottle in a small pool a safe distance from the whitewater; afterward, he came back and sat down next to her on the blanket.

They smoked cigarettes, were silent and looked around at the scenery. In the parking lot below them, next to Lögberg, there hadn't been any cars or tourist buses, and they hadn't seen a single person in the ravine. So unusual on such a nice day in May—though it was a Wednesday. Everyone must be stuck at work.

"Aren't there any midges at Thingvellir?" asked the boy and looked around. "I can't remember if I've ever seen midges here."

The girl couldn't decide how she felt—she was simultaneously sad, angry, and frightened. The sadness came on when she'd decided to break up with Baldur, which was the boy's name, although now it was changing to hate. She thought he was very intelligent and often funny, handsome too, but there was something about him that she just couldn't stand—probably it was all his *brightness*, which bordered on what some women might see as smugness. With him, everything was always *good*. He was a man who marched ahead, who didn't seem to harbor so much as a speck of self loathing, self destructiveness, not even a hint of any unbridled, conflicted angst that might need to find some means of expression. They couldn't have been more different.

In the end, she was frightened because she thought she might not find the words, the courage to end the relationship before the day was over, and to do it with dignity. Otherwise, there would be a fight: someone would get hurt. She would simply have to ignore the beautiful weather and scenery until she decided what to say.

"I want to take a nap," she said, and lay down along the edge of the blanket.

"We just got here!" he said.

"I have a hangover," she said. They had gone to a cocktail party at Vigdis Finnbogadottir's office, where the girl worked, the previous afternoon, to see off a staff member who was moving overseas for a job. After the party, they'd gone to a bar and then to another party. And it was at the second party that she decided that they couldn't be together anymore, just before she passed out on someone's bed. She wasn't certain how her reasoning went, exactly, she just knew. They'd been together for three months. It had been pretty good, so breaking up after three months shouldn't be a problem. Three months was nothing.

He decided not to say anything, she could do whatever she wanted to do, probably she'd be more fun if she slept her headache off. He closed his eyes and listened to the lazy drone of the insects that rose and fell like an unfinished melody. Unfinished melody, he thought: a title. A composition for buzzing bees, broken up by a ridiculous, over-the-top heavy-metal drum solo, nothing else. Maybe a little flowery, sentimental, lisping baby-girl singing, too. The drone quickly became irritating, an intolerable thrumming, a communiqué from nature about frost or a trip to the country.

He stood up, ate a piece of dried-out baguette that he had picked up at a bakery, went down to the river to check on the bottle, and saw a patch of snow below the cliff face, across the river.

"Last snowdrift in the ravine," Baldur mumbled to himself. "Alone. Nothing but sun and death all around ... A vampire that didn't make it home."

He grabbed the cooler, stepped carefully across on the river stones, and filled it with snow. When he looked over to the blanket, he saw that Ella, which was the girl's name, was awake, sitting and smoking another cigarette. He crouched over the snow which was thin and covered with grit, made a snowball, and threw it at her. The snowball blew apart in the rocks next to the girl but she said nothing, just continued to smoke.

He didn't know what was going on, but the night before, at the party, something had changed. It was as if there was a distance between them, or that he had moved closer to her and she had stepped away. A coldness had come into her eyes, or a hardness that hadn't been there before—not a single time in the past three months. Her eyes had always lit up when she looked at him. The first time he remembered her eyes going cold, he had been standing and talking to someone—but it didn't register at the time. He had looked across the room to where Ella was sitting and smoking and realized for the first time that he loved her, undeniably. This sensation was warm. He felt his frozen sense of trust begin to thaw, melt through him, spread through his chest, then bubble up into his mind. He loved everything about her: her eyes, her long eyelashes, her smell, how she smoked—everything. It was unimaginable for him to try and pinpoint one thing out of this totality that was Ella and try to identify it as the primary reason. He couldn't, so he stopped trying. He had wanted to put his arms around her right then and tell her he loved her, more than he'd ever loved anyone, but decided to delay. He was drunk. Anything he said would come out slurred and pathetic, and she would have thought he was making it all up, would've looked right through him and laughed, would've asked him to tell her all about it in the morning when they were in his bed, and then when he repeated his confession it would've made her uncomfortable. The first time would have been awkward, and everything that followed would be clumsy, compromised. All the delicate nuances that should really have been the foundations of an anecdote they could have told all their lives about how they met and first fell in love would be ruined because of his drinking. And then, the next time he looked over at her, after having just roared with laughter—probably too loudly—over some tidbit in the general conversation, he saw Ella looking at him with drunken eyes, deliberately cold, as though she'd just caught him in a lie, or was seeing something loathsome in him. But it was probably only his imagination. The glance had lasted only a second, and then she looked away.

No, she was angry about something, he thought. He had to fix it. But he was still certain that he was in love with her—probably he'd known for some time now, two or three weeks perhaps, or at the very least he'd been pretty sure since he'd filled the wicker basket for their trip, bringing along the gift that he intended to give her—arranged with the help of a friend. This was the perfect day to give it to her, and for her to read what he had written on the label.

He tiptoed back across the river, stuck the white wine into the snow in the cooler, and sat down next to her.

"Last snowdrift," said Baldur, pointing over to it. "Smart snow. A survivor." She didn't reply, looked at the rainbows in the waterfall's mist. She had noticed them as she was lying down for a nap. Hundreds of small rainbows were scattered through the mist. There hadn't been any when they arrived, she thought—the sun must be higher in the sky.

She put out her cigarette, lay down again, and closed her eyes. Behind her eyelids she saw halo bursts, distorted faces that seemed familiar—people's faces she had known in previous lives, perhaps, over the course of some other short existential interval, sneering children blowing around in a nuclear mushroom cloud. There were also dead suns, and jellyfish, and skates swimming in the cold murky depths.

"Did you see the tree up there, up on the rim?" he asked, and she made a noise. "Or I should say, dwarf tree. I came here once when I was trying to cultivate a bonsai. Iceland is teeming with dwarf trees. The Japanese would kill for them. All their highlands and beaches have been picked clean of trees that grow in poor conditions—in the cold or wind or salt. The conditions stunt their growth, and you can make any stunted tree into a saleable bonsai in two to three years, if you know how to do it. Trees can grow everywhere in Iceland in a few months. One hundred thousand bonsai-starters right here. In grams, a good bonsai is as valuable as gold. We could open a major factory here, have compressors, wire, and hydraulic equipment, and people with little scissors, and export bonsais to the States or Japan. Bonsais are in right now."

"What a practical dream," she said without opening her eyes. "And you can employ little elves to do the trimming, little Sigur Rós androgynes with iPods."

"I also got a pine tree from Thingholt, stole it from a garden on Bergstastræti, a dwarf pine that I wired up for three years and sold on the Internet."

"To Japan, I assume," she said and felt a wave of nausea, a terrible ennui about their conversation. If he said one more word about dwarf trees, a vein would burst in her head.

"California," he said, "but to a Japanese company." She jumped to her feet and grabbed the bottle out of the cooler, was about to reach over to the basket for the corkscrew, but he shouted at her to leave the basket alone. She wasn't allowed to look in it yet. He stood up, retrieved the corkscrew from the basket, and contemplated his dull outline against the bright sky reflected in the silver, shining wrapping paper around the gift.

He removed the cork, poured some white wine into plastic cups, and they drank and looked out over the Thingvellir plain, toward the west. The sky was blue and empty, but in the opposite direction toward Skjaldbreidur, some glint in a black cloudbank made it seem to him that it was heading their way.

"Clouds . . . Are those clouds over there?" he asked and pointed over to Skjaldbreidur, but she didn't respond, sat down again on the blanket. Her face was drawn, eyes distant and bright, as though she were thinking about terrible things. He didn't know why he didn't let her just have the package right away. He didn't know what he was waiting for. Maybe he'd give it to her after she drank off her hangover.

"Clouds over Skjaldbreidur," he said and looked into her eyes. "... Our thoughts are clouds," he added, feeling that he wanted to provoke her—she was treating him as though he was simple or stupid, which he wasn't, but he could tell that's what she thought of him.

"You're an expert on the sky now?" she asked, and handed him the glass to refill.

"The sky doesn't exist," he said and filled her glass. "It's distinct layers of atmospheric densities fracturing the sunlight, harmonizing, making it all appear blue. The layers diminish gradually until there's nothing left but emptiness. The sky isn't like a glass dome over us—it's like a complex melody."

"*Distinct layers, harmonizing*," she said. "What a surprise for a musician to talk about nature like that. It's like you just can't see anything except yourself, mirrored everywhere you look."

"What do you mean?" he asked.

"You even said that the sky was *like a melody*."

They both fell silent.

"Have you heard about the Copenhagen interpretation?" he asked.

"Have you ever heard of psychological projection?"

"It's always the same with literalists," he said, ignoring the girl's rejoinder, "people who claim to be 'grounded,' who consider themselves to be practical and, in general, use *science* as an excuse for everything, are always the same people who turn out to be the loudest objectors and archconservatives, who still believe in antiquated nineteenth-century philosophy and wander around in a dense fog, denying everything that's been discovered by *real* scientists in the first half of the twentieth century, and that musicians and artists have always known. There is no reality. Everything is beauty. Impressions are made on our neural receptors—across clouds. We're clouds wearing pants! The earth we're sitting on is a cloud, and our brains are crackling clouds full of lightning! Niels Bohr investigated the double nature of light particles, for which Einstein received the Nobel. Light behaves both as a particle and as wave, or to put it another way, like a ball, for example, and a water ripple after a stone has been dropped into the water. This was considered incomprehensible, but Bohr designed an experiment where light particles were shot or pushed in the direction of a partition with a photosensitive screen on the other side that had recorded their journey."

"I know this," she said, wishing she had a gloomy Heathcliff-type man, someone who was capable of ordering her around like a parent one minute and fucking her on the floor the next. Someone she could handle—someone she could keep right at the brink of violence without ever pushing him over. "There were two slits on the partition, just like on a woman."

"*Two* slits?" he laughed.

"The mouth and the pussy, Baldur! The ass just has a hole. And when the particles were fired off, some of them were all hot for the slits in the partition, but their path through it was recorded by a voyeur, drooling over their every move—you won't find *that* fact in the overwrought erotic science-for-laymen love stories called textbooks. The light particles manifested as a pattern on the screen and this was wave oscillation, meaning that the light particles flowed through *both* slits *at once*, which is just like pushing your cock into one slit but somehow splitting it in two along the way so that it goes into both. If it had been possible to view this phenomenon in slow motion, the scientists would have seen the particles move through the partition by going through each slit simultaneously, behaving like a particle and wave all at once. It's all so cliché!"

"Everything is cliché!" he yelled. "You can't avoid it! To be born is a cliché: we're all born at the same level and die at the same level! Life's challenge is to learn about clichés—which also happens to be a cliché—and to figure out how to handle them on our own terms. And look, that slit thing was an important experiment! It should be on the FRONT PAGE of the newspaper every goddamn day of the year! It demonstrates that the timeless, formless breath of existence, or whatever it's called—life or God or music!—isn't subservient to any law of nature except those that we've imposed on it. The possibilities are endless! Reality doesn't exist beyond what we make of it! Everything is POSSIBLE!"

"More clichés," she said, and found that she was uncomfortable with this debate, or whatever it was that they were having. "And clichés—both yours and the ones even guys like you find trite: guys who actually enjoy sitting around and spouting off about this shit—don't change anything. People need to understand that. If the possibilities really were endless, we wouldn't all sit around feeling impotent all the time—people could change, learn to cope with their problems, go to a monastery, do asanas, reflect on life, whatever. I know for a fact that we can't do a thing to reality—all we can hope to do is carve out a small plot of land for ourselves in the formless, gigantic universe around us, pretend that we deserve it, and call it truth or knowledge or good or a 'real experience.' That's obvious! But at least I see things as existing within some kind of framework, while you just want to blow everything apart, as usual—you just go on making everything meaningless over and over again, and that's all you'll do as long as you live. You fixate on your premise so much that you can't even understand what I believe in. And this makes you a slave to your own language. You talk and think and only practice what you preach when it comes to work or money. In Asia, for example, *no one* discusses the Copenhagen interpretation. There are no representatives of recreational culture who go around talking about 'formlessness' on the level that you do, who want to subsume all religions and systems and disciplines into their nothingness —who want to own thought."

"Don't even try to talk to me about Asia," he said, suddenly irritated. "I know everything about Asia."

"We live within a framework, and always will," she said. "It's meaningless to talk about what's outside of it—probably it'll even be impossible in the future, after this framework has collapsed, but it's certainly impossible today. Nothing exists but the framework. Some guy in the sixteenth century sat next to a lake and played on his guitar—a small lute—and then, presto! He invents the electric guitar and then a Van Halen solo. Why would he do that? Electricity hadn't even been discovered yet. There were no plugs or amplifiers. In order for his life to be complete, he perfected the technique of playing what was in his hands, *at that moment*—and he did it well."

"Or he could have discovered electricity, wired up his guitar, and then plugged it into an amplifier. You prefer to live life in a box—just know your limitations and never try to get past them. But there's no difference between art and science. All of these things are just different ways of approaching the same end."

"And I'm saying that it's all meaningless. When you lump everything together like that, you come up with nothing. You learned to read by figuring out the individual characters, one by one, despite the fact that each letter, by itself, has no meaning. Then you moved forward by picturing words, and later, sentences. If it were up to *you*, everyone would be illiterate and incapable of writing—they'd just be staring at clouds. What does music actually mean to you, for example? Just another thing to play around with? What do you want to *do* with music, though? Aren't you afraid that one of those cloud-with-pants naïve musicians out there, those idealists— the people who pretend to be *something*—might appropriate you and use your music for whatever fascist or Nazi campaign they've cooked up, maybe pipe your ridiculous music into people's rooms at night to brainwash them—infusing sentiment into ordinary communication, into the very framework that you reject, keeping them from knowing *reality*? People who reject reality always lose! Besides, your logic is all founded on narcissism, which owes no allegiance to anyone—it only attaches value to things that it can use to make itself look better."

"Are we fighting?" he asked. "For the first time? Buddha rejected reality, does he lose too?"

"We *are* arguing," she said, "and not for the first time." She sipped from the glass and began to rip the grass next to where she was sitting.

"When have we ever argued?" he asked. Then they were both silent. She looked at the clouds over Skjaldbreid, they flowed down the mountain and she couldn't see the peak anymore. She tried to say something, but could only say, "We're different. Maybe too different."

"What I was about to say . . ." he began, attempting to calm the situation down without giving in. He couldn't really address the problem as long as she couldn't understanding what he was getting at. "I'm not talking about escapism, or being some kind of pathetic conformist. I just wanted to say that, in practical terms, as far as our understanding of the world, everything is separate and well-defined and is, therefore, in complete harmony—everything is matter. A comes before B, and the light goes through both slits at the same time. Everything is good. And so, in order to control the world, humanity naturally sees itself as just another machine, we think we're all individual little engines built to portion out eternity—to feed, even while we're still young and unformed, off the corpse of life, creating a reality for ourselves that is itself a kind of machine: a machine world, full of machine nervous systems, machine brains, and machine love. Everything is a machine. But that doesn't have anything to do with truth or *happiness*, you see?"

"Do I see?" she said and giggled. "So now you're going to 'you see' me to death?"

"What's the matter with you? What's wrong with 'you see?' "

Squinting into the sun, blushing with anger, she said, "That expression should never be used to finish a sentence. It's just an empty placeholder, a different way of saying 'you know what I mean' or 'um'—like shaking your fist when you're yelling at someone."

"And another thing," he said, also angry, "sarcasm, something you're clearly familiar with, is *evil* and originates in fear, a wall that people erect between themselves and life because they can't find the strength to confront it—they're defenseless in the face of the limitless possibilities of life, which only appeal to the imaginative and *courageous*. Evil is *submission*, contempt for both the world and the self, bound to figures of speech born in the powerful European courts of the past hundred years and which, like a nightmare, has insinuated itself into the whole of Western culture! Let's talk about the Asia of the future! One and a half ZILLION CHINESE DO NOT UNDERSTAND SARCASM!" A small bird whistled up out of the shrubs beside them, but Baldur didn't notice it, he was beginning to shake with emotion—and not in a pleasant way. In fact, he hadn't lost his temper like this in more than a year.

"Don't talk to me about Asia," she said, mimicking the way he had said it earlier, though she didn't risk making her voice quite as strident and needy as she would have liked. "And another thing. Let's talk about the women's rights struggle of the future. In order for women to understand men better, to better control them, they all only need to understand one thing: that men are more emotional than women are. The reason for this is that women are all so much more *self-assured* than men, women have evolved away from their subservient status only to find themselves still subordinate to men when it comes to money, property, and so forth. Ergo, women's emotions are now, generally speaking, centered around practical matters—profit, health, equilibrium—while in the meantime our marvelous, wild, mercurial, over-privileged men have managed to get themselves all worked up over the unlikeliest of phenomena—the Copenhagen interpretation, God, air, rocks, whatever's at hand!"

"Why are you telling me this? What the hell does that have to do with me?"

"Because you're just another example of the kind of man who always makes his way into my life. Men invented romanticism, you know—they like to make women into symbols, into unearthly beings! Nothing so ethereal and absurd has ever been written by a woman. Austen, Emily Dickinson, Sylvia Plath, and Doris Lessing are each about the coldest and most elemental stylists that you can find. No man could ever approach the deliberate, cold-hammered styles of those *women*. Whining idiots like Schopenhauer or Michel Houellebecq are just pubescent boys, by comparison. Men simply can't escape their own emotions. The books on the best-seller list are all written by frustrated middle-aged men who want to force their pessimism on us, want to tell us all how dissatisfied they are with their bodies, want to proclaim their latest theories about self-love or moan about the universal gestalt of WESTERN CULTURE. It's nothing but hysteria! Men need to figure out how to vomit up their emotions once and for all, to purge themselves of whatever it is that'll be their next crisis—now *that* would be a real form of *cultural criticism*! Until then, women will just have to learn to walk away from the problem, if they want to get ahead: men are pale, humorless, and thin-skinned—always resorting to suicide, alcohol, and depression. Men ooze emotional bullshit. They've become exactly what people used to call *old crones*."

"I don't have a clue what we're talking about anymore," the boy said, holding his head in his hands and closing his eyes. "Or maybe I should say, we're not talking about what we're pretending to talk about . . . *You* aren't, anyway . . ."

She stood up, grabbed the bottle, and poured wine into the glass, putting the half-finished bottle back in the cooler and walking away from the blanket, from the small postage stamp that they'd fastened to the earth there, just for the pleasure of making each other suffer.

"I want to go back to town," she said loudly, walking back to the blanket and standing over him. He didn't reply but reached over to the basket and took out the small package. The package was silver, thin, and rectangular. He handed it over without looking at her. There was a small, red label on the front of the package. She turned the package over in her hand, saw the label, and read: "To Ella, the woman that I love." A dark cloud welled up inside her, as well as an incomprehensible blend of surprise and despair. The fucker, she thought, *the goddamn fucker*, is he saying he loves me? It had never occurred to her that he might be capable of this, not once, but now, after giving it some thought, it seemed perfectly normal. Some people fall in love in a minute, a second, in a fraction of a second.

She tore open the package and found a black-and-white photograph in an unpretentious ebony-wood frame. The image was a grainy, out-of-focus photograph. Along a wall, she could make out something that looked like a person, and a lamppost, maybe one or two cars. At the bottom, on the right corner, were numbers: 02.11.19. A delicate flower-filigree ran over the border of the frame.

Something about the photograph made her think that this was a *scam*.

After she had inspected every centimeter and every grain of the photograph, searching for a clue about what it was she was looking at, or what it could have to do with her or *them*, she realized she had to say something. "What is this?" she asked, the setting sun tearing into the lazy buzz of nature all around them as she turned back toward him. He was looking over at Skjaldbreidur, he seemed tired or maybe he was daydreaming; he said that he had arranged this with the help of his friend, a pastor.

"He worked for the police during the summer. I've told you about him. He left a few telephone messages for me . . . Do you recognize anything about the photograph? The people there, or . . . ?" He pointed to two shadows up by a wall—it seemed to her that the figures might be exchanging something, a package, or they could be shaking hands.

"Will you please just tell me . . . ?"

"This is the exact second that we met," he said. "The photograph was taken from a security camera. You can see there at the bottom—that's the time it was taken: eleven minutes and nineteen seconds after two, Sunday morning, February 20th. We're the shadows there. The third shadow, between us and farther off, is your girlfriend, the one who introduced us. We're shaking hands . . ."

She brought the photograph up to her nose and peered at their shadows there. After he'd told her what she was looking at, the picture became clear. She recognized her own silhouette, the nose, eyelashes; recognized his blond hair and profile outlined in the cone of light under the lamppost. The corner of Posthusstræti and Austurstræti. The second they met. Exactly two o'clock, eleven, nineteen . . . You *goddamn whiny pathetic piece of shit*, she thought and finally noticed the dimming light around them, looked over at the waterfall and said:

"Do you know why no one paints landscapes in our country?"

"No," he said.

"Midges."

"Midges?"

"Midges. Midges everywhere. And while I've seen paintings of every form of wildlife on this pathetic island, I can't recall ever seeing a painting of midges."

"What are you talking about?" he asked.

"You know that a midge," she continued, "is as significant and real or beautiful or ugly as everything else. When you go into the Icelandic countryside during the summer, midges are the first thing you think about, and more often than not they become your main focus. You move around the landscape in particular ways because of them, contort into the most amazing shapes, swing your hands and legs around, hope for a breeze or rain. And finally you just want to go home. Maybe when you're painting you're supposed to get so caught up in yourself and your easel and in what your *eyes* tell you that you don't notice them buzzing around your ears, flying up your nostrils, or biting your skin. The landscape painting becomes the goal—a memorial to the victory of your eyes! But only a very small—actually, an unreasonably miniscule—number of painters actually understands that nature is in as much pain as we are, and even fewer manage to get this into their pictures! And I'll tell you why that matters." She lifted up the photograph he'd given her. "Because the one thing—perhaps the *only* thing that the security cameras of this sad, compromised, apathetic little world are still unable to capture in photographs is *love*. So, even if someone's love was meant to be photographed in this picture here—this ridiculous gift, this memorial to *dread*—whatever piece-of-junk machine was scanning and buzzing at us from outside someone's house never managed to capture it. So I understand that you couldn't tell that there's no love in this picture—that love didn't happen in the moment this photograph was taken. I'm trying to tell you, in other words, that I don't love you. That I'll never love you." She tore the photograph down the middle, tossed it onto the ground, and walked away up the ravine without looking back.

The boy watched her walk away and opened his mouth to yell something, but nothing came to him except "I love you." He began to shake and then cry. He threw himself onto the blanket and cried until he couldn't cry anymore.

When he stood up again his body was numb. His head buzzed like all the midges in Iceland that went unpainted on a calm summer day. But we won't examine his thoughts and feelings any more closely than we already have. Perhaps these will end up in some other book, someday . . . for now, they don't much matter. (Or else: they'll never matter.) The boy gathered up the food and dishes and put them into the basket, then he folded the blanket and laid it on top. He slipped the basket under his arm and walked down the trail toward his car.

Back in the grass, where they'd been sitting, in among some torn blades of grass, there was a red thread from the blanket and some breadcrumbs that the flies immediately dissolved with their saliva and ate. In the air, the faint odor of the boy's shaving cream and the girl's body odor were carried off into the afternoon by the breeze. Then the clouds arrived, the rainbows disappeared from the waterfall mist, the flies quieted down, and it began to rain. Two black-and-white halves of the moment in time when the boy and the girl first met were blown into the river, carried into the depths, and turning in an occluded whirlpool throughout the summer, autumn, winter, and into the next spring. The river finally carries them all the way down to the lake where they sink into the silt bed and slowly dissolve. This is how the two of them spent their lives—they lived, died, and all traces of their existence vanished from the earth.

But it seems that on one certain beautiful spring day in a small hollow by a little waterfall, one tiny human being was able to see all this in the palm of his hand, and realize how important it is to express oneself decisively, to try and break free from the chains of the slow, inevitable death that concludes human life. For one fleeting second in the eternity of the cosmos, a girl by the name of Ella demanded truth—and received it. Her efforts exposed her to our scrutiny—but perhaps, in that moment, she understood that this report might one day be written about her. Our story is another kind of confrontation. Also doomed to failure, in all likelihood. As such, we will withhold any further explanations, withdraw, and head straight back up into the sky—not just over Thingvellir, but over the entire globe. We'll let that suffice. There's nothing left to say—except, let us all remember that (as has often been said during one or another of the pathetic, pretentious errors that we call a human life) even a broken clock is right twice a day.

TRANSLATED FROM ICELANDIC BY CHRISTOPHER BURAWA

JULIAN GOUGH

The Orphan and the Mob

If I had urinated immediately after breakfast, the mob would never have burnt down the orphanage. But, as I left the dining hall to relieve myself, the letterbox clattered. I turned in the long corridor. A single white envelope lay on the doormat. I hesitated, and heard through the door the muffled roar of a motorcycle starting. With a crunching turn on the gravel drive and a splatter of pebbles against the door, it was gone.

Odd, I thought, for the postman has a bicycle. I walked to the large oak door, picked up the envelope, and gazed upon it.

JUDE

THE ORPHANAGE

TIPPERARY

IRELAND

For me! On this day, of all significant days! I sniffed both sides of the smooth white envelope, in the hope of detecting a woman's perfume, or a man's cologne. It smelt, faintly, of itself.

I pondered. I was unaccustomed to letters, having never received one before, and I did not wish to use this one up in one go. As I stood in silent thought, I could feel the orphanage coffee burning through my small dark passages. Should I open the letter before or after urinating? It was a dilemma. I wished to open it immediately. Yet a full bladder distorts judgement and is an obstacle to understanding.

As I pondered, both dilemma and letter were removed from my hands by the Master of Orphans, Brother Madrigal.

"You've no time for that now, boy," he said. "Organise the Honour Guard and get them out to the site. You may open your letter this evening, in my presence, after the visit." He gazed at my letter with its handsome handwriting and thrust it up the sleeve of his cassock.

I sighed, and went to find the orphans of the Honour Guard.

I found most of the young orphans hiding under Brother Thomond in the darkness of the hay barn. "Excuse me, sir," I said, lifting his skirts and ushering out the protesting infants.

"He is asleep," said a young orphan, and indeed, as I looked closer, I saw Brother Thomond was at a slight tilt. Supported from behind by a pillar, he was maintained erect only by the stiffness of his ancient joints. Straw protruded at all angles from his wild white hair.

"He said he wished to speak to you, Jude," said another orphan. I hesitated. We were already late. I decided not to wake him, for Brother Thomond, once he had stopped, took a great deal of time to warm up and get rightly going again.

"Where is Agamemnon?" I asked.

The smallest orphan removed one thumb from his mouth and jerked it upward, to the loft.

"Agamemnon!" I called softly.

Old Agamemnon, my dearest companion and the orphanage pet, emerged slowly from the shadows of the loft and stepped, with a tread remarkably dainty for a dog of such enormous size, down the wooden ladder to the ground. He shook his great ruff of yellow hair and yawned at me loudly.

"Walkies," I said, and he stepped to my side. We exited the hay barn into the golden light of a perfect Tipperary summer's day.

I lined up the Honour Guard and counted them by the front door, in the shadow of the south tower of the orphanage. Its yellow brick façade glowed in the morning sun. We set out.

From the gates of the orphanage to the site of the speeches was several strong miles. We passed through town and out the other side. The smaller orphans began to wail, afraid they would see black people, or be savaged by beasts. Agamemnon stuck closely to my rear. We walked until we ran out of road. Then we followed a track, till we ran out of track.

We hopped over a fence, crossed a field, waded a dyke, cut through a ditch, traversed scrubland, forded a river and entered Nobber Nolan's bog. Spang plumb in the middle of Nobber Nolan's Bog, and therefore spang plumb in the middle of Tipperary, and thus Ireland, was the nation's most famous boghole, famed in song and story: the most desolate place in Ireland, and the last place God created.

I had never seen the famous boghole, for Nobber Nolan had, until his recent death and his bequest of the bog to the state, guarded it fiercely from locals and tourists alike. Many's the American was winged with birdshot over the years, attempting to make pilgrimage here. I looked about me for the hole, but it was hid from my view by an enormous car park, a concrete Interpretive Centre of imposing dimensions, and a tall, broad, wooden stage, or platform, containing politicians. Beyond car park and Interpretive Centre, an eight-lane motorway of almost excessive straightness stretched clean to the horizon, in the direction of Dublin.

Facing the stage stood fifty thousand farmers.

We made our way through the farmers to the stage. They parted politely, many raising their hats, and seemed in high good humour. "Tis better than the Radiohead concert at Punchestown," said a sophisticated farmer from Cloughjordan.

Once onstage, I counted the smaller orphans. We had lost only the one, which was good going over such a quantity of rough ground. I reported our arrival to Teddy "Noddy" Nolan, the Fianna Fáil TD for Tipperary Central, and a direct descendant of Neddy "Nobber" Nolan. Teddy waved us to our places, high at the back of the sloping stage. The Guard of Honour lined up in front of an enormous green cloth backdrop and stood to attention, flanked by groups of seated dignitaries. I myself sat where I could unobtrusively supervise, at the end of a row. When the last of the stragglers had arrived in the crowd below us, Teddy cleared his throat. The crowd silenced as though shot. He began his speech.

"It was in this place . . ." he said, with a generous gesture which incorporated much of Tipperary, ". . . that Eamon de Valera . . ."

Everybody removed their hats.

". . . hid heroically from the entire British army . . ."

Everybody scowled and put their hats back on.

". . . during the War of Independence. It was in this very boghole that Eamon de Valera . . ."

Everybody removed their hats again.

". . . had his vision: a vision of Irish maidens dancing barefoot at the crossroads, and of Irish manhood dying heroically while refusing to the last breath to buy English shoes . . ."

At the word "English" the crowd put their hats back on, though some took them off again when it turned out only to be shoes. Others then glared at them. They put their hats back on again.

"We in Tipperary have fought long and hard to get the government to make Brussels pay for this fine Interpretive Centre and its fine car park, and in Brünhilde de Valera we found the ideal minister to fight our corner. It is with great pride that I invite the great granddaughter of Eamon de Valera's cousin, the Minister for Beef, Culture and the Islands, Brünhilde de Valera, officially to reopen . . . Dev's Hole!"

The crowd roared and waved their hats in the air, though long experience ensured they kept a firm grip on the peaks, for as all the hats were of the same design and entirely indistinguishable, it was common practice at a Fianna Fáil hat-flinging rally for the less scrupulous farmers to loft an old hat, yet pick up a new.

Brünhilde de Valera took the microphone, tapped it, and cleared her throat.

"Spit on me, Brünhilde!" cried an excitable farmer down the front. The crowd surged forward, toppling and trampling the feeble-legged, in expectation of fiery rhetoric. She began.

"Although it is European money which has paid for this fine Interpretive Centre; although it is European money which has paid for this fine new eight-lane motorway from Dublin and this car park that has tarmacadamed Toomevara in its entirety; although it is European money which has paid for everything built west of Grafton Street in my lifetime; and although we are grateful to Europe for its largesse . . ."

She paused to draw a great breath. The crowd were growing restless, not having a bull's notion where she was going with all this, and distressed by the use of a foreign word.

"It is not for this I brought my hat," said the dignitary next to me, and spat on the foot of the dignitary beside him.

"Nonetheless," said Brünhilde de Valera, "grateful as we are to the Europeans . . . we should never forget . . . that . . . they . . ."

The crowd's right hands began to drift, with a wonderful easy slowness, up towards the brims of their hats in anticipation of a climax.

". . . are a shower of foreign bastards who would murder us in our beds given half a chance!"

A great cheer went up from the massive crowd and the air was filled with hats till they hid the face of the sun and we cheered in an eerie half-light.

The minister paused till everybody had recovered their hats and returned them to their heads.

"Those foreign bastards in Brussels think they can buy us with their money! They are wrong! Wrong! Wrong! You cannot buy an Irishman's heart, an Irishman's soul, an Irishman's loyalty! Remember '98!"

There was a hesitation in the crowd, as the younger farmers tried to recall if we had won the Eurovision Song Contest in 1998.

"1798!" Brünhilde clarified.

A great cheer went up as we recalled the gallant failed rebellion of 1798. "Was It For This That Wolfe Tone Died?" came a wisp of song from the back of the crowd.

"Remember 1803!"

We applauded Emmet's great failed rebellion of 1803. A quavering chorus came from the oldest farmers at the rear of the great crowd. "Bold Robert Emmet, the darling of Ireland . . ."

"Remember 1916!"

Grown men wept as they recalled the great failed rebellion of 1916, and so many contradictory songs were started that none got rightly going.

There was a pause. All held their breath.

"Remember 1988!"

Pride so great it felt like anguish filled our hearts as we recalled the year Ireland finally stood proud among the community of nations, with our heroic victory over England in the first match in group two of the group stage of the European football championship finals. A brief chant went up from the young farmers in the mosh pit: "Who put the ball in the English net?" Older farmers, farther back, added bass to the reply: "Houghton! Houghton!"

I shifted uncomfortably in my seat.

"My great grandfather's cousin did not walk out of the Dáil, start a civil war and kill Michael Collins so that foreign monkey-men could swing from our trees and rape our women!"

Excited farmers began to leap up and down roaring at the front, the younger and more nimble mounting each other's shoulders, then throwing themselves forward to surf toward the stage on a sea of hands, holding their hats on as they went.

"Never forget," roared Brünhilde de Valera, "that a vision of Ireland came out of Dev's Hole!"

"Dev's Hole! Dev's Hole!" roared the crowd.

By my side, Agamemnon began to howl and tried to dig a hole in the stage with his long claws.

Neglecting to empty my bladder after breakfast had been an error the awful significance of which I only now began to grasp. A good Fianna Fáil ministerial speech to a loyal audience in the heart of a Tipperary bog could go on for up to five hours. I pondered my situation. My only choice seemed to be as to precisely how I would disgrace myself in front of thousands. To rise and walk off the stage during a speech by a semi-descendant of de Valera would be tantamount to treason and would earn me a series of beatings on my way to the portable toilets. The alternative was to relieve myself into my breeches where I sat.

My waistband creaked under the terrible pressure.

With the gravest reluctance, I willed the loosening of my urethral sphincter.

Nothing happened. My subsequent efforts, over the next few minutes, to void my bladder, resulted only in the vigorous exercising of my superficial abdominal muscles. At length, I realised that there was a default setting in my subconscious which was firmly barred against public voidance, and to which my conscious mind had no access.

The pressure grew intolerable and I grew desperate. Yet, within the line of sight of fifty thousand farmers, I could not unleash the torrent.

Then, inspiration. The velvet curtain! All I needed was an instant's distraction and I could step behind the billowing green backdrop beside me, and vanish. Once hidden from sight, I could, no doubt, find an exit off the back of the stage, relieve myself in its shadow, and return unobserved to my place.

At that second a magnificent gust of nationalist rhetoric lifted every hat again aloft and in the moment of eclipse I stood, took one step sideways, and vanished behind the curtain.

I shuffled along, my face to the emerald curtain, my rear to the back wall of the stage, until the wall ceased. I turned, and I beheld, to my astonished delight, the solution to all my problems.

Hidden from stage and crowd by the vast curtain was a magnificent circular long-drop toilet of the type employed in the orphanage. But where we sat around a splintered circle of rough wooden plank, our buttocks overhanging a fetid pit, here a great golden rail encircled a pit of surpassing beauty. Its mossy walls ran down to a limpid pool into which a lone frog gently plashed.

Installed, no doubt, for the private convenience of the minister, should she be caught short during the long hours of her speech, it was the most beautiful sight I had yet seen in this world. It seemed nearly a shame to urinate into so perfect a pastoral picture, and it was almost with reluctance that I unbuttoned my breeches and allowed my manhood its release.

I aimed my member so as to inconvenience the frog as little as possible. At last my consciousness made connection with my unconscious; the setting was reset. Mind and body were as one; will became action; I was unified. In that transcendent moment, I could smell the sweet pollen of the heather and the mingled colognes of a thousand bachelor farmers.

I could hear the murmur and sigh of the crowd like an ocean at my back, and Brünhilde de Valera's mighty voice bounding from rhetorical peak to rhetorical peak, ever higher. And as this moment of perfection began its slow decay into the past, and as the delicious frozen moment of anticipation deliquesced into attainment and the pent-up waters leaped forth and fell in their glorious swoon, Brünhilde de Valera's voice rang out as from Olympus:

"I hereby . . . officially . . . reopen . . . Dev's Hole!"

A suspicion dreadful beyond words began to dawn on me. I attempted to arrest the flow, but I may as well have attempted to block by effort of will the course of the mighty Amazon River.

Thus the great curtain parted, to reveal me urinating into Dev's Hole, into the very source of the sacred spring of Irish nationalism: the headwater, the holy well, the font of our nation.

I feel, looking back, that it would not have gone so badly against me, had I not turned at Brünhilde de Valera's shriek and hosed her with urine.

They pursued me across rough ground for some considerable time.

Agamemnon held them at the gap in the wall, as I crossed the grounds and gained the house. He had not had such vigorous exercise since running away from Fossetts' Circus and hiding in our hay barn a decade before, as a pup. Undaunted, he slumped in the gap, panting at them.

Slamming the orphanage door behind me, I came upon old Brother Thomond in the long corridor, beating a small orphan in a desultory manner.

"Ah, Jude," said Brother Thomond, on seeing me. The brown leather of his face creaked as he smiled.

"A little lower, sir, if you please," piped the small orphan, and Brother Thomond obliged. The weakness of Brother Thomond's brittle limbs made his beatings popular with the lads, as a rest and a relief from those of the more supple and youthful Brothers.

"Yes, Jude . . ." he began again, "I had something I wanted to . . . yes . . . to . . . yes . . ." He nodded his head, and was distracted by straw falling past his eyes, from his tangled hair.

I moved from foot to foot, uncomfortably aware of the shouts of the approaching mob. Agamemnon, by his roars, was now retreating heroically ahead of them as they crossed the grounds toward the front door.

"Tis the orphanage!" I heard one cry.

"Tis full of orphans!" cried another.

"From Orphania!" cried a third.

"As we guessed!" called a fourth. "He is a foreigner!"

I had a bad feeling about this. The voices were closer. Agamemnon held the door, but no dog, however brave, can hold off a mob forever.

"Yes!" said Brother Thomond, and fixed me with a glare. "Very good." He fell asleep briefly, one arm aloft above the small orphan.

The mob continued to discuss me on the far side of the door. "You're thinking of Romania, and of the Romanian orphans. You're confusing the two," said a level head, to my relief. I made to tiptoe past Brother Thomond and the small orphan.

"Romanian, by God!"

"He is Romanian?"

"That man said so."

"I did not . . ."

"A gypsy bastard!"

"Kill the gypsy bastard!"

The voice of reason was lost in the hubbub and a rock came in through the stained-glass window above the front door. It put a hole in Jesus and it hit Brother Thomond in the back of the neck.

Brother Thomond awoke.

"Dismissed," he said to the small orphan sternly.

"Oh but sir you hadn't finished!"

"No backchat from you, young fellow, or I shan't beat you for a week."

The small orphan scampered away into the darkness of the long corridor. Brother Thomond sighed deeply and rubbed his neck.

"Jude, today is your eighteenth birthday, is it not?"

I nodded.

Brother Thomond sighed again. "I have carried a secret this long time, regarding your birth. I feel it is only right to tell you now . . ." He fell briefly asleep.

The cries of the mob grew as they assembled, eager to enter and destroy me. The yelps and whimpers of brave Agamemnon were growing fainter. I had but little time. I poked Brother Thomond in the clavicle with a finger. He started awake. "What? WHAT? WHAT?"

Though to rush Brother Thomond was usually counterproductive, circumstances dictated that I try. I shouted, the better to penetrate the fog of years. "You were about to tell me the secret of my birth, sir."

"Ah yes. The secret . . ." He hesitated. "The secret of your birth. The secret I have held these many years . . . which was told to me by . . . by one of the . . . by Brother Feeny . . . who was one of the Cloughjordan Feenys . . . His mother was a Thornton . . ."

"If you could speed it up, sir," I suggested, as the mob forced open the window-catch above us. Brother Thomond obliged.

"The Secret of Your Birth . . ."

With a last choking yelp, Agamemnon fell silent. There was a tremendous hammering on the old oak door. "I'll just get that," said Brother Thomond. "I think there was a knock."

As he reached it, the door burst open with extraordinary violence, sweeping old Brother Thomond aside with a crackling of many bones and throwing him backwards against the wall where he impaled the back of his head on a coat hook. Though he continued to speak, the rattle of his last breath rendered the secret unintelligible. The mob poured in.

I ran on, into the dark of the long corridor.

I found the Master of Orphans, Brother Madrigal, in his office in the south tower, beating an orphan in a desultory manner.

"Ah, Jude," he said. "Went the day well?"

Wishing not to burden him with the lengthy truth, and with time in short supply, I said, "Yes."

He nodded approvingly.

"May I have my letter, sir?" I said.

"Yes, yes, of course." He dismissed the small orphan, who trudged off disconsolate. Brother Madrigal turned from his desk toward the confiscation safe, then paused by the open window. "Who are those strange men on the lawn, waving torches?"

"I do not precisely know," I said truthfully.

He frowned.

"They followed me home," I felt moved to explain.

"And who could blame them?" said Brother Madrigal. He smiled and tousled my hair, before moving again toward the confiscation safe, tucked into the room's rear left corner. From the lawn far below could be heard confused cries.

Unlocking the safe, he took out the letter and turned. Behind him, outside the window, I saw flames race along the dead ivy and creepers, and vanish up into the roof timbers. "Who," he mused, looking at the envelope, "could be writing to you?" He started suddenly and looked up at me. "Of course!" he said. "Jude, it is your eighteenth birthday, is it not?"

I nodded.

He sighed, the tantalising letter now held disregarded in his right hand. "Jude . . . I have carried a secret this long time, regarding your birth. It is a secret known only to Brother Thomond and myself, and it has weighed heavy on us. I feel it is only right to tell you now. The secret of your birth . . ." He hesitated. "Is . . ." My heart clattered in its cage at this second chance. Brother Madrigal threw up his hands. "But where are my manners? Would you like a cup of tea first? And we must have music. Ah, music."

He pressed play on the record player that sat at the left edge of the broad desk. The turntable bearing the orphanage single began to rotate at forty-five revolutions per minute. The tone-arm lifted, swung out, and dropped onto the broad opening groove of the record. The blunt needle juddered through the scratched groove. Faintly, beneath the crackle, could be heard traces of an ancient tune.

Brother Madrigal returned to the safe and switched on the old kettle that sat atop it. Leaving my letter leaning against the kettle, he came back to his desk and sat behind it in his old leather armchair. The rising roar of the old kettle and crackle of the record player disguised the rising roar and crackle of the flames in the dry timbers of the old tower roof.

Brother Madrigal patted the side of the record player affectionately.

"The sound is so much warmer than from all these new digital doohick-eys, don't you find? And of course you can tell it is a good-quality machine from the way, when the needle hops free of the surface of the record, it of-ten falls back into the self-same groove it has just left, with neither loss nor repetition of much music. The arm . . ." He tapped his nose and slowly closed one eye, ". . . is true."

He dug out an Italia '90 cup and a USA '94 mug from his desk, and put a teabag in each.

"Milk?"

"No, thank you," I said. The ceiling above him had begun to bulge down in a manner alarming to me. The old leaded roof had undoubtedly begun to collapse, and I feared my second and last link to my past would be crushed along with all my hopes.

"Very wise. Milk is fattening and thickens the phlegm," said Brother Madrigal. "But you would like your letter, no doubt. And also . . . the secret of your birth." He arose, his head almost brushing the bulge in the plaster, now yellowing from the intense heat of the blazing roof above it.

"Thirty years old, that record player," said Brother Madrigal proudly, catching my glance at it. "And never had to replace the needle or the record. It came with a wonderful record. I really must turn it over one of these days," he said, lifting the gently vibrating letter from alongside the rum-bling kettle whose low tones, as it neared boiling, were lost in the bellow of flame above. "Have you any experience of turning records over, Jude?"

"No sir," I said as he returned to the desk, my letter white against the black of his dress. Brother Madrigal extended the letter halfway across the table. I began to reach out for it. The envelope, containing perhaps the se-cret of my origin, brushed against my fingertips, electric with potential.

At that moment, with a crash, in a bravura finale of crackle, the record finished. The lifting mechanism hauled the tone arm up off the vinyl and returned it to its rest position with a sturdy click.

"Curious," said Brother Madrigal, absentmindedly taking back the letter. "It is most unusual for the crackling to continue after the record has stopped." He stood and moved to the record player.

The bulge in the ceiling gave a great lurch downward. Brother Madrigal turned, and looked up.

"Ah! There's the problem!" he said. "A flood! Note the bulging ceiling! The water tank must have overflowed in the attic and the subsequent damp is causing a crackling in the circuits of the record player. Damp," he touched his temple twice, "is the great enemy of the electrical circuit."

He was by now required to shout on account of the great noise of the holocaust in the roof beams. Smoke began entering the room.

"Do you smell smoke?" he enquired. I replied that I did. "The damp has caused a short circuit," he said, and nodded. "Just as I suspected." He went to the corner of the room, where a fire axe rested in its glass-fronted wooden case. He removed axe from case and strode to beneath the bulge. "Nothing for it but to pierce it and relieve the pressure, or it'll have the roof down." He swung the axe up at the heart of the bulge.

A stream of molten lead from the roof poured over Brother Madrigal. The silver river flowed over axe and man, boiling his body while coating him in a thick sheet of still-bright lead that swiftly thickened and set as it ran down his upstretched arm, encasing his torso before solidifying in a thick base about his feet on the smoking carpet. Entirely covered, he shone under the electric light, axe aloft in his right hand, my letter smouldering and silvered in his left.

I snatched the last uncovered corner of the letter from his metal grasp, the heat-brittled triangle snapping off cleanly at the bright leaden boundary.

Snug in that little corner of envelope nestled a small triangle of yellowed paper.

My fingers tingled with dread and anticipation as they drew the scrap from its casing. Being the burnt corner of a single sheet, folded twice to form three rectangles of equal size, the scrap comprised a larger triangle of paper folded down the middle from apex to baseline, and a smaller, un-creased triangle of paper of the size and shape of its folded brother.

I regarded the small triangle.

Blank.

I turned it over.

Blank.

I unfolded and regarded the larger triangle.

Blank.

I turned it over, and read . . .

gents

anal

cruise.

I tilted it obliquely to catch the light, the better to reread it carefully:

gents

anal

cruise.

The secret of my origin was not entirely clear from the fragment, and the tower was beginning to collapse around me. I sighed, for I could not help but feel a certain disappointment in how my birthday had turned out. I left Brother Madrigal's office as, behind me, the floorboards gave way beneath his lead-encased mass. I looked back to see him vanish down through successive floors of the tower.

I ran down the stairs. A breeze cooled my face as the fires above me sucked air up the stairwell, feeding the flames. Chaos was by now general and orphans and Brothers sprang from every door, laughing and exclaim-ing that Brother McGee had again lost control of his woodwork class.

The first members of the mob now pushed their way upstairs and, our lads not recognising the newcomers, fisticuffs ensued. I hesitated on the last landing. One member of the mob broke free of the mêlée and, seeing me, exclaimed, "There he is, boys!" He threw his hat at me and made a leap. I leapt sideways, through the nearest door, and entered Nurse's quarters.

Nurse, the most attractive woman in the orphanage, and on whom we all had a crush, was absent, at her grandson's wedding in Borris-in-Ossary. I felt it prudent to disguise myself from the mob, and slipped into a charming blue gingham dress. Only briefly paralysed by pleasure at the scent of her perfume, I soon made my way back out through the battle, as orphans and farmers knocked lumps out of each other.

"Foreigners!" shouted the farmers at the orphans.

"Foreigners!" shouted the orphans back, for some of the farmers were from as far away as Cloughjordan, Ballylusky, Ardcrony, Lofty Bog, and even far-off South Tipperary itself, as could be told by the sophistication of the stitching on the leather patches at the elbows of their tweed jackets and the richer, darker tones, redolent of the lush grasslands of the Suir Valley, of the cowshit on their Wellington boots.

"Dirty foreign bastards!"

"Fuck off back to Orphania!"

"Ardcrony ballocks!"

I saw the sophisticated farmer, who had seen Radiohead at Punchestown, hurled over the balcony and his body looted of its cigarettes by the infants.

The crowd parted to let me through, the young farmers removing their hats as I passed. The other orphans shouted, "It is Jude in a Dress!" But the sexual ambiguity of my name served me well on this occasion, as it helped the more doubtful farmers take me for an ill-favoured girl who usually wore slacks.

Escaping the crowd down the final stairs, I found myself once again in the deserted long corridor.

From far behind me came the confused sounds of the mob in fierce combat with the orphans and the Brothers of Jesus Christ Almighty. From far above me came the crack of expanding brick, a crackle of burning timber, sharp explosions of windowpanes in the blazing tower. My actions had led to the destruction of the orphanage. I had brought bitter disgrace to my family, whoever they should turn out to be.

I realised with a jolt that I would have to leave the place of my greatest happiness.

Ahead, dust and smoke gushed down through the ragged hole in the ceiling through which the lead-encased body of Brother Madrigal had earlier plunged. I gazed upon him, standing proudly erect on his thick metal base, holding his axe aloft, the whole of him shining like a freshly washed baked-bean tin in the light of the setting sun that shone along the corridor, through the open front door.

And by the front door, hanging from the coat hook in a more alert posture than his old bones had been able to manage in life, was Brother Thomond, the golden straw bursting from the neck and sleeves of his cassock. And in the doorway itself, hanged by his neck from a rope, my old friend Agamemnon, his thick head of golden hair fluffed up into a huge ruff by the noose, his tawny fur bristling as his dead tongue rolled from between his fierce, yellow teeth.

What was left for me here, now?

With a splintering crash and a flat, rumbling, bursting impact, the entire façade of the south tower detached itself, and fell in a long roll across the lawn and down the driveway, scattering warm bricks the length of the drive.

Dislodged by the lurch of the tower, the orphanage record player fell, tumbling three stories, through the holes made by Brother Madrigal and landed rightway up by his side with a smashing of innards.

The tone arm lurched onto the record on impact and, with a twang of elastic, the turntable began to rotate. Music sweet and pure filled the air and a sweet voice sang words I had only ever heard dimly.

"Some . . .

"Where . . .

"Oh . . .

"Werther . . .

"Aon . . .

"Bó . . ."

I filled to brimming with an ineffable emotion. I felt a great . . . presence? No, it was an absence, an absence of? Of . . . I could not name it. I
wished I had someone to say goodbye to, to say goodbye to me.

The record ground to a slow halt with a crunching of broken gear-teeth.
I looked around me for the last time and sighed.

"There is no place like home," I said quietly to nobody, and walked out
the door onto the warm bricks in my blue dress. The heat came up through
the soles of my shoes, so that I skipped nimbly along the warm yellow
bricks, till they ended.

I looked back once, to see the broken wall, the burning roof and tower.
And Agamemnon dead.

ORNA NÍ CHOILEÁIN

Camino

Ramón sat cross-legged on the wooden portico. He picked up a chunk of asphalt from the pile against the wall and started on the final shift of the afternoon. Some chunks he struck against each other to break them up. The remainder he had to whittle with a blunt tool. He threw the fragments into the tatty old basket beside him.

When the basket was full he would take it and empty its contents into the wheelbarrow. That full, he would make a longer trip up the mountain, where he would sell the pieces as filler to the developers. If he were fortunate, the crew would refill his wheelbarrow with additional large rocks. Usually, he had to do the work himself.

The bypass was well under way. On completion, the engineers would have no further need of Ramón's labor. He would then need to find some other work in order to earn money for himself and for his aunt. There was no question of living off the contributions they received from the well-intentioned visitors who came to see her once in a while. Only the most desperate people would undertake the arduous trek to their home in the Andes.

He glanced over to the other side of the portico, where Espie sat in her rocking chair—asleep, he thought. Even blind as she was, her inner eyes saw far more than Ramón ever would.

She sensed his eyes on her. "The weather will turn," Espie announced from her chair.

Ramón smiled. "I don't need a clairvoyant to tell me that much."

"Is your knee bothering you?" she asked, though she knew the answer.

"My knee aches, I ache all over, just as I always do when the weather is about to change. I don't remember a dry spell lasting longer than this one. I suppose the rainy season will be fairly heavy when it comes, whenever that might be."

Ten years before, Ramón, while working on the road, skidded and dropped through a deep, narrow gap in the undergrowth. There were no emergency rescue services nearby at that time, not even a telephone to raise the alarm. He lay in a hollow, semi-conscious for nine hours, until a rescue team came. His knee never healed properly. On account of the injury Ramón was unable to compete for work on the bypass with the other men downtown. On the bright side, he was in a position to keep his aunt company during the day.

"I'll have to look for other work soon. The bypass will be finished before the rain comes, and the engineers will leave."

Espie was not of the same opinion. "Folks have been saying for some time now that the weather is about to change, but here we are still waiting."

Ramón knew what she meant. The weather had outstayed its welcome. Locals had been saying over and over that the dry season would surely end soon; that the rain would come the next week. In much the same way, the bypass had been "almost finished" for a number of years now.

This time however, the developers had the advantage of the long drought, and they really were approaching the end of the project. The workers endured the heat of the day to feed their families. They depended on one another. If rain did not come soon, there would be no crop to harvest. If there was no crop, they would have no work, and hence no food for their families.

Espie's face was a sudden expression of anguish. "Are you in pain too?" Ramón asked worriedly. He rose to tend to her. She remained silent, and Ramón understood at once that a vision was taking place. The lines on her aged face grew deeper as she was drawn in.

While it did happen on occasion, Ramón was aware that it was unusual for visions to occur without some forewarning. Normally Espie would be given someone's picture or a personal possession to interpret. Such items invoked thoughts, images, strong emotions, and she gave direction to her audience wherever possible.

Ramón stayed beside her until the vision faded. He did not ask what she saw. He never did. She would tell him if she wanted to tell.

Finally Espie let out a sigh, though there was always tension in her body. Ramón raked his mind, in search of something to say. "It's almost seven. I'll go get the chocolates."

Espie's expression changed, she looked more relaxed and the worry receded from her face. "That would be nice," she said.

Ramón rubbed his weathered hands on his faded jeans and limped into the kitchen, which also served as both their living room and sitting room. He opened the dresser and took out the small golden box of Belgian chocolates. Espie was intuitive, but she had not expected this dainty gift prior to receiving it last week.

Each chocolate had a different flavor. They were magical. Far better than the coca leaves Ramón would chew from time to time, if he needed to stay awake.

Outside, Ramón removed the green ribbon. He opened the cardboard. Three left. "Tía," he called to his aunt, "There are three left. You have one now and we'll each have one tomorrow night." As he spoke, he saw the same dark shadow of distress draw across her face once more. Then, in the blink of an eye, all trace of it was gone. Perhaps it was nothing, Ramón thought, but a ray of sun dancing on her face.

Espie took a chocolate. Ramón returned to the kitchen without another

word, where he tied a new bow in the ribbon as he had done every afternoon this week, and returned the box to the dresser for the last time. He
went out to watch his aunt while she ate the chocolate. Sunlight glinted off
the foil. The chocolate was already melting in the heat of the afternoon.
Ramón's thoughts lingered on the couple who had brought the box of
chocolates to the house the week before. He wondered if they'd found what
they were searching for.

■　■　■

Mrs. Nolan and her husband came to speak with Espie about their daughter Hayley, who had been missing for eight weeks. Ramón felt a piercing
stab of pity for the couple when he saw them. They clutched one another
fiercely, as though one might lose the other if they lessened their grip.

They had exhausted every possibility, searching for their daughter. The
police had given up the investigation. The social worker told them that it
was time for them to "move on," that there was "every possibility that Hayley had just eloped to the continent with some boy." The Nolans refused to
accept this theory. Determination to discover the truth spurred them on to
make the difficult journey across the world to speak with Espie in her
kitchen.

Ramón went about the housework, always keeping one eye on the conversation between his aunt and the Nolans. They gave Espie a photograph
of Hayley, hoping she would give them a clue as to the whereabouts of their
daughter. Espie revealed that their daughter was dead.

Mr. Nolan held his wife to him and let out a woeful wail. It was harsh,
but better for them to hear the truth, Ramón supposed, than to conceal it.

Espie told them that Hayley's body could be found in a forest, not too
far from a large white manor. Did they know of such a large white manor?
There was a manor nearby, they said.

"You're not thinking of the right one," Espie insisted. "Go farther west.
This house is on a large plot of land. The murderer hid her under some

leaves, knowing that no one would set foot on the estate until springtime when the residents would resume their annual hunt."

Espie revealed to them that the man had not been quite as clever as he'd thought. In her mind she saw what appeared to be some small shiny item, which lay embedded near the stump of a large oak tree. The killer had been in a desperate hurry, and he'd tripped. As he fell, this little trinket slipped out of his pocket. What was it? A ring, perhaps? Or a lighter? They would have to find it as soon as they reached home, or some curious animal or bird would steal it from them for good.

"If you find that, justice will be done. But hurry. The murderer is en-raged. He is ready to kill again."

Perhaps it was a rifle cartridge, the little shiny trinket, Ramón sur-mised. They had computers in those places, and records of the people who owned guns, and which cartridges fit which model. If they found the car-tridge, they would know who the culprit was.

Although the couple was utterly grief-stricken as they bade Espie good-bye, they had embarked on a new beginning. They had a strength of mind about them that had not been present when they first arrived.

Usually visitors would leave Espie vegetables or clothes, to show their gratitude. These two had left Belgian chocolates.

■ ■ ■

James Scorley was incensed. Fifty hours ago he had left his flat. London, Chicago, Miami, and Santa Cruz had not been on his list of places to visit, but he'd passed through every one of them during those past fifty hours. Now a fool in La Paz was trying to take him in because James was foreign: the fool thought he could get a lot of money out of him.

"I could *buy* the car for that price!" James barked.

The attendant shook his head and held out his hands, indicating he did not understand what James was saying. James hissed, but gave him the dollars. He had no choice. He was in a hurry.

"Don't expect to get it back," he muttered, having no intention of bothering with La Paz on the return journey. He'd dump the car on the way to Santa Cruz. He had an open ticket onward from there. He would go through Dallas, Amsterdam, and then home. Or perhaps he would stop for a while in Amsterdam.

The attendant ignored him, pleased to get the dollars. The vehicle he gave him was a black Yugo. One of the best cars on the lot, James decided with disdain.

It was a long, complicated trek he had ahead of him. He was not familiar with the route but had done his research, having had plenty of time during the first leg of his journey to contemplate the execution of his plan.

He hadn't dared risk bringing a knife or a gun onto the plane unnecessarily. Any object had the potential to be a weapon, if he wanted to use it as such. The flight attendants had given him towels. These he would use to smother the old woman. They wouldn't leave much of a trace on her throat. People would think she'd had a heart attack. She was old. She was weak and brittle. She was living in a remote area. There would be nobody to come to her aid. She was blind too. She didn't stand a chance.

He had heard the news on television. Police had found the body of that Nolan tramp in the wood. The parents said in an interview that some "wise woman" in South America, of all places, had told them where their daughter could be found. Nonsense, some people said, but it startled James. What else had this contemptible woman said about the incident?

The police claimed to have a "fresh lead" that would help them catch the killer, that they were aware he was responsible for other crimes in the region. James knew that they often made statements of this nature in order to unsettle the perpetrator and to reassure the community until such time that they turned their minds to some other topic. Even so, he had better mute that ruinous tongue lest it give rise to any more "leads."

■　■　■

"They're looking for workers for the rescue services," Ramón told Espie. "I'm planning to go down to the town tomorrow morning so they can interview me."

"Good," said Espie. "It would be better for you to find a steady job like that, in the town. I may not be long for this world, and you will probably leave this place once I'm gone."

"What sort of talk is that?" Ramón asked her.

"Ah, only talk. I think you would make a fine officer."

He looked at her curiously, but she said no more to him. Since she had given her blessing, he assumed it safe to go to town in the morning. Perhaps he would even succeed in getting the job.

"Will you be all right here alone the whole day? I don't really need to go. I could get someone to stay with you, or you could come with me.'"

"I'll be fine, Ramón, off you go to town tomorrow."

■   ■   ■

James was sick of driving. He was sick of passing through rotten godforsaken shanties. He was sick of sitting in a stifling old car. He really was sick. But he was close. His heart pounded with a depraved excitement in the knowledge that he was fast approaching his destination.

He braked alongside a tired old woman sitting in a rocking chair on the wooden porch-front of a ramshackle house. She had a water basin beside her, filled with chontaduros. One at a time, she picked up a fruit, peeled it, and dropped it into a bowl.

James suspected that she might know where he could find the blind woman, assuming she herself was not the one he was after. He addressed her from the car. "Excuse me, I'm trying to find a woman." The woman paused to direct her attention towards the stranger. "I'm looking for a particular woman," he snickered. A thought struck him and he stopped laughing. "I hear that this woman is wise—she can speak with the dead. A friend of mine has died and I'd like to find out if she's with the gods."

For a moment neither of them spoke. Then the woman raised a finger and pointed further up the road.

"A bit further up," she advised. "You will find people who can speak with the dead. They will put you on the right path." Then silence. James remained uncertain about this peculiar character.

"What does her house look like?" he asked, trying to catch her out.

"Large," she responded quite simply. "A red door."

"Red, is it? Like the fruit in your hand?"

"Far redder."

■　■　■

Ramón arrived home and let out a long sigh. He crossed over to his aunt who was sitting in the armchair. He kissed her forehead, but she didn't stir. He peered at the basin of half-peeled palm fruits. Sitting back on his haunches, he took a good look at his aunt, at this blind woman.

"Tía," Ramón called, laying a hand on her. She woke from her sleep and opened her eyes.

"Oh, Ramón. I needed that siesta." Espie yawned. "How did it go?"

"I didn't get the job," said Ramón glumly. He yawned too. "They said that I'm too far from them up here, that my response in the event of an emergency would be too slow. They said to come back when we have better roads! Ha! That will be the day! How about you—did you have a good day?"

"Indeed I did. Now don't you worry about that job. Is the bypass finished yet?"

"No."

"You'll get another year out of those industrial developers. They won't finish it this season. The winds are changing."

"We'll stay here another year or so. Now, let me fix a bite of food for dinner and afterwards we'll have chocolate."

■　■　■

James continued the upward climb. The road became narrower, if it could be called a road. A dirt track, rather, barely three meters wide. He kept as close to the left-hand side as he could possibly manage. The rocks on that side soared towards the heavens. On the passenger's side was a sheer vertical cliff. At the bottom of the canyon he spotted a tiny stream.

He scowled. He had to be close to the old crone by now. The entire trek had been a real nuisance to him, a waste of both time and money. He drew on the rage that was burning inside him. He wanted to get worked up, to steep himself in tension; he needed to force up his blood pressure, needed the strength to embrace his horrible goal. His resolve grew as he drew nearer.

A thick blanket of fog obscured the view ahead. James drove even slower along the treacherous trail. He turned right and then left, right, and a sharp left again.

Peals of thunder roared in a deafening command and lightning scarred the once perfect sky. The long drought ended abruptly: rain cascaded down the chasm walls. Mud sloshed and oozed over the surface of the perilous path.

James veered right once more, and then he and the car skidded into the fatal abyss.

TRANSLATED FROM IRISH BY ABIGAIL MITCHELL

Orna Ní Choileáin 157

GIULIO MOZZI

(AKA CARLO DALCIELO)

Carlo Doesn't Know How to Read

Carlo (that's me) doesn't know how to read. He reads a great many books. When he reads these books, Carlo doesn't remember a single word. All Carlo remembers from the books he reads is what he sees. When Carlo reads, he often shuts his eyes. Sometimes he falls asleep. When he sleeps, he sees things. When he wakes up, he goes back to reading. He doesn't always start reading from the same place, because he doesn't always remember the exact place he left off at when he fell asleep. Sometimes when Carlo sleeps, the book closes, or the pages turn, or the book falls off the armrest or the bed. With some books, Carlo hasn't read even half the pages; others, he reads the same pages over and over. When he reads a page he's read before, sometimes over and over, Carlo doesn't recognize the words. Carlo doesn't recognize the words because he doesn't see them. If the page includes the word "door," Carlo doesn't see the word "door." He sees a door. If the page includes the word "blue," Carlo doesn't see the word "blue." He sees something blue. Every time Carlo rereads a page with the word "door," the door Carlo sees is a new door. Every time Carlo rereads a page with the word "blue," the blue things he sees are different shades of blue. When proper nouns show up on a page, names like "Mario," "Raymond," "Liz," "Evelyn," or "Alioa," this is the only time Carlo doesn't see anything at all.

He doesn't see the words "Mario," "Raymond," "Liz," "Evelyn," or "Alioa," and he doesn't see anybody who might correspond to the words "Mario," "Raymond," "Liz," "Evelyn," or "Alioa"—not in the same way that a door—an ordinary door—might correspond to the word "door." And so, every time a word like "Raymond," for example, shows up in a book, Carlo doesn't recognize—doesn't see—that word, and so he sees things being done in a scene, but he doesn't see who does them, and he doesn't know—he can't know—that the Raymond who does these things is the same Raymond—as indicated by the word "Raymond"—who appears in other scenes: so all that he, Carlo, knows how to do is imagine himself, Carlo, in that scene doing these things. To be more precise, what Carlo sees is a series of actions that frame a space, and using his imagination, he, Carlo, sets someone inside this space framed by actions, someone like himself, like Carlo, and so—you might say—that someone *is* Carlo. As a result of all this—that is, because Carlo doesn't know how to read and reads a great many books and reads them in the way that's been described—Carlo, every time he reads, sees himself inside this framed space. When he tells his friends about his experiences when he reads—because Carlo has some friends he likes to talk to about his experiences when he reads, hears, or sees—there comes a point when his friends always say, "Okay, so it's like this, Carlo: you really identify with the story you're reading." When Carlo hears this, that is, every time he tells his friends about his experiences when he reads, he answers, "No, I don't identify with the story. I can't identify with a space that's framed by a series of actions. The best I can do is see a space, a space where I fit, and stick myself inside." When he tells his friends about his experiences when he reads, Carlo never mentions the words in the book—especially not the characters' names, since he never remembers them, since he never sees them—instead, he talks about what he sees. What almost always happens, for Carlo, is that when he talks about what he sees when he reads a book, or sleeps on a book, he realizes, while he's talking, that he remembers things, can see many more things in his memory than he seemed to be able to remember before he started talking in the first place. When he tells his friends about a book (if the memory's strong enough: if not, he gets confused, lost, and says, "I don't remember anymore"), Carlo imagines himself reentering the space where he was the first time he read the book, and from there, within that space, the action going on around him, Carlo looks all over, looks at things, notes what's there, what he didn't notice before when he was reading, and he names these things, comes up with words—apparently, for Carlo, spoken words are completely different from written words—and so as he sees these things, bit by bit, he realizes that they're there. If his friends don't interrupt—and sometimes they do interrupt, saying things like, "But I read that one—none of this was in the book!", or, "But how can you give us a whole scene when there's only one sentence about . . ."—but if his friends don't interrupt, Carlo can go on for a half hour or more about what's in the room—the furniture, the knickknacks, the doilies, the lamps, the curtains, the windows, the floor, the blank spot on the wall where a picture used to hang, the fingerprints on the glass of the small china hutch, the water stain in the corner over the door, the dent in the plaster from where the doorknob always hits it, that curl of dust just peeking out from under the sideboard, the crack in the base of the tiny porcelain statue on the sideboard, the stitching coming undone on the pocket of the tan raincoat thrown over the chair. Once, in a bookstore, there was a reading by one of Carlo's favorite writers, and an influential critic introduced the writer, and then the man read a little from his book, and then, when the audience (barely anyone showed up, like always) was invited to ask questions, Carlo stood up and thanked the writer for the stitching coming undone, and he, Carlo, stood there talking in the tiny, nearly empty room about that stitching coming undone on the pocket of a raincoat that appeared in a scene in the book by this writer, one of Carlo's favorites; and he, Carlo, spoke for so long that the critic finally interrupted him, thanked him, and pointed out that someone else in the audience might want to talk too, and that's when the writer (one of Carlo's favorites), looking embarrassed but also a little annoyed, told Carlo, "Look, I really don't remember anything about any stitching coming undone. Besides, I don't see what's so interesting about it anyway." This was the event that spurred Carlo to find himself some friends so they could share their experiences with reading, and it was during these discussions (usually held in the small back room in the bar by the Poggio Rusco train station, where the friends—a few from Poggio Rusco, a few from surrounding towns—could find some peace and quiet) that Carlo realized, while they talked, that he really couldn't read—he could only see—and while his friends could read, could look at books and read them, read the words, words like "door" and "blue," even proper nouns like "Raymond" and "Evelyn"—while his friends could do all this—they really couldn't see. "When you talk about a book," one friend told him, "it's like you're talking about a dream. And it's always hard to tell with dreams if you're describing what you saw or if the act of trying to describe a dream has set your imagination off in a new direction so that now you're actually adding new things to what you remember, things you're dreaming up right there on the spot, even if you don't know that's what you're doing, until everything's mixed up, and you can't keep what you remember from the dream and what you've invented around the dream straight, and you wander around inside your vision of the dream—or book, in your case, Carlo— and it's not like you're wandering around inside a memory, it's like you're exploring an entirely new place full of entirely new things." That's it exactly, Carlo answered. And from that time on, Carlo (who for years had kept a *Dream Diary* where he didn't describe the dreams he had the night before—he didn't describe them because he didn't remember them: Carlo's the type who never remembers dreams—instead he'd describe what his body was like when he first woke up, and what his bed was like—pillow, sheets, blankets—in those moments right after he rolled himself out of bed), he, Carlo, decided to keep a *Reading Diary* where he'd jot down what he just experienced while reading, not in words—he doesn't see them—

but in drawings. And sometimes, when he's with his friends at the bar by the Poggio Rusco station, Carlo shows them his *Reading Diary*, and his friends laugh a little, but they find it moving, too, when they see how Carlo reads—Carlo, who doesn't know how to read—and how he takes these books and turns them into sequences of scenes, and the elements from a book keep coming back—the doors, the blue things, the shirts, the telephones, the men playing cards, the fish coming up from the water then falling back, the lit windows, the rain, the cars with their headlights on at dusk—and there's no question that these are always the same things, the things that make up the story, the objects and things that motivate the action going on in the story; and yet they're never really the exact same things: a door's a door but never the same door; an evening's an evening but never the same evening; a kitchen table's a kitchen table but never the same kitchen table; a fork next to a plate's a fork next to a plate but never the same fork next to a plate. And even Carlo, his friends realize, when they meet for one of their evenings at the bar by the Poggio Rusco station, even Carlo's not the same exact Carlo; no, he's really not the same Carlo; he's always a Carlo but never the same Carlo; he's always recognizable as Carlo—the Carlo they all know—but every time, before they recognize him, before they perk up and say, "Ciao, Carlo," or say to one another, "Here he is, here comes Carlo," they hesitate, aren't quite sure—they recognize him and they don't recognize him—and it's only through (but this is in just a fraction of a second) some gesture from Carlo, something he'll say, or some distinctive piece of clothing he's wearing that his friends finally come to recognize that what's in front of them, what's walking to their table, is what they've always called "Carlo"; it's only then, after this Carlo joins them at their table and finally fills his empty space, the space that was empty before and that Carlo's friends had been maneuvering around, it's only then that his friends are able to say "Carlo," and give this object a name, and through the name, "Carlo," they can tie this object, Carlo, to all the Carlos that through all the weeks and months and years now they've called "Carlo" every time. And it's through this recognition, through this name, "Carlo," that Carlo's not some stranger for them; he's not some apparition who's appeared between the tables and the men playing cards; he's a friend of theirs, he's Carlo, and they know him well, have talked with him a thousand times, and they love him, really love him, because Carlo, eccentric and confused Carlo, Carlo with his head in the clouds, is always Carlo, the Carlo who gets their imaginations going, and without him, without Carlo, they, his friends, would only have words and names in the lives they're so attached to, and never any visions.

TRANSLATED FROM ITALIAN BY ELIZABETH HARRIS

INGA ĀBELE

Ants and Bumblebees

Father wanted to go to Ventspils. And right he was—they hadn't been there for almost two years. Marta told Father to be ready early on Saturday. It's hard to drive during the heat of the day, but in the morning it's a whole different story. Look—a dog's been run over during the night near the concrete factory; the dog was large and gray, it's lying in the sand but its head is still on the asphalt. Marta and a hundred others like her make up a mob that rolls itself over the bodies of dogs, deer, hedgehogs, and so forth, every single day, as though these were just bloody rags in the road the drivers have neither the time nor space to pull over and inspect. Still, seeing this sight so early in the morning, Marta suddenly wants to stop the car, to sit down next to the dog in the sand, to be with it for a while. A strange wish— Marta hasn't stopped for years. She just keeps going forward. In other words—she lives.

Father is sulky when he greets Marta, for some reason. He limps up to her car and examines it critically. "Not very impressive," he says, "it's too low." "Take it or leave it," Marta snaps back—"I want coffee!" "Well, go and make some then, the water's already boiled." Marta enters the small kitchen, which smells of mildew and damp wood, and where the window is plaited over by pale creeper plants. An endless, shining cargo train is moving past the window, and the black oily surface of her coffee is trembling in its cup. Marta stands by the window, sipping her coffee and count-ing the cars. She's had an obsessive need to count train cars ever since she was a child: if you can count them all, everything will turn out all right.

Father appears wearing his good suit. In the eighties a derailed train car had crushed him against a stack of wooden planks. Since then he's been receiving a disability pension, and year by year he's been getting increas-ingly lopsided—and petulant. He can't get his limp arm inside the sleeve of his jacket. Marta helps. He yells at her—"I don't need your help!"—once the jacket is safely on. Father refuses to sit in the front seat of her car. He folds himself into the back and disappears as if sucked under by the cur-rent. Marta searches for his face in the rearview mirror, but can't find it. Men are only happy when they're free to disappear, she thinks to herself. Clear glistening drops of morning dew fall onto the windscreen from two nearby trees: a sallow and a goat willow. The car radio is long gone.

'We could go through Jurmala," Marta says aloud, to break up their pro-longed silence. "Why go through Jurmala when we need to get to Vent-spils?" Father grumbles, watching the scenery rushing past out of the cor-ner of his eye. "Jurmala is beautiful. Nice buildings and that sort of thing," Marta says, not giving in. "Jurmala is disgusting," Father replies. Marta clenches her fingers even tighter around the steering wheel. She senses that the trip isn't likely to get any easier. "Jurmala is beautiful, Dad. You know that. You're just being difficult." "Jurmala is disgusting. The news-paper says there's more piss in the sea there than water." "Fine. We don't have to talk if you don't want to," Marta says. The expression on Father's face remains unchanged.

Horseflies and a bunch of hungry kids greet them at Lucija's—Mom's sister's place. Half-naked, the kids attack the sacks of food Marta's brought and pull them into a pergola to divide. Marta hasn't even managed to get out of the car when, accompanied by a few burr-covered dogs' heads, Fran-cisks sinks into her lap. He grabs Marta by her cheeks and kisses her gen-tly on the eyes. "Marta, Marta," he says, "finally!" Marta has no idea what's happened to her brother. As she opens her eyes, she realizes he's dyed his hair black. There's a dark streak around his forehead still—he must have dyed it pretty recently. "It doesn't suit you," she says, "you look like a woman." Francisks stops being demure and dismisses her comment with a wave. He hadn't expected much else from Marta. Father, on the other hand, is acting in a strangely tolerant manner. He tries not to stare at Francisks's hair and asks about life, school, the animals, and finally asks Marta to take a picture of them. She finds her mobile phone and takes a picture of the two—her asymmetrical father and her brother with what looks like a black wig—feudal-era ruins in the background.

Then Lucija shows up and gives Marta a cuddle. Marta asks if she's been growing those beautiful round cemetery plants again this year—those plants that are so patient they can even be planted in sand. "Oh yes," Lucija replies, "I just happen to have a box left over from what we brought to sell at the market." She gets out a wooden box full of hen-and-chicks houseleeks. Marta hands her some money. "I don't really want to charge relatives," her aunt objects, but immediately enquires, "how much do you have there?"

Marta puts the box into the trunk of her car and yells out at Francisks, "Get ready!" "Get ready for what?" he asks. "Aren't you coming along to the cemetery?"—"I can't go running around cemeteries during working hours," Francisks says. "I was five when she died and I don't remember her at all. I have to mow grass for the cows." "For God's sake," Marta says, "Lucija will do that, Francisks!" "Fine," Francisks says, "but only if you let me drive through the forest."

Marta lets Francisks drive for a while. He's good at it. When some people see a ditch coming, they hit the breaks. Francisks knows to keep going, knows how to straighten out, how to correct for it as much as he can. Marta decides to stop for some gas. She asks if anyone wants ice cream. Father does, but Francisks declares: "I just want you to get me my favorite drink."

He fills the tank and goes with Marta into the dusky gas station. "So

Francisks, what's this drink you want?" she asks. He points at some Aldaris beer. "That's alcohol," Marta says. "Barely two percent!" Francisks says. Marta tells him to forget it. "Take me home then!" he yells. "You can walk," Marta snaps back. The station's door slams shut. Marta buys three ice-creams and exits into the midday heat. Father is sitting quietly in the back of the car.

"Where's Francisks?" Marta asks. "Took his bag and left," Father says. Marta pulls around the gas station and notices a small determined silhouette walking uphill through the fir-tree forest. She drives up next to Francisks on the sun-heated road. He picks up his pace. Marta beeps. He flips her off. Marta puts the car in park and steps out into the sweltering dust.

Tears start streaming down her face, on cue, as if she were an old actress. "Why are you doing this?" she wails. "I'll never, and I mean never, buy you alcohol or cigarettes or any other shit that'll kill you. How can you not understand that? You promised to come along if I let you drive for a bit—what are trying to pull? You're going to abandon us because I won't buy you beer? You traitor!"

Francisks glances at his sister's dust-covered face and gets into the car. Marta wipes the tears off her face and sits down behind the steering wheel. "I'll come along," he says, fastening his seatbelt, "but I won't say a word for the rest of the day." "Eat your ice cream before it melts," Marta orders.

Father manages to get ice cream all over himself, and Francisks gobbles his up like there's no tomorrow. Still fuming, he's left holding an empty wrapper and a naked popsicle stick. Naturally, Marta has neither tissues nor a plastic bag in the car to clean up with. She stops near a lonely white bus stop on the main road. Without saying a word, she steps out and opens the trunk. Nothing there either—not a single trash bag. What to do with the garbage? Marta looks back at the bus stop. There must be a trashcan there. She opens the back door of the car, where Father is sitting. "Give me the wrappers," she says and he puts the warm, wet paper into her open palm. She opens the door on Francisks's side. "You too," she says. "I put it down," he says indifferently, without looking at his sister. "Where?" she asks, looking around his seat. "Nowhere," Francisks snaps back. Marta gets down on her bare knees on the sharp pebbles on the road and looks under the car. It's shady there, there's a bit of a draft, and yes, Francisks's stick and wrapper. With difficulty, Marta manages to get the wrapping back. "Litterers are disgusting pigs," she declares and slams Francisks's door shut. Francisks sticks out his tongue. Marta brings the wrappings over to the bus stop. Disaster: there's no trashcan. People have been throwing their garbage right on the ground. There's a thick layer of it all around, being blown here and there by the breeze kicked up by passing cars, under and over the single brown bench. Marta gives it a moment's thought, then drops her trash on the ground and returns to the car.

In protest, Francisks goes to sleep. He droops in his seatbelt with his black-painted head bobbing around like a flower mown down by a storm. Occasionally his head sways right over into Marta's lap or the gear shift. She pushes it back, touching his soft cheek. Francisks doesn't wake. A tiny dribble of sweat is streaming down from his temple in the heat. Father is quiet in the back. "Father," Marta says, smiling, "you still know some people around here, right? People you don't speak to anymore. You haven't seen them for years. Should we stop by, while we're here?" Father can't believe what he's just heard and goes a little berserk: "What relatives," he hisses, throwing himself repeatedly against the rear passenger door, "we're going to the cemetery! Drop me there and then you can go wherever you want! I'll take the bus home!" "Calm down," Marta laughs, "I get it, I get it—we're just going to the cemetery."

At the cemetery all three stand in the hot sand gawping at the reed canary grass-covered graves. They cast short, stocky midday shadows. "Let's get cracking," Father says and takes off his jacket—but it's only Marta and Francisks who get cracking. Father can't bend down very well. Marta takes out the box with the bright green houseleeks and hands Francisks a chisel. Uncle Fricis's tombstone is overgrown with moss and lichen; it's cracked and sunken now like a well-worn stepping stone. Francisks begins tearing strips of moss off it. "You see Francisks," Marta says, relaying a family legend to him while planting the houseleeks on the other grave, "Uncle Fricis is under there, Fricis who cried his eyes out when his wife passed away even though they were both so old." "It wasn't Uncle Fricis, that was Uncle Ansis," Father tells her. "Keep quiet if you don't know what you're talking about." "But did he at least cry his eyes out?" Francisks asks impatiently. "Of course," Father replies.

The big forest ants have built a nest in a nearby ivy bush. Marta happens to be crouching in their way. Soon her legs are covered with shiny black spots. Still planting the houseleeks and brushing a handful of ants away from time to time, Marta raises her head and sees her mother coming toward her—though perhaps not with the eyes in her head. Her mother is dressed in a light cotton suit and has a blonde curl in the middle of her forehead; she's holding a cherry-red handbag in her hand. She is young-looking, unconstrained; before Father, before Marta, before Francisks, before Lille, before the disaster. "Mom, save yourself," Marta whispers. The trembling trees, the narrow path, the heat—Marta stares into empty space for a moment, and then looks back to her work.

"Anybody home?" Francisks asks jokingly, banging the stone on his uncle's grave. A swarm of dark fluffy balls flies out at this provocation and chases Francisks away—some bees must have taken up residence nearby. "How about I just carry the water?" he shouts. Marta agrees. She won't give up, however. The bees go after her instead as she continues to plant the expensive houseleeks. There's about half a box left. The insects keep flying close to her face but don't sting. Is it true that bumblebees don't sting? Either way, they keep landing right on Marta's nose. She screams whenever they do. "Be quiet," Father rumbles. "I'd like to see you keep quiet, down here between the ants and the bumblebees!" Marta says. When she screams again, a nearby funeral takes notice. The attendees jump and look in her direction. "You idiot," Father says. Marta removes Father's rail worker's jacket from the nearby thuja and puts it over her head. It smells like her childhood under the jacket—it's dark and nice. Marta can see just enough of the ground to continue planting. The bumblebees can't bother her now, and she doesn't feel the ants stinging her legs. "Don't you dare get my jacket dirty in the sand!" Father mutters somewhere over her head. "It's my only good jacket." After a while he can't take it any longer—he grabs the jacket and puts it on, then walks off to have a cigarette outside the cemetery.

"Here, take a picture of my grave." Marta hands her phone to Francisks and crouches next to Uncle Fricis's or Ansis's plot. Francisks asks why Marta's calling that narrow strip of land her grave. Marta replies, "Because Father once told me he'd bury me here. He said, 'Here, my dear daughter —here is where we'll plant you.' And I always believed him. He said it gently, but firmly too. Like it was a promise." Then Marta smiles and shouts "Now!" Francisks takes her picture together with all the ants and bumblebees, with the wind and the sand and that funeral procession in the background; and perhaps Marta isn't his sister after all, maybe she's really Francisks's mother, or maybe their mother hasn't even been born yet; maybe their uncle wasn't named Ansis or Fricis but was actually Francisks, and Father has long since cried his eyes out over them all. Who knows—it's all so easy to mix up when there aren't any inscriptions. "We need to do some engraving," Marta tells Francisks, staring at the wind-and-sand-polished headstones. Father comes and asks if maybe they could all leave the cemetery already.

They get in the car and start the return journey. The heat has broken and the sun is far away in the west. Nevertheless, Marta keeps her sunglasses on. Her window is open and the wind keeps blowing her light blue silk scarf up against her neck. Marta is quietly humming a song about perfect mates who nonetheless never cross paths. Francisks is hanging asleep in his seatbelt again. Just before they reach a bridge, a long cargo train passes by. Marta laboriously counts up to fifty-seven cars. She's been counting train cars since she was a child, but never quite figured out what to do with the numbers she obtained by doing so. She texts a friend of hers that she's just counted fifty-seven carriages but has no idea what the significance of this might be.

Once the exit to Lille's house appears, Marta gets jumpy. Father hasn't said a word since they left the cemetery. His silence has a kind of superhuman tension in it. She swerves off the main road, and then Father's silence intensifies so much that he might as well be giving her directions, pointing out the right house. Marta takes a side road, braking suddenly— sand goes flying in the air, Francisks hits the dashboard, and Father sighs.

"Did we really have to?" he asks quietly, the house's front gate having settled directly out his window. "Go on, stop in for a chat," Marta says quickly, almost angrily.

Father pulls himself out of the car, straightens out his jacket, and opens the gate. A massive crowd of geese is running around in the dust. Father splits the flock down the middle and, accompanied by their honking, proceeds toward the entrance at the other end of the house. He disappears around a corner. Red geraniums are growing in bunches on the windowsills.

"Who lives here?" Francisks asks. "Dad's old lover Lille," Marta replies. "Jesus fucking Christ," Francisks mumbles, then falls back asleep. There's nothing to see—just the evening, a pine forest, sand, some geese, and a lonely white house. Marta remembers the view from her childhood—how Mom took Marta's hand and they both walked to this house; they stood quietly behind the gate after Father had been away from home for a couple of days; he was inside the house, behind the curtains, which were and are blowing around in the wind—he was wearing a white shirt and sitting behind a full table and Mr. Lille was pouring vodka into his glass from a glass carafe. The nearby gravel pits radiated heat. Father glanced at his wife and daughter—so did Lilija. Mother turned around and they both went home. And usually not long after these incidents, Father came home too. Marta's cell phone beeps, and she jumps. Her friend has sent her a text message: "57 carriages means that you have 57 summers ahead of you!" Marta says, "Jesus fucking Christ."

Father emerges from the cloud of geese; he closes the gate uncertainly. "It would have been so easy to avoid this place," Marta thinks. "In fact, I'm not sure I had any real reason to stop here." Father climbs into the back seat and finds it necessary to explain: "Wasn't home." "It would have been so easy to avoid this place," Marta says once the bluish road is flashing past underneath them again. Father doesn't say anything.

Marta isn't quite sure how they left Francisks. It's something like an avalanche—time accelerates like a massive stone rolling down a cliff, and suddenly you realize you're alone again. Everything that matters slips right through your hands. Marta remembers that Francisks hugged her; she sees his eyes up very close to her. She's already gotten used to his black hair. "You're smiling," Francisks says. "Are you going to go cry your eyes out once you're alone?" "Yes," Marta replies. Francisks nods with satisfaction. "Don't," he says. "I'm not dead yet."

When they reach the seafront forests, Father coughs. "I want to have a smoke." Marta stops the car, gets out, waits until he pulls himself out of his trench like a fragile, lopsided whale and lights up; then she confiscates a cigarette and his lighter. "Me too," she says. "Are you sure you should?" Father asks. "You already quit once."

Marta walks into the woods and sees the daylight melting at the far end of a long path. This view is perfect. Father shouldn't worry. Nothing else is necessary. If at one point it had seemed to Marta that she was always bound to feel two ways about her life, never quite knowing what it all meant, she now realizes that whatever it is she's approaching has no meaning at all. Yes, it's quite meaningless. Which could be good or bad, depending.

TRANSLATED FROM LATVIAN BY LAURIS VANAGS

MATHIAS OSPELT

Deep In the Snow

"Is it still far?" Günther asked his friend, Wachter. Since he didn't receive a response in what he considered ample time for such a response to be given, he yelled again to his companion, who was stamping in the snow in front of him under the still-dark blue of the icy night. Wachter mumbled something through his over-the-mouth scarf, which most probably meant "no." Then again, perhaps the most likely interpretation would have been: "How should I know!"

Wachter didn't know anything at all. Nevertheless, he always came up with all the best ideas. An example: while he was busy insisting that the masked ball was supposed to be held up in Triesenberg, the others were positive that the Shrove Tuesday festivities were actually taking place in the Lowlands. Somehow or other, though—as usual—he'd got them all convinced, but when they finally arrived at the supposed venue after hitchhiking all the way there, after one of them read the piece of A4 paper stuck to the front door of the bar, which said that the place was "closed due to being closed," Wachter just shrugged and told them that he couldn't possibly have foreseen that. It's not like they put that sort of thing in the news. And with this pronouncement, he absolved himself from all reprimands that might have followed. "What—you think I know everything?" he asked them. That was Wachter's style.

And yet, he was always ready to make suggestions. If the others came up with seven good ideas for having fun on a given weekend, Wachter would, like clockwork, immediately offer an eighth: "I've heard ..." he would tell them. Or, "They say that ..." Or, "In such-and-such town, it seems they've got ..." And most of the time, he got his way: without further adieu, the entire evening, their entire valuable Saturday night, was risked on Wachter's plan.

This particular evening, Wachter and Günther had set off by themselves. They were heading for Ruggell. Deep into the Lowlands. At the northern end of the country. A new bar had opened in the "Ochsen," Wachter announced. Topless. Practically bottomless too. Günther was easily convinced. The prospect of a topless-and-almostbottomless bar made him forget all his anxieties regarding Wachter's brilliant ideas. Thus, the twosome began their bus journey from the Oberland to Ruggell with the highest expectations and enthusiasm. They paused in Schaan, one of the stopovers on the route, and drank a couple of beers; when they eventually arrived in Ruggell, however, the bartender had just locked the door. Eleven P.M. Closing time. That was it. Out! And, anyway: nobody in there was naked. Thus, they had to drag themselves to Nendeln. But weren't they a bit too young for that sort of thing? Günther and Wachter laughed.

Nendeln. How could the not-yet-eighteen-year-old twosome get to Nendeln from Ruggell, on a wintery Saturday night, after eleven P.M.? The typical route could well have been a simple walk along the highway, or else a little hitchhiking to cover the same distance. If they managed to get to Bendern, the worst part of the trip would be behind them—you could always find a way to reach Nendeln from Bendern. Wachter had a better idea, of course. His motto was: there has to be a shortcut. He wasn't at all happy with the idea that, first of all, you had to take a long, roundabout route that involved covering a certain distance, making what amounted to a ninety-degree turn along with the highway, and then covering more or less the same distance again. There *had* to be a shortcut. A straight line is the short-est distance between two points. He had learned that at vocational school. That there happened to be a mountain range called Eschnerberg between the two points in question on this particular night carried no significance whatsoever, according to the geometry classes he'd taken.

"We walk through the fields and then take the best first street, which goes to Gamprin, and from there we go through the wood to Eschen and abracadabra, we're in Nendeln." "Abracadabra." It sounded good. Wachter liked talking like that—it helped him get his way. Yes: "Abracadabra" and they would be in Nendeln. They would be surrounded by women, and get to see all their "abras" and "cadabras" up close. And so, they set out. They left the main street, climbed over the fences, arrived at some snow-covered fields, and walked across. New snow started falling. They walked. It snowed harder. They walked. And walked. As it snowed. And snowed. And they walked. And walked.

They had been en route for two hours now. Günther was sure of this, since he'd checked his watch at the time of departure. He'd been curious how long their march would take. He wanted to be able to give a precise account of the adventure to their friends later on. But the longer they walked, the less impressive the story became.

"Shouldn't we have arrived in Gamprin a while ago now?" shouted Günther. Wachter acted as though he hadn't heard him. As if the question didn't concern him. As if he, Wachter, was stamping through the snow only because of Günther. As if it weren't entirely his doing that they were out there in the cold; as if he, Wachter, would—if it had been up to him—be happily at home watching TV. Thus, they stamped farther through the snow, ever-deeper, and straight into the ever-rising wind. It got more and more difficult, and they began to feel acutely uncomfortable. The booze they'd been drinking all evening had left their systems ages ago. Every difficult footstep made it clearer that they were not, in fact, enjoying themselves. Besides, all the bars would already have closed by the time they eventually arrived in Nendeln. All of Günther's desires had long since abated. He just wanted to go home. To be in bed. Sleeping.

"Hey! Wachter!" Günther shouted. "Let's go back. We can't keep going like this!" Yet neither changed course. The night had been inhospitable enough, but the raging snowstorm had made the situation impossible. Günther couldn't see a thing—looking into the evening around him was like staring into a television tuned to a dead channel. There was nothing: no road, no light, no house. The snowflakes were like little fireworks—they glowed and popped in his eyes. He kept himself from feeling entirely blind by stubbornly focusing on the footprints of Wachter, who was getting further ahead of him. He had to move faster. The footprints were filling up almost as soon as they were made, now. Günther was trying hard not to lose contact.

Then, suddenly, the wind and the snow stopped. Günther, who'd been fighting his way through the night almost horizontal to the ground, stood upright again. His legs shook as he tried to get his bearings. Through a fissured hole in the clouds he saw the starry night sky and recognized what his father had once told him was the Kreuzberge mountain range. But now it was in entirely the wrong direction. It should be in the northwest. In Switzerland. But they were heading southeast.

"Wachter! Look over here!" Wachter was no where to be seen, though. The hole in the clouds had already closed, the wind started up again, and the snow picked up where it had left off. Günther had lost his guide. "Shit!" he yelled. And: "Hey! Wachter! Where are you?" His friend remained mute and out of sight. Günther wanted to cry. But what if Wachter appeared just then and caught him losing his nerve?

He fought through the snow for five hours, barely making any progress. With every other footstep he sank deeper into the snow, and it soon reached up to his knees. He sweated. He was wet all over. He was scared. It was the end. But no giving up, he said to himself. He forced himself on.

And, in the meantime, he called up to all the saints he could remember from school. He begged them for help. No more, he promised, would he sleep through Sunday Mass, luxuriating in his bed, fantasizing about naked women and all their "abras" and "cadabras." No more beer. No more cursing. No more stealing mopeds. He was going to lead a holy life. But none of this helped. Exhaustion and weakness covered him like a lead-lined cloak. His last conscious thought was, "Have I prayed to St. Martin?" Then he lay down on his side and fell asleep.

As Günther woke up at noon, he was lying curled up under the porch of a barn in Gampriner Feld. He felt frozen but capable of moving. He was very thirsty, but beyond this seemed to be more or less healthy. No sign of Wachter. Günther got up, looked around, and walked to the nearby bus stop, swaying. He took the next bus home.

When he met up with Wachter days later, all he asked was where the hell he had been. He had really missed out on something. Nendeln was brilliant.

TRANSLATED FROM GERMAN BY SEVINC TURKKAN

GIEDRA RADVILAVIČIŪTĖ

The Allure of the Text

I have several criteria for determining the quality of any effective text. *First,* after the text has been read, the narrative must force its way back into memory involuntarily, and not necessarily because of its plot or its characters—perhaps only thanks to its details, similes, metaphors, or other unexpected aspects: "Her farm had been destroyed by a bomb during the war, and all her relatives had perished in the fire. Because of that, she temporarily lost her mind. A doctor had told her to walk against the wind, against a moderately cool wind, and that helped her" (Emil Tode). *Secondly,* the text cannot be far removed from experience. It should make it seem as though I've lived through its contents; that I've been in its landscape; that I've quaffed the mead or ale in question; that I've spoken the very same words: "Once, I recall, you asked me: 'Do you know what's there, there where Polocko Street ends?' I cringed, even shivered a little, but you gazed stubbornly into my eyes: 'Tell me, what's there?' And I answered, 'A forest, of course. A forest, what else? And . . .' No, you shook your head vigorously— it's that head-shaking of yours I almost miss the most. 'There's only fog and sky there, understand?'" (Jurgis Kuninas). *Thirdly,* while reading the text, I must forget everything around me—sometimes just for a moment or two, but at other times, this state should last longer: "A tiny moth blew in from somewhere and fluttered about like a scrap of paper. The moth ended up on her breast and stayed there before flying off again. Once the moth had flown off, she looked the slightest bit older." (Haruki Murakami). *Fourth*, when the narrative touches on things that are well-known, or perhaps even banal, it must reveal something new about them: "At that time it first occurred to me that there was nothing one could say about a woman; I noticed how they left her out whenever they talked about her, how they named and described the others, the surroundings, the localities, the objects, up to a certain point where all that ceased, gently and as it were cautiously creased with the casual, never retraced contour that enclosed them." (Rainer Maria Rilke). *Fifth*, whenever I want to formulate something completely, in its totality, I panic. All the assertions I've voiced become arguable and ephemeral. The ultimate truth becomes a mystery that I can't reveal without obvious hesitation. Not long ago, I watched a film that at first tells and later shows us how people in the countries of the ancient Far East, after hearing a thing that upset them, would go into the woods, find a tree with a hollow, go right up to it—lips almost touching the bark—and, having spoken their secret into that dark hollow, would then seal it up with earth, dried grass, or moss gathered from nearby. In the film, a man narrates the story of his love for a woman—he loves her so much that he can't make love to her. Her silhouette is almost like a rosebud, and the zip of her silk dress, stretching from the small of her back to the nape of her neck, keeps her from releasing her blossom.

I didn't start thinking about what makes an effective text just off the top of my head. I don't do anything without a reason. I had come to a small Lithuanian town to take part in a forum on contemporary literature. I had been forewarned that, before the readings that would be held in the evening, I would be expected to say a few words to some television journalists who hadn't arrived yet. The forum was called: "Nordic Summer. The Allure of the Text." In addition to writers from Lithuania, authors from neighboring Baltic and Nordic countries were taking part as well. At the previous year's forum, a terrible cross-draft had risen in the old manor house during the readings. Framed photographs fell off the walls and sand plugged up one musician's saxophone. A particularly strong gust of wind tore a sheaf of papers from the hands of an Icelandic writer and hurled them straight into the fireplace. The writer wasn't upset, however, because in his country fire is seen as a miracle. He said it's so cold in Iceland that only one species of insect is capable of surviving there—*Phthirius pubis* (the crab louse). There were two hours to go before the readings were supposed to begin, so I decided to use the time to track down a distant relative of mine in the town. I only knew her address, and a few details of how we were related—our places on the family tree: she was my grandfather's brother's granddaughter. Grandfather's brother had had two daughters, but one had died in her teens. Šermukšnių Street wasn't far away; it was just past the old and somewhat shabby manor-house park.

The two brothers had been fighting almost until they died. After the war, my grandfather was sentenced to five years in prison. He had been working at a flour mill where he'd ostensibly (or actually) stolen some flour. He stole the flour for his family, skimming a few hundred grams from each sack. Several decades later, I was born into our family, whose offspring all seemed to have been made from this same flour: in the hospital, when I was brought over to be breastfed for the first time, my mother said there was still flour in the creases of my face. Grandfather would always swear to God that he was innocent and that he should never have had to serve time in prison. But his brother, when drunk, would tell him he had been a gang-leader, a crook, and a cheat from an early age. He used to reminisce about their brawls. My grandfather, who was five years older, would throw his brother to the dirt floor, pinning him down by his wrists crucifixion-style, leaning over his face, swearing at him and threatening to drool all over him. He used to harness toads to little carriages made from spools. And he would press his brother's face into a bowl of flour to make death masks. After the war, he sprinkled two packages of saccharine into the village well. He would leap onto the table when it was set with a good holiday tablecloth. He also kept a gun around his entire life—sometimes legally, other times not. "You stole flour for Elena and your children so that you could live better," his brother would say, caught up in his moment of audacity, and then, almost immediately, to soften his accusation, or perhaps simply because he was worried he'd get a punch in the nose, he would burst into song: "Step on a stone, mount your steed . . ." Grandfather was shipped off to serve his sentence in Zagorsk, past Moscow. While he was being transported there, while his group was changing trains, another inmate sidled up to him from behind and suggested they have sex: "It'll be good for you and good for me." I don't know what my grandfather told the man, but that was the last time anyone made that suggestion to him for the next three years of his incarceration (thanks to an amnesty, he wasn't required to serve his full five years)—and he'd been put away with criminals who, at breakfast, would unbutton their pants under the table and display their genitals to all the new inmates. To this day, I don't understand how my grandmother managed to visit him there in those Russian forests. She told me many times how she got lost in the marbled Moscow subway, carrying a cardboard suitcase packed with smoked bacon fat. "That was when your grandmother lost her mind . . . but she started walking against the wind, into a cool refreshing wind, and this helped her." I can't imagine her in a Russian blizzard, the same way I can't imagine myself at the Frankfurt Book Fair, for instance. My mother would send photographs of herself to Grandfather while he was in the prison camp—until she received her first reply, also with photo. It wasn't from Grandfather but from an inmate to whom he had shown the photographs. The man in the mustache wrote: "Even though you are far away, I am always with you in spirit." When my grandfather returned, he told us how he'd had to live in that place—not only with that man, but also with the two murders the man had committed. Grandfather also enjoyed retelling the scene of his homecoming, in later years. He entered the house unexpectedly, causing Grandmother to drop the skillet she was holding, along with its freshly poured potato pancakes. My grandfather's brother never sent a care package to his sibling while he was in the camp. But they made their peace before dying.

Grandfather came to this town, the site of the contemporary literature forum, onto which all these writers from Baltic and Nordic countries had descended, in order to make peace. But other events intervened before the two brothers' fateful meeting could take place. One of Grandfather's brother's granddaughters died, and then later—according to this particular existence-of-God-refuting sequence of events—so did his daughter. I can still recall the photograph of the dead granddaughter: a teenage girl lying in a casket in her own bedroom, it seems. She holds a book in her hands—a prayer book, too large. And, standing by the casket, there are the bereaved mother and a ficus plant. I was the same age as the deceased girl at the time. Perhaps it was precisely this that overwhelmed me. I was constantly reminded of that girl lying in her casket and the lifeless (wooden) braids lying on either side of her—when I brushed my teeth, when I squeezed the pimples on my forehead in front of the mirror, when I took out my jewelry from a little apple-shaped box, and when I cried after reading stories about true love. On Grandfather's fiftieth birthday, someone from the town sent him a ham wrapped in newsprint. I remember it: a ham marbled like a Moscow subway station. But it hadn't been sent by any of the relatives we knew.

I had exactly two hours. The trails in the park weren't paved or covered with gravel or pebbles. I had nothing with me except a box of truffles for Emilija, under my arm. Maybe I was going to have to call her by her pet name—Emiliute—as Grandfather did when he opened the last letters he received from his brother, who had dictated them to her. The sun was already setting; slanting filaments from it still shone, however, and on the other side of each of these rays, one was instantly attacked by swarms of flying insects. Only a kind of yellow flower was in bloom. Small, perfectly round clouds of pollen-mist hung around their blossoms. I was afraid a sandstorm might suddenly erupt; those are common in that area. A woman who sews blouses from dried jasmine petals and hair in Vilnius asked me recently if I enjoyed being in nature. Not alone—definitely not alone. I told her that the sound of barking dogs echoing in the distance seems mystical to me, that each blade of grass takes on a separate existence, while the sky above seems to close in like a lavender suitcase with a false bottom in which dangerous, apocalyptic things are hidden. A small bug flew into my eye, irritating it. To the left stood the cemetery fence, and it felt strange knowing that a girl had been laid to rest there, at some precise spot, in a white casket, holding a prayer book—a thin droplet of my own flesh and blood.

The local museum on the right was bathed in red light. I approached a woman who was smoking in the doorway; she seemed to me like a little gray mouse who might have used her fur to dust the dreary exhibits in their display cages every morning, but who was too small to block your line of sight to them. When I got closer to her, "it . . . occurred to me that there was nothing one could say about a woman." Her nails were lacquered a rich cherry color, and she wore a silver chain around one ankle. She lisped when saying *ermukni*, the name of the street I was looking for. This woke a German word from my memory: *verführen*—to seduce. I noticed a long time ago that people with lisps, or even people who are cross-eyed, can give rise to an odd erotic effect.

"Watch out for the pond on your left," she said, gesturing in the direction of Šermukšnių Street. "We call it 'The Queen's Eye.' It's three meters deep, but from far away it just looks like a meadow that's completely overgrown."

As I left, it crossed my mind that the woman could probably only bear the museum in summer (and her eyes were three meters deep, too).

Emilija met me in her orchard, wearing an old nurse's gown that was old but still white over her clothes. I didn't recognize any of Grandfather's features in her face. But I felt at home when she asked me to take off my shoes and prepared us some tea. She never got around to showing me around her single-story house; all I glimpsed were two cats perched on top of an old-fashioned stove. And out in the "orchard chock-full of plums," there was a man naked from the waist up who was mixing cement. Emilija began telling me about herself in a way that made it seem as though we simply hadn't seen each other in a while, when in actual fact I'd never seen her before in my life. Not even in photographs of relatives. Emilija worked at the municipal hospital, in the dialysis ward. People with kidneys that no longer functioned were driven there by relatives to get their blood cleaned. Husbands would accompany their wives two or three times at the most, she told me—usually very polite, but scared. Later, their wives would seem like bruised and horribly jaundiced pears to them. "It's no one's fault," said Emilija, "it's simply Mother Nature at work. I understood long ago that a man only loves a woman as long as he desires her. Women, meanwhile, will sometimes love their men even after they've died." Wives would accompany their husbands to these treatments, sometimes lasting up to four hours, until the day they died—which was what happened if a kidney donor couldn't be found in time, making the situation hopeless. Men and women cried in exactly the same way when their wrists and legs got so butchered by the treatments that you couldn't find a place to jab in a needle. Emilija was an old hand, though: sooner or later, she would always manage to find the right spot. She took a skeptical view of peritoneal dialysis because of the frequent infections it gives rise to. Though, of course, when it was possible to perform the procedure at home ... Until six months ago she'd still worked at the clinics in the city of Kaunas. At the time, Riardas—she motioned toward the man out the window who was mixing cement—had been working at a fish processing plant in Ireland to earn money.

"I'm getting married this autumn. I was tired of coming in from Kaunas on the weekends. It doesn't really matter what you do. I had an affair with a doctor from another ward while Riardas was away. I slept with him, and he slept with other nurses in turn. Somehow, right up to the end, I could never bring myself to address him with the familiar *tu*—I would use the formal *jūs*. And even his kids would use *jūs* when speaking to him. We made love in his old Benz once. In the winter. I opened my eyes only to see a person next to me whose breath stunk of the rags people use to wipe windows. A snow-covered signboard that read 'Catholic Summer Camp for Children' stood nearby, beside a path in the woods. I should have felt young, with two functioning kidneys to boot—I should have felt alive. Past the signboard there was a pine forest blanketed with snow and marked by the spoor of rabbits and dogs, and now stained with coffee from our thermos too; further on there were the outskirts of the city, then Kaunas itself, people, noise; but to me it seemed as though there was nothing at all beyond that signboard ... *only fog and sky, understand?* It suddenly became clear to me that I couldn't go on saying *jūs* to that doctor. And that I wouldn't need to anymore, since I'd stopped loving him. After Riardas came back and I was already working here, the doctor called me one last time, at night, from the casino in Kaunas. He was a little drunk. 'Emilija, you always know what you want, right? I never figured you out completely, but I know that much. Quick, tell me what color to bet on, red or black—choose one or the other, and give me a lucky number too!' Riardas was lying next to me. I whispered: 'Red. Seven. And please, Doctor, you should call the other nurses in Kaunas too: it's not worth risking so much on one person's opinion.' Meanwhile, my Riardas was talking in his sleep, telling me what an important job I had: at night the staff were all lost without me, lost among the bottles of our laboratory."

"Emilija," I said, "love lasts three years. Like jail. Then you go home."

"How do you know?" she asked.

"From the French writers," I said.

"Don't be offended, but I have no interest in literature, you know. Chemistry is more my speed. I read about the conference going on at the manor, but I won't be attending. Maybe just the evening sessions, to take in some music. The hospital wears me out so much that I sometimes can't even manage to get through a newspaper. And we need to make plum jam tonight. And we need to work on the honey. The honey helps get us through autumn. My sister, though, would probably have studied litera-ture—though that's just a guess, of course, since she was only twelve when she died. During the worst parts of her illness, Mother carried home the entire municipal library for her in bags; later, she had to haul all those books back again. My parents found my sister dead with a book in her hands, in the morning, and we buried her with it, a 1972 edition of *Pan*. Our idiot neighbors told us that God-fearing folk would have pressed a prayer book into her hands, not a novel, but Mother didn't give a damn. Women who bury their children bury God along with them. And it was probably a consolation for her to imagine that my sister would finish read-ing that book in Heaven. The effect my sister's death had on me was to force me to live in the present. Though maybe that wasn't because of her death—I was too young to understand it at the time—but because of all the patients I see. Riardas thinks of things in an entirely different way. For him, the past doesn't exist—only the future. He came home from Ireland with some money; now he's building an addition. He says there'll also be a separate entrance for our kid. What he doesn't know is that I had surgery when he was in Ireland and that I probably won't be able to have any chil-dren."

There wasn't a single picture of my grandfather with his brother among the photographs Emilija showed me. It was almost as though their one-upmanship meant they could only get along in other people's reminis-cences. But her album did have a print of the same photograph I had torn up as a teen, out of fear—a teenage girl with wooden pleats, lying in a cas-ket, holding Hamsun's book, that ficus plant and the mother who had to bear her death standing next to her.

Later, we went out into the orchard, because Emilija got it into her head to pick some plums for me and to give me a one-liter jar of honey. Without bothering to introduce me to Riardas, she climbed up a ladder and placed an enamelware bowl on my head; I balanced it with one arm, thrusting the other out to my side, which made me look like one of those women on old Soviet-era wine-bottle labels. A sweaty cat rubbed its head against my calf. Plums thudded directly onto my skull. *A tiny moth blew in from somewhere and fluttered about like a scrap of paper. The moth ended up on her breast and stayed there before flying off again. Once the moth had flown off*... then I could imagine Emilija's future. Riardas would build the addition to their home, but afterwards he wouldn't be able to find work in town and would have to go back to Ireland, since all of his work contacts were still there. He would package frozen fish that came down a conveyor belt and, in a half-year, he would begin to feel that his heart was freezing over too. One evening, hungry after a night at the pub, he would meet another Lithuanian woman in a café; one who had moved there for a year to make some money so she could arrange for a nice headstone for her son, who had been killed in a car crash. He would escort her to her apartment, telling her about the addition, about the shitty standard of living in Lithuania, and he would even tell her about Emilija. A day or two later, he would get a letter from Emilija, who had been emboldened by the distance separating them, in which she would admit that she can't have children and is feeling guilty for not having told him sooner. He would remember the town; that is to say, the home awaiting him—the orchard "chock-full of plums," the autumn honey, Emilija, the old white gowns draped on the floor in place of doormats, and ...

"Enough?" Emilija asked, perched among the branches. She had removed her nurse's gown and wrapped it around her head to guard against the bees. She bent down, looking at me sideways. I lowered the bowl and looked back up at her, which was when it hit me that she reminded me of someone: a white pallid face in half profile, plump moist lips, no hint of any past, a perfect state of anticipation (although she might have thought the opposite)—swirls of white drapery instead of hair—yes, through the branches of the tree above, Vermeer's girl with a pearl earring was peering at me with her enormous eyes. Only, instead of an earring, a heavy plum surrounded by an opal haze hung next to her ear, trembling.

After this, we went to the cemetery. I carried the bag of plums and the liter of honey under my arm and struggled to show an interest in Emilija's sister's grave; though all I could think was that whenever I visit such places, it always seems to me that I'm seeing them for the first and last time. Several layers of our family lay buried in that soil, but I lost the thread right after Grandfather's brother. A linden stood next to the grave. The sap coming off the linden had darkened the headstone, which was odd since it was already the end of August. It must have been that the stone had drunk that midsummer syrup for many years. We kissed when we said goodbye. And I felt as though my lips had stroked a warm, freshly painted canvas.

I returned to the manor by another path, taking less time than the journey out. I knew it had rained in the park in the interim: crushed strips of fallen yellow petals lined the edge of the path. Theoretically, it seemed to me, Grandfather and his brother could have walked here together. Though, who knows? Country folk didn't have the luxury of walking for the sheer pleasure of it.

Catching sight of the wall of the manor house through the trees, I took a nearly overgrown trail leading in that direction. Long ago, it had probably been an avenue. At the end of it there was a dilapidated and faded traffic barrier that served no purpose. I crouched and passed underneath it because it was surrounded by stinging nettles, sticking up like the battlements of old castles. Striped traffic barriers, for me, have always called to mind those dotted lines labeled "cut here" that appear on bills received in the mail. At the top of such documents there's usually some general information, and beneath the "cut here" line is the date, your telephone-company account number, and a breakdown of local and intercity calls, showing absolutely astonishing amounts of time. In a word, dreary abstractions that become present-tense irritants once they've made their appearance below the dotted line.

As I made my way across a field, I could see two journalists and a camera they had set up on the lawn from afar. "Thanks for being on time," said a friend from the town of Anykiai sarcastically. I felt bad. I knew that she was never late for anything and that she had left her little girl, just a few months old, at home for two days—mother's milk frozen in little cubes— so that she could take part, unencumbered, in the conference. Her husband thawed the milk in little portions and fed it to the child as needed. My friend was convinced that babies needed mother's milk during the first six months of their lives, six months at the very least, and that this staves off all illnesses until the age of three. Another acquaintance—a poet— stood there drinking coffee from a plastic cup, a men's sock protruding from the pocket of his blazer. I still owed him five litas and one quotation, but I didn't even look at him. I don't like poets because they're all flighty people who usually come from large families, and they usually have several kids in several different cities with several different poetry-crazed women.

In a bit of a panic because I couldn't come up with a more precise way to formulate my fifth criterion for effective texts, I forgot to greet the journalists. For some reason, I walked right across the lawn toward the camera, which was switched on, as though I were about to accept an award. (A ham wrapped in newsprint.) I only stopped when I couldn't go any further, because my lips were pressed against the glass of the camera lens. I pressed against it the way snails press themselves against tree bark, and without further ado I launched directly into my final criterion for a text:

"*Fifth*. A good text is obliged to draw you back to it many times. Just like old parks—in which you can always lose your way—beckon you to go for a stroll in them. But notwithstanding the tangle of trails and the mystical sound of barking dogs echoing in the distance; and despite the pollen mist rising from the flowers, the overgrown ponds, the sky above us closing in like a lavender suitcase hiding dangerous things, and the stinging castle-nettles, you forge ahead, sensing that, at some precise place, something vital, like a denouement, is awaiting you. Like a blood relative of yours—one whom you've barely, or never, known . . . until this moment . . ."

After I had spoken these words, the man standing behind the camera stood stock-still. This wasn't the sort of nonsense people were supposed to spout on television if they wanted to leave an impression. A singer—I had seen this with my own eyes—even went so far once as to say that his favorite time for making love to his girlfriend was at the crack of dawn, in a sitting position, while his favorite song was playing: . . . *even though there are only three million of us on this Earth.* Afterwards, in full view of the interviewer and his girlfriend, the singer removed his underpants, which had been hand-woven for him by a designer. The reporter standing next to me looked a little exasperated. She could see that I was no longer young, that I was no longer photogenic, that I was a little too skinny (from crawling under traffic barriers, perhaps), and that I was basically a bundle of nerves. She took my elbow in a motherly manner and guided me a few steps away from the camera, drawing me nearer to her, saying, "Perhaps we can move away from textual and theoretical considerations and come back to the subject of the conference itself. You probably have some personal impressions of it, since you've been coming here for years. Do you have any anecdotes you'd like to share with us from the prior years of the conference?" This provided instant relief. The words poured from my mouth, smoothly and without hesitation:

"These last few days, I have been sitting and thinking about the northern summer, with its endless day . . . two years ago, I remember, the time passed quickly—beyond all comparison more quickly than time now. A summer was gone before I knew. Two years ago it was, in 1855. I will write of it just to amuse myself—of something that happened to me, or something I dreamed."

After mentioning the year, I realized that I wasn't speaking my own words. They had come from a passage in the notebooks of Lieutenant Thomas Glahn, which, in turn, came from the first page of *Pan*—the book Emilia's sister was holding in her hands when she was buried here in this town. I felt a sudden compulsion to tell the journalist about that girl. It would have been a truly personal impression and anecdote—from prior years. I glanced at the reporter but she was looking at the cameraman now and no longer smiling. Not feeling I was getting the kind of life-support I needed in that sort of situation, I choked up. Hoping to avoid the camera's eyes, which from this distance seemed remarkably like the hollow in a tree, I crouched down. I touched the springy, emerald-green grass. I saw four legs belonging to two people, which now seemed as though they belonged to a single being. I could find neither a handful of hay nor any moss, nor even a tuft of some dry foliage. Then, hurriedly and without rising, I peeled the seal off the one-liter jar that was slipping from my grasp, stuck four fingers into the honey Emilija had given me—the honey that helped get her through autumn—scooped out a generous handful, and smeared it on the lens of the camera. (Exactly what the people of the ancient Far East would have done—telling their secrets to a tree whenever they needed to stifle what they knew in the darkness.)

TRANSLATED FROM LITHUANIAN BY DARIUS JAMES ROSS

GOCE SMILEVSKI

Fourteen Little Gustavs

All his sons bore his name. When he died he left behind fourteen little Gustavs. Gustav Klimt had a face of a good-hearted man and the body of a warrior and he would sometimes get into fights with the male models in his studio; it was during one such fight that he accidentally broke his arm. Almost certainly the bed was a battleground for him, a place where pleasure and anger became indistinguishable—and, as the creation of his paintings advanced, large bruises sometimes appeared on the bodies of his female models. Even his paint wasn't safe from attack—he would jab his brush into his palette and then swipe it over his canvas like the victor in a duel magnanimously granting a foe his life. If there was one word to sum up his existence, it would be "fight": he fought the people who bought his paintings, the mediocre critics who misevaluated his art, and then the bankers, merchants, and workers whose wives hung around his studio. He won all his fights except one: the fight with his mother. His mother was determined not to let him leave the family home. Even though he could have bought a quarter of Vienna with the money he earned from selling his art, he went on living with her, staying to protect his sister Klara from his mother's abuse and to listen to the offensive, familiar words, said over and over, until they reached number fourteen: "I heard a whore bore you a son!"

It was the models who posed for him, the women he met at the receptions held at his patrons' houses, the prematurely aged women who looked ten years older than they actually were and who cleaned his studio, it was these women who gave birth to his children, and all these children were male and they were all called Gustav and they all had different last names: their mother's. The only woman he really loved never bore him a child; her name was Emilie Flöge. She saw his infidelities as his way of deceiving his mother and thus a way to remain faithful to her alone, and in her childlessness she didn't see a cruel trick of nature but her determination not to split the love she felt toward the artist between the man and his child. For her, this relationship with Gustav was something holy, even back in 1891 when she was seventeen years old and the artist painted the portrait that her father ordered for her birthday, even when she found out that Gustav already had several sons, as the days went by in his studio while he was painting, even when she sometimes arrived there unannounced and found him between the legs of the ladies who were posing for him. This dedication continued even after she asked him to marry her and he responded that two people as free as they were didn't need the formality of marriage and even after she asked him to move in with her and he replied that he needed to stay at Westbahn Street #36 to protect his sister from his mother—the same house where he remained even after his mother died in 1915 so that he could continue to take care of Klara. Emilie Flöge took all of this with faith and devotion, even when one after another of his sons continued to be born . . . It's possible that her faith and devotion resulted from her realization that of all the women Gustav had slept with, she was the only one he loved. That same faith was in her eyes even when, in winter, at the beginning of 1918, he suffered a stroke and fell on the floor of his studio; he lies unconscious, she sits by his bed, and for the first time she's looking at him not as her husband but as her child, she's trying to wake him up and she talks to him not in the voice of a lover who's been devoted to him since she was seventeen years old, not in the voice of a woman who had been seducing him for nearly three decades, but in the voice of a mother trying to comfort her own child in his silent pain, though her voice is different from his real mother's voice, it's a voice in which Emilie Flöge is trying to convince her child that everything is going to be all right, that all of this will pass, forgetting while she says these things that it's she herself whom she would like to comfort with these words. And even after he dies, she goes on saying these things, and even after his body is removed from his bed, she goes on sitting by his bedside, she goes on staring at his pillow, at the sheets on which twenty-seven years have passed as though in a second, and indeed, she thinks, all those years passed by just like the single moment of her staring at the pillow and sheets and there's no fear or desperation in her look, only a kind of shattered resignation, and it's with this same look in her eyes that she will bid him farewell at his grave.

And nothing that strayed into her field of vision after his death changed that look in her eyes. Her view of the world didn't even change when the Nazis marched into Vienna in March 1938; what could have brought her back to life when her inner world had already languished? Yes, something in her cringed whenever she heard that a child had been murdered, that an old man had been beaten, that thousands had been put on trains and transported who knows where, but this feeling was fleeting, it only lasted a second or two, her terror a testament only to her continued presence among the living, after which her whole body resumed its usual languor.

Sometimes she would try recreating his image in memory, and with her eyes closed she would build his image out of fourteen tiny children's heads, fourteen children's heads that—she presumed—all looked like Gustav had when he was a child; fourteen heads combining into one big head, Gustav's head in profile, a turned-up nose, wide cheeks, large forehead, thinning hair, fourteen children's heads like stones in a mosaic creating the image of Gustav Klimt in Emilie's imagination ... And yet, his image remained incomplete, there was still a space in it, room for one more child's head, for one more son, for the fifteenth child, the one she was supposed to bear him.

■ ■ ■

In 1907, on one of the hills in the western part of Vienna, an entire small town had sprung up with sixty separate buildings housing five thousand people. At the time, this was the world's largest psychiatric clinic. The inscription above the entrance read: "Steinhof: Institution for the Cure and Care of Mental and Nervous Disorders." A path that started at the entrance and led up to the top of the hill had patients' pavilions on either side. Gardens and pine trees separated the pavilions. During the opening ceremony, the institution's director said that Steinhof was going to put an end to the barbaric treatment of psychiatric disorders, and that from now on humane and scientific methods would be used for the treatment of patients with mental and nervous illnesses. The patients worked in the gardens around the pavilions, sculpted in clay, and prepared dramatic performances that they then performed in front of an audience in the small theater built inside Steinhof.

In the spring of 1918, Klara Klimt's name appeared on the list of the patients admitted to Steinhof. Klara was the eldest child of the gold engraver Ernst Klimt and his wife Anna. After her father died, Klara continued to live with her mother, brother, and one of her sisters. Her brother painted, and with the money he made from his art they lived modestly in their house on Westbahn Street #36. They continued living modestly even after Gustav's paintings were no longer considered the work of a skillful artisan but started being recognized as "high art," and when he could, it was said, have bought an entire district of Vienna with his earnings.

Gustav Klimt never asked about his sons, the fourteen little Gustavs. For him, his sons were just the product of some old, long-completed act.

His sister, however, went from one part of Vienna to the other, helping the mothers of fourteen Gustavs. Once she even went to the prison to plead for the release of a sixteen-year old Gustav who'd been arrested after injuring a peer in a fight. Every month, Klara went from home to home with the money she'd received from her brother, leaving some at each. When one of the children got sick, she took them to the doctor.

After her brother's death, Klara Klimt became silent and inert. When somebody asked her how she was, she wouldn't answer. She lay in bed without speaking a word. Her sisters took her to Steinhof. When the eldest of fourteen Gustavs found out that Klara was in the hospital, he went to ask for permission for his brothers and he to visit their aunt.

"Come on Wednesday," said Dr. Mann, who numbered Klara Klimt among his patients. On Wednesday, fourteen little Gustavs showed up at Steinhof. Dr. Mann took them to the twelfth pavilion. They went through a long corridor with six doors, each an entrance to a large bedroom. They entered one of the bedrooms. There were more than ten beds, each with a woman patient lying in it—some of the women lay motionless, some mumbled while they tossed and turned, one woman had her arms and legs tied down. Toward the end of the room, on a bed in a corner, they found Klara. She was wearing a white nightgown. She was lying curled up on the bed, legs pressed together, knees beneath her chin, her feet pointing outward. Her arms were folded and pressed to her chest. She was staring at the wall. Fourteen little Gustavs stood by her bed. The eldest brother sat next to her.

"Aunt Klara," the eldest, seventeen-year-old Gustav said.

Her expression didn't change at the mention of her name, nor at the sound of a familiar voice. She continued breathing and blinking at even intervals. "We came to see you," he continued. "We are all here. All fourteen of us."

Klara didn't move. She went on staring at the wall. The youngest Gustav, who was four years old, walked up to Klara's bed and stroked her hair. The eldest brother, the one who was sitting by her, put his hand on the back of her hand. Her fingers were curled up in her palm, forming a fist. But this was a loose fist, peaceful.

A woman from the other part of the room started screaming. Others followed. One woman threatened to set them all on fire. Only Klara Klimt remained silent. The fourteen little Gustavs who stood around Klara's bed thought that her silence was the loudest sound in the ward.

The eldest brother turned to Dr. Mann:

"Isn't this too loud for her? Everybody's screaming. She doesn't make a sound . . ."

Dr. Mann raised his index finger and wrote a "no" in the air, he then said "no" aloud a couple of times and continued:

"Until now she's been assigned to the quiet pavilion, with the patients who usually don't speak unless spoken to. She spent several weeks there without saying a word. Silence isn't good for her—it's making her numb. She needs provocation. I think that the screams here will break her silence."

"Screaming like this can only force her further into silence," the eldest brother said.

"You are wrong," said Dr. Mann.

"It doesn't matter whether I'm right or wrong. What's important is that you stop torturing her by keeping her in the middle of all this screaming."

"I don't think she considers this torture. Look at her face. When I first brought her here from the quiet pavilion, where she'd spent several weeks, she looked quite anxious. Now she radiates calmness."

And, indeed, Klara Klimt's face had a corpse-like tranquility. Gustav Klimt's sons looked at their aunt on the bed, curled up like a fetus, her face likewise as expressionless as an embryo's. The youngest Gustav touched her feet, which were as cold as death. She continued staring at the white wall, breathing evenly.

"Come on children," said Dr. Mann. "You saw your aunt. It's time for you to go home now."

And fourteen Gustavs started leaving, each to a different home. The youngest Gustav went back to the bed before going; he wanted to kiss his aunt, though she had her back turned to him and the bed was too high and he couldn't reach her face. He went to the other side of the bed and kissed his aunt's feet. Then he ran toward the exit to catch up with his brothers in the hall.

TRANSLATED FROM MACEDONIAN BY ANA LUCIC

STEPHAN ENTER

Resistance

Hans Jurgen Roelof Wiesveld is dead. I never even realized that that was his name. I knew him as Mr. Wiesveld, the man who, for three winter months, had taught me and eight other boys chess at the Brevendal Chess club, *En Passant*.

I just happened to see his death notice one day: I would never have known, otherwise. It reminded me of the time I found myself back home in my attic bedroom after years of being away. In the twilight by the tilting window, broken-spined volumes of Karl May suddenly appeared beneath a pale layer of dust—and shoe boxes too, containing that sky-blue *Märklin* model train, those pieces of track, and the damaged signal-box-and-trees, once trod upon by my father's giant foot. They had waited for me, motionless, breathing in that unmistakable wood scent to prove that nothing moves on, except for time.

How long had it been since I'd last thought of Mr. Wiesveld? Decades. But now he's back. Not as a corpse, nor as the sixty-seven-year-old that the dates on the death notice tell me he must have been—he's there just as he was when I first saw him, when I was thirteen. He's so very clear to me; once again I can see the way he moves, his stiff little gait. His thin voice is in my head, as well as his asthmatic cough. And yet there's something else too: a sense of shame and regret. This is no ordinary memory. This is a splinter that's been left.

■

Every Saturday morning at half past nine, we would gather in a side room at Café Centraal, near the Old Church. Chessboards, double-faced clocks, and sturdy wooden boxes holding chess pieces were laid out on the tables, which were all pushed together. In the corner, on a tripod, a magnetic demonstration board was displayed like a painting on an easel. The room was deep and narrow, with a window high up on the street side and two matte-glass sliding doors leading to the barroom with its ethereally green billiard table and chestnut-brown bar, polished until it could serve as a mirror.

I can remember the stale smell of the cigars smoked by the farmers on market day. I can hear how the sliding doors rattled discreetly as they were being opened. The only person who ever came in during our lessons, however, was Lina, the proprietor's eighteen-year-old daughter—an unapproachable and mythical figure. She would serve glasses of cassis and Fanta and we would only be able to tear ourselves away and get back to chess tactics after her body had once more dissolved behind the rippled glass. I can see how the morning sun would pierce the stained net curtains in horizontal beams, and how the dagger-shaped leaves of the sansevieria intensified the glare; my eyes and mouth dry up as I recollect the fierce heat of those cumbersome, gurgling old radiators. But what I remember most is how good, how cared for, I felt. A delicate seed in a firm, hard husk.

One December morning after we had all settled down to games of speed chess and tandem chess, a strange man emerged from between the sliding doors. He looked at us; we looked at him.

"Good morning, boys," he said. "My name is Mr. Wiesveld. I'm afraid Mr. Vink will be away for a while. I'm his replacement." He laid his slim leather case on an empty table, mumbled, "Let me just get some coffee," then nodded shyly and returned to the bar.

We exchanged looks; a couple of us began to giggle. This man would be replacing Mr. Vink? What a joke! Mr. Vink was a major in the army and everything a thirteen-year-old boy could imagine an officer to be: broad-shouldered with incredibly hairy hands and a red, curling mustache. Above his caterpillar-like eyebrows was a deep groove set in a severe and permanent frown. But he was never severe to us: without his having to say a word, we would sit there attentively, as quiet as mice. Mr. Vink smelt distinctly of outdoors, of oak wood and sandy paths, as though he had only briefly interrupted his military exercises to teach us about chess, after which he'd return to maneuvers immediately. There was no doubt in our mind that he was unparalleled in his ability to jump from a parachute, fight, shoot, and kill the enemy.

The new teacher came back; we went on playing. Only when he had finished his coffee and clinked his cup twice with a teaspoon did we bother looking up.

"Mr. Vink has unexpectedly been dispatched to Lebanon," he said in a soft, almost frail voice. "He'll be returning in three months time. Until then you're going to be stuck with me." He ventured a smile but no one responded.

"So where have you gotten up to? Have you finished *Chess for Young People* yet?"

"Oh ages ago!" replied a familiar voice. "We've already got our kings diploma! Even the little kids have."

It was Jan Boot, the oldest of our group. He was fifteen, and would often come yawning into the Saturday morning class and claim with a smutty grin that he'd been to The Comet, the village disco, the night before, and that he'd really "painted the place red." We were cowed by this, even though he spared us the details. Still, when he casually remarked one day that he'd "felt Lina up," we laughed in his face.

"Okay, so what are you up to now?" Mr. Wiesveld asked him. "How far have you gotten?" He clicked open both locks of his case and pulled out a little pile of books. "Which book are you using?"

"We're not," said Jan Boot, slouching in his chair. "We just get exercises. And at the end we're allowed to play."

"Exercises. Yes . . . what sort of exercises?"

Jan Boot stood up and strode over to the demonstration board. He removed a number of pieces, repositioned a few others, turned round, and smirked: "White mates in four."

We sniggered. We'd been given that problem last week and Jan Boot had been the only one to solve it within the ten minutes allowed.

"Yes ..." said Mr. Wiesveld, not really paying attention to the board. "Yes, I'll have to have a little think about that. I'll need to find out what you're all capable of. I tell you what we'll do: we'll arrange the tables in a circle—or better still in a horseshoe. Yes ... today we're going to play a game of simultaneous chess, and you're going to take notes on all the moves. Okay?"

Hesitantly, we did what we were told. But when we sat down, notation books at the ready, and he began to play against us, we could hardly keep our eyes on the game, intrigued as we were by our new chess teacher. We exchanged knowing looks, clearly all thinking the same things: what a funny little man with his jumpy little movements and those ridiculous clothes! A black blazer worn over a light-blue lozenge-patterned jumper with a V-neck revealing a pink, thin-collared shirt! Spindly legs squeezed into a pair of skinny jeans, and those clean, smooth nails we got a good look at every time he stretched out his hand to make a move. We lost piece after piece, but barely even noticed, since we kept on discovering new details about Mr. Wiesveld that we immediately divulged to the rest of the group with nods and other such signs. Mr. Wiesveld affected a cough and muffled it with his fist. He had black hair—so black and shiny it made you wonder whether he had dyed it. He smelled of something—wasn't it eau-de-cologne? He was as skinny as a rake; his jacket fell from his shoulders as though from a hanger. His muted eyes lay sunken in their dark sockets. And he was so dreadfully pale, especially in comparison to Mr. Vink's boundlessly healthy, ruddy complexion.

After beating us all effortlessly, Mr. Wiesveld stared into the distance, three fingers on his chin. Suddenly, his face broke into a cheery smile as he asked us to go over our notes at home and come in next week prepared to tell him at what point we might have tried a different move.

"Yes . . . I think that's enough for today. Would you like to play against yourselves now?"

We stood up, rearranged the tables and chairs, picked up the clocks, re-set them to five minutes—all the while casting silent looks at the man and then at one another. He coughed into his hand again, rasping, yelping, like a dog. With thumb and forefinger, he flicked a piece of fluff off his pants. He was clearly uneasy. But as soon as one of us accidentally made eye con-tact with him, he smiled encouragingly. After Lina had come in with soft drinks for us and another coffee for him, he clinked his teaspoon again curtly on the rim of his cup. He hadn't meant anything by this, however; he just sat there, not saying a word until the Old Church bell struck twelve heavy strokes, telling us the lesson had drawn to a close.

He helped us put the chess sets back into the cupboard, then locked it. He replaced his books in his bag, returned the cupboard key to the bar, and accompanied us outside.

I can still picture how, while we were unlocking our bikes, he cycled off, coat flapping in the wind, and then looked back to wave good-bye.

"See you next week! And yes . . . remember to think about those games we played."

No one reacted—until he had turned a distant corner. It was then that we heard Jan Boot snort. Normally he was the first to leave with a cheerful "Bye-bye babies!" or some such taunt. But this time he stayed where he was. Standing astride his bike, clutching the handlebars, he stared straight ahead.

"A fag," he said, disconcerted. "We're being taught by a fag."

In the weeks that followed, none of us could think of anything other than the new chess teacher. We kept a beady eye on him, and as soon as one of us spotted something new, the rest of the group was informed. There was the time Mr. Wiesveld smoked a cigarette, which he held like a TV actress between the tips of his fingers, wrist cocked back. The time he swept his hair into place—a gesture we imitated enthusiastically after each class. "He's got thick lips," whispered Jan Boot one day when Mr. Wiesveld had left to use the facilities. "Have you seen them? Queers always have thick lips." Later on we all took a discreet but very close look at those lips.

We laughed our secret, disdainful laugh, but at the same time we were almost grateful to Mr. Wiesveld for his peculiarities, which lent themselves so well to detailed examination. He was like an extremely rare species of animal we figured was worth our closest scrutiny—given that we were going to be stuck with him regardless.

The members of our group were culled from numerous different grades at our secondary school on the outskirts of Brevendal. The fact that we all belonged to the same club hadn't, until then, meant we ever spoke at school. A casual "hi" if you happened to bump into a chess-class member was about as far as our friendship went. Playing chess did not endear you to your classmates, and certainly not to girls. But now, whenever you stood in the lunch line, you might be surprised from behind by Mr. Wiesveld's little cough (mimicked to perfection by another member of the club) or by the word "yes" pronounced in that silky voice of his. Or else you might be greeted in the corridor by an effeminate flick of the wrist that you would respond to in kind with a deadpan expression on your face. It wasn't long before our other schoolmates took an interest, and we satisfied their curiosity, exaggerating a little when we imitated his walk, for instance, with our frantic little steps. The other pupils laughed too, so we felt less embarrassed and sometimes even challenged each other to a game or two on miniature sets during recess.

What Mr. Wiesveld thought of *us*, however, wasn't something I ever considered. What I do know, though, is that from his second Saturday with us, he threw himself into our lessons, making his approach completely different from Mr. Vink's good old method of assigning clear exercises (mate-in-*N* was like a math equation—either you could solve it or you couldn't), posing less definite questions, such as: "How is White developing his queenside?" or "How is Black going to foil the threat to his bishop's diagonal?" or "Is White really right to castle here?" Often we were unable to come up with an answer, but what confused us the most was that, after having let us puzzle over a problem for a good half hour, Mr. Wiesveld was often unable to come up with a good answer himself. Or, if he did, he might suddenly cross his legs tightly (hooking a foot around the opposite ankle), place his fingers on his smooth chin, and then announce in falsetto: "But, on second thought . . ."

The boys began to grumble—especially Jan Boot. Although he had once been the best student in the class, now he was more and more at a loss. He stopped paying attention and dedicated even more of his time to poking fun at Mr. Wiesveld. Whereas he used to slam the chess-timer during matches with the flat of his hand, now he pressed it preciously with a forefinger saying "Dearie me!" in mock surprise. Outside on the gravel next to the bike racks he would mince around between us, hand on hip. He made a game out of using every derisory word for that type of man he could think of: not just calling Mr. Wiesveld a "fag," but also "queer," "queen," "pansy," "fairy," "poof," and "nancy"—not to forget his favorite: "hairdresser." Occasionally he tried something new, like on the fourth or fifth Saturday, after we'd been served our drinks and could see Lina's form fading behind the glass ripples, he blurted out: "What a beautiful sight, eh?" with a big wink at Mr. Wiesveld, who reacted, as always, with a half-timid, half-encouraging smile.

In the beginning, the others took little notice of Jan Boot's jokes. I don't think anyone much cared for him, and we were pleased that he was no longer the best in the class. But once we saw that our lessons would never get any less confusing, when we were given complex problems and convoluted game analyses to take home (something unheard of under Mr. Vink), we too began to rebel: we started to affect that little cough and begin all our sentences with a contemplative "Yes . . ." Once, we even concocted a plan to turn up at Centraal en masse with neatly parted, gelled hair. But it never came to that.

It was February, about eight weeks after our first class with Mr. Wiesveld. During a sports day at school, when all the teams were supposed to do demonstrations, we all sat around four or five boards in the assembly room playing chess with our geography teacher and some older boys: a group from the upper as well as the lower sixth. There had been a similar event about three months earlier—"The Chess-heads" versus Everybody Else—and that time it had been a close call. But not now. We won every single game inside of ten minutes. And when our opponents demanded a rematch, we did it again. We exchanged looks: they hadn't stood a chance! And then we discovered that this was not an isolated incident: suddenly, there were all sorts of stories floating around about our beating our fathers, grandfathers, next-door neighbors, anyone who, up until then, had been a challenging opponent—slaughtered where they stood.

With Mr. Vink, chess had always been exciting, but never more than an exciting *game*—a game like any other. The best player was the first to complete his calculations. With Mr. Wiesveld, however, calculation had largely been replaced by something more akin to instinct, and this became obvious during speed chess, those five-minute matches that before had always been a matter of gambling and bluffing: you'd make an opening move, learned by heart, select the pieces for your attack, pause for a second's thought, and off you went. It was like a stag fight, really: whoever managed to smash their pieces against their opponent's the hardest would, nine times out of ten, emerge triumphant. But all this changed. Just like it's impossible to stare up innocently at the night sky having learned about its various constellations, so we were no longer able to look at a chess board without being struck by key configurations, pinnings, center control, and vulnerable pawns. Where once we had seen a tangle of possibilities with tens of potential moves, now we saw only two or three, into which we funneled all of our attention.

We must have realized somewhere deep down how brilliantly Mr. Wiesveld was teaching us, how profound his explanations were about tempo, opposition, and potentially passed pawns, along with twenty other subjects, which up until then, even if we'd heard of them, would have seemed like gobbledygook. We must have realized how admirably patient he was with us, pubescent and adolescent as we were, sitting there gawking, failing to do our homework and never letting him know what we were actually thinking. Perhaps we sensed, albeit vaguely, the opportunities he was giving us when he said: what's true of chess (it being interesting only when difficult—only when one encounters resistance) is also true of life in general. His lessons contained all the ingredients to help move us forward, perhaps even to give us a little character.

Things didn't turn out that way, however. Speaking for myself, I see now how the shell in which I had felt so cared for, so protected from the outside world, had been transformed by Mr. Wiesveld's presence into a suit of armor against which all his kindness rebounded impotently. And yet he remained inspired, class after class. Each week he had prepared something new, along with subtle illustrations of his point. Whenever a boy was unable to attend, Mr. Wiesveld was more upset about it than the absentee himself. Whenever a boy had been sick, Mr. Wiesveld found extra time to get him back on track.

Once we realized that we owed our progress to Mr. Wiesveld, we stopped impersonating him. But we still kept him at a distance. After all, what choice did we have? He was a man who wore raised heels, and whom —in order to amuse your brothers, cousins, and friends—you would mimic by slapping your left wrist a couple of times with the limp fingers of your right hand.

■

March arrived and Mr. Vink was due to return two weeks later. At the end of the morning (it had been snowing and we were dying to get out and throw snowballs at each other), Mr. Wiesveld asked us to stay behind for a moment. Coats on, we sat back down.

"Would you mind," he began, more timidly than ever, "coming an hour earlier next week? I've put your names down for a tournament. Yes . . . I do believe that none of you have ever participated in a tournament before."

A few of us shook our heads. Jan Boot asked suspiciously: "What sort of tournament? Where?"

Mr. Wiesveld smiled. It was to be a speed tournament, in other words, one where each player would play for twenty minutes at a time. It would be held in Schoonhoven, somewhere in the province of South Holland, but there was no need to worry about transport. He did advise us, though, to bring some sandwiches, seeing as the event might go on all day. And yes, of course we'd need to get permission from our parents.

"I don't know," said Jan Boot, standing up. "I've got other things to do." He looked round provocatively, but failed to win our support. Even if we'd also had other things to do, we would have cancelled them for the adventure of a real tournament—something we'd only read about in newspapers and chess books.

The next Saturday, an hour earlier than usual, Mr. Wiesveld was standing waiting for us next to a light-blue Volkswagen minivan parked outside Café Centraal. Just when we'd all found a seat and Mr. Wiesveld had pulled the sliding door shut with a slam, Jan Boot showed up. Utterly shocked by the idea that we might actually leave without him, he fell to the gravel from his bike as he was trying to dismount it. He climbed into the van quickly, bludgeoning and elbowing himself into a seat, us laughing at him all the time.

I remember very little about the trip or about Schoonhoven itself. By contrast, I vividly remember the moment I entered the hall with the others. It was a gigantic sports auditorium, the size of a football field, smelling of pencil shavings; it had a varnished wood ceiling with lightning-white neon tubes, and a green floor on which squeaky shoe-soles would occasionally resound. Chessboards, chess pieces, chess clocks were laid out on row after row of tables. And in between all those tables, teeming like ants, were hundreds of boys and a few girls, all aged twelve to sixteen. But the scene was chaotic only in appearance: each participant had been assigned to a pool of six players, each of whom were tied to a well-regulated schedule.

I am there in the midst of all those other children and the electric murmur of ticking clocks, holding on to a corn-colored card with a grid filled in with my name and the names of five unknown opponents. All of a sudden, I'm terribly nervous; maybe that's why it seems so warm and stuffy in here. When I get to my table, my opponent is ready and waiting. He's wearing glasses with some tape over the left lens, which makes me feel even more insecure. I hang my jacket over the back of my chair and we shake clammy hands; he looks at his card and asks whether I've also played in Rotterdam; I'm so nervous, I can manage no more than a silly shake of my head.

I'm Black. I touch the pieces just to make sure they're right in the middle of their squares. I blow a hair off the edge of the board, look up to assess my opponent (although I can barely take him in), then press the button on the clock. After a couple of moves, my concentration improves. Mr. Wiesveld walks by; when I look up he raises his thumb. A little later I notice that he's left, and I'm grateful to him for his tact; we had been worried that he would prance around like he was our leader, afraid of being instantly branded "those kids with the queer teacher." But that isn't happening: even when Mr. Wiesveld does have a word with us between matches, he does so quickly—nothing more than a little remark or piece of encouragement as he wanders from table to table . . . that's all.

After a couple of rounds, I realized that I was not only a formidable opponent at school; this was my first tournament, my very first opportunity to test my skills against children from other clubs, and I had beaten them one by one! My nervousness returned, but in a different way now: I was becoming fanatical. After each game, I could barely sit still, waiting for the next to begin. I felt a tingling pleasure with every piece I robbed, with every combination that cleaved my enemy's defense in two. And with each victory I realized more and more that without Mr. Wiesveld, I would have cut a far less impressive figure.

At the end of the afternoon I found that I hadn't been the only boy in the club to have had a successful day. We'd all won more matches than we had lost. But I was the only boy to have won a prize: a thick bronze coin with an image of a rook on the front, and on the back an inscription that read "11th Schoonhoven Junior Tournament: Eighth Place." While we were walking to the Volkswagen, with me clasping my medal, Mr. Wiesveld said that it had been a long day and that we must be tired and hungry and could probably do with some French fries. He'd treat us.

"Yum yum . . . paid for out of his own *back* pocket, I'll bet," I heard Jan Boot mutter under his breath, after the others had cheered. But he wolfed the food down the same as the rest of us.

Through the fries and on the way back I kept on thinking about my accomplishment, and how I owed it to Mr. Wiesveld. If I'd had to rely on what I'd learned from Mr. Vink, I would have become a laughing stock—so shouldn't I thank Mr. Wiesweld? Thank him today, this being his last Saturday. But how? Perhaps I could say something—speak on behalf of us all. Because I was the oldest, not counting Jan Boot, and hadn't I done the best?

Sitting in the rear of the van, I stared at the back of Mr. Wiesveld's head. Any negative thoughts I might previously have had about him had been replaced by a feeling of gratitude. So as we drove back to Brevendal through the dark country roads, I tried to think of what I was going to do.

After a while I could make out the familiar houses and street corners illuminated by the orange glow from the lampposts. Our van drew up in front of the café; we slid open the door and jumped out. I stood there looking at the others, then took a deep breath.

"Mr. Wiesveld—" I began. But he raised a hand.

"Sorry Norbert—just a moment. Boys, could I have your attention for one minute please? Gather round, if you wouldn't mind."

Mr. Wiesveld climbed out of the van and stood in the light. A circle formed around him.

"Boys," he began again, his voice trembling. "Umm . . . as you know, today was our last session . . . last lesson rather . . . although it might not have felt like that to you. I do hope that you got something out of it—out of all the lessons I mean—because I for one am very, very proud of you. Proud of every one of you! You were fabulous today. And above all, you Norbert—go on, show us your medal again—yes Norbert, you surprised me enormously. Eighth place—who would have thought! A big hand for our champion!"

I didn't know where to look. A slow, forced, applause followed. As Mr. Wiesveld continued, I couldn't concentrate on what he was saying. What I did notice, though, was Jan Boot standing half-concealed behind him, staring me in the eye as he clasped the fingers of one hand into a ring through which he stuck the middle finger of his other hand, to move it slowly back and forth. And then his thick, pasty tongue poked out from in between his lips.

"Norbert, what was it you wanted to say?" asked Mr. Wiesveld with a friendly look.

Now that I could see him clearly, his smooth complexion, the straight part in his hair, and his narrow shoulders, my courage deserted me. What could I possibly say? Thank you for everything? But what did I have to gain? Next week he wouldn't be there—but Jan Boot and the others would.

They were staring at me. I felt a dull ache rise up deep inside. For months to come, they might call me a fag-friend—or worse.

The evening breeze touched my face and the church bell struck once. I looked sideways into the dark café windows. Although there was nothing to see other than the pale sheen of the net curtains, I was overcome by a desire to crawl right behind them—to be covered, as it were, by a lovely warm thick blanket.

I looked at Mr. Wiesveld, the taste of the fries still in my mouth.

"Nothing," I said. "Just—see you next week, guys."

I dropped the medal casually into my coat pocket, turned around, and walked across the gravel to my bike.

It was Saturday morning. We were in our room in the Café Centraal, its dry air reeking of cigars. Soft drinks within arm's reach and Lina in our thoughts, we sat looking at Mr. Vink and the demonstration board. He hadn't wasted any time in Lebanon, he announced in his loud military voice, but had devised dozens of new exercises just for us—enough to keep us going for the rest of the season.

He stepped aside so that we could view the first problem.

"White mates in three," he said. And as a severe frown formed above his caterpillar-like eyebrows, he added: "Ten minutes to solve it."

Jan Boot solved it first.

TRANSLATED FROM DUTCH BY IMOGEN COHEN

JON FOSSE

Waves of Stone

I sit in my boat. I'm alone. It's twilight. I look toward the land and there, on a black cliff, on the top of a cliff that loses itself in the sea, I see them standing, the man and the woman. She stands in front of him. They both stand there completely still, they stand there as if they're a part of the cliff. I watch her, and suddenly she moves, she steps toward him.

This was the place you wanted to show me, she says

and he glances at her and he glances at the ground and he tries to think of something to say, because what does she mean, it's like she means something else, something other than what she's saying, but he doesn't know what she means by it, and since she's asking he thinks he has to say something

This is the place, he says

she steps toward the edge

Because you remembered it from your childhood, she says

Don't go so near the edge, he says

and he sees a dark and transparent man rise up and stand a little behind her, and the man reaches out with one arm and a black wave of stone raises itself up and spreads itself out and clouds and mountain and sky and sea are all rolled aside, as if they're afraid of his gesture, and he stands there and he sees the man who's looking at the light in his breast

Don't go any closer to the edge, he says

Everything's hidden, she says

Most things are hidden, he says

But hidden things reveal themselves, as much as they can, she says

They don't reveal themselves, he says

she steps closer to the edge

Don't go any further out, he says

Why not, she says

Just don't, he says

Aren't you afraid, he says

and he sees the man extend an arm toward her and he grabs the man by the other arm and tries to keep the man away from her, because the man shouldn't come any closer to her, he thinks, but the man tears himself free and moves toward her and so the man stands there and reaches out with his other arm and a new black wave of stone raises itself up and moves along with the first, and the waves of stone crash against each other, and the man suddenly lowers his arms and the waves of stone sink and then they're like cliffs slowly darkening

Don't be afraid, she says

and she moves closer to the edge of the black cliff

Please, for my sake, don't go any closer, he says

and he watches as the man strikes out with both arms now and the stone waves raise themselves up again and again they crash against each other

It's not dangerous, she says

and the two waves of stone crash and crash against each other and he sees the man lower his arms and the waves of stone fall back, they become two black cliffs, and he sees the man stand there and look down, and suddenly the man is calm and still and unthreatening, simply calm and earnest, that's how he looks, and the waves of stone are serene though filled with unrest

It's so far down, he says

I won't go as far as the edge, she says

and the man comes toward him and the man says to him that he can't just stand there, that he has to go to her, that's what the man says and so he begins to move toward her and he passes the man

Are you coming closer or not, she says

and she doesn't move, she just stands there and looks and looks at the cliff on the other side of the inlet and at the sea and at the sky and clouds

I'm coming closer, he says

and the man grabs him from behind with both arms and holds him where he is

You sound worried, she says

and still she doesn't turn toward him

I'm not worried, he says

It isn't dangerous, she says

Don't go any closer, he says

and he feels the man tighten his grip, and he sees her hair, her long, gray hair, and the man tightens his grip, tightens and tightens until the whole world turns black, not still and black, black and wild

Why not, she says

and she doesn't turn toward him, she just stands there and looks and looks

Why not, she says again

It's a long way down, I've seen it, it's such a long way down, he says

Yes, she says

What's down there, she says

It's only the sea, he says

Oh yes, she says

and he sees her back, her hair, her long, gray hair, and he sees how the wind lifts her hair and how it becomes a golden snow drifting above the cliff on the other side of the inlet and he sees her and she's a part of the cliff and she blends with the cliff and he stands there and the man loosens his hold and he sees how she blends with everything, with the sea and the cliff and the sky

I bet it's beautiful on that cliff, she says

I don't know if it's beautiful, he says

It's like it's hiding something, she says

Yes, he says

and he looks at the black cliff

It's your own light you're seeing, he says

My light, she says

Yes, your light, he says

No, she says

It's our light, she says

Your light and my light, she says

That's what it is, she says

It's a long way down, he says

and the man puts a hand on his shoulder

Let's go down, he says

I'm ready, she says

and he sees her move and he moves toward her and he pauses and he watches her and she pauses and turns back

Come away from there now, he says

I'm coming, she says

and he begins to move toward her and he looks at the water below and he moves toward her and the man follows with a hand on his shoulder

Don't go any closer, she says

and he pauses and he remains standing and he looks down below and she comes to him and she stands next to him

Let's go down to the water now, she says

and so they begin to descend and I see them descending and he goes first and she follows him. I look again at the shoreline, the evening is still, it's white, it's blue, it's the colors of the sea, the evening is peaceful, but it might as well be gusting and storming, since I'm protected by a cliff that stretches itself high over the inlet. The water around me is calm. There wasn't another soul around, not until I saw him and her standing way up on top of the cliff, the two that are now descending. It's evening, the sun is going down, but it's not quite dark at this time of year, not dark like it should be. I sit and look at the water. Everything is still. It's still like only an ocean can be. I'm also still. I look at the land, and on the nearest out-cropping I see that he stands and beside him she stands, they both stand and look at the cliff on the other side, the cliff under which I'm sheltered, and they begin to descend toward the water, and he goes a little in front of her.

Don't you see that? he says

and I turn and see that he's standing with arm outstretched and point-ing out across the water

Don't you see that? he says again

and I see her look in the direction he's pointing and I look that way too, I look out across the water, and I see a stream of light, the light's steady and transparent, pouring out from the land and spreading itself to cover sky and sea, and the stream of light persists, gathering itself into a single steady beam that hangs in the air and at the same time flows overhead, and the beam of light is genial and joyful and I see how it spreads itself over the water and how farther out it dissolves and becomes a laughing blend of mist and light and I turn back to the shore and I see his knees collapse under him and he falls to one knee, as if he's kneeling down to pray, that's how he falls, I think, and I see him crumple to one side and I see that he remains lying there on his side and she sinks to her knees next to him and she grasps his shoulder and she turns him over and she stands up and she stands there and she seems both desperate and lost and I wonder what's happening, if the man is sick, what can it be, and perhaps I should go to her and what was the stream of light that hung in the sky and that was so childishly joyful when it dispersed to become a palette of mist and light, I wonder, but he's simply lying there, and he's probably sick, you know, and I should help, I think, since he's sick, I should certainly help, there's no one else around, we're so far away, maybe I could do something, I think, as I sit motionless in the stillness and I think that I can't bear to sit here, I think, I should row over and ask if I can help, if there's something I can do, I think, and I begin to row toward the shore and around me I see the water, so still and blue and white in the evening, that's the water, and I can still see the remnants of that laughing palette of mist and light, but it's weaker now, as if it's about to disperse, that's how it looks now, and I turn and look toward the shore and I see that she's kneeling beside him and it doesn't seem she's noticed me, nor heard the sound of the oars, she simply kneels beside him and gazes vacantly in front of her, and what could have happened to him, what was it he saw, you saw it too, you saw what he saw, was it that, I think, and what did he mean, I think, when he saw it and pointed out across the water, I think, no, no that wasn't what he saw, he saw it but you didn't, that was what he saw, I think, and I row and row my boat quickly toward the shore, that was what he saw, but you didn't see it, that must have been what he saw, I think, and that's why he fell to his knee, and that's why he crumpled down, and that's why he's lying there on the outcrop. I row toward the outcrop. I see that the water around me is peaceful and that the sky is blue. And now there's a blending of weak gold and a glimmering mist of light overhead. There are only one or two clouds in the sky. I turn my head and I see that she's stood up and that she remains standing and that she looks out over the water, she simply stands there and looks and looks, she's full of anxiety as she stands there. I row my boat toward the outcrop, reach the shore, tie up the boat, and then I approach her. She simply stands there and looks and looks out across the water. And there, at her side, in a crevice between two black waves of stone, there he lies, unmoving. I move toward her. I should say something to her, should ask what happened to him, if I can do anything, I should ask, I think, but why doesn't she say anything to me, why doesn't she look at me, why is she just standing there, I think and move toward her

Is something wrong? Is he sick? Can I help? I say

and she doesn't look at me and she doesn't say a word and I move toward where he lies and I put my finger over his mouth and I part his lips and I see he's not breathing. He's not breathing. I look at her and think that I should say he's not breathing, should actually say it, of course I should say it, I think

He's not breathing, I say

and she simply stands there, she doesn't answer

Something must be done, she says

and she looks at me

He's not breathing, I say

and she looks at him and she looks at me

He's not breathing? she says

No, no I can't feel any breath, I say

He's not breathing, she says

We should, yes, yes, we should do something, I say

and I look at her and I see her kneel down beside him

and she lays her hand on his forehead and he thinks, you, those are your hands, and he can still see her hands, he thinks, but now her hands are on his forehead, her blessed hands, he thinks and he sees her stand there with the other, together with another man she stands there, and she's small, she's the smallest of the two people standing there, the most fragile of all, that's her, and it's the other who's talking, she simply stands there, stands in place, but she looks as if she'd rather be no place at all, but no one can do that, she simply stands there, but mostly she looks as if she'd rather be no place at all, he thinks, and he sees her hands, her small fingers, her hands! and he feels her hands on his forehand and he's already far out over the water, in the palette of mist and light that seems about to disperse, that's him, but she's there too, and her hands are there, and her hands are the palette of mist and light that he is now, he's the palette, shimmering and joyful, the blending of mist and light that becomes an unseen glimmer, he thinks and he's a part of the unseen glimmer, and those are her hands, her hands and she's standing there, the day, the moment, and her hands that she rests on his forehead, which is no longer his forehead, but which is the sky and the water, he thinks, and she looks at me

He's not breathing? she says

No, no I don't think he's breathing, I say

Is he dead? she says

Perhaps, I say

and I see how she moves her hand toward his mouth and how she rests her fingers lightly on his lips and now, I think, now, now he's the wind in her long gray hair, now he's the water she sees, now he's the sky she walks under, I think, because now he isn't, because now he's a part of the unseen glimmer that gathers water and sky into one, that's him, I think and I see that she raises herself up

No, he's not breathing, she says

and she raises herself up and looks toward the water, and she stands there motionless and looks out at the water and then she turns to me

We should get help, we should do something, she says

and she begins to walk along the outcrop

Should I go with you? I say

No, no, she says

and I see her walk slowly along the shore and I see her long gray hair blow and blend with the gray, soft clouds over the black cliff across the way, and I see him lying in the crevice between two black waves of stone, and at the same time he's the wind that lifts her hair. I think that I can't just stand here. But someone has to watch over him, I think. He can't just lie here alone, I think. I should stay with him, I think. But I can sit in my boat, it's not going anywhere, I think, and I go down and sit in my boat. I look out at the water. I see that everything meets in the unseen glimmer on the horizon. And it's as if I'm a part of the glimmer, I think, and I see the glimmer spread itself out and vanish at last from water and sky.

TRANSLATED FROM NORWEGIAN BY KERRI A. PIERCE

MICHAŁ WITKOWSKI

Didi

had scars on her wrists and came from Bratislava:

"Only an hour away from La Vienne!"

Her name was Milan. A drop-dead gorgeous, sixteen-year-old blond with blue eyes, long eyelashes—like the boy next door from a comic book for good little kiddies. But inside, inside that boy next door, an old, smutty harlot was hiding. A bit of a sloth, too. She worked in the metro, at the Karlsplatz-Oper station. There was a glassed-in bar there, which we called the "Aquarium": it had a view of the public toilets. Scads of teenaged Poles, Czechs, Romanians, and Russians would circle around—and geriatric Austrians, too, of course. A few of them were beautiful; others, hideously ugly! There was no middle-of-the-road there . . .

Didi couldn't forget the pervasive stench of citrus-scented disinfectant, which mingled with the smell of shit from the toilets there. She hated standing in front of the urinals, waiting for clients, so usually she would sit drinking beer in that glassed-in, subterranean bar, and watch, glassy-eyed, as the old men circled the facilities. I said to her:

"Back to work, Didi! *Arbeiten!* Even if it's just for fifty schillings." And she said:

"Ja sem žena leniva . . ." *

* *Slovak*: I'm a lazy woman.

Once she finally did get her ass in gear, all she'd do was sit and drink beer with the fellow. Then she'd say to me, out loud since he didn't understand anyway:

"*Konečne som nasiel toho pravého chlapa . . .*"*

Didi wasn't really suited for this kind of work. Once, exhausted by a client, she phoned ahead for a cab. She had a hard time finding the stairwell, the stairs were steep, and through the open entryway she could see the car waiting for her. So she hurried, started running down the stairs, carefree and happy that she had it all behind her and had a decent wad of cash in her pocket. And suddenly, just as she got to the last step, the world disappeared and there was a terrible thud! Didi blacked out. Coming from Slovakia, she wasn't used to such clean, translucent windows. She wasn't used to a lot of things. And later it pained her to no end that the cabdriver had seen her fall, had seen her careening head slam against the windows at full force; and she was embarrassed.

Things went downhill from there. She had less and less money. She even started living on the streets, which made her look like shit. It was a vicious circle: she had no money, so she looked awful, but in order to make any money, she'd need to get a bit of rest, bathe, and put on some clean clothes.

She was on her own, in the metro, and her shoes chafed her feet, so she couldn't go roaming around Vienna. She hobbled over to Alfie's, a bar for boys like herself (rent boys), sat down in the corner, and without drinking, without smoking, without eating, simply watched the goings-on, quietly humming Slovak rock songs to herself.

It was like a game of roulette: one day you might earn fifty schillings, but to do that you had to invest something first. Because most of the time you'd sit there for hours before picking up a client. During that time you'd end up drinking five coffees, five Fantas, five beers, five whatevers, because the waitstaff made sure that the rent boys ordered at least one drink per

* *Slovak*: I've already found my stud . . .

hour. So what you made in one day, you'd spend over the course of five just sitting and waiting. Didi watched with envy as the successful ones up at the bar stuffed themselves on enormous schnitzels with fries and salad or cutlets covered with eggs, sunny-side up. With beautiful halves of lemons for squeezing on that meat, those fries, on all that wonderful grub! She swallowed her own spit and smoked a cigarette she'd bummed off someone, which tasted like shit on an empty stomach. She wondered how long before they threw her out, since she couldn't invest any money in their business. Even if she did dig up a few schillings, she knew what would happen: she'd trick once, then have nothing five nights in a row; she could lose everything. Even the Romanians—they've been dry for two weeks! And what Romanians they were! Oh my God! Through their oversized, baggy white trousers they showed Didi their gorgeous, fat cocks. Stretching the stained fabric around them. In their broken German mixed with Russian, they asked her to see for herself, starved as they were—two weeks. They wanted schillings, cigarettes, but what could she give them? They were handsome and masculine, none of that anesthesia in their eyes, like the Austrians, Swiss, and Germans have; they're straight. Eighteen years old, swarthy, with bushy, black eyebrows!

An elderly john named Dieter, a copy of Günter Grass's *The Rat* wrapped in brown paper under his arm, makes the rounds of the bar like a professor. Wearing a threadbare sports coat. With a little pipe. But he doesn't know what he wants. Once he called Didi over to his table, bought her drinks, and then he said:

"*Heute bin ich müde, lass mich in Ruhe* . . ."* And then they made a date for Wednesday, though Didi really wasn't sure he'd live that long.

Vincent is behind the bar today, a tall, likeable Austrian; Didi and her ilk are good for business. Old torch songs waft out of the stereo speakers, even Edith Piaf. In the other room the rent boys play the slot machines.

* *German:* I'm tired today, leave me alone.

There's one hideous, filthy African there who smells like shit; Didi knows she's homeless, that she fell into the vicious circle, and that she'll end up the same way, too, if a miracle doesn't happen tonight. Then that sweetheart Vincent gestures to the security people to escort the African discreetly off the premises. Suddenly a raucous band of local playboys bursts in: middle-aged, wearing colorful handkerchiefs on their heads, chains around their necks, rings on their fingers. Noisy and cheerful, straight from a land called Miami, a land of movie stars, cocktails, and red convertibles pumping music at full blast. A land of moonscape wallpaper and faded dreams that's only as far away as the mind of the next playboy. They order whiskies and smoke Marlboro Reds—they don't care if smoking kills. Bald and monstrously obese, in the way that only wealth can bring about, because wealth always exaggerates a person's personality—thinks Milan, the philosopher of the Bratislava council estates. Because if someone likes to eat and he's poor, all he does is get fat; but if he's rich (and for Didi all Austrians were rich), then he ends up looking like one of these behemoths. And if you have a really campy queen who's loaded, she's probably got on an entire jewelry shop, a coat of gold, furs—enough to trump any opera diva. The playboys' bellowing fills the bar; they're completely out of control, but of no use at all to Didi as long as they're occupied with each other. She's been around long enough to know that only the shamefaced, solitary daddies stuck in their corners were worth eyeing. The bald men unleash another volley of rowdy guffaws. While the real "rowdies"—the beautiful young Russians—sit quietly in the corners, fumbling in the pockets of their grubby jeans, counting out their last coins. There was yet another kind of john deformed by wealth: the middle-aged queens with their faces, their grimaces, each reminiscent of a different animal species: weasel, parrot, owl . . . Dripping with bracelets and hair transplants. A moment later, those poseurs are joined by beautiful, six-foot-five lads from the land of glittering lights and cheap entertainment, who come to take their coats, move their ashtrays closer, light their cigarettes, who exchange their

Michał Witkowski 225

place at the door for a chance to be taken. They even pull out their chairs for them, seat them at the table.

But even as those lads are rushing to serve them, the queens bat their eyelashes and slap them—clumsily, tenderly—or make indignant faces: "You look like a turd. I'm taking someone else home tonight! Pooh!" Even though they were old and ugly, they didn't show the least sign of balding (thanks to those transplants) or graying (dye), they had no wrinkles, they were tall, well fed; it was only the jaded expressions on their faces that gave away their real age. They'd already had everything replaced. But they acted all snooty like those Czech actresses, those old girls with frizzy perms . . . Old gazelles with their bracelets and rings and cigarette cases and lighters, and everything smothered in diamonds, rubies, a hoard they'd spent years building up. Right next to them was a table of strapping bears with huge bald pates—a gang of taxi drivers. They're tossing back beers, smoking those little brown cigars, cracking up for the whole bar to hear. They wear tin rings with skulls on them. And if one isn't bald, then he invariably has his hair cut in a mullet, sometimes down to his ass in back, but a crew cut up front, with highlights. Now one of them swaggers to the jukebox like an old sailor and picks out a whole variety show of bad German dance songs about love. With choruses. A woman's warm voice oozes out of the jukebox. All they need now are beer and schnitzel, thinks Didi, chewing her nails.

The macho breadwinners are playing billiards in the other room. Ad nauseam, for six hours already. As if they didn't need to work at all. Oh, they're ordering sandwiches! The expensive ones . . . Garnished and served right at the billiards table, with an extra charge for service . . . Those sandwiches with sausage and pickle and tomato . . . Sometimes they leave the door to Alfie's open and a breeze blows in. Some of the boys are always getting calls on their cell phones—they're actual call boys . . . They put ads with their phone numbers and photos in the gay papers. They pick up their calls and walk slowly past the bar toward the door, chatting away. Hi, this is Eros; hi, this is Hyacinth . . . Their names are always made-up. Later, from pay phones, they call their girlfriends in Prague and Moscow, their fiancées:

"Hey Baby, I got a job in a restaurant. I can hardly wait till I've made the money for our wedding . . . Yeah Baby, I got the socks and clean sheets you sent, thanks a million . . ."

Every now and then a skinny, nervous, bald queen walks in, sits at the bar, orders a beer, and spends the whole evening igniting and extinguishing her lighter. When you ask her for a light, she looks at you for a moment with a completely vacant stare. Later a group of Polish yobs walks in. Heteros. Their eyes brimming with banality, hostility. They're here to make money; they suppress their disgust. They wear tracksuits with POLSKA in enormous red letters emblazoned across the back. Right off they say:

"Jesus fucking Christ, I'll fucking pulverize that piece of shit!"

Didi is deliriously afraid of them. But there's one agreeable Pole amongst them. She hears him telling someone else how he's just gotten back from France, from Cannes, how he didn't make a cent, and in fact got cleaned out, and if his friend hadn't cashed in on a slot machine, they'd have had no way to get back, would've gotten stuck in the old vicious circle there. At that, he stops; there's no need to explain to anyone in that bar what the vicious circle is.

Now Didi gets up and walks out of the bar, out of its heavy air thick with the smell of cigarettes, schnitzel, beer, and cologne . . . She walks to the little park next door, where others are stomping their feet on the ground from the cold. They're like her—so broke they can't even sit in a bar. Out on the street, it all looks just like it must have in the past. People stand there; old, fat, and bald, the johns walk between the parked cars along the street; sometimes someone beats someone else senseless, or else the cops come round and everyone vanishes into thin air.

And that's when the lawyer turned up, who for the next three months would make her his domestic whore. In exchange for cleaning and sex, he tended to Didi's legs, which were chafed to the bone, and all of the diseases she'd contracted during those five days when she'd been homeless. When she'd had to sleep . . . no, in fact, she hadn't actually slept anywhere. Because they lock up the metro with those grilles that drop down from the ceiling like in old castles. They shut everything down; they raise the drawbridges; it was red lights everywhere for Didi of Bratislava! The first night seemed like it would never end. Milan stood in the freezing cold from midnight until daybreak. And nothing happened. Snowflakes fell against a backdrop of lit streetlamps. Was that all? Was that all that was going to happen? Sometimes an elegant, streamlined Mercedes would drive by; but Didi no longer wanted a Mercedes—all she wanted was her own room, in her apartment, in her block, in Bratislava; for her mother to make her tea; to be doing her homework. It's just that her passport . . . Well, basically, there was no passport. So why did Milan leave? Because the soup was too salty. Didi came here a year ago because she was having troubles in school, and she couldn't stand the food at home, the smell of burned food in the kitchen . . . Things like that. Because they made her go to vocational school, and she was getting bad grades and stuff. Because life was something that happened somewhere else; life meant dancing with millionaires and drinking champagne, not the smell of burning all the time. The idea came to her suddenly. She started stealing this and that and sold it, and as soon as she had enough, she left town. Later, once she'd disembarked in Vienna, she swore she'd arrived in Paradise, that she'd never go back, and she tossed her passport down a manhole.

Around five in the morning she started eating snow. From the lawns, because she thought it had to be cleaner than the snow in the street. She hobbled down one of the main streets, studied the shop windows, and got a taste of that unique and inimitable flavor that the West takes on when you don't have a cent to your name. She tried to sneak into an underground garage, thinking that even the cars must have it better than she had; but she tripped the alarm and had to run for it. And so, for five days and five nights she shambled over the whole of that fucked-up city. When she went down the less-frequented streets she would take off that awful shoe of hers, in the winter, in the snow. She wanted to freeze. She'd station herself on bridges and watch the Danube with its enormous, slow-moving ice floes. She inspected all the curbs and gutters, filled with a beggar's certainty that at any moment she was bound to find some money there, that it was statistically impossible for her not to find anything. In the metro station there was a vending machine, and in it, behind the glass, chocolate bars and hot chicken wings. Everything. She just needed to find some money, and she spent every night searching for it. Every single bottle cap looked like a coin, and every stone embedded in the asphalt begged to be picked up. When she had only a few coins left . . . That was awful. Three days earlier she was about to call home, her parents, and ask them to come with their car and pick her up, to arrange for a provisional passport at the embassy, but the phone ate her money. She pounded it with her tiny fists, but nothing came out. There was a sign with a toll-free number to call and report such incidents, but of course it didn't work; all she got was an automatic message with some bitch's voice rattling off whatever. To get her revenge on those Austrian fuckers, Didi stuffed the payphone with sticks and matches (matches that would've come in handy about now).

She came to despise all the people getting into their cars, driving off to their Opera, reading the newspaper in their little Eduscho cafés, carrying their packages, running through their snow, kissing under their statues, and giving each other chocolates embellished with the heads of their Great Composers. Didi glared at the huge boxes of chocolate like a starving dog. Whole window displays of chocolate, each one individually wrapped in gold paper, painted with the profile of some musical fuckwit in an enormous, gray wig. Open round boxes of chocolate the size of carriage wheels shimmered in the empty street's nocturnal light. Didi had crossed a boundary in her hunger and was feeling it less and less now. But she looked at those boxes of sweets and couldn't pull her eyes away: the luxuries of the world had become so improbable and fascinating to her. A poor man dreams of work and enough money to get by; a beggar dreams of nothing less than millions! Bells were ringing in the distance; crimson garlands lit up, then went out; and Didi had the feeling that, at any moment, a carriage drawn by a legion of reindeer would come for her, here in front of the shop, and whisk her off into some fairy tale or other. She wasn't quite sure which story best suited her: the one about the little girl with the matches, who froze in the snow? She'd stuffed her last matches into the payphone, and anyway, smoking was just awful! It did nothing at all to make the hunger go away. Or maybe the story of Kai and Gerda was better? That must have been one of those Scandinavian fairy tales, because Milan remembered only that it was full of ice, whiteness, blue skies, and lucre. Just like Sweden. And just when it seemed things couldn't get any kitschier . . . Hmm, how to explain? There were these lights set up everywhere, and Didi figured, to her surprise, that they were rigged with photosensors, because whenever she got near them, they would start playing this one especially inane American Christmas carol. And in that empty, bitterly cold night, little bells really were ringing, but instead of reindeer a combination street-cleaner and garbage truck drove by, which in Austria all look like something out of a science fiction war game. Didi was feeling a lot like garbage herself, and couldn't help thinking they must be coming on her account.

Eventually Didi stopped walking, because every time she took a step, her shoe would cut into her foot, practically to the bone. At least that's how it felt. Those beautiful loafers—how she hated them now—were a reminder of the life of prosperity (Ralf! Alex!) she'd had not long before, when instead of saving her money for times like this, she'd spent it all on heaps of new clothes. (*Geld sparen, Geld sparen, Didi! Du musst Geld sparen!*)* But later, when she was kicked out of her apartment by her Brazilian fag landlady (Sierra Ferreira da Silva), she stashed them all in a locker

---

* *German*: Save your money, save your money, Didi! You need to save money!

at the train station, threw in a coin and . . . and they were still there, but in order to get them out she'd have to deposit fifty schillings or something, because the meter was still ticking! The blinking display kindly informed her that if she didn't remove her things within twenty-four hours, she wouldn't be able to get them out at all. Or something like that—she didn't entirely understand what those Austrian pigs had written there.

Didi was no longer able to walk or stand up, nor could she put up with the sadness emanating from all the Christmas trees and lights and jingling, caroling bells everywhere. She was so over that whole green-and-red festival of kitsch.

But then: a miracle! Didi, filthy and hungry though she was, snared a john in the metro. A fat, sweaty, unshaven Arab. Who smiled lasciviously at her nineteen years and fawn-colored hair. Milan thought she might kiss him for joy, right there in the subway! She was already figuring how many cutlets, French fries, and sandwiches he'd be good for . . . How much could she get out of a guy like that? Not much. But there was a shower at the Bahnhof; you just tossed in some coins and the doors parted. Only a few inches, though, so that two people couldn't make it through at once. You had a half hour entirely to yourself. Washing up was wonderful, but being entirely by yourself for a whole half hour—that was pure bliss! To be off the street, finally; finally, to be alone! She'd go and wash up there and put on a pair of fresh socks, which she would buy. It would be a holiday.

The Arab didn't have a place. She asked him, "You got a place?" But as if to spite her, the Arab didn't even have a place to go. Didi wanted to get the whole thing over and done with as soon as possible, and was about to drag him off to the bushes in the park or the toilet in the metro, but the Arab (Ahmed) insisted that he knew the perfect spot. He took Milan to an underground parking lot that had some public toilets in it. They zigzagged between the variously colored cars. It was dimly lit; the only bright thing was a green sign with the word "exit." They shut the door, and Ahmed sat down on the toilet. It was enough to make you throw up. He had breasts like a woman's, except they were covered in hair, and he reeked of sour sweat. Every few minutes he would break into idiotic laughter and order Didi to lick his corrupted body from head to toe. Or else he would fart and laugh as if it were the funniest joke he'd ever heard. Didi did lick him, but all the while she fantasized about those cigarettes and cutlets, which allowed her to forget what she was doing. Suddenly someone started pounding against the door of the stall—it was the guard! The parking-lot guard! The guardian of all those underground garages, one after the other, deeper and deeper, leading all the way down to hell! One of those guards in the fluorescent vests, yellow, maybe orange. He banged against the door and bellowed. Didi didn't understand a thing because he was yelling in German, and for her to understand he would have had to be yelling in Slovak, which he wasn't. Instead he yelled in German, but Milan had no problem imagining the contents of his communiqué. In a word, they needed to get the fuck out, because the *Polizei* was on its way.

"*Verdammte Schwule! Verdammte Schwule!** Open up!"

Well, the Arab managed to get away (without paying!), but Didi was grabbed by the even fatter and more repulsive-looking guard. Without so much as a how-do-you-do, he lands his fist in her face and blood begins flowing. She falls on the floor, on the tiles. The guard grabs her by the collar, screams something about the police, then throws her a bucket, a mop, and a rag. Didi tries to escape, but the fucker grabs her by the ear and holds her with all his strength. He keeps holding her by her tiny ear, like she was a schoolboy. She was afraid she'd never escape, our Didi—she'd end up as cheap labor, washing the floors. The guard cries *"Polizei!"* and "washrag!" in turn. It's her choice. Eizer you gonna putzen zis whole parking lot for me right now, or I call ze police! Fucking faggot! Didi chose the rag. Bawling to high heaven, hungry and filthy as she was, she had to clean the entire multilevel garage, and then she had to clean the toilet where she'd been

---

* *German*: Goddamn queers! Goddamn queers!

caught, the cause of everything. Finally she walked out into the night, with nothing, wiped out. That's what they call it. She lifted her head and noticed an enormous luxury hotel in front of her. Hilton or Carlton. Snow was falling. Only one room had a light on in it. She'd seen her share of hotels like that with clients, their laptop computers loading on their king-size beds, Chanel perfume in the bathroom, and room service bringing up champagne on silver carts. The light went out, and Didi thought to herself in Slovak how unjust it was that so many rooms should go to waste, stay empty all night, while she was freezing and had nowhere to sleep.

How many times had I told her:

"Didi, drop it. This job is for people with the steel nerves. Who learn Deutsch, collect the Geld, and fuck men from the Mercedes and the underground parkings! But not here—you must to go to München, to Zürich! No bleiben here! Nicht gut, here *kein Geschäft*,* Didi. You will be surprised if I say you the many clients I have! Because I know how it is done! I even make little CDs mit the photos of me! *Ponimaesh?*† You understand, little tart, Milan, *ptishku?*"‡

Now, at five in the morning, in front of the shop with the chocolate composers, my words must have been drifting through her head like flakes of snow. That night, Didi realized that the entire West was like an electric amusement park wired on high-voltage. The little lights kept blinking regardless, whether you were having fun or biting the dust in the metro, dear Milan, you lovely, you beautiful angel. Perfectly indifferent. Forever happy. As long as the plug stays in its socket. And Didi was a hair's breadth from turning into a Socialist that night.

But the lawyer. He took pity on Milan. He locked him in at home for the whole day and went to work. Didi had to do the kitchen, and all the other

* *German*: No business
† *Russian*: You understand?
‡ *Russian*: Sweetie [little bird]?

work, dust off the computers ... Bored, running the vacuum, digging through wardrobes stuffed with boring suits on hangers wrapped in plastic. Eventually she started to regret that she'd ever run away from home and come to Vienna, where she thought she'd be quaffing champagne every night, where the streets were supposed to be full of hot boys and fast cars. In the meantime, there was Jürgen, this old, balding attorney, who got upset over everything, shouting and all—when someone wipes his ass with chamomile-scented cotton pads, how normal is that? Didi looked suspiciously at all the unfamiliar contraptions. What, for instance, was that enormous toothbrush plugged into the socket for? It looked like it was for cleaning bottles, but it had some kind of setup on the handle, buttons, *nerozumiem tomu.** What a laugh that "toothbrush" got when she turned it on! It was a vibrator, for heaven's sake!

Or one time she washed her hair with some shampoo she found in the bathroom, and Jürgen threw a shit fit because it was a special shampoo for gray hair—his—and was very, very expensive, and she absolutely must stay away from it. And once he beat her to a pulp, for no reason at all! That too! He'd told her countless times not to use the metal spatula when scrambling eggs in the Calphalon pan, she needed to use a wooden spoon! So what, big deal ... Because wherever the coating gets scratched off, the pan will get burned. Didi really got it for that scratched pan. That's when she realized that the first commandment of the urban professional middle class was: "Thou shalt not use metal utensils on Calphalon, only wood!" And these commandments had been revealed to the urban professional middle class by their Yuppie god, scratched into the surface of two Calphalon frying pans ...

Well, eventually Didi rebelled. She began doing things wrong intentionally, just to spite him: she used his shampoo, moved his underwear around in the wardrobe, and—although he'd expressly forbidden her to—

* *Slovak:* I don't understand it.

she called up Edwin, her friend from the good old days, her American . . . And she told him that she was going to slip out and visit him that evening, told him to wait. And Edwin once again explained to her how to get there on the U-Bahn, because Didi didn't really understand how it worked. She waited until evening. That's when she had her daily walk, when she could be alone for one hour outside the house. But if she didn't come back at the agreed-upon time, she'd have all hell to pay. Edwin was a playboy of the first degree. Tall and slender, hair dyed blond, cowboy boots, jeans, chewing gum, and poppers, which were already illegal then and you could only find in porn shops labeled as "CD-washing fluid." He waited for her near Hammergasse and took her to his place; then, an hour later, he sent her off. Still dazed from the poppers, Didi bounded down the stairs and bashed her head against a completely transparent pane of glass. When she came to, she was in the vestibule. The glass doors to the stairs had snapped shut behind her automatically; the exterior door was still in front of her, and it turned out to be locked. She tried to open the glass doors, but they were equipped with an intercom. What the hell was Edwin's last name, what floor was he on? She hadn't paid attention when they went in—how was she supposed to know she was going to need that information later? So there she was, trapped in just a few square feet and with time ticking away. Jürgen was probably already home, bitching her out in her absence. And probably no one would come through the vestibule before morning, because all the Austrian yuppies had gone to bed hours earlier. She rang one of the buzzers for the first floor; a woman answered. But Didi's German wasn't the best . . . She tried to explain her situation in the same language she spoke with me, a mix of Slovak, German, Russian, and Papiamentu, but the voice started shouting something about the police, so Didi stopped. She made herself at home on the stone bench and thought about how everyone in Vienna, really everyone in that rotten city, lived in old buildings . . .

When she got home, Jürgen refused to let her in. He'd thrown all her clothes out the front door. In the end, though, Didi whined so much that he gave in and let her sleep there until morning; he was afraid of the neighbors, and Milan kept sobbing louder and louder. But he wouldn't let her sleep in his bed; he told her to sleep on the floor. That night Didi slipped into the bathroom, took the blade out of his safety razor, and . . . that's how she got those cuts on her wrists.

TRANSLATED FROM POLISH BY W. MARTIN

VALTER HUGO MÃE

dona malva and senhor josé ferreiro

dona malva had prayed so fervently that her dead husband would come back, she'd wished for this so passionately, that she started hearing voices coming from the attic one night. the voices seemed to be whispering, whispering words she couldn't understand, words that floated down in dry spirals and then seemed to fall through the floor as guttural grunts.

dona malva ran through the house yelling and rosa woke up but couldn't get to her feet. mom, mommy, why are you yelling. and dona malva, bitter, furious, said that the dead had entered the house and that they were coming to take rosa away. after that she took her own head in her hands and didn't know what she was saying or doing. sometimes she said one thing and did the opposite. the dead are in the house because they want to return someone to me. it's my husband, she said to herself, they're calling me to the attic because of my husband, and rosa started crying, she refused to believe it, until the voices in the attic finally went quiet. after a few minutes, dona malva quietly climbed the stairs, tears leaking down her face as from an old faucet. she couldn't stop herself, though fear was tight around her chest, and every second seemed to bring her closer to death, closer to heaven, or better yet, closer to eternal hellfire.

dona malva had hardly grasped the handle of the attic door when the noises began again, sending her rushing back down the steps. the dead struck the walls of the attic with such force that tremors reverberated throughout the whole house. they were speaking again too. when rosa and dona malva realized this, they both went quiet and listened. one dry voice whispered incessantly, and to dona malva it seemed gentle, full of tenderness. it seemed to be saying, i'm your father, i'm your father. but how could she be sure? after death, it's easy to impersonate anyone you want, even a woman or an innocent child. as the voice continued whispering and the dead went on striking the walls, dona malva and rosa struggled to give definitive shape and sense to the words, but they weren't comprehensible, weren't understandable, and they made no progress. perhaps the dead only persist in the shadows of the mind, hidden from the human eye. and perhaps they'd leave the house if no one there ever wanted the dead to return again.

but no. as the days passed, the voices in the attic were heard more and more often. eventually dona malva and rosa thought it quite normal to see the sun shining outside while listening to the dead banging on the attic walls. something would fall because of the vibrations and dona malva didn't bother asking why. silently, with trembling hands, she'd put the fallen objects back into place. she knew of course that supernatural beings could cause things to fall. and sometimes objects would be hurled with such force that anyone passing by the house would jump in surprise. and on the third day, the walls began to weep. it's the blood of the dead, dona malva said to herself, though their blood is only an exhalation of vapor, a fine curtain of water that evaporates as soon as it touches the walls. but the water didn't evaporate. it seeped through the whole house, from the attic down to the rooms below. they pulled rosa's bed away from the walls so that she wouldn't have to smell or touch it. dona malva even opened the windows in the hope that fresh air would cause the blood of the dead to dry. i watched as she gathered flowers from our garden and placed them on the windowsill, trying to make the house more cheerful. but every hope eventually gave way before the relentless dead.

on the seventh day, someone saw the figure of the dead man on the roof. people came running, but only a few could actually make him out, the others strained their eyes but saw nothing. even dona malva went out into the square, rosa crying in terror at being left alone. no one thought to enter the house and keep the girl company. maybe they didn't care, or were too afraid. but there, though only visible to a few, was the ghost of senhor josé ferreiro, larger than life, standing on the roof, terrible in the gathering wind. then the gathering wind gathered in a storm, and the rain chased everyone back into their homes.

it's true that dona malva had wanted senhor josé to return. at the same time, she wasn't sure if she was all that comfortable with the notion of being a wife to the undead. come to think of it, she wasn't even sure what she'd really seen on the roof that night. there had been such confusion. although she could hardly rule out the possibility that rooftop apparitions were an entirely normal part of the process of a dead person returning to the living. all in all, she was at a loss, and even my grandfather, who was, at heart, an ignorant and thoughtless man, tried to do what he could to spare her any more pain. anyone who hears and sees things that aren't there is probably a liar, he said, but someone who encourages that kind of insanity is even worse than whatever evil thing has possessed the liar in the first place. sometimes when dona malva went out, we'd all stop whatever we were doing and crane our necks toward the street to see the crazy woman as she passed. eventually my grandmother changed the kitchen curtains for a darker linen. that way we wouldn't have to see what was going on in the neighboring garden. that way, we wouldn't have to think so much about the threat next door.

a short time later, senhor josé ferreiro appeared in the kitchen, a phantom giving off a weak and intermittent light. he sat down at the table and didn't move or speak. dona malva watched him in the hope that he would eventually give her some sign or other, but he remained perfectly still. he was like a strange refraction of light, a dull reflection of what he'd been in life, or perhaps a television channel only partly tuned-in. rosa called for her mother and her mother ignored her. during this time, no one in that house paid the slightest attention to other people. it seemed they'd become ghosts themselves. all the members of the household, senhor josé as well as the insane mother and daughter who could see him, no longer bothered acknowledging the presence of anyone else in the neighborhood.

word still spread, however, and neighbors crowded into dona malva's house to see if senhor josé really was sitting at the kitchen table. no one else besides an old widow could see him. most people just caught a strong scent of mold coming from the shadows. no weak refraction of light, they thought, no nothing. they told themselves that the old widow who'd corroborated senhor josé's presence was probably just overtired, and while they wouldn't rule out the possibility that something strange was going on, it certainly wasn't that senhor josé ferreiro, they said, was back from the dead and sitting at his kitchen table as though waiting for his supper. after that, dona malva longed for someone to see him on the roof again, like they'd seen him the first time, looking like a rooster crowing at the night. that's right, thought dona malva, he looked like a rooster, crowing at the night instead of the day, because it stands to reason that night is like day to the dead. though even then not everyone could see him. i certainly didn't.

i went into rosa's room and sat down on her bed which had been pulled into the middle of the room, away from the walls whose colors had started to blend and run. it's vapor from the attic, she told me. my body is disappearing. my mother will find me evaporating too, i'm going to disappear forever. when we die, i said to her, we become nothing. it's your imagination. she sat up so abruptly it shook the bed. my father is sitting at our kitchen table and one day he's going to speak and he's going to make everyone understand him.

the two crazy people in the house were due to get a few more surprises. one night dona malva went to bed late. she'd been begging senhor josé ferreiro to say something to her or at least to silence the other voices still coming from the attic. suddenly she heard the sizzle of something burning and thought the house was on fire. she got up and looked around but nothing seemed wrong. just the noise. the only other thing out of the ordinary was that the ghost of senhor josé had moved. he appeared right in front of her, and dona malva thought she was going to die of fright, but instead fell into a profound sleep. she dreamed that the voices had deepened, that they surrounded her, thick, tangible, capable of swallowing a person whole. she sank into the voices and then there was nothing but the sensation of being enfolded by them, suspended within them. rosa is screaming, she thought, and the voices are entering me. all at once, she woke up with her stomach enormous, bloated. she woke up pregnant, in the final weeks, needing to throw up.

the next day, my grandmother visited dona malva's house and didn't touch anything. dona malva was weeping in terror, and my grandmother waited to see how the lunatic was going to react to her famous empty chair today. that's all we saw, an empty chair. but dona malva was overcome, begging, josé josé, tell me what you want from me, what are you doing to me, and it's true that dona malva's skirts were giving off a little smoke, smoke that writhed downward and disappeared before reaching the floor. of course, my grandmother didn't want to believe that a ghost could get a woman pregnant, or that a woman could have spirits leaking out of her body like excess gas. dona malva put her hands on her stomach and stumbled to the front of her house. i myself went into their house then and made my way slowly and fearfully toward the kitchen, determined to prove to myself that senhor josé ferreiro didn't exist. though it was getting harder and harder to know what to believe. as rosa said, if her father had returned and gotten her mother pregnant, who else could it be in her mother's stomach right now. i saw dona malva at the end of the hall surrounded by my grandmother and some other women now and i imagined senhor josé ferreiro bursting out of her gut so that he could live again and buy himself nice things. that was the sort of nonsense filling my head. it was hard to keep oneself thinking sensible things when a ghost-birth was about to take place.

dona malva vomited and then the other women got sick too. chaos. the women were screaming and i thought, well, this sort of malicious impossibility might very well destroy the world. dona malva herself yelled and swore and then fell into a stupor. without realizing it she opened her legs wide so that something could pass or be passed through, like gas being expelled. the smell was overpowering and the other women rushed to open the windows, screaming in unison. after that they drew together into a circle, facing outward, watching for any sign of evil. a few men came in too, but left quickly enough thereafter, since dona malva with her legs spread wasn't a fit sight to be seen. if they watched her from the back, however, the married men were allowed to stay. as the smoke leaked from between dona malva's legs, the men turned their faces away and called to each other for comfort. all was confusion and it became obvious that the men couldn't handle the situation as well as the women. they either lacked courage or a natural tolerance for such occurrences. so finally they gathered together in the doorway and reminisced about how senhor josé ferreiro had been a good man and, truth be told, had never hurt anyone in life. they said that senhor josé must have come back like this because dona malva had been such a bitch to him. he'd been a peaceful man, they said, but now apparently he'd become a little impulsive. no, said someone else, once you're dead it's like you're deaf and dumb. josé ferreiro is nothing more than a deaf, sad spirit now. he doesn't know what he's doing. another disagreed. death isn't like going to sleep, it's like waking up, he said. it's like a blow to the head that gets all your senses going at last. dona malva vomited again and the men turned their eyes down the hall to the kitchen and then turned back, frightened, disgusted, numb, saying, that senhor josé, that son of a bitch, he's really there, he's sitting at the kitchen table, just sitting there while his widow succumbs to this insanity. and then everyone began to file out again and i went into the small backyard with my grandmother.

the blossoms on the orange tree perfumed our walk, my grandmother behind me. we didn't talk about anything important for a while. sometimes your grandfather seems so rude, she said, that son of a bitch. i've learned to expect anything. if he gets hungry, he demands to be fed on the spot. and i asked, grandmother, can you see senhor josé. and she said no, but fear can make him real. fear can make people think they see him. we had a good talk until my grandfather got back from the market and then we stopped as if we'd been switched off and pretended we were occupied with unrelated things. my grandfather came into our house looking preoccupied, went up and rummaged through the drawers in his room, and finally left again via the backyard. perhaps he needed to kill some bugs out in the garden, or perhaps two cats were wandering around out back and he wanted to give them a good kick. he was as hard as a rock, or like iron hardened in water.

dona malva's belly stayed distended for a few days and our daily life in the neighborhood took on a rather improvised, hurried pace. at the market, we loaded ourselves down with vegetables for soups and herbs for tea. there was a hand on dona malva's stomach most of the day to measure her progress and check for changes. dona malva waddled around like an old woman, sad and with an enormous stomach, though she moaned convincingly enough like a new mother about to give birth. fumes constantly leaked from out of her skirts. slowly, very slowly, the days would darken. small children trailed behind her, frightened and fascinated, expecting her to act like a witch from their fairy tales. they told each other that she was going to mix vegetables with hair and nails, with dirt from new graves or else from some holy site, that she was going to cast a spell to drive away the fire in her belly. dona malva ignored their taunting and hurried on her way. rosa, left alone in the house, began to starve, and eventually the solitude ate away at what was left of her sanity. the more alone she was, the more the voices tortured her, and the more the blood of the dead seeped into the walls of her room.

one day dona malva collapsed in mid step and more smoke began to seep out from between her legs. the black fumes thickened and eventually hid the moaning woman as people ran all around her calling for help. dona malva emptied out her belly right there and then, and in the darkness no one could tell if she was giving birth to anything living. when the smoke dissipated, only the groaning woman was there, obviously in agony, broken, as if she'd been carrying a whole house in her body. people approached cautiously, refusing to believe that all dona malva had held inside her was fire. people looking closely saw that her clothes were charred. it was ridiculous. there she was, alive and smokeless now, although she'd certainly smelled like smoke from time to time. dona malva was still moaning, begging for someone to help her. she said her soul had escaped between her legs and that she couldn't stand up.

a few terrified men picked her up and threw her into her house like a sandbag over a cliff. when she heard rosa calling out, she finally moved a little. it was late in the day, the sun was just a sliver in the sky. finally, my courageous grandmother went over and helped the disgraced woman get up, leading her to senhor josé's old chair and telling her to rest while she saw to rosa. i stood in the doorway but didn't enter. everyone else stood behind me and said that a house so corrupted by evil should be burned to the ground. they said that dona malva's remains would continue to smoke even after everything else was ash. they stepped back then as my grandfather arrived, hoe in hand, crying out, you there, it's only idiots like you who waste time being afraid of things that don't exist. then he shook his hoe and threatened to split their heads open if they came any closer. like potatoes, he said. any one of you.

dona malva stood up and pushed senhor josé's chair against the wall. she looked at it a long time. she said, we'll never move it. she said, and we'll never see each other again. then my grandfather came right in and moved the chair. dona malva protested. be quiet, senhora ferreira, for god's sake, my grandfather said, and he pushed her to the floor. she went quiet and seemed to doubt herself, rubbing her stomach, now shrunken. when nothing else happened, my grandfather approached the chair again, thought a moment, and then left to bring back bricks and cement. dona malva didn't object. she watched him wall in that chair, and as she watched she seemed increasingly defiant. you're not going to move from there ever again, josé. you're going to be trapped between these walls. yet as soon as the bricks reached the ceiling, the noise in the attic started up again, louder than ever, and then louder still, until it seemed as if all the dead of the world had squeezed into the top of the house. dona malva cried out in desperation and collapsed. i looked for rosa. no one had the courage to acknowledge what was going on. an impossible wind began to blow through the house, picking objects up and then smashing them apart. again, chaos. objects began to revolve around rosa, knocking her to the floor. i grabbed her and held her against me, and i thought, what if this wind never stops, we'll spend the rest of our lives like this, or else, what if we get ripped to pieces, they'll have to search for us among the flowers. it was as though life had stopped. in that moment, life felt suspended.

the following day was christmas eve. whenever someone tried to enter the house, they'd hear a soft snarl. rags were stuffed in the chinks in the walls and all the curtains were drawn. the members of the household worried that this supper would be their last, especially since the blood of the dead had begun descending from the attic again, seeping into every wall of dona malva's house, except the one my grandfather had built. soon the dead too began coming down from the attic again. this is apparently what the dead do.

TRANSLATED FROM PORTUGUESE BY KERRI A. PIERCE

COSMIN MANOLACHE

Three Hundred Cups

If you find yourself hoping for something exceptional from a wholly ordinary day, wanting much more, that is, than you would ordinarily, had your expectations been at their usual modest and patient level, then it's probably a good idea to forget the precise meaning of the word "exceptional." At least until evening gradually settles its coolness over half the globe. Forget the person you were at the moment of formulating your desire. Forget everything that led up to that moment. And, even after evening falls, it's probably still a good idea not to remind yourself that you'd wanted much more from that particular day. At most you should say a simple, homely prayer of thanks for yet another twenty-four hours siphoned out of the intangible flux of time. Let a week go by, maybe more. Then, and only then: roll up your sleeves—be the bookkeeper of your own fate—and erase the dividing line between ordinary and exceptional days once and for all. Because every single day is ordinary or exceptional in almost equal measure. What was an ordinary day yesterday—whichever day it might have been— will be promoted to exceptionality only after its wounds have healed, only once the sun is setting at last . . . or perhaps only after an even longer interval, when, inside us, all that remains is a few vague memories, mingled together now and indistinguishable from the residue of countless other exceptional or ordinary days.

That was what I was thinking yesterday evening, submerged in the late-autumn coolness, allured by the feast-day fervor of Bucharest around the Cathedral of the Patriarchate and the relics of St. Demetrios the New, having stowed the priceless *Notebook No. VI 1965*, (or, to be precise, *Notebook Containing a Part of the Novel of My Life*, by Potocianu) containing the memoirs inscribed (evidently) in Potocianu's own tremulous handwriting, its cover emblazoned (evidently) with a pen-and-ink patron-saint-effigy of our national poet Mihai Eminescu (based on the well-known photograph from the poet's youth, but marred by ham-handed draftsmanship, visible above all in the elongated eyebrows, which make it resemble that other well-known photograph, from the end of Eminescu's life, the one with the big moustache), carefully into my knapsack.

Yesterday was a day I somehow have to record. It was a day I had dedicated to myself. I probably should have spent my two weeks of freedom at home, or anyway, somewhere other than where I was (two weeks after a month of isolation, posted between the two shores of the southeastern extremity of the country), and above all according to a rigorous, organized timetable. Two weeks poking my head around the Danube Delta wilderness, for example—like the heads of the writers or statesmen who peek out from the pages of schoolbooks. (This is the only way, after all, that our national heroes can escape from the afterlife—our dreary lessons and homework assignments are, for them, brief holidays, dotted throughout the year: their only means of exacting revenge against the tyranny of the present day, mingling them all together in its—often false—histories.)

And yet: what could be more hopeless than a period of "planned freedom," however long it lasts? The last time I went away on leave, I spent the first week withdrawn, wasting the days in introspective confusion. It wasn't until the second week that I realized the danger I was in. I had to start paying attention, had to put myself in an analytical mind-set, had to use my time judiciously—a revelation that struck me in a private art gallery. I had wanted to see as many seascapes as I could—no more, no less. Even without an expert's eye, however, I had begun to notice that some of the huge, mostly second-rate canvases there resembled the ones I had seen in a book I owned called *Dutch Paintings in Soviet Museums*. And I finally understood. The gallery was full of imitators who were hoping to earn a good living off the ignorance of people like myself. I was wasting my time. I had to change my approach. I headed off to the National Museum of Art instead. I'd learned to spend my time wisely, then. But what about now? What was I supposed to do for the length of a day as vast as the Black Sea?

Yesterday morning, at something past six A.M., I was already in the center of town, on Magheru Boulevard. It was still quiet out. A quiet that went well with the wind. For a couple of minutes—as long as the traffic lights kept the few buses running at that hour away—it seemed to me that I was in the middle of an abandoned city. In a city where there were no human beings left to keep me from investigating the remains of this world, which had only just ceased to exist. A city whose demise only I could have borne witness to—or written the obituary for. But the green light flashed at last and unleashed the rumble of car engines, shattering the silence once more. In that moment, I thought of my mother's aviator friend. Dumitru, Doru for short—my secret godfather, whom I'd never met: a clandestine, outlaw figure. Maybe even my real father. In any case, a patron, a twin—imagined in every possible way, depending on my mood at the moment. And then I thought about how, up there, on a flight path his company had assigned him, there must have been the same sense of abandonment, of crushing silence, of solitude.

He had been in the air force, which probably meant that he only flew on really big missions, or for training, but not often as an ordinary pilot. Or maybe he sat out most of his career in some personnel office or other. This last thought brought me back down to earth.

Consequently, I decided to spend my day according to three simple, efficient watchwords: *organization, planning, rigor;* that's what you end up with after a life in the barracks. I quickly decided on my mission goal: satisfaction of an affective need. Procedure: one of two options—either investigate a certain air-force base, or else visit the Military Museum. Execution: the Military Museum is closer.

When I'd been at the academy, our visits to sites of military-cultural import were only intended to ensure that we obtain the maximum benefit from a trip into town—back then, the getting there and the getting back were the only parts of the trip that excited me. I couldn't look at a halberd, a painting, or a two-hundred-year-old building with any degree of concentration. They meant absolutely nothing to me, nothing at all except their passage through time—and the grim efforts of the people who were employed to dust them day after day, week after week. Thus, my visit to the Military Museum—for once of my own volition, without having been ordered to stop there, without some commandant watching my every move—seemed all the more peculiar to me.

I entered the courtyard containing the greatest number of statues in all of Bucharest. Our greatest national heroes, guarded—as is only fitting—by the most modern pieces of artillery. A good foretaste of the Last Judgment for our particular nation. I imagined us all lining up at the Throne of Judgment carrying our history books—so that we would actually be able to identify the various legendary figures being judged ahead of us—and reciting Matthew, chapter 12, verse 18. I imagined our forefathers' shock at seeing their disappointing descendents. What would King Burebista of Dacia think if he caught sight of me somewhere at the back of the line? *Where'd that fucking half-breed come from? Get out of here! You're unworthy of the great history I founded! What worthless pagan tribe dumped this nonentity here in the bosom of my nation?* Yes, Burebista wouldn't be very pleased with the likes of me. (According to the history books, his kingdom's borders hadn't even reached to where I was stationed, in Portia, or as far as Musura, opposite the Isle of Snakes. Burebista was something like a sheriff, cleaning up the Wild East near the Crimea.) And he certainly wouldn't be pleased to see what a good time I'd be having standing in the same line as St. Stephen the Great, Radu the Handsome, St. Constantine Brâncoveanu, and the Cantemir Brothers, all of whom, during their lives, never missed an opportunity to do a little sacking and burning, and all of whom would be standing around waiting for the same redemption as myself. And he certainly wouldn't be pleased to see that I wouldn't know which of these great men to offer my services as lieutenant to. A month ago I heard a priest—trying to persuade his parishioners that the apocalypse was nigh—say that all the weeping and wailing we see in soap operas is salutary, as it serves to prepare us for the weeping and wailing and gnashing of teeth every one of us will witness at the end of the world. Back in military school, however, they never taught us anything about the horrible events we're all, apparently, hurtling towards (at least according to the Bible). I'm willing to bet that the director of the Military Museum never once made the same association I had—between the row of statues in the courtyard and a catechism on the subject of the Judgment of Nations. A pity. If he'd seen things my way, he would have been able to attract new visitors: not just academy cadets, but seminary school students, theology scholars, and even humble parishioners. If they got the proper encouragement, they could have brought new life to the cold and empty rooms of the museum. But: life and increased ticket sales? Probably too much to ask. In any event, as an officer on active duty, I didn't have to pay full price to get in, and soon I was revisiting the sinful and bloodstained past of the Romanian people, on my way to the *Aviation and Aeronautics* room. I was on the trail of Doru the First.

The hall was like an immense insectarium. I think so many bugs would have been a comfort to Kafka. Fighter planes from both world wars, early prototypes of crash-prone flying machines, fuselages fragile enough to scare you out of any future flights to visit relatives abroad, manifold models of helicopter rotor blades, bombs and bomblets, a rocket nacelle, and the landing capsule of Romania's only cosmonaut, Dumitru Prunariu—in which he and his copilot, Leonid Popov, had returned to Earth at mind-boggling speeds. The capsule was accompanied by a cutaway diagram on a metal stand. The tiny, to-scale outlines of the two cosmonauts in the picture looked as though they were about to emerge from the womb after nine months of working to acquire human shapes. In the diagram, the capsule itself looked rather like an eyeball, or maybe the insides of a camera. I loitered around the vessel for an hour or so, finally reaching out to touch it—as though an object that had traversed the heavens would have to be imbued with some unsuspected talismanic powers; as though all I needed to do was entrust myself to it in order to pick up my aviator's scent. If I saw that monstrosity plummeting to Earth, I don't know what message I could relay to my regiment. Perhaps only a single code word, HEAVEN, HEAVEN being the emblem of fear, a cipher for both beginning and end, for α & ω, HEAVEN signifying a whole succession of heavens (how many are there again? nine?), the ascent through the aether, through the celestial tollbooths, each manned by an angel and a demon that vie for one's soul, not at all like the Fall, not at all a descent from the glory of heaven, a plum dropping scorched and shriveled by the sun. Touching the capsule, it was as if I had entered a church and leaned my head against an icon during some precise, efficient prayer. Finally I copied the diagram down with as much talent as I could muster on such an emotionally trying day.

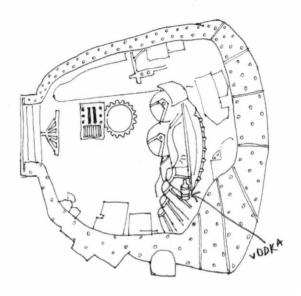

The museum guard was obliged to follow me around—it was like having a bodyguard. She wouldn't let me out of her sight for a second. Maybe she had special instructions concerning people who insisted on getting so close to the historic capsule, sole evidence of Romania's cosmonautical endeavors. So as not to seem suspect, I tried to strike up a conversation with her:

"Excuse me . . ." And the lady, dressed as though for a winter that would last the rest of her life, waddled over to me like a penguin, immediately rattling off a speech she'd probably had to memorize in order to get hired:

"If you're interested in the Interkosmos Soyuz 40 mission, then I can tell you that it lasted a total of seven days, twenty hours, and forty-two minutes in space. Ever since he was a little boy, Dumitru Dorin Prunariu had wanted to fly, little knowing his dream would one day come true. As a schoolboy he took part in the state Minitechnicus Competition and won prizes that fueled his ambitions. If you look at the photographs on the wall over there, you can learn all about the training Dumitru Dorin Prunariu underwent at the Yuri Gagarin Cosmonaut Training Center in Zvyodny Gorodok, also known as 'Star City,' near Moscow. There he learned Russian and became acclimatized to cosmodrome life together with his family. Then, on May 14, 1981—at exactly 20:16:38 Bucharest time, to be precise —the Soyuz 40 rocket was launched from the Baikonur Cosmodrome, weighing three hundred tons and carrying a combined Romanian-Soviet crew: Lieutenant Major Pilot Engineer Dumitru Dorin Prunariu and Colonel Cosmonaut Leonid Ivanovich Popov. Dumitru Dorin Prunariu was and is the first and only Romanian in the history of space exploration to have gone into orbit, a flight that lasted, as I said, seven days, twenty hours, and forty-two minutes, between May 14 and May 22, 1981. During the flight, twenty-two scientific experiments were conducted, including those designated 'Capillary,' 'Bio-dose,' 'Astro,' and 'Nano-balance,' but the most significant was a study of the earth's magnetic field. I should also mention that the vast majority of the experiments carried out were Romanian in conception. During the almost eight days he spent in space, Dumitru Dorin Prunariu crossed from night to day sixteen times every twenty-four hours, which means he orbited the earth one hundred and twenty-five times. Dumitru Dorin Prunariu has said that he passed over Romania around 7:30–8:00 P.M. every day, and that from that altitude our country looked like—and was about the size of—a loaf of crusty homemade bread. In his free time, around one and a half hours per day, he watched cartoons and listened to music, and when he wanted to relax, he has said that he used to 'go to the beach': looking out at the cosmos through the capsule's porthole."

Her speech went on, including numerous other technical and administrative details connected to Romania's great achievement in space exploration. The museum guard had hit her stride; she was beginning to warm to her subject, standing there in front of her favorite object in the museum. I wondered what would have happened if I'd asked about some other exhibit. I thanked her and asked her to allow me another five minutes to admire the great capsule of the Romanian people in silence. Reentry, at those infernal speeds, had scorched the super-resistant materials of its hull. It looked like a football that had been kicked around by every kid on the block. Looking at the diagram again, I noticed that there was a canteen by one of the cosmonauts' feet—the same kind they give you in your conscript's kit when you join the army. A canteen in which these two heroes of socialist space exploration probably kept water or their national drink (either tzuica or vodka). Maybe they even conducted an experiment about the effects of alcoholic beverages on the human body in space. (Really, one could justify conducting a space experiment on just about any human activity or experience, from mystical ecstasy to masturbation. But a drinking bout is still in a class of its own.)

After leaving the museum, and then for the rest of the day, I found myself thinking of all the things to which the two cosmonauts might have raised a cup of their customary liquor, and so I finally sat down and wrote out a list of three hundred cups for as many perfectly human motives, namely: the cup of banality (1), the cup of compassion (2), the cup of confession (3), the cup of the spirit (4), the cup of the clouded mind (5), the cup of death (6), the cup bathed in sunlight (7), the cup of moist sensations (8), the cup of distance (9), the cup of acquisition (10), the cup of modesty (11), the cup of wandering (12), the cup of silence (13), the cup of solitude (14), the next cup (15), the brutal cup (16), the disposable cup (17), the cup of friendship (18), the previous cup (19), the cup of depravity (20), the cup of the week (21), the cup of laziness (22), the concentrated cup (23), the slanted cup (24), the meaningful cup (25), the final cup (26), the cup of indignation (27), the authentic cup (28), the cup of doubt (29), the complicated cup (30), the cup of judgment (31), the cup of understanding (32), the cup of wasted mornings (33), the cup of the gloaming (34), the cup of itchiness (35), the cup of desire (36), the cup of idleness (37), the cup of infamy (38), the approximate cup (39), the slippery cup (40), the indefinite cup (41), the infinite cup (42), the cup of discovery (43), the possible cup

(44), the cup of continuation (45), the careless cup (46), the cup of occlusion (47), the cup of communion (48), the cup of cold (49), the cup of fury (50), the cup of repulsiveness (51), the prudent cup (52), the cup of fear (53), the cup of liberation (54), the cup of abandonment (55), the traditional cup (56), the cup to go with a cigarette (57), the brisk cup (58), the balanced cup (59), the experimental cup (60), the rhetorical cup (61), the cup in itself (62), the cup of politeness (63), the cup of contrast (64), the cup of optimism (65), the suitable cup (66), the populist cup (67), the precarious cup (68), the cup of decline (69), the false cup (70), the cup of university professors (71), the comparative cup (72), the polemical cup (73), the cup of immigration (74), the cup of vehemence (75), the critical cup (76), the cup of the body as a whole (77), the relative cup (78), the cup of knowledge (79), the cup of the cupbearer (80), the spilt cup (81), the useful cup (82), the controversial cup (83), the cup of valuation (84), the cup of seeing (85), the studious cup (86), the cup of maturity (87), the cup of cynicism (88), the cup of concubines (89), the insatiable cup (90), the cup of parting (91), the cup of betrayal (92), the cup of absolution (93), the cup of piety (94), the cup of indignation (95), the cup of pain (96), the cup of water (97), the cup of skillfulness (98), the concave cup (99), the cup of the tip of the tongue (100), the unregistered cup (101), the cup of occurrence (102), the cup of pleasure (103), the ritual cup (104), the cup of courage (105), the unfinished cup (106), the cup of conviction (107), the cup of tribulation (108), the empty cup (109), the cup of astonishment (110), the cup of relief (111), the cup of ordeal (112), the cup of rebellion (113), the successful cup (114), the cup of good business (115), the cup of vision (116), the lucid cup (117), the cup of gentleness (118), the cup of the end attained (119), the chalice cup (120), the cup of return to first principles (121), the cup of forgetting (122), the illusory cup (123), the cup of blindness (124), the cup of failure (125), the cup of sin (126), the cup of revenge (127), the cup of bitterness (128), the cup of silence (129), the cup of poets (130), the cup of excess (131), the chipped cup (132), the lingering cup (133), the cup of the building site (134), the improvised cup (135), the scandalous cup (136), the wedding cup (137), the cup of night (138), the cup of futility (139), the cup of inequality (140), the inevitable cup (141), the partisan cup (142), the cup of submission (143), the cup of trust (144), the cup of essences (145), the bathing cup (146), the archetypal cup (147), the cup of impressions (148), the cup of presence (149), the febrile cup (150), the cup of harmony (151), the cup of the apogee (152), the alluring cup (153), the subtle cup (154), the cup of shadows (155), the cup of opulence (156), the luminous cup (157), the cup of insinuation (158), the cup of memory (159), the cup of captivity (160), the echoing cup (161), the cup of appetite (162), the cup of getting drunk for the first time (163), the symbolic cup (164), the cup of observation (165), the passport cup (166), the atypical cup (167), the social cup (168), the cup of nationalism (169), the cup of skepticism (170), the cup of resistance (171), the surplus cup (172), the omniscient cup (173), the cup of truth (174), the cup of levity (175), the reflexive cup (176), the cup of misfortune (177), the cup of Lucifer (178), the cup of pride (179), the grave cup (180), the pedagogical cup (181), the cup of survival (182), the capable cup (183), the serious cup (184), the equivalent cup (185), the civilized cup (186), the cup of innocence (187), the cup of altruism (188), the explicit cup (189), the cup of abundance (190), the cup of all trades (191), the cup of invective (192), the cup of nations (193), the cup of the absurd (194), the cup of harmony (195), the resounding cup (196), the inimical cup (197), the cup of metabolism (198), the cup of influence (199), the cup of functional disorders (200), the adjuvant cup (201), the cup within the reach of children (202), the cup that does not require an administrative hiatus (203), the cup recommended by a physician (204), the cup of ghosts (205), the cup of watchfulness (206), the contra-indicated cup (207), the cup of fatal injury (208), the cup of kings (209), the cup of the proscribed (210), the difficult cup (211), the cup over the sea (212), the cup of the heart (213), the invited cup (214), the cup of substrata (215), the cup of fragrances (216), the cup of promise (217), the clever cup (218), the cup of vagrancy

(219), the cup of wilting (220), the cup of old age (221), the cup of freshness (222), the limpid cup (223), the enchanted cup (224), the cup of suffering (225), the cup of glory (226), the tainted cup (227), the cup of uncertainty (228), the rejected cup (229), the cup of calm (230), the cup of abuse (231), the cup of steadfastness (232), the cup of the coast (233), the empirical cup (234), the cup in a small railway station (235), the cup of discrepancies (236), the cup of curiosity (237), the interrupted cup (238), the efficacious cup (239), the cup of libation (240), the wellspring cup (241), the sluggish cup (242), the cup for the prosecution (243), the cup of magnanimity (244), the cup of tears (245), the overture cup (246), the cup of camaraderie (247), the paired cup (248), the soft cup (249), the cup of wounds (250), the cup of the history of taste (251), the balanced cup (252), the collector's cup (253), the virtuoso cup (254), the cup of the well-said (255), the bewildering cup (256), the cup of the future (257), the bloodied cup (258), the technical cup (259), the cup of stubbornness (260), the discourteous cup (261), the cup of monologue (262), the dirty cup (263), the cup of the single woman (264), the asexual cup (265), the purely religious cup (266), the profound cup (267), the cup untouched by reality (268), the synonymous cup (269), the cup from a dream (270), the unknown cup (271), the missing cup (272), the energizing cup (273), the cup of concession (274), the cup of a hell of a day (275), the cup of abatement (276), the not-just-one cup (277), the old cup (278), the hygienic cup (279), the sophisticated cup (280), the cup for the road (281), the cup of my angel (282), the perfect cup (283), the cup of indebtedness (284), the sticky cup (285), the cup of reflections (286), the cup of reduced speed (287), the easily maneuverable cup (288), the cup of prudence (289), the cup with white gloves and a corkscrew (290), the cup for a picnic (291), the oppressive cup (292), the instructive cup (293), the healthy cup (294), the cup of decay (295), the cup of accompaniment (296), the cup of mystification (297), the thermos cup (298), the cup of the reading public (299), and the cup of beginnings —the three-hundredth.

In the evening, my nerves exhausted after a day dedicated to this unique Romanian aviator and astronaut, I decided to pass by the Military Museum one more time—just as a murderer is always tempted to return to the scene of his crime. The heroes of the nation were illuminated by rather dim searchlights, and the courtyard was guarded by conscripts bumming cigarettes off passersby and sniggering among themselves. The rest of the street had been plunged into a suspect and alluring darkness. Heading toward the other end of the street, toward the Dîmbovia River, I began to make out the glinting eyes of pimps offering me one or more "girls" at excellent prices. I was overcome by an explicable fear, and, simultaneously, a lust that had begun to radiate from my solar plexus to my extremities. I trembled at everything, at every sound, at every voice or whistle around me. Finally, I went into an alley and I was allocated—naturally—a Russian girl. Climbing the stairs of her two-story building I thought again about that great Romanian-Soviet friendship, about that capsule diagram like a pregnant belly from which twins were about to emerge: Dumitru and Leonid. And about how my Russian girl would give our twins a middle name, a patronymic: my name, Doru. Just like what had happened to me. And before opening her door, I remembered—how strange!—that Romania's first astronaut, Dumitru Prunariu, did indeed have a middle name, Dorin, which is more or less the same thing as "Doru." My Russian girl was called Sonia. But I rechristened her, I named her Mother Russia before getting on with the business I was there for. Unfortunately, I don't remember much of what came next. Then: a new Romanian night, black, profound, Walachian.

TRANSLATED FROM ROMANIAN BY ALISTAIR IAN BLYTH

VICTOR PELEVIN

Friedmann Space

Experts agree that a sizable portion of contemporary popular culture func-
tions according to a principle they've dubbed the "windmill": the merely
comfortable selling the poor fantasies about the lives of the rich, the very
rich, and the fabulously rich. Often this pattern varies by way of some colorful true-life detail coming out: one of these merely comfortable individuals showing the tabloids around his actually rather modest house in the
opulent Rublev neighborhood of Moscow, for instance, all the while par-
roting some legitimate example of a famous oligarch's conversation that
he's managed to overhear (like the sacramental phrase such powerful men
always repeat on arriving in London, fresh from visiting their goldmines
in the far north: "Why, the Siberian winter was really quite mild, this
year!").

This rather consistent and, in its own way, beautiful mechanism has,
however, one dangerous shortcoming—not infrequently, the rich themselves want to find out how the rich live, and thus are forced to study the
existing literature on the subject, without fail produced by these same,
merely comfortable arrivistes, who are, by comparison, if not entirely des-
titute, then still rather close to this condition. This is the only way to explain the Babylon of mansions in the Rublev neighborhood, or the fright-
ening number of Maybachs stuck in Moscow traffic.

So, is there any truly reliable and scientifically proven method of seeing into the world of the megarich?

To this question, we would like to present a firm reply in the affirmative.

But we have to begin our story in the distant past, going back to the nineties of the previous century. It was in those days of primitive accumulation that it suddenly occurred to one Chinghis Karataev, a particularly energetic figure of this era (who, aside from business, was also a big fan of the Strugatsky Brothers' science-fiction epics) that the proverb "money attracts money," found in nearly every language in the world, could be taken literally.

It was easy to substantiate such a theory in those wild days. Karataev took a big shoulder bag, put three hundred thousand dollars into it, and, having given his Chechen guards the day off, set out for a stroll around the city. His hypothesis was that the fairly large amount of cash he was carrying would somehow attract even more money to itself. He spent about three hours wandering the Moscow streets. During his stroll, he found two wallets—one only had a few thousand rubles in it, small change at the time, while the other one contained four hundred-dollar bills. In addition, Karataev found a gold ring with a topaz in it, as well as a schoolbag holding a stamp album, which, as it turned out later, held two rare "Straits Settlements" stamps from the British colonies. His total take for the day equaled about three thousand dollars—not itself a massive sum, of course, but clearly exceeding the threshold of the statistically significant, as far as a brief walk around Moscow went.

Two days later, Karataev repeated the experiment by putting five hundred thousand dollars in his bag. This time, the result was much more impressive—aside from wallets, coins, and jewelry, Karataev found a plastic bag with forty thousand dollars in it hidden under a bench on Gogol Boulevard (an ultraviolet light revealed that the word "bribe" had been written on the bills, but this in itself didn't alter the implications of the find).

Thus, his strange, even absurd supposition had been confirmed in practice. This frightened even Karataev, and he decided to figure out exactly how it all worked.

A few days later, in a Moscow suburb called Dolgoprudny, Karataev tracked down a certain Professor Potashinsky: a theoretical physicist who had fallen on hard times, and who had once worked for one of the classified space programs. After Karataev scrubbed down and fed the professor, he told him about his findings and demanded an explanation: for one thing, he wanted to know why nobody else had ever noticed this effect. The professor answered that from the point of view of experimental science, this particular question was simple: during the transportation of a large sum of money, an ordinary person would only be thinking about delivering it to its destination along the safest possible route; it was unlikely that he would push his luck by wandering up any dark alleys.

—Besides, added the professor, what do you mean "nobody else ever noticed"? How do you think the proverb you were testing out got coined in the first place?

Then the professor gave Karataev a short lecture.

—The effect that you have discovered, Chinghis Platonovich, he said, can only be explained by analogy with gravity. First of all, one has to keep in mind the fact that money in its essence is a social mediator: it does not exist in and of itself, separately from the people whose behavior it affects. In this particular case, it was probably not your money that attracted more money. It's more likely that the huge social magnet represented by the sum you were carrying influenced your consciousness in such a way that you started perceiving the world slightly differently from how others see it. It was you, not the bag on your shoulder, who discovered the wallets and the plastic bag under the bench—just you! You out of the hundreds of people passing by!

Karataev had to admit that this made sense. What Potashinsky said next, however, stunned him:

—We've observed, said the professor, that sums of money behave like gravitational masses. The only difference being that the source of the financial gravity is not money in and of itself, but the consciousness of its owner. The behavior of large gravitational masses has already been studied by contemporary physics in great detail. It is not difficult, therefore, to deduce the financial corollaries to these discoveries. Have you heard about black holes?

Karataev said that he understood the general idea—they are, they say, stars that have collapsed under their own weight into tiny invisible points; science doesn't really know much about them.

—Precisely, said the professor. In the vicinity of a black hole, all the properties of space and time as they're known to us become distorted. But there are certain things we do know about them. If you, Chinghis Platonovich, were falling into a black hole, everything would end rather quickly as far as you were concerned—your body would cross the event horizon, beyond which even light can't escape; then, torn into particles, it would be sucked into a singularity. But for an external observer, it would look like you'd approached the boundary of the black hole and then frozen there forever. From the point of view of an external observer, you would never cross that boundary—time, for you, would have stopped. It's impossible to fully comprehend this paradox: it can only be accepted.

Later, the professor would remember that Karataev was simultaneously inspired and frightened by what he had heard.

—Well, he said. Well, let's continue the experiments then.

First they decided to see how Chinghis Karataev's subjective time would be altered when the sum he was carrying was increased to a million dollars. The cash was divided into two identical red Puma bags. Their straps crisscrossed over the entrepreneur's chest like bandoliers (he was outfitted in this fashion not only for convenience, but also to the even distribution of financial gravity). Professor Potashinsky also hung an electronic chronometer, borrowed from his old lab, on Karataev's chest. An identical chronometer was synchronized with the first and kept in Karataev's office. The goal of the experiment was to compare the readings of the chronometers after a three-hour walk around the city. Potashinsky was supposed to walk ten meters ahead of Karataev in order to find out whether he would be able to spot—before Karataev himself—whatever valuable things would be attracted by his employer's financial gravity.

Unforeseen circumstances, however, interfered with the experiment. When Potashinsky and Karataev left the office, a bomb went off in a nearby trash can. It killed Karataev on the spot and threw Potashinsky aside, damaging the professor's spine. Potashinsky saw a masked man come running up to Karataev's body, grab both bags, throw them into the trunk of a parked car, and drive away.

A few years later it turned out that the attack had been carried out by a professional hit man from the Vyborg criminal syndicate named Sasha "*Der Soldat*": the gangsters had found out that a significant sum of money was about to pass through Karataev's office. But in the first days following the tragedy, suspicion fell on Potashinsky.

While the Department of the Interior was investigating, Potashinsky had a hard time of it: sleepy Moscow cops failed to comprehend any of what he told them about the planned experiment, and even began to suspect that the professor was feigning insanity. Later, however, in view of the enormity of the sum that had been stolen, the Federal Security Service joined the investigation, and there, the professor found a very attentive audience indeed. The legendary General Slipa, who at that time headed FSS department #6, dedicated to paranormal and neo-scientific affairs, got personally involved. After his discharge from the hospital, Potashinsky was taken on staff as a consultant for a project that Slipa poetically dubbed "The Green Corridor."

In the late nineties and at the beginning of the new millennium, work on the project was moving very slowly, and was basically limited to repeating the experiments already conducted by the late Karataev: there was a shortage of money in the country, and it was only whatever cash happened to be seized as material evidence in criminal cases that allowed the research to continue. The experiments were conducted on young volunteers from among the FSS officers, who with Slipa's blessing became known as "lucrenauts."

It was finally determined that "the Karataev effect" did indeed exist, and that large sums of money had the ability to transform reality. Two additional points were clarified as well, at this time. First, said transformation took place only in cases where the money in question had actually become a lucrenaut's own property, however briefly (a convoluted plan was developed to provide temporary cash flow through their accounts—but we need not concern ourselves with its intricacies). Second, the effects of the money were entirely internal to a given lucrenaut, and couldn't be registered by any scientific device. For instance, in the experiment that had led to Karataev's death, the chronometers would not have shown any difference, no matter how long he had walked the streets. But Potashinsky refused to believe that the entrepreneur's death had been in vain.

—His glorious sacrifice was like those of the heroes of our childhood, he said in a video-recorded memorial speech, the characters in *Andromeda Nebula*, *The Magellanic Cloud*, and *The Country of Crimson Clouds*. Romantics like him are the ones who once made our country great . . .

As their scant financing didn't allow them to conduct any serious experiments, Potashinsky devoted himself passionately to theoretical issues during those years—and made several important discoveries, as they say, on the tip of his pen. Some physicists still consider his calculations to be pure fraud, though even they agree that the mathematical approaches he brought into play were witty and unconventional. His attempts to connect the theory of relativity as well as quantum mechanics to such fields as the neural mechanisms of perception are still considered highly dubious: "like an iron and beef sandwich," as one imaginative specialist put it. Nevertheless, the conclusions the professor reached are astounding.

But let's turn the floor over to Potashinsky himself (here the professor is trying to speak in simple terms, so that even you and I can understand him):

A simple parallel with black hole theory allows one to see that there must be a certain sum of money, the personal possession of which would lead to something resembling a gravitational collapse within the boundaries of one's consciousness. By analogy with the Schwarzschild radius, which is the radius a given mass must be compressed to in order to generate a black hole, let's call this particular sum of money the "Schwarzenegger threshold." Its amount can be calculated on the basis of the nonsteady solution to Einstein's field equations, as put forward in 1922 by A. A. Friedmann. In memory of the great mathematician, let's call the mysterious dimension entered by a person whose holdings exceed the Schwarzenegger threshold, the "Friedmann space."

The nonsteadiness of the solution means in this case that the sum total of the threshold has to be recalculated every year due to a multitude of economic indicators. Its exact value is classified at the moment. I can only say that many Russian businessmen have managed to cross the Schwarzenegger threshold.

Our calculations indicate that, after crossing this threshold, it is impossible to acquire any factual information about the inner life of a superrich subject, though an external observer will still think that the subject is capable of initiating contact and, indeed, discussing a broad range of subjects, from soccer to business. It may be hard to grasp this from an everyday perspective, but it is nonetheless true that, in such cases, the external observer will be dealing with a relativity illusion, similar to the seeming cessation of time at the boundary of a black hole; except that in this case, everything will be reversed: time will stop in the lucrenaut's consciousness (American physicists call this effect "the end of history"), but not the observer's. Moreover, beyond the Schwarzenegger threshold, all lucrenauts perceive one and the same singularity—Friedmann space is the same for everyone! But what exactly a lucrenaut sees while there, we, most likely, will never find out. And here's why.

A superrich person can, of course, lose all his money and once again become

just like you and me. But here another paradox awaits us: when his conscious-
ness returns to the normal human dimension, he, no matter how he tries, will
be entirely unable to tell us about his experiences in Friedmann space, because
he won't remember a thing. A lucrenaut crossing the Schwarzenegger threshold
in the opposite direction, returning to earth, as it were, will retain only the so-
called "false memory" that corresponds to the illusory trajectory of his life as
recorded by the external observer. The symmetry of the space-time continu-
ums—financial and physical—remains intact, in this respect, and all the fun-
damental Einstein-Friedmann equations are still valid. In practice, this means
an absolutely amazing, not to say terrifying, thing. That is, only a lucrenaut
personally present in Friedmann space can see what happens there—and he'll
only be aware of it as long as he remains there. He can never bring this infor-
mation back and share it with the rest of us . . .

A few years later, the first opportunity to check Potashinsky's theoretical propositions arose. Two undercover researchers were placed into the
cell of a former oligarch serving his sentence in a prison camp (out of compassion, we won't mention his name). Their goal was to find out what, if
anything, the prisoner remembered about his past. The researchers insinuated themselves into the former oligarch's confidence and soon determined that he retained no memories of Friedmann space—just as the theory had predicted. Potashinsky's assumption regarding the existence of a
"false memory" turned out to be valid as well: the oligarch's recollections
coincided with the external pattern of his biography, as an observer would
have recorded it, in every detail. Thus, one of the cornerstones of
Potashinsky's hypothesis was confirmed. After this, the highest state authorities took an interest in the scientist's experiments.

At that time, even the most audacious dreamer couldn't have imagined
that scientists would soon have the ability to see into Friedmann space. It
happened, of course, thanks to rising oil prices. And yet, the primary fac-
tor in this achievement was the technological progress of humanity.

By 2003, a group of Japanese scientists succeeded in developing a set of microprobes that, implanted directly into the brain, allowed them to objectify human perception, if imperfectly. The Japanese equipment couldn't determine what its subject was feeling or thinking, but it could generate a multicolor (though blurry) image of what the subject was seeing at a given moment—not only while awake, but also in the active phase of sleep. This was possible because the signal was received directly from the areas of the brain responsible for unmediated representation, rather than from the optic nerve. This equipment was immediately purchased by Potashinsky's team.

The probes could transmit wirelessly, which allowed a lucrenaut to carry on with his daily life unhampered by his participation in the experiment. The only requirement was to keep relatively near a signal receiver, which transmitted all information to the laboratory computer in real time.

Potashinsky's experimental procedures could be summarized as follows: First, a set of test electrodes was implanted into the brain of a lucrenaut-researcher (for this role, as usual, volunteers were selected from among the young officers of the FSS). After this came the launch, fueled by a tractive network of offshore accounts all working according to the recoilless financial principles invented by Potashinsky: the volunteer's private property was augmented until it reached the sum guaranteeing that he would pass beyond the Schwarzenegger threshold.

Many of the large transfers of capital that have been noted by international currency regulation committees over the last few years—all of whom were at a loss to account for them in any coherent way—were associated precisely with these experiments. Similar to how ballistic missile launches can be detected from all over the world, the lucrenaut launches conducted by FSS with the aim of studying Friedmann space were registered by all sensitive economic sensors, of course. But the majority of observers peering into the financial universe mistook these tremors for the redistribution of wealth after the privatization of Soviet property. This isn't surprising, however—the launches were conducted in absolute secrecy, and there was no way for anyone not directly involved with the project to tell which members of the pleiad of new superrich might be one of the FSS research vessels.

Now it has been revealed who they were, of course—not all of them, but the first pair. The first ever controlled leap beyond the Schwarzenegger threshold was made by Russian lucrenaut Yuly Kropótkin. A month later he was followed by Sergey Timashuk. The payload sent with the second launch was more or less the same as the first—approximately six hundred million dollars (of course, in the "real world," these new financial stars rose into the stratosphere under cunning pseudonyms).

The lucrenauts led the lives of rich sybarites—flitting from continent to continent in Boeings refurbished as flying palaces, drinking rare and expensive wines, yachting, playing cards, transferring their genetic material to gentle creatures who sold themselves so expensively that the transaction already resembled love—in a word, they denied themselves nothing. And all this time, the signal relays registered the transmissions coming from the probes implanted in their brains, sending these to the FSS computer center in Moscow, where they were gone over as thoroughly as possible.

When this first expedition into Friedmann space came to an end, the lucrenauts' accounts were closed, and the process of returning them to the human race was initiated. Yuly Kropotkin successfully touched down at Domodedovo Airport. But Sergey Timashuk was not so lucky.

When making his approach to terminal 2 at Sheremetevo Airport, he entered a semi-comatose state onboard his Global Express XRS, which was making its final flight at his expense. The welcoming party decided that he'd simply had too much to drink, but the lucrenaut's condition did not improve the following day. He was practically incapable of communicating with anyone around him, and was heard to be muttering the same mysterious phrase over and over again: "The moon is the sun for the poor!" (Scientists suggested that this might have had something to do with the unknown visual phenomena that he might have observed during his passage through the Schwarzenegger threshold—similar to the apparent distortion of heavenly bodies in close proximity to a black hole.) It proved impossible, in the end, to return Sergey Timashuk to normal life. But his sacrifice—made in order to acquire this unique scientific data—was not in vain.

For the first time in history, Friedmann space had been photographed by means of two probes, absolutely independent from one another, completely eliminating the possibility of error. As a result of this unprecedented breakthrough, the project scientists acquired the second experimental confirmation of Potashinky's theory.

If you recall, the professor's calculations had established that, having crossed the Schwarzenegger threshold, all lucrenauts would start perceiving one and the same reality. The very first telemetric data showed that this was true: the video signals from Kropotkin's and Timashuk's brains coincided completely. Moreover, Potashinky's theory had predicted that time in the Friedmann space must come to a stop. This too was confirmed: the image from both video probes was static and hadn't changed during the entire experiment. Thus, Professor Potashinsky's hypothesis was vindicated. Theoretical science hadn't enjoyed a similar success, perhaps, since evidence of black holes—which had also been discovered on the tip of someone's pen—were actually found in space.

Not everything went so smoothly, however. The very first photographs of Friedmann space astonished and amazed the researchers: the flickering screen of their monitor displayed a blurry, washed-out image of . . . a corridor.

No single image from the surface of Mars, no radio telescope image of the galaxy ever underwent such intensive analysis as these images. Unfortunately, the low resolution supplied by the first-wave neuro-optical implants precluded study through magnification. But as far as they could tell, using every possible reference point, it was a typical institutional corridor—with linoleum tiles and walls in chrome green up to two meters (above two meters they were white). A few meters ahead, the corridor turned right, into some sort of unlit area; it was difficult to tell what might be over there.

Viewing the image using infrared or ultraviolet didn't add much to their initial impressions; all they could establish was that there was something very hot around that corner.

So-called scientific journalists immediately started printing guesses as to what kind of a corridor it was and where it led, but the serious scientists strongly disapproved of this approach.

"None of this actually indicates that there is any such corridor or source of heat," writes one of the researchers. "All we know for certain is that the received video image of Friedmann space looks *similar* to a corridor. If you thought you saw a human face made up by geological features on the surface of Mars, this would not imply that it had been carved by Martians. It would just be your own interpretation of a natural geological formation."

To settle everyone's mind, Professor Potashinsky at last consented to a long interview. The camera framed him with Chinghis Karataev's recently opened monument in the background: it is a light aluminum structure, featuring two swan-like red Puma bags with crisscrossed straps, and, soaring over them, as though suspended in the air, a sandglass, reminding future generations about this brave man who gave birth to a new form of science at the expense of his own life.

—Why a corridor? asked Potashinsky, a gawky, shriveled-up giant with an enormous shock of gray hair (sitting in a wheelchair: the consequences of the old explosion bother him more and more often, these days). "You know, the so-called 'anthropic principle' in contemporary cosmology helped me to understand this. Why is the universe around us exactly as it is, and not different? Why are we living on this strange globe half-covered with water? It is because, my friends, that if our universe was some other universe and did not contain this strange, wet globe, we ourselves wouldn't be here either, asking this very question. The world is what it is because we are in it. And if it was different, we would not be us, and it's not certain that any such question would ever come into anyone's head—or whatever they'd have instead of heads. So: why does Friedmann space look like it does? There can only be one answer: because it does! We can't know what's there in reality. But for some reason we see it precisely as we do—in the form of a half-darkened corridor.

—You don't have any idea at all? begs the interviewer. Not even the slightest guess?

Potashinsky sighs and smiles.

—Possibly. The problem is that, from the quantum point of view, the question itself determines the result of the experiment. The first name given to our project was "The Green Corridor." They ask me every day: Professor, what's there, around the corner? As a scientist I can only give one reply—from the scientific point of view such a question doesn't make any sense in the first place . . .

—It is, certainly, he continued, difficult to come to terms with the now scientifically proven fact that all multifaceted creative activities of all the individuals populating the summit of the human pyramid is simply an illusion of relativity, and that, in fact, the consciousness of every one of these individuals is nothing more than a static peephole, peering into the dimness of a corridor leading who knows where.

—Most likely, it is precisely our psychological repugnance to such a thought (or else the resulting intensification of our struggles for power) that stands behind the rumor so persistently spread by the tabloids: that a simple computer error led to the telemetry received from our lucrenauts getting mixed up with the input from the security camera in the secondary boiler room of the Metropol Hotel (under which, as is well known, the secret FSS computer center was located). Well, we can all believe what we like.

—One only hopes that new expeditions beyond the Schwarzenegger threshold—which our civilization, lost in the unimaginable stretches of the universe, anticipates with baited breath—will help to clarify this question once and for all.

TRANSLATED FROM RUSSIAN BY ANASTASIA LAKHTIKOVA

DAVID ALBAHARI

The Basilica in Lyon

1.

The story begins in Lyon, but it could end anywhere. There are four men in the story, two policemen, five women, a couple of cameras, a bicycle (not visible), and an old soccer ball. The story has ten parts of differing lengths. The longest stretch of the story, covering more than one part, takes place in front of a basilica; the shortest part passes in almost total silence; all the parts are figments of the imagination. At one moment, even before it began, the story was out on the edge of town. It stood there for a while, until rain began to fall. It brushed away the drops that were coursing down its face and stuck out its thumb. Two women were in the car that stopped. Both were chewing gum. "You can sit in the back," said the woman who wasn't driving, "or here between us, as you like." She shrugged and blew a bubble. The story thought it would be sad sitting alone in the back so it sat between the two women. The woman who was not driving slammed the door shut and the car pulled away. "Where were you headed?" asked the story. "Anywhere," answered the woman who was driving. Good, thought the story, I started in Lyon and I could end anywhere. She smiled first at one of the women, then at the other, then she closed her eyes and dropped off to sleep.

2.

She dreamed of ants crawling around on her, but when she opened her eyes she saw it was the fingers of the woman who wasn't driving. The woman had unbuttoned her blouse and was touching her skin with the tips of her fingers. The girl pushed the woman's hand away with disgust and buttoned up her blouse.

"What's wrong?" said the woman. "All I wanted was to see what your skin is like. You have nice skin," she continued, "but you already knew that, I'm sure."

The girl said nothing. She went on buttoning up her blouse and then she tucked it into her pants. Lucky thing I didn't wear a skirt, she thought. That morning she had spent nearly two hours deciding between a skirt and jeans, and though she'd been angry at herself at the time, now she was glad. She turned to check whether her backpack was still on the backseat: there it was, perhaps a little shoved to the side, but the lock, as far as she could tell, hadn't been tampered with. The girl then looked out through the windshield and saw it wasn't cloudy outside, as she had thought it was when she first woke up, but that it was actually just getting dark. Headlights were illuminating the road, but when the girl looked to the left and right, she saw no other lights. Who knows how far they had gotten from Lyon, she thought, and told herself that she mustn't ask them to stop. Then she heard herself say, "Stop, I want to get out."

The woman who wasn't driving began to whimper.

"For God's sake," blurted out the other woman, "will you shut up?"

The woman who was driving looked at the girl. "And you, what did you say you wanted?"

"I want to get out," said the girl.

"Here?" said the woman who was driving, "Are you sure?"

"Yes, I am," answered the girl. Actually, she had never been so *un*sure.

The woman who was driving put her foot on the brake. "I won't be coming back for you," she said to the girl, "is that clear?"

"Yes," said the girl. She turned and reached for her backpack.

The woman who was driving touched her hand. "The backpack stays," she said.

The girl couldn't believe her ears. "What do you mean it stays? All my things are in it."

"Exactly," said the woman.

Then the woman who wasn't driving started whimpering again. She whimpered louder than she had before, and with each intake of breath the whimpering got louder still.

"Okay," shouted the other woman, "Okay, let her take her fucking backpack, who cares!"

The girl dragged her backpack over the back of the seat with effort. She waited for the woman who wasn't driving to get out of the car, then she got out after her. "Thanks," she said to her, and extended her hand. The woman who wasn't driving stared at her hand and whimpered even more loudly.

"Come on," shouted the woman sitting in the driver's seat, "get back in already!"

The car started up before the woman who wasn't driving had had a chance to sit back down. The girl watched the car move off into the distance, saw its lights get smaller and smaller, and then, when they vanished altogether, she turned in the opposite direction, put her backpack back on her back, and set off with a sure step, as if she knew where she was going.

3.

She woke up, huddled, on damp grass, in a ditch by the road. She didn't know how she had gotten there. She remembered the fear that had gripped her more and more as her steps rang out in the dark. She'd have given anything, she thought, to be back there between those two women, a little touching never hurt, but it was too late to change her mind. She could only walk and hope that a car would pass by, which she had begun to doubt, while meanwhile she had to get used to the sounds of the night, which she heard all around. For a while she was convinced that someone was walking along the other side of the road, then she heard some branches snap right next to her and she stopped, frantic with fear. The branches continued snapping for a while longer, but she persuaded herself that the sound was moving away and she kept on walking. An assortment of night birds could be heard, but she couldn't tell them apart. They were all owls to her, though as for the creature that flew right in front of her face, she quite decided, quite correctly, that it was a bat, not a bird. If only she could be a bat, she moaned, and so find her way in the dark. Her exhaustion draped over her like a ragged dress and she probably stumbled over something at that point, sat down beside the road, and fell asleep. She stood up and looked around. It was early yet, a mist slid over the fields, the leaves on the trees shuddered, the road was damp. She didn't dare imagine what her hair was like, and her makeup was probably smeared, she must look horrifying. Then she heard the sound of a motor and saw a car. She raised both her arms high, felt her blouse pulling out of her jeans, and wondered whether this was some sort of sign, but by then the car had stopped and out of it peered a middle-aged man, graying hair, gray moustache.

"We're out early this morning, aren't we," said the man.

"It's a long story," said the girl.

"Will it take us all the way to Lyon?" asked the man. "Or at least to the city limits?"

"No problem," said the girl, "it can take even longer than that. My stories are always entirely under my control."

"Fine," said the man, and only then did he look her up and down. He told her to put her backpack in the back, he waited for her to sit beside him and fasten her seat belt, and then he drove off. He drove courteously, perhaps even slower than necessary, because at first the fog was extremely dense. Later, when it thinned and then lifted, he drove faster, but still cautiously, avoiding every risky traffic situation, so the girl felt her eyes closing. If I fall asleep, she thought, will he unbutton my blouse? She imagined his palm on her stomach and it didn't really bother her, but she didn't want to test him or herself.

"How are you?" asked the man. "Have we woken up at last? A night spent in the woods can definitely throw off one's mental and physical rhythms."

The girl rubbed her eyes. The facades of houses were moving past them and she realized that she had, indeed, dropped off to sleep. She looked down at her blouse, but not a single button was undone. She checked the buckle on her belt, though she immediately felt that was overdoing it a bit. She yawned once, twice, and asked where they were.

"In Lyon," said the man, "where else would we be?" He looked over at the girl. "You asked to go to Lyon, I hope I didn't get that wrong?"

"Oh, no," answered the girl, "I mean, oh, yes, sure I wanted to come to Lyon, you weren't wrong."

The man smiled and said, "Where should I leave you?"

"Leave me?" asked the girl. "Why?"

"Well, presumably you're going somewhere," said the man, "and I thought I would take you there."

The girl caught sight of a little cluster of white tents. Colorful flags were hanging on many of them. Some of the tents were open and there were people gathered out in front. "Here," said the girl, "this is where I was going."

The man didn't say anything. He slowed down, then he stopped, he waited for the girl to get out and then he handed her the backpack. He took out his wallet, found a business card and gave it to the girl. "I work in a museum," he said, "if you're done before lunch with whatever you came to do, come and find me, perhaps we could have lunch together." He watched the girl studying the business card and smiled. "The museum isn't far from here," he said, "everyone will be able to show you the way."

David Albahari 277

4.

The girl waved to him as he pulled away, then she turned toward the tents. She had no idea what was going on here. The tents gleamed in the morning sun, somewhere there was sad music playing, pebbles rolled around her sneakers, it occurred to her that she didn't even know what she looked like and she ran her fingers through her hair, then she passed by some security people and wandered from tent to tent. A different country was represented by each tent and the girl soon picked something up to read explaining that this was a consular exhibition, that all the countries were displaying their economic and cultural achievements, including folk art, music, and dance. The girl put down the brochure and continued her stroll among the tents. She tried to distinguish some sort of pattern in which tents were open to the air and which tents were closed, she tried seeing this pattern as related to national traits, but soon she saw that there couldn't be any such pattern. The Croatian and Serbian tents, for instance, were open, while the Bulgarian and Greek tents were closed, though they all belonged, if she was not mistaken, to the same Balkan region. She went into the Serbian tent and studied reproductions of medieval frescoes. A young man who was sitting at one of the tables coughed softly, which was a sign that he was available to answer her questions, if, of course, she had any.

"I don't have any questions," said the girl.

She spoke over her shoulder, in a half-turn, so the young man didn't hear her properly. He got up and went over to her. "If I understood you correctly," said the young man, "you had some questions?"

The girl turned and saw that the young man had the same eyes as one of the angels in a fresco. "No," she answered, "I said I don't have any questions."

The young man shrugged and smiled. "Sorry," he said, "it's the music."

Sure enough, one of the tents across the way had music blaring. The girl didn't know what sort of music it was. She thought of China, of Korea, of Indonesia, and later, when the music ended, she no longer thought of anything. She turned and saw that the boy had sat down again by the table. She went over to him, quickly, as if she didn't plan to stop, and he looked up at her with his angel eyes. "I do have one question after all," said the girl. "Where is this museum?" She took out the business card and handed it to the young man.

"Oh," said the young man, "it isn't far, you can walk there from here." He turned to look around him. "I should have a map of Lyon here somewhere," he said, "I'll show you."

"If it's so nearby," asked the girl, "couldn't you take me there yourself?"

The young man stopped shuffling through the things on the table. He stared at his hands for a minute, as if he was expecting an answer from them, then he drew a mobile phone from his pocket and dialed someone's number. While he spoke in a language she didn't understand, the girl leafed through books about the monasteries in Serbia. The young man finished the conversation and stretched. "As soon as she comes," he said, as if the girl knew whom he was talking about, "we can leave. You'll see, it really is nearby," he continued, "but if you aren't sure, no point in risking it. People get lost in Lyon easily and disappear without a trace."

5.

The young man headed back as soon as they got to the museum. He said he had to hurry, that the secretary of the consulate could only stand in for him for half an hour, that the consuls of Japan, Canada, and Australia had made appointments to visit the Serbian tent, and that the girl had only to cross the courtyard and she'd find herself at the museum entrance. The girl wanted to ask about something else, but he was already hurrying away and disappeared among the passersby. She took out the business card and then, while the ticket seller at the cash register called the man the girl wanted to see, she sat on a chair in the corner to wait.

The man who appeared ten minutes later, who went over to the ticket seller at the cash register and then, when the ticket seller gestured toward the girl with her chin, came over to her and asked how he might help her, was not the man who had driven her to Lyon that morning. The girl took out the business card again and gave it to the man.

"Yes," said the man, "that's me."

"No," said the girl, "that's not you."

The room was silent.

"I think I know who I am," said the man. His voice had grown inflexible and hard.

"Then how," asked the girl, "did I get your business card?"

"I'd like to know that myself," said the man. He turned to the ticket seller and shouted: "She doesn't even know where she got the business card!" The ticket seller nodded in sympathy.

"I got it from a man who drove me here to Lyon this morning," answered the girl.

"You only arrived in Lyon this morning?" exclaimed the man, surprised. "Why that's incredible!" He turned to the ticket seller again and shouted: "Can you believe it, she only arrived in Lyon this morning!" The ticket seller nodded again in sympathy.

"What's so strange," asked the girl, "about me only getting to Lyon this morning?"

"You got here this morning," said the man, "yet you're talking just like a native. That's unbelievable. Would you allow us to test you?"

"No," said the girl, "I've got to go."

"She has to go," shouted the man to the ticket seller. The ticket seller only blinked and picked up her phone.

The girl suddenly realized where all this might be going. She stood up abruptly, shoved the man away from her with all her strength, and as he tumbled across an armchair, she ran outside. There was no one in the yard, full of greenery and shadows; the only thing on a bench by the entrance was an old soccer ball. The girl didn't stop; she kept going, out into the street, she turned right, away from where the young man from the Serbian consulate had gone, then she turned into the first street on the left, then again to the right, then again to the left, until she felt she was lost. Then she came out into a little square and thought she'd like to sit down.

6.

The girl sat at a table in a restaurant in the little square. The chimes of church bells reached her from time to time, but she was never able to count from the first ring, so she had no idea what time it was. Most recently she counted out three chimes, but when she counted before that, she'd counted five. She raised a hand to call the waiter, but when she asked him, he too had no watch.

7.

Then night fell. Abruptly—though the day, the girl thought, still hadn't actually ended—but perhaps that was how night fell in Lyon, as if it had been waiting in ambush. From the place where she sat having her third espresso, she couldn't see across the square. The darkness was dense and tangible, so she kept brushing it off her face and picking it out of her hair. She wanted to pay, but she could no longer see the waiter (just as he, probably, couldn't see her), so she got up and looked for the door to the restaurant. She found a door, which she hadn't seen before, opened it and stepped into a room full of people. They were standing in groups of three and four, deep in conversation and paying no attention to each other. Someone did notice when she came in, stopped talking and stared at her, and soon all the little groups were standing there, silent, staring at the girl, and the only thing audible was the pat of her footsteps, which continued, though she had no idea of where she was. Since I got to Lyon, thought the girl, I know less and less, and soon I won't know anything at all. There are cities like that, she thought, in which you seem to disappear, as if you melt into the houses and streets, unlike those cities in which you grow and multiply and you're always becoming someone else. She couldn't remember any of the latter sort of city, though there was a wisp of memory hovering in her of a small town in which she saw herself as if she were slipping around a corner, but now she was in Lyon, or at least she hoped she was in Lyon, and she had to forget everything else. By now she had made her way back to a narrow door on which the word "Exit" was written and when she reached for the doorknob, the room became noisy again. No one looked at her anymore. And she didn't look at them. She opened the door, went out, shut it behind her, and leaned against the wall. Her heart was pounding so loudly that the pounding echoed off of something. The girl thought: Finally I have arrived. On the floor, between her feet, she noticed a crumpled envelope and now she reached for it. On the envelope were the words: "For You—Open Immediately." "How did they know," said the girl, "that I'm here?" She looked to her left, she looked to her right, but there was no one nearby who could answer her questions. There was a slip of paper in the envelope on which was written: "I am waiting for you by the basilica."

8.

"Excuse me," the girl asked a policeman the next morning, "where is the basilica?"

The policeman raised his eyebrows, clearly surprised, and then gestured skyward with his head.

The girl laughed. "I didn't mean the heavenly basilica," she said. "I meant, is there a basilica here in town, in Lyon?"

The policeman kept on gesturing with his head and making faces, until he realized he was getting nowhere. "Not in the heavens, my dear," he said, "right there on the hilltop, up on the hill!"

The girl looked up and, sure enough, straight above her, up on the hill, she could see the basilica. It seemed as if all she needed to do was jump up to touch it, but later, as she panted as she climbed the steps and steep paths, she cursed the basilica, and the letter, and whoever wrote the letter, and herself, and especially Lyon, which, so harmonious and beautiful, was stretching out before her more and more, gradually filling the whole horizon.

So what now, thought the girl when she finally reached the basilica, which was surrounded by large and small groups of strolling tourists, how will I recognize the person who wrote to me?

"Sorry," said a youngish man, "would you be willing to take a picture of me in front of the basilica? Everything is all set," he said and handed her the camera, "all you have to do is press the button."

The girl took the camera, looked it over, and asked: "This button here?"

"No," said the youngish man, "the other one."

The girl placed her index finger on the button, waited for the youngish man to strike his pose, and then she pointed the camera in his direction, but when she looked at the little screen, she saw only the basilica. The youngish man stood on the steps and grinned, but no matter how much the girl tried, his figure wouldn't appear in the image.

"Are you done," asked the youngish man, "can I move?"

"Sure," said the girl. If she handed him the camera quickly, she thought, and then turned and went, maybe he wouldn't notice anything, or, by the time he did notice, it would be too late. She couldn't say why she was feeling guilty about this, but she was already fed up with Lyon and everything that had been happening to her there. What a story she could put together out of all of this!

The youngish man was quicker than the girl had figured, however, and, without breaking the movement with which he took the camera, he brought it to his eyes and looked for the picture the girl had taken. "Brilliant," he said, "you take photographs like a professional, we came out beautifully!"

The girl walked over to him slowly. She looked at the little screen and saw what she had seen before: the steps and no one standing on them. Yes, she thought, high time for me to leave Lyon.

"Would you like me to take a picture of you standing in the same place," asked the youngish man, "or somewhere else?"

"No," said the girl, "I want to go home."

"All of us want to go home," replied the youngish man. "But really, it's no trouble, it won't take a minute—not even that."

The girl didn't like it when people pleaded with her. "Fine," she said and went over to the steps. She didn't know where the youngish man had been standing exactly, so she decided on the sixth step.

"Great," said the youngish man, "exactly where I was standing."

"Strange," said the girl, and raised her hand to her face. "That's what I was thinking."

"Coincidence," said the youngish man. He kept holding the camera pointed at the girl.

"There is no such thing as coincidence," replied the girl, "there's just someone's willingness to believe in coincidence."

The boy shrugged and said that he did believe in them.

"I figured as much," said the girl, and sighed. If he believed in coincidence, then he wasn't the man who had left her the message. But, she stopped herself, why am I saying "man"? Couldn't it have been a woman? And while the flash went off on the youngish man's camera, the girl began to look at women out on the terrace in front of the basilica.

9.

"I see you're looking for me," said a small woman who resembled a mouse. She came up to the girl slowly, first on one step, then the next. She stopped on the second step. Then she moved up to the third.

The girl wasn't crazy about anyone standing so close to her on the steps, least of all a person she didn't like, but she also knew that if she herself went up a step or two, the small woman would just keep coming closer. That's how it is with mice, thought the girl, you can't stop them. And then she said, "I'm not looking for you, you're looking for me."

The small woman stopped on the fourth step. She said, "Who is looking for whom is not what matters, believe me." She breathed with effort, as if she'd only just climbed up the hill to the basilica. "What matters is who will find whom."

"Was it necessary," asked the girl, "to climb all the way up here to the sky, just beneath the clouds?"

"We are far away from the clouds," said the small woman, "and farther still from the sky."

The small woman raised her right foot, lowering it onto the edge of the fifth step, and the girl felt herself breaking out in a sweat. I can't let myself pay any attention to this, she said to herself, though she didn't stop staring at the woman's foot for so much as a second. "So, what now?" she asked. "Is this all?"

The small woman said nothing for a moment, then suddenly moved up to the fifth step, lifted her face to the girl, and said, "I have a bicycle."

The flash that went off just then was not on the camera of the youngish man, who, the girl concluded, had disappeared without a trace. The flash that went off just then was on a camera held by a fat woman who, obviously, had been listening to the conversation on the steps. "In Lyon," said the fat woman, "everyone has a bicycle."

"Who asked you?" snorted the small woman. "Get out of my sight this minute, before I claw your eyes out!"

"How dare you talk to me like that!" said the fat woman. "I'm trembling. Look at her, would you?" She turned to the girl. "If I were to sit on her there would be nothing left."

"With an ass like that," said the small woman, "you're lucky you can get up at all."

"Midget freak," screamed the fat woman.

"Elephant," shot back the small woman.

"Ladies, ladies, calm down," a voice could be heard behind the girl's back, "what will our guest think of us?"

The girl turned and saw a policeman. He was the same policeman who had shown her where the basilica was. Or, even if he wasn't really the same one, thought the girl, he looked enough like him. Anyway, there was no difference between one policeman and the next.

"Oh," said the policeman, "you're wrong about that. Sure," he said, "all uniforms make the people wearing them look alike. After all, that's the whole purpose of uniforms, but that doesn't mean that each of us isn't different, distinct, full of various emotions, love, joy, and sorrow." His voice began to quaver, so he stopped for a moment. "There," he said after a moment, "for instance: this morning my rabbit died."

"What an awful shame," said the girl.

"Poor bunny," said the fat woman.

"So sorry," said the small woman.

"And now?" asked the girl. "Will you buy a new bunny rabbit?"

"Ah, now," said the policeman, brushing away a tear, "that would be too soon. First I need to grieve, overcoming the pain so I can face reality, and only then, after all that, I might decide to buy a nightingale."

"Oh," said the small woman, "I've always wanted a nightingale."

"I'm not sure," said the fat woman, "it's such a good idea."

The girl said nothing. Everything happening in front of the basilica made her feel like she should be on her guard. Simply put, she could not believe that all these people just happened to find themselves near her, and she couldn't understand why such a large group of people would be working to draw her into a game—a game, furthermore, about which she understood nothing. And, on top of all this, the policeman had read her thoughts a moment before, after which, in fact, she was doing all she could to think about nothing at all, to be an empty mirror, until the moment came when she could slip away and leave for somewhere else. That's the way it is with stories: they could begin in Lyon and end anywhere, leaving traces everywhere along the way, just like the way a dog trots around and marks its territory. One of these days, who knows when, the story would come back this way and pick up the abandoned fragments just as a person picks ripe fruit. And when she thought of this, the girl raised her hand, signaling to the policeman and the women to stop talking.

"You don't have to talk anymore," said the girl, "because there is no rabbit, nor has there ever been a rabbit."

The women were shocked, the policeman tried to object, but the girl, with a grin, cautioned them, wagging her finger.

"There's no cause for dismay," said the girl, "because life, even though it looks as though it only belongs to us, is actually a story being told by someone else. That's why we met here in front of the basilica—there's a story for each of us in which we each play a role, but all these stories are different, and we all need to walk away from here and go find our own. The story in which we've all found ourselves is the wrong story and we got here because our storyteller was careless, but if we leave now, and if we hurry, perhaps we can all still catch the ones we really belong in. A story, after all, which begins in Lyon, needn't necessarily end there. The real basilicas are inside, not outside, of us."

10.

Nice job, said the girl to herself once the policeman and women had gone. She didn't know what she'd do, but if she was patient enough, something would occur to her. Good, she thought, I'll wait, what matters is that the story is coming to an end. The end may not seem like an ordinary ending, but then again Lyon is not an ordinary city. She understood this as she climbed up the stairs and looked for the way up to the basilica. Her legs shook with the effort, sweat coursed down her face, her throat was dry as sandpaper, and she didn't like Lyon at all, but when she got to the basilica and looked down at the city from the surrounding terrace, she believed she would stay here forever, curled up under a tree or on a bench, in a darkness she didn't fear. A story can't feel fear, it thought, it can only shiver at the thought that it might be interrupted or chased downhill, but at least as far as the latter was concerned, after the long climb, this was no longer really a cause for concern. When a path leads downhill, everything is much easier.

TRANSLATED FROM SERBIAN BY ELLEN ELIAS-BURSAĆ

PETER KRIŠTÚFEK

FROM The Prompter

The preparations for the summit took over a month. The whole of the city center, where the meeting was to be held, was completely rebuilt. Facades of disintegrating buildings were renovated and faded brickwork of old walls touched up; wooden doors received a fresh coat of paint and the statues were all restored. The result of this monumental effort was that the city now contained numerous phantom doors that led nowhere and false windows that could not be opened. However, the important thing was the final impression made: the city should fit the modern view of historical style, and come as close as possible to resembling the photographs the drunken mayor once discovered in a family album of holiday snapshots.

Of course the houses behind these splendid facades were left to rot and decay as before, because the honored visitors would never go inside.

The mayor personally arranged for the loan of brand-new buses and trams from neighboring towns, but understandably no passengers were allowed to travel in them in case they might wear out or damage the furnishings. Instead of passengers, these excellent vehicles transported dummies, which from a distance looked convincingly real. They were all fitted with mechanisms to enable them to move, and they even leaned out and waved joyfully at the foreign delegations.

Technicians from the Cinecittà and Babelsberg film studios were hired to lay down new paving in the streets. The primary aim was for these to resemble the originals as far as possible, and to produce the most genuine sounds.

The hired extras (for security reasons, of course, the hustle and bustle of normal city life was excluded from the venue of the summit) were to be organized by a world-renowned film director, whose famous name was, however, kept a closely guarded secret.

And, indeed, everything went smoothly, along these lines, looking just like the genuine article. The only problem was with the woman who'd been contracted to play the blind flower girl (the director with the famous name hadn't been able to resist including this little tribute to a certain classic auteur): having fallen ill with infectious hepatitis, she was unable to appear in the production, and they had no replacement.

The city's budget wouldn't allow for a sufficient number of extras to be hired, so the players all had to rush from one spot to another at breakneck speed, depending on where the members of the delegation happened to be at that moment. In order to achieve the most realistic effect, they were often forced to run alongside the delegates' limousines and dash through hidden passages and secret courtyards, to hide the fact that the street around the corner was entirely deserted.

While conducting sightseeing tours of the city, the guides led their foreign guests in circles around four streets, relying on their own eloquence to keep the dignitaries from noticing this deception—after all, *you only need to see a statue from three sides for the fourth to be implied!*, as the great Belgian architect Le Fantin used to say. The guests admired the "consistency" and "homogeneity" (yes, these were their exact words!) of the architecture in the capital.

On the eve of the summit itself, a banquet was held at which Prime Minister Berger was to deliver a formal speech. The grand hall in the presidential palace was filled to capacity, everyone smiling and bowing respectfully.

The Grand Inquisitor—a conservative Catholic politician with a face that seemed carved out of stone (called Gee-Aye by his friends ... and he was particularly proud of this nickname)—tapped on the window of Berger's Lincoln limousine.

"A word with you, Prime Minister!" he said in his grating voice, brooking no refusal.

Berger lowered the window.

"Yes?"

"I just want to remind you that our country stands on firm Christian foundations!" He lowered his voice and leaned close to Berger's fleshy ear. "There are an awful lot of left-wing liberals, feminists, communists, and— I'm told—even some prostitutes and homosexuals in the hall. I know that if Inquisitors Sprenger and Institoris—may God grant them lasting glory —had done their work better, more thoroughly, the whole of Europe wouldn't now be lousy with that sort of person ... but what can we do?" He raised his hands emotionally and rasped: "All I'm concerned about now is that your speech emphasize the proper values! Please keep that in mind!"

"Will do, boss!" Berger said. He rolled his window up again and leaned over to Krištof. "Did you hear that?"

The time for the speech was getting uncomfortably near. The limousine had been driven indoors and pulled up to the main table so that Berger's window was aligned with his place setting. Thus, he had a good view of everything, and could preside over this elite gathering without leaving his car.

He adjusted his diamond tiepin, cleared his throat, and tapped on a glass with a gold teaspoon. Further taps on glasses were heard as the five interpreters—Spanish, French, English, Russian, and German—discreetly followed suit. Everyone got to their feet. Except Berger, who remained sitting on the backseat of the Lincoln, smiling radiantly.

"A great day ... !" whispered the prompter. "Some days ..."

"A great day . . . !" Berger spoke up. "Some days are greater than others, of course . . . This is one of the great ones . . . One of the greatest, perhaps. But what if this day really is the greatest? Does this make the rest of our days insignificant? Less worth our whiles?"

The corner of his mouth twitched and he leaned over to Krištof, who was sitting on the seat next to him. "Can't we cut this short?" he muttered surreptitiously.

Krištof shook his head. "The punch line, sir . . . You have to give them the punch line. 'And what is greatness and insignificance?'"

"And what is greatness and insignificance?" Berger forced through his clenched teeth. "What can we measure them by? Is greatness the measure of insignificance and insignificance the measure of greatness? Or is there one standard . . ." he broke off.

The guests wriggled uncomfortably.

"That's really too much . . ." Berger exclaimed furiously, grimacing. "Shit, can't you stop feeding me this ridiculous nonsense?"

Krištof's stoical face convinced him that more nonsense must follow. The prompter shook his head.

". . . by which we must measure greatness . . . !"

". . . by which we must measure greatness . . . and another by which we must measure insignificance. But let's turn this question around . . . Let's ask ourselves, is insignificance, true insignificance a suitable measure for greatness? The answer is yes . . . without a doubt!" Berger recited, more and more disgustedly.

"The sea is great. The world is great. This is a great day! We are all great! Greater than the planet! Than the sea! Thanks to ideas! Thanks to great ideas!"

The hall filled with a storm of applause.

Krištof smiled. Berger shook his head in disbelief. He raised a glass of Mumm champagne, then hesitated for a moment before pulling the microphone towards him once more and gesturing for silence.

"Ehm ... God is great! Thank you ...!"

When all the five interpreters translated this, the applause reached new heights ... It was like a typhoon. Gee-Aye nodded in satisfaction.

Skirkaničová was the only one to look remote; to make sure no one—for heaven's sake—would be able to get a photograph of her smiling. Everyone thought she must be someone exceptionally important, given her aloofness. And they weren't far wrong.

The official banquet went as expected. A total of one hundred and forty-five bottles of Mumm champagne were drunk, along with two hundred and thirty of Piper-Heidsieck and one hundred fourteen bottles of Dom Pérignon. These—now empty—were carried away to the recycling center by one of the waiters, for which task he received a remuneration of nine hundred and ninety-six crowns.

Part of the program accompanying the summit was to be the planting of a memorial tree in the president's garden. Several of the foreign participants suggested that, given the topic of the summit ("The Sea"—despite this country being landlocked), it should be some coastal species. After an exceptionally dramatic vote, taking two long days, with the choice being made from among two hundred and fifty-six suggestions, of which fifteen reached the final round, the olive tree won in the end, because the olive branch is a symbol of peace. A few months later—on the fifteenth of February of the following year, at four in the afternoon, to be exact—the tree froze and never recovered ... but none of the participants in the summit ever learned of this.

Well, of course, the delegates couldn't forgo the traditional ceremonial ascent of Hump Hill, which rises majestically over the capital. This hill, with a height of one hundred twenty-five meters and twenty centimeters above sea level, was hardly chosen by chance. Many of the participants in the summit were of an advanced age—including Baron Salzundpeppär, who was nearly eighty—and Berger's secretary Felix didn't want to risk any of them having sudden heart failure or an asthma attack. When they reached the very top, the delegate from Austria muttered scornfully under his breath, "Well . . . At least it's above sea level!"

By contrast, the Dutch people present praised this beautiful massif, since it reminded them very much of their distinctive hills, Watchman, Dreamer, and Sleeper, created by mistake from three piles of earth during the construction of dikes to prevent flooding. As Hump evoked nostalgic memories of their homeland, all five were moved to tears and together they sang their national anthem.

The person who was happiest to reach the summit, however, was Baron Salzundpeppär himself. He particularly appreciated the beauty of the young girls in folk costumes who were keeping him company day and night.

"It's vunderful, vot your girls vill do, ven they meet a real man at last . . . !" he exclaimed enthusiastically. "I feel zo young! Zo young! Zeventy, maybe zixty-five!"

Since folk costumes are easy to take off, but hard to put on, the foyer of the Baron's hotel was crossed at regular intervals every night by half-naked maidens drifting like fairies under the gaze of the accommodating porters and receptionist, who had received strict orders not to intervene. Finally, when the summit was winding up, it was decided to convene the delegates in the bedroom of the Baron's own suite, so that the participants wouldn't be forced—as had been the case until then—to wait hours for him to appear. He presided over them in elegant striped pajamas and a velvet dressing gown, designed especially for him by Jean-Paul Gaultier.

TRANSLATED FROM SLOVAK BY HEATHER TREBATICKÁ

ANDREJ BLATNIK

FROM You Do Understand?

AND SINCE I COULDN'T SLEEP

I've left. I know I have to leave a note. I know it's not right for a girl to walk out like this after you've taken her to dinner, or rather, after you've been wining and dining her for three months, virtually every night, and after she's said, for the first time, after your nearly one hundred dinners together, that yes, tonight she would like that nightcap. I know it's hard to wake and find an empty bed when the night before you were so sure it wouldn't be empty in the morning, to wake up to an empty apartment when you thought it wouldn't have to be empty anymore. But I had to leave, I couldn't sleep, you do understand, don't you.

What can I say? That it was a lovely evening? You know that already. I always told you so. It was always lovely. That I couldn't stay? You know that too. You can see I'm gone. All those dinners—I wasn't really that hungry, you know. But it was nice afterwards, when they'd cleared away the dishes and we just sat there, chatting. I liked the way you always slowly shook your head no when I offered to pay the bill. I could have paid, you know, almost every time, not just once, but I liked your slow head shake. It made your hair undulate.

Yes, I know we'd had too much to eat already and it was time to move on to other things. That's why I said we could go to your place. But the moment we walked in through your door I knew we shouldn't have come. All that stuff in your apartment! There was no room for me. While we were out eating it was less—personal. Here, though—I don't know, maybe we should've gone to a hotel, maybe that would have worked. Like in a restaurant, you come and you go. This, though, was your home. All those things on the walls, objects you and your wife had brought back from trips. You even showed me your kids' room. Yes, that was a mistake, as I'm sure you realize. I know they're grown up and on their own. But they still have a room at your place. They can come back, anytime. And what would I do then?

I felt bad when you cried. I wish I could've been more of a comfort to you, but I couldn't. Yes, I know you care about me. I care about you, too. And I'm really sorry, because you're a nice guy. Other guys wouldn't have made up a bed for me in the living room. But I really couldn't. Sleep. Too many things. Those books that can't really belong to you. That music you never listen to. Too much for me, sorry.

You know something? I'm very full. I don't think I'll be able to eat anymore, at least not for a while. And what else is there for us to do? You're not offended, are you? You do understand, don't you?

A DAY I LOVED YOU

I lay there with my eyes closed, waiting for my husband to vacate his half of the bed. To go to work, of course. He'll get a sandwich on the corner. He'll have a coffee during his first meeting. Then he'll call home. To make sure that I'm still here, and haven't run away. I'm not going to. I'm going to open that box of old snapshots again. There were no hard drives back in those days. I'll go through it all photo by photo, and with each one think: That was a day I loved you.

THIRTY YEARS

It's awful how time changes things, she thought. Everything used to be open, it seemed like everything was still ahead of us, but then it's all over and it all comes down to a moment when there are no longer two paths in front of you.

It's awful how a man you've loved for so many years changes, she thought. His skin used to be smooth as glass and warm as cotton. Now it's furrowed like the earth and cold as ice.

It's awful how a woman who's loved someone for so many years changes, she thought. Her hand used to caress, now it holds a knife.

THE POWER OF WORDS

They say: you can't blame the tiger for eating the antelope. Eating antelopes is its nature. It's nice, being a tiger: the endless grasslands, plenty of antelopes waiting for you to get hungry. Night is coming; you'll fall asleep, sleep, and dream of being a tiger. Now test your power in a different way: explain to another tiger that an antelope is a living, sentient being. Tell him: picture this: you're not a tiger anymore, you're an antelope now, running from a tiger, your strength is failing but you run, you run, the tiger is gaining on you, you think you should've run in the other direction but it's too late now, the tiger is coming from that direction. And when your legs buckle and the tiger finally catches up, as is bound to happen, you, the antelope, say to the tiger: "You're not going to eat me, are you? Meat is murder. Your steak had feelings once, you know." And the tiger stops. Thinks. The power of words.

Andrej Blatnik **297**

CRACKS

Many stories have happened. This is one of them. You have a wife, you have kids, you have a job, you have a car, you have a house in the suburbs. It looks like you'll die happy, your children will cry at your funeral, and your neighbors will be sorry you're gone. Then one night as you're driving home in the last evaporating tendrils of light, going no faster than usual, there's a thump, you hit something. You haven't seen anything, there was just this thud against your car. You stop, you get out to see what's happened. There's a child lying under your car, seven, eight years old, you've got one just like him waiting for you at home, he could've been yours. He doesn't move. A pool of blood is forming under his head.

You cry out, bend down, feel for his pulse, find nothing. You look around, there's no one there, the street is deserted. You drive along this street every day without knowing anyone, a housing development, gray and disheveled. There's no one watching, all the lights are out.

What now? What do you do when something like this happens to you? You know: if the child were to moan a little, it would all be simple. You'd load him in your car and rush him to the hospital. Or call for an ambulance. But you can see there's nothing to save. When you calm down a little you see the streetlights haven't even come on yet. You see there are no cars in the street. You turn and look around to see if anyone's coming, if anyone's lurking behind the dumpsters, watching. But there's no one anywhere.

You'd like to call someone, but whom? Besides, your phone battery has suddenly run out and you realize that nobody would answer even if it did still work. You look at the child again. He seems to have been lying there for hours, his face has grown colorless, the blood under his head has dried. You look around again and the buildings along the street seem to be crumbling, the asphalt crackling, huge fissures appearing in the night sky, through which the void will begin to seep in at any moment. You're still holding your car keys, you look at them, you look at your car, and you know it will never move again. You drop the keys, they slowly fall into the dark beneath you and you're not even surprised when you don't hear the metal strike the asphalt. There's no sound left anywhere. No dogs barking, no televisions buzzing, no phones ringing. Again you bend over the child. He's getting tinier and tinier and more and more dried out, you look at your hands and wait for the cracks to appear on them. You think: I had a wife, I had kids, it seemed I would die happy. Now things will happen differently. Many stories don't have happy endings. This is one of them.

THE MOMENT OF DECISION

The man decides that things can't go on like this. The man realizes all the women he knows only want to be friends, even the ones who sleep over only sleep over because they've been rejected by his best friend. The man quits his job, leases his apartment. The man goes abroad. The man travels a long time and is silent, people speak to him, he answers as briefly as possible. The man is finally tired, the man stops somewhere, the man rents a room. The man watches the girl making his bed. The man feels something inside him stir, something he thought he had left far behind in the past. The man tells the girl she is beautiful. The man is glad when the girl laughs and thanks him. The man asks if she has time for a drink after work. The man is pleased when the girl says she does. The man thinks it perfectly all right when, after the drink, or rather, the drinks, the girl declines to come up to his room, or rather, the bed she has made. The man tells himself it's really too soon. The man is glad when he sees the girl in the hallway the next morning and she smiles. The man is in love. The man decides not to travel anymore, this place is just as good as the next one, or rather, better, far better. The man takes the girl out to dinner many times, out for drinks, out on trips on her days off. Then, when she has two days off, the man invites her on a longer trip. After dinner in a faraway town the man asks her if she feels like staying, like spending the night. The man is happy when she says she does. The man knows: it has to be in some other hotel chain, not hers. The man pays for the room, leaves a tip, orders drinks up to the room. The man enjoys feeling the looks of envy on his back as he climbs the stairs to their room. The man doesn't understand why the girl starts crying when she sees the bed meant for two, them, and not one, him. The man thinks: this is love, a surprise, it always catches you by surprise, and it did her too. The man tells himself: you have to live for something larger than yourself. The man walks up to her, places his hands on her shoulders. The girl looks at him, she looks at him for a long time, then she crosses herself and starts undoing her blouse. The girl asks him: will you always love me? The man thinks: yes, this is the right question for this moment. The man is happy.

THE MAN WHO DIDN'T THROW
HIMSELF UNDER A TRAIN SPEAKS

I didn't want to fall in love. But I did. It didn't work out. I remember everything. How I threw the rings I'd bought us in the river and she got scared I'd hurt her if she refused me. Each and every note I stuck behind her windshield wipers. I wrote so much, on every one of them, even though the pieces of paper were so small. I gave all of myself. Burned my bridges. My wife said I was crazy, the kids were still small, I used to have a good job, what was I thinking, roaming the city all day long. I know what I had in mind. Running into her. But I never did. And even when I did, I pretended not to see her. Because I didn't know what to say. Because she'd told me: no more. So I didn't. I didn't want to. But then, after she'd thrown herself under the train, I heard. They said I had goaded her into it. That she cried every time the phone rang. Because she always thought it was me. But it wasn't. Not always. That it was my fault. But I didn't want that. I only wanted her to hear me out. So I could tell her about us. Once and for all. One more time. But she wouldn't have any of it. She left and never said she was leaving. If she had, it would've been different. I would've told her. But I didn't. Because she didn't say. So now I go to the station, every day, to see if maybe I can leave town. My wife won't let me near the kids anymore. She has it in writing, too. It says I'm dangerous. Likely to do something. But I'm not going to do anything. It wouldn't change a thing. Maybe she never really died. I didn't go to the funeral; they said I'd better not. Maybe there never was a funeral. Maybe she's waiting at some station, waiting for me to arrive. I just don't know which train to take. I look at them and can't make up my mind. I just look.

SEPARATION

It's odd to wake up in a strange apartment. You look at the woman lying next to you. How did you get here? You can't strike up a conversation with a woman reading Coelho on the train, really. And yet, it happens. Now you're here. She's asleep. You listen: she's still breathing. It would be awful if she wasn't. Who would you call? How would you explain? As it is, everything can be repaired. On the floor, the remnants of last night, leftover food and drink. You feel like cleaning up, you don't want to be useless, last night seems to have been nice, you didn't talk much, it all went ahead without words. But: it's not easy to clean up when you're on strange turf. How do you figure out what's garbage? You used to assess strange apartments by the books and the records. Wherever you went: a quick glance cast along the bookshelves. And you knew. But you can no longer rely on that. Everyone's books and music are increasingly alike. Waste separation is the thing, now. Where do you put the paper, the glass, the organic waste? You look all around, you peer under the sink, but there are no options, just a single container. No other choice. Quietly, you put on your shoes.

SUNDAY DINNERS

A long time ago, before the war, generals, good friends of my grandfather's, used to attend my grandmother's dinners, she remembers. Those days are over; a lot of time has passed. The generals of today couldn't care less about congenial Sunday dinners; they sit in their offices, clicking on screens, they don't seem to care about my grandmother and her famous stuffed duck. Understandably, these days, my grandmother can't just sit around waiting for the next war. Frantically she hoards the ingredients for stuffed duck in her cellar, her deep freezer is full of headless bodies in plastic wrap, she's bought an oil generator because it's common knowledge that electricity is one of the first things to go in wartime, and the oil should last for a few Sunday dinners at least. On Sundays, my grandmother calls up her grandchildren, one by one. "Will you come when the war starts?" she asks. "Will you come?" We explain that there could be complications, there could be roadblocks, there could be shooting, someone might even be drafted. "I'm not eating my duck by myself," grandmother sobs into the receiver on her end, "not all by myself, dinners like that make no sense. I hate war, I hate wars like this, wars used to be *comme il faut* in the old days, they didn't interfere with my stuffed duck." Those days are over, Grandma, we explain patiently, it's all mixed up now, no one knows what it will be like when it happens. Grandmother's whimpers slowly subside, we put down the receivers and go over to our closets, concerned, wanting to make sure that everything is in place, the weapons all loaded and the safeties all off, ready, we must be ready now, nobody knows when it will happen, when it happens.

QED

"So you're saying you've traveled a lot," says the woman I met yesterday, three hours and quite a few drinks ago.

"A lot," I say. *I have, actually.*

"You must be used to everything then, nothing can come as a surprise anymore," she says.

"Nothing whatsoever," I say securely, "I'm used to absolutely everything." *Okay, more or less.*

"So you're saying that," she says, "if that kid by the bar stripped, if she dropped all her clothes on the floor, that would be something totally ordinary for you, something you've seen hundreds of times?"

I look at the kid. She's cute all right, not wearing much, but too drunk to do much of anything, she can barely hold on to the bar. *The only trick that girl's likely to pull is falling over.*

"Oh, that would just break me up," I say superciliously. "Because, you know, there are limits, I'm a decent man, there are things I can't stand, this rampant nudity everywhere, it's really disgusting—" *I'm getting into the part now, just a little more and I'll end up believing myself.*

"Oh come on," she says. "It's just skin, it's no big deal. Look."

She pulls up her shirt. *She has nothing underneath it, nothing but—*

I can't look, though it's a pleasant sight, but—*everyone can see! Is she nuts? How can they just carry on drinking, how can the guy behind the bar go on rinsing out glasses while this woman here . . . Is this normal for them? Does she do this regularly? With a different guy every time?*

She gives a mock smile, only turning up the corners of her mouth.

When I calm down a little, when my eyes stop flitting all over the place and I stop blushing, she gives me a penetrating look: "So, of all the places you've visited, which was your favorite?"

MELTING POINT

Pressing the stop button on the tape recorder, she was nervous. Legend had it that he'd slept with every woman who attended his famous pottery class, even those who didn't care for men, even those who didn't care for anyone. What would happen now that they'd done the interview? How would he make his move? His swelling ceramics bulged towards her, she felt she couldn't think straight with all those exposed, polished curves around. Legend had it that she'd never slept with anyone, not even the people who never gave interviews to anyone, the people who never gave interviews to anyone but her.

Smiling, he said: "I really enjoy listening to you, you know."

Aha, here we go. "You—you listen to the radio?"

"It's quite lonesome here in the studio for the most part—" *Getting personal.*

"—and I'm always so happy when I can fill the room with such a sensuous voice . . . like yours." *Do you really think I'm as easy as all the others?*

"The thing is, I'm rather lonely." *Sure, and I really feel for you, shithead.*

"I've had a lot of women, you know—" *I know, I know, they all know.*

"—but none of them turned out to be the right one." *Now he's going to say, "Until I met you!"*

"You're just the opposite, I hear. There haven't been many—"

Haven't been many? Who on earth could he have heard about?

"—so I'm sure that when you find one, it'll be the right one for you." *Now he's going to say, "Are you sure it isn't me?"*

"Well, it was nice of you to come by. See you around. Good-bye."

She stood in the street, listening to the recording, smart questions, evasive answers, and couldn't believe it.

That was it? Just that?

She went back and said:

"I'm sorry. Something went wrong. The tape is blank. We'll have to give it another try."

LET'S SAY THAT

Let's say that you're kissing a strange girl. Yes, things like that do happen. Let's say that you'd gone to a bar, you'd drunk even more than usual, let's say you hadn't gone along with your colleagues this time, remembering your wife sneering as you picked up your suitcase: "Do all these meetings have to end up in a strip joint? Couldn't you go, I don't know, pick up used needles around the train station instead?" So you'd thought of her and told your colleagues you wouldn't be coming with them today, and then you'd ended up in this bar. And when this girl joined you at your table because all the other seats were taken, it didn't feel wrong. And when you'd paid for the drinks and she thanked you and lightly touched your arm, it didn't feel wrong. And when you leaned close to her and spoke into her ear because it was getting noisier and noisier and her skin was nearer and nearer, it didn't feel wrong. You thought: if you look down into an abyss, there's a force that pulls you in, you can't help it, there's nothing wrong with that. But when you caressed her knee, sort of inadvertently, and then a bit more and a bit higher, you felt that there might be something there, something possibly slightly wrong. That things might not be what they seem.

Sure, you'd read that funny dating-advice book. *How can you tell the gender of your date in advance? In men, the ring finger is longer than the index finger, the knuckles are hairy, the Adam's apple is prominent, the shoulders are broader than the hips.* That sort of thing. But the bar is dark. Too dark. And you don't know if perhaps something might be terribly wrong.

These things happen, things that are terribly wrong. Your wife doesn't like you going to strip clubs, you think. But there, in a strip club, things are clear. They are what they look like. Everything's in plain sight. You're told the prices at the bar. But what about now? What now? You reach for your cell phone. No, your colleagues won't give you advice, they'll laugh at you, they'll say: "Go for it, go the whole nine yards. If you can't tell the difference it doesn't matter anyway." But it does matter. There is definitely a difference. Who can you call? What would your wife say if you called and

Andrej Blatnik 305

said: "I'm not at a strip club, and I'm not picking up used needles either, I'm kissing someone and I'm not sure—"

No, this isn't acceptable. That's why the warm lips moving up your neck fill you with dread: it's nearly closing time, and maybe even then they won't turn up the lights, maybe you'll just both rise to leave and probably that's when that little question will be posed: "Coming with me?" What do you say then? There are, as always, two options. But which one's the right one? You wish you were in a strip club with your friends, you'd know what to say, you'd say: "Check, please!" and leave, everything would be all right. When they asked you if you were coming along, you should have said: yes. Soon now the same question might get asked. And what are you going to say?

MARKS

All my lovers give me bookmarks. They seem to think I must read a lot. I put all the marks into the same book, the one I never open. When I can't sleep at night I think about how I should, how I *ought to* open it and see what I've marked. What would a story made up of only my marked pages be like? I never do, though. Perhaps I don't—or so I think when the night feels just a little too long—because whatever this story might be like, it would be about its being all over already, and about the impossibility of adding any new marks. About there not having been any sense in reading this story in the first place. Because it's all happened before. That's why I just look at the tops of the bookmarks peeking out of the book. Thinking.

TRANSLATED FROM SLOVENIAN BY TAMARA M. SOBAN

JULIÁN RÍOS

Revelation on the Boulevard of Crime

Our sulfur-scented scene is set in Paris among the marvels of the Romantic era, amid all the attractions and the crowds of curiosity-seekers who flocked to the Boulevard of Crime—or, as it's now known (melodramatically enough; perhaps in honor of its many theaters), the Boulevard du Temple; Aparicio, however, didn't hear the story until a little more than a century later, in 1969, as he was returning from London on the train, on the leg of the journey between Calais and Paris, as he was trying to photograph the dawn cloud-forests in the sky outside, through his compartment's tiny windows, when his traveling companion first broke his silence.

The stranger spoke in English, spoke in dreams—or so it appeared to Aparicio at first. Later he would come to understand that the stranger was speaking a perfect, if somewhat hesitant, and thoroughly old-fashioned, French. The story he told was equally strange, mixing extraordinary events with the most mundane details imaginable. It was in the peculiar atmosphere of their compartment—almost like a confessional—that Aparicio admitted to the stranger that he wasn't a photographer, at least not in the usual sense. Still, because he was just finishing a degree in radiology, you might say he was a photographer of interiors. The stranger, dressed in a dark oversized coat, had propped his feet on the seat across the way.

When he spoke, he didn't change position. He neither gestured nor cocked his head, but simply remained in this virtually horizontal pose. His long face stayed in shadow, making it difficult for his traveling companion to judge his age. Perhaps he's no older than me, thought Aparicio, who at that time was around thirty, tall and bony; and who, after some consideration, thought that he could discern a certain resemblance between his body and the other—the stranger's—stuck in the same compartment. The stranger unfolded his story slowly, lingering at the most unusual places . . . or so it seemed to his listener.

Aparicio repeated the whole tale to me the following summer, imitating the stranger's labored, though somehow urgent voice, as we were on call one night at Saint Mary's hospital in London. I told the story myself on the eve of a new millennium to Delsena in his studio in Paris. Throughout my narration, Delsena listened without blinking, without moving, adopting the relaxed posture of someone listening to a tall tale by the light of a campfire.

As I talked, I noticed how the white hair and dark skin of the photographer Delsena blended with the chiaroscuro of his studio—which is on Rue Daguerre—and was duplicated again, as if in a negative, by the painting hanging over the mantle of the fireplace, a painting by Mons, the tenebrist.

What Doctor Aparicio heard on the train that early morning required a certain suspension of disbelief, as it was a tale that left itself open to all sorts of criticism and conjecture—not least that it was the result of drugs, delirium, or outright fabrication. Nonetheless, thanks to Delsena, we were able to ascertain a number of years later that the events in question did indeed take place, on the Boulevard of Crime, in the afternoon hours of a splendid early May in 1838.

The protagonist of our story was a budding actor, though at one time or another he had also been a playwright, musician, painter, and had even experimented with several different branches of science. He was an indecisive young man, convinced that he would find success and a place in history no matter what discipline he turned his hand to. The only problem was, he couldn't decide on a path.

Be number one in whatever you do. This was his personal motto, his mission—instilled in him since birth.

And it was with this motto in mind that he directed his steps through the fragrant flower market on the Plaza del Château d'Eau (now called la République) on his way to the crowded Boulevard, struggling to control his impatience as he walked, contemplating the brilliant future that awaited him.

He paused before a large mirror hanging next to the door of a café, studying his artificially elongate figure and making sure that his suit still gleamed like new under the early spring sun.

He walked a few more paces and then, stopping suddenly, pulled out a handkerchief and bent down to wipe some dirt off his shoes. It was then that an old man, wearing a worn, checkered vest, stepped out from behind a water pump and sank to his knees in front of the young man. He then took our protagonist's right foot in his hands and it seemed for an instant that he was about to beg for mercy; what he did, however, was simply place the young man's foot on a black box adorned with gold ornaments and take out a large can of shoe polish that likewise gleamed in the sunlight. He promised to make the young Monsieur's shoes glisten like the glory of Solomon.

The bootblack began to practice his magic, blending his polish with saliva, rubbing back and forth, back and forth as the minutes stretched on and twelve o'clock passed, and yet the old man continued to daub at the young man's heels, even revisiting the places he'd already polished; meanwhile, with his hands at his back and his right foot balanced on the box like a statue, the young man became engrossed in the coming and going of the fiacres and cabrioles, the multicolored parade of ladies and gentlemen, women with small dogs, children with hoops, decorated soldiers, vendors who cried *Voilá le plaisir*, beggars and dentists.

The young man had plenty of time. Later he had an appointment to meet with Frédérick Lemaitre at the Théâtre des Folies-Dramatiques, who would arrange his debut as a captain of industry in the sequel to the adventures of Robert Macaire, and could even set him up as a a playwright—that is, if he wanted to talk to the celebrated actor about his sketch for a proposed play to be entitled *A Visit to Beau Brummel* (about the famous ex-arbiter of fashion, now spending his final, miserable days in an asylum in Caen).

In order to secure a role in the revue *Les Folies Dramatiques* and introduce himself to Lemaitre, the young man had had to submit himself to an affair with an infatuated *grisette*, a vile vaudevillian who called herself a ballerina, but who had both connections and influence. (You know what they say: *Lemaître bien vaut la maîtresse . . .*) Even after so many years, in that train compartment which resembled a confessional, the stranger still remembered that she was blonde and slight; that she jumped for joy whenever she received a present; that she had danced with spirited elegance in a dress made of rose percale. Her name was Rosette and she smelled of the rose water sold by a perfumist in the Rue du Faubourg Saint-Honoré. At the same time, he couldn't remember her frequent exclamation, *Hélas!*, nor any of the verses he'd composed to immortalize her.

He had other projects, of course—something in the sciences—though I'd prefer not to mention that quite yet.

By the time he reached his thirtieth birthday, he'd still been unable to settle down, was still pulled in various directions—he obsessed about mechanical laws, about celestial bodies, about terrestrial formations; his restless genius continued to encourage him to set his feet on several paths at once. He pursued various arts and explored several branches of science, because—as I've said—he was also gifted in this area.

A few years earlier he'd spent some time as a *pensionnaire* in the Villa Médicis and had vacillated between painting and the violin—he'd studied the latter under his increasingly disconcerted master, Ingres—but had soon realized that he would never be the best painter, nor violinist, in Rome; and, anyway, he had little chance by way of either discipline of paying off his debt to a certain young woman with certain cravings and her moneylending husband. As such, he decided to move back to France and follow in his father's footsteps by enrolling himself in the military school of Saint-Cyr, near Versailles. It wasn't long before he left this school, however, because—according to a gypsy who read palms and played the mandolin out in front of the cafés on the boulevard—his day of glory hadn't yet arrived, and, moreover, would never arrive via the military. Your lifeline's too long for an adventurer of that type, she pronounced in the garden of Café Turc as he tried to remove his hand from her grasp. And anyway, he hadn't followed in his father's footsteps with much conviction—since his father had never actually known he was going to be a father: the man had been promoted to grenadier captain during the Battle of Friedland, where eight thousand of his comrades lost their lives, only to die of typhus at the gates of Warsaw two months later.

Although more people die by the scalpel than the sword, occasionally he regretted abandoning his medical studies after the disillusionment he'd experienced when he couldn't heal the people dying of cholera during the cruel April of 1832. Along with his indefatigable colleague, Labrunie, he had worked tirelessly day and night. He could still remember their endless debates, the way they'd argued over actresses and the daily news, how they'd always returned to the theme of Dr. Faustus and Mephisto, to Rosicrucians and mystical transubstantiation. In vain Labrunie had tried to bring him back to reason with help from Holbach, La Mettrie, Helvétius, and other materialists and encyclopedists. Dry theories, he'd reply, theories only fit for the fire. And then he'd return the discussion to the pact Faust made with the devil, how he signed the contract with a single drop of his own blood. What nonsense, though, to waste a piece of paper on a pact with the devil, he'd thought. Selling something that doesn't exist to someone who doesn't exist. There's only one eternity open to us mortals:

posterity. And Aparicio imitated how his traveling companion had lingered over every syllable of that word. Glory is the sun of the dead, he'd recited. You have to strive to be the best at what you do. He'd repeated the words then as he'd repeated them to his stern tutor, as he'd repeated them distantly to his distant mother, totally absorbed by her devotions. You have to be number one at what you do and then you'll be remembered forever. This made perfect sense. He didn't regret that he'd spent his entire inheritance—it's too bad it was so insignificant—on this quest for glory. The goal is to remain when everything around us has vanished, he thought as he considered the crowds passing by on the Boulevard. He'd gladly trade his poor soul for enduring fame. The transaction wouldn't cause him the least inconvenience.

Perhaps he'd spoken this last thought aloud, or else the old bootblack knew whose shoe he was polishing, for he said immediately, as if it were nothing at all: "How about right now? Would you like to trade it this very moment?" The old man raised his head and, shading his face with one hand, waited for his customer's reply.

A syncopated laughter rose in the young man's throat as he considered how to respond to this joke, but the bootblack made an insistent hiss that demanded of the young man with anxious precision: You want to be number one at something, right? Yes, I want to be remembered in a hundred years, be immortalized in encyclopedias worldwide, for instance in England and Germany. That's what he'd demand before he'd barter with the old peasant, he thought, trying to hide his fear. Trying to keep his eye on the prize.

From his black, ornamental box the bootblack had removed a large book the color of old bone. (In the center of the cover was a round golden seal with the number 1768 stamped in gilt.) He opened the book and offered it to the young man who found himself face to face, as if in a mirror, with a man who had managed to pass into posterity.

It was volume seventeen of the *Encyclopedia Britannica*, and bore the date 1969, though the dazed young man couldn't comprehend what that might mean. But that was exactly the point: many years, editions, and generations would have to pass before that deceptive golden number was reached.

Nor could the young man understand what the image, engraved in copper, representing the Boulevard du Temple, completely deserted, was supposed to represent.

It's not deserted, the old man explained, because if you look here in the lower left-hand corner you'll find the man who is just now finishing having his shoes shined—frozen forever.

That's the one, the small figure there with his left foot raised, posed on the edge of the Boulevard.

We can imagine what he thought, how he felt, to see himself there, hardly the size of a pin, the shape of a miniscule *H*, a manikin, a homunculus . . .

Life had vanished from the boulevard, all movement had ceased, abandoned houses stretched toward the horizon, not a soul appeared in the doors and windows, the double lines of trees with their immobile crowns stood firm and cast shadows across an empty street from which all carriages had disappeared, the light-flooded pavement had swallowed all pedestrians and he remained alone, a tiny doll riveted in place.

It's not exactly an engraving, the old man continued amicably, even though it appears on copper, or rather, on silver-plated copper. As he spoke, the old man pulled on a robe and a black velvet biretta that gave him the appearance of an alchemist or antiquarian. Mercury works its magic and the latent image appears. It involves a new procedure that allows the perfect and permanent reproduction of images obtained using a camera obscura. He then pointed to the encyclopedia where that miniscule figure with its raised left foot appeared in its image in the middle of the page. Below the image was a caption in English that explained that this was the first man to be photographed—a new art invented by the painter and set designer Louis Jacques Mandé Daguerre, who waited a year before divulging his secrets. His patron, the learned astronomer and minister François Arago, would later refer to these images as "photographic drawings." The new art would be baptized after its inventor: "daguerreotype"—small, magical mirrors to contrast with his huge, fantastic set designs. I suppose you've seen his *Diorama*, with its spectacular views of Paris and Venice, or the burning of Edinburgh and the inauguration of Solomon's temple? But all that's already going out of style. From his elevated studio on Rue de Marais, near here, Monsieur Daguerre has been able to seize, to capture this luminous boulevard forever with his camera obscura. The image in the book doesn't do justice to the beauty of the original, the silver gray of the metallic plate, the special mirror. The *Encyclopedia Britannica* simply titles it "Paris Boulevard," but we know it's the Boulevard of Crime, or rather, Boulevard du Temple. Now it remains fixed, an empty stage. Everything that moves is in the process of vanishing, dissipating without a trace. You see, nothing that moves can be captured in the daguerreotype. That part has yet to be perfected, because right now the art requires a long exposure to light. With my modest collaboration, you sir, my young gentleman, have paused long enough to pass into posterity. That is, your image will be passed, printed, and reproduced in volume after volume, as you can see, for example in this encyclopedia from the rather interesting year of 1969.

What a lot of nonsense! the astonished young man exclaimed, gesturing in disbelief at the bootblack who'd delivered this strange monologue on the Boulevard of Crime.

Did someone drop something into my drink when I stopped for refreshment in the flower market? The witch had been so persistent that he'd drunk what she offered him just to get rid of her, as he was making his way toward the Boulevard . . .

He'd go back and review the path that had led him here detail by detail. But that would have to wait until the revelation on the Boulevard was complete.

The old man was standing in decorous silence, dressed in his new robes, suddenly a rather imposing figure.

As a last resort, it occurred to the young man that he might save himself by playing for time. The book hasn't appeared in print yet, he said. Only its future readers would be able to confirm that it's not a hallucination or the work of some sorcerer or mesmerist. In order to truly see if the book is authentic, one would actually have to be alive in 1969 and be able to physically hold the encyclopedia and read if the printed image was really the first of its kind . . .

The old man gave him a look of contempt, but he nodded in silence. So be it, he said, and disappeared.

So hell's been biding its time . . . and Delsena stirred the last embers in the fireplace.

Aparicio, who was leaning with his Kodak against the small window in the train compartment, would never forget the way he'd jumped when the dark figure confessed what his mind couldn't immediately comprehend.

I was the first person to be photographed.

The man's pompous tone was somewhat ruined by his dreamy slurring, like someone who'd had too much to drink.

And Aparicio realized he hadn't seen the stranger among the group of Englishman who had huddled together on the ferry, drinking their last beer shortly before they'd docked in Calais.

The stranger, masked in shadow, continued speaking in his monotonous, merciless voice, which seemed to be striving to make his extraordinary tale sound as insignificant as possible.

After the pact, he continued walking along that Boulevard known for its melodrama, arguing with himself out loud, pulling his hair, beating his breast, and crying out toward the azure afternoon sky.

He didn't remember his appointment with Lemaître because now he had another lord and master. One he fully intended to flee.

He indulged in countless calculations, figured that he had 47,579 days and nights before his time ran out. But perhaps he was wrong . . . Time is an illusion, an interior voice whispered.

He spent many days severely agitated, wasn't able to sleep, and at the end of the seventh night he reached a terrible conclusion: he'd never sleep again. That precious oblivion, the escape into dreams, was denied him; instead, he'd be awake day and night, alone with his conscience, suspended in perpetual nightmare. At the most, he could relax *as if* he were sleeping, like at the beginning of this train trip, which was coming to its end.

A few months after the fateful encounter on the Boulevard, he was sent to an asylum in Montparnasse run by a doctor called—and this is not a joke—"Esprit Blanche," the "white spirit." White, because his was a mind in which the darkest of thoughts could be recorded—a silver-plated surface like that in which the stranger's tiny, living image was imprisoned. The haunted mirror of Daguerre.

Time passed, and the invention of Daguerre remained a secret. Perhaps the whole thing was a cruel, elaborate joke, the work of a hypnotist disguised as a bootblack?

But the press lost no time in divulging that the renowned Daguerre was about to unveil a sensational new experiment.

Eventually, the young man began to think that if he could destroy the unique view down Boulevard du Temple that Daguerre had captured—while the old man was shining his shoes—along with the figure of his homunculus, then he could break the spell as well.

On March 8, 1839, at one in the afternoon—he'd never forget the day or the hour—he slipped into the Diorama on Rue de Marais with a candle beneath his coat and started a fire. He waited until the doors were open to ventilate the hall before crowds gathered for the evening show. The ticket seller was talking cheerfully with the doorman, allowing the young man to slip between them without attracting any notice.

The flames immediately caught the thin, colorful curtains and drapes. They began to climb and in no time at all had arrived at the fourth floor of the adjacent building, where Daguerre had his studio and laboratory. The firemen, egged on by Daguerre himself, finally arrived upon the unfortunate scene. Daguerre begged, screaming, that they should forget the Diorama and direct their hoses at his study. He threw himself boldly at the gigantic flames and was finally able to reach the narrow, smoke-filled stairway, hack his way through the garret door and, with the help of a chain of neighbors, succeed in saving his optical instruments, plans, diverse manuscripts, and some metal plates that would shortly thereafter receive the name of daguerreotypes.

The stranger had watched in dismay as his plans were ruined. He decided it was better to meet the eternal fire sooner rather than later. After a nearby wall collapsed in upon itself in a cloud of rubble and embers, making a terrible noise and eliciting numerous cries of panic, he made his way through the cloud of smoke and walked right into the spectacular flames —which, he soon realized, simply caressed his skin like a warm breeze.

It occurred to him then that if he wasn't mortal, he could at least enjoy immortality as a hero. With great effort he was able to drag a fireman with a broken leg out of the flames, and immediately thereafter rescue a volunteer who, thanks to the young man, sustained only minor burns.

In the midst of the chaos, the confusion of shouts and cries, he answered the questions of a couple of reporters and left them his name.

The following day every newspaper in Paris contained exhaustive news of the Diorama fire, which had destroyed the theater in less than a half hour, but *his* heroic action remained unanimously ignored. In vain he read and reread *Le Quotidien, La Gazette des Tribunaux, Le Constitutionnel* ...

Since he had an abundance of time ahead of him, he decided that if he was going to be number one in something that was actually worthy of being remembered, he'd have to reduce that insignificant figure on the deserted Boulevard du Temple to nothing, thereby destroying his debt and with it the pact that he had made with the old bootblack.

He traveled the world, covered every continent, and tried everything that came his way, including the most reprehensible things he could think of, for example murder, treason, and theft, not excepting such mercenary occupations as flatterer and social climber. In the grip of his ambitions he lived the high life in London, Madrid, Berlin, Rome, Prague, Brazzaville, Buenos Aires, New York, Mexico, Macau, Tokyo ...

We must have heard of him by way of one of his false personae, said Delsena. The names may have changed, however, but the man was always the same.

Time didn't fly. 1969 didn't arrive before he knew it. In a library in London, in Dillons, in Bloomsbury, he could finally touch and see volume seventeen of the same *Encyclopedia Britannica* that he'd examined with such confusion on the Boulevard of Crime one hundred and thirty-one years before.

Of course, back then he had no way of knowing that the encyclopedia had erroneously dated Daguerre's picture of the boulevard a year later than it had actually been taken. Perhaps the devil had noticed it and perhaps not. No one's perfect, Delsena commented; he'd concentrated his attention onto several trees—no doubt lindens—on the left side of the Boulevard, which didn't have any leaves in their crowns. The lindens in Paris, he said, begin to sprout leaves at the beginning of May.

Good, we've arrived, the stranger said with complete calm as the train entered the Gare du Nord. He offered his hand to Aparicio and left with his bag.

No doubt he's going to go back to the scene of the crime in time for his meeting, concluded Aparicio. A few minutes before they arrived in Paris, he'd asked the stranger: What are you going to do now? Ask for an extension, the man had said. Or perhaps not. He'd shrugged and crossed his arms. The only thing Aparicio would remember about his appearance afterwards was that his face was long and sad, and that the man was as tall and thin as himself.

He lost sight of him on the platform among the flocks of rowdy Belgians who celebrated the triumph of Eddy Merckx in the Tour, and, to a lesser extent, the arrival of a man on the moon.

TRANSLATED FROM SPANISH BY KERRI A. PIERCE

JOSEP M. FONALLERAS

Noir in Five Parts and an Epilogue

AT THE BROTHEL

Dabo Joanàs always wondered why the sign and the business cards for Chez J. Sussane had that *J* in the name. Were someone to ask him, he would have been able to say where the name "Sussane" on the façade came from, and he knew that "chez" means someone's house. Yet, while he was able to understand that "Chez Sussane" meant "Sussane's house," he just didn't understand what that *J* was doing there. Dabo Joanàs was the kind of guy who always came up with these types of questions while drinking a beer in a brothel. Which is to say that he was more interested in the world's little mysteries than in getting to know any of the girls. He should have asked about the sign the first time he came in, but he'd been struck dumb—he remembered his first impression of the place: the wide sitting room, the lamp-covered ceiling; it was bigger and better-lit inside than he could've imagined—yes, he should have asked about the sign that first time, but he was struck dumb by all of those girls in bikinis: there must have been thirty of them. That was his first impression, but it was dispelled just as quickly when he learned that quantity didn't necessarily lead to enthusiasm. It was the sheer number of girls that had left him dazzled: seeing them all there together, gathered in the lounge. None of them were, by his standard, interesting—not a single one. Yes, he should have asked Papà Cess what that *J* was for. He could think of a few explanations. He could imagine, for example, that the madam, who we may suppose was named Sussane, also answered to a *J* name, like Jacqueline or something. And so, in order not to make the place sound like a dermatologist's office instead of a brothel, she'd decided to hold back on "Jacqueline Sussane" and thus shortened her Jacqueline to *J*. Another possibility was that a long time ago there was a brothel named "Chez J.," and the new madam, determined to make her mark, but hesitant to make too much of a change, simply added her "Susanne" to the house's old J.

Anyway, Dabo Joanàs didn't ask about it. Papà Cess would just have confirmed whatever suspicions Dabo Joanàs had by providing him with the real truth; or maybe he would have thrown a new hypothesis into the mix. Maybe he would even have told him that the madam wasn't the aforementioned Susanne at all but that a brothel just gets called whatever the hell you want to call it. "What's important about a brothel is that you can fuck there," Papà Cess would have said. He was fat and tough, extraordinarily tough. He'd still be a bouncer at the front door if it weren't for his age. Now he serves beer from behind the bar. After a while, he became Dabo Joanàs's confidant. And he can still remember the first conversation Dabó Joanàs ever had with a whore. "You asked where the fuck she was from—and she didn't understand you at first. Then she told you that she was from Romania, and you told her that Romania is really beautiful, and that you'd been to Lake Constance. And, shit, she didn't say anything because there's no Lake Constance in Romania: you made it up."

Dabo Joanàs had confused Lake Constance—which is located at the border between Germany, Austria, and Switzerland—with the Port of Constantza, which is in fact in Romania. But what happened is that the girl, uninterested in anything that wasn't a direct request to retire to one of the upstairs bedrooms, just looked at Dabo Joanàs with an expression best described as stupefied.

Josep M. Fonalleras **321**

Thus went Dabo Joanàs's life at the brothel: sitting at the bar, asking girls where they were from, and then relating some misremembered feature of their homeland to some similarly named but unrelated location. Not one of them ever asked him where he was from in turn. It would only have annoyed him. Reis Pequés—who also sometimes tended bar, her eyebrows retraced with eyeliner, her upper lip bearing the slight suspicion of a moustache—asked him once whether it was true that he'd been a journalist in Belgrade. Dabo had answered yes . . . and said that it was never to be brought up again.

JANA POLAN

Jana Polan was German and had once been Dabo Joanàs's lover. She was a photographer and a war correspondent in the Balkans and in Belgrade, where she met Dabo Joanàs, who was working as a translator at the time. Their relationship didn't last long: Jana Polan was also keeping company with a dentist from Stuttgart, a fact she confessed to Dabo Joanàs, after which—knowing then that he was only sharing her affections—he stormed into the hotel she was staying at and beat her up in front of whatever guests happened to be in the bar at the time. Jana Polan had known that her relationship with the dentist wasn't going anywhere. He was married and didn't have any intention of destroying his social status by cutting himself loose from his "ball and chain"—though, as tends to happen in such situations, he had indeed promised Jana Polan that he would separate from his wife and move in with her.

She hadn't counted on her affair with Dabo Joanàs going any further than a few intense but sporadic rolls in the hay. She hadn't counted on Dabo Joanàs reacting so violently to her confession. This incident ended up being a definitive push toward a decision she had already half made in her mind: to leave the Balkans.

Back in Germany, after taking a few days off, she decided that she'd do a report on the lives of truck drivers who take on international routes. She got the green light from her boss and joined a driver who was delivering oranges to Valencia. The driver was actually the owner of a small fleet he'd christened with a rather pretentious name: NO TIES TRUCKING. He thought it gave an impression of competence, let people know they could handle any freight or travel any distance. Nevertheless, his entire empire—if we can use this expression, since it was really a rather small and modest empire—had been founded, naturally enough, on loads having been tied down in the back of his trucks . . . and he accepted this contradiction with conviction and ignorance in equal measure. The driver's name was Nam Plujao: he was from Hong Kong. He hardly knew a word of German, and even less of anything even slightly resembling a Romance language.

Jana Polan saw all of Europe at Nam Plujao's side. After submitting her article, with its photographs of highways and truck stops, of the restaurants and hostels where they'd eaten and slept, of Nam Plujao's Chinese customs, of the cab of his truck, of the kilometers they'd crossed, Jana Polan continued to hang around Nam Plujao. She rode with him a second time—this time for sport, like a game. It was the worst decision of her life.

THE POLICE

"The identified vehicle, a Mercedes-Benz Atego 1223 L, 4×2, white, Dortmund plates, was discovered unoccupied at the 735.6 kilometer mark on highway N-11. The vehicle was on the highway meridian and showed no evidence of having suffered an accident or any type of violent intervention. The following items were found in the truck: a cargo of tin toys, one mustard-green backpack, and a scribbled note reading: JUA REME PSO D. Said vehicle matched data previously received from the Criminal Investigation Unit, which intervened at this stage, ending the involvement of the Highway Patrol. This report will be incorporated into file 9/foundry/07."

"Excerpt from file 9/foundry/07: Two bodies, both Caucasian, were found in the forested region of the township of Mediynà. Two females: one of the women approximately forty years of age, the other approximately twenty, the first wearing a white T-shirt and jeans, the second a black leather mini-skirt and a top with straps, also black. Evidence of violence and probable cause of death in both subjects: deep wounds in the front cranial regions, severing of spinal cords."

THE TIN TOYS

Jana Polan was sure that the purpose of Nam Plujao's current trip was to collect a shipment of tin toys in order to take them to Belgium. And it actually was. She saw for herself how they loaded the toys into the truck and how Pim Jo Saleveros, a Vietnamese employee whose mother was from Brazil, checked over the order. Once all of the paperwork was done, the three of them got in the truck for the return trip. Jana Polan found something magical about these long hauls—they soothed her. She'd had plenty of experience with complicated situations and so wasn't in the least bit anxious about whatever unexpected problems might crop up on the trip. She was more interested than ever in the kind of life that truck drivers led. She was even thinking about expanding her original article into a novel. A documentary novel, a verisimilar one filled with real faces and protagonists made of flesh and bone—not a historical novel full of bizarre museums where nonsensical characters dig out medieval mysteries thanks to the help of just-as-bizarre archives; not a novel full of political conspiracies and corrupt lawyers; not a novel stuffed with the kind of literary detritus that a common reader wouldn't even be able to follow ... No. A novel about a truck driver. Jana Polan honestly thought that writers shouldn't be people who stay at home being quietly astonished by the perplexities of the world, but out in the world, wading through it themselves. What she didn't realize was that it was just as possible to be preoccupied with all those perplexities when you were on the move. She'd heard noises in the truck on their way to pick up the toys. They sounded like groans. She didn't pay any attention. The two truckers had the radio on, and the music was always up loud. They screamed over it when they talked to each other. On the way back, she heard the moans again. She decided they were coming from the tin toys rubbing against each other.

She had no way of knowing that there was another passenger inside the truck.

CHARLEMAGNE'S RING

The real shame of it all is that Jana Polan was never able to write about all the things she experienced that afternoon: it would have been exactly the real-life story she wanted; the violence with which the Vietnamese with Brazilian roots (or was it the other way around?) forced the other girl out of the truck; how he dragged her by her hair and told her that she had no rights whatsoever, that she'd do whatever she was told, and that she'd better keep her mouth shut. But the girl fought back. That's when Jana Polan came on to the scene, and became another victim of Pim Jo Saleveros.

The last image that Jana Polan's mind retained, the last image of her life, was the serene visage of Nam Plujao. She would have put an excellent description of it into her novel.

At the brothel, Dabo Joanàs didn't usually get into conversations with other clients. One night, however, he asked Nam Plujao and Pim Jo Saleveros whether they'd ever heard of Lake Constance. "It's not in Romania," he said, "it's at the border between Germany, Austria, and Switzerland." Then, he told them about the legend of the lake.

It was when he was telling them that Charlemagne had fallen in love with the lake, and that he'd stayed there gazing into it forever and ever, that two police officers entered Chez J. Sussane to ask Papà Cess and Reis Pequés if they had ever heard of NO TIES TRUCKING and Jana Polan; they wanted to know if they might somehow be able to connect the murder of the two women with that piece of paper, tossed like a ring into a lake, that read JUA REME PSO D.

AN EPILOGUE

Dabo Joanàs asked one of the prostitutes if she was Romanian. She said yes. He made another reference to Constance and wondered what type of foundry made rings like the one that still rests at the bottom of that lake.

TRANSLATED FROM CATALAN BY ROWAN RICARDO PHILLIPS

PETER STAMM

Ice Moon

It wasn't until I locked up my bike that it dawned on me that something had been out of the ordinary. I went back on foot to the entrance of the industrial compound and saw that the blinds of the gatehouse were closed. I had forgotten in the Christmas confusion that Biefer and Sandoz would go into retirement at the end of the year. At the beginning of December somebody had collected money for a good-bye gift. I had thrown in some money and signed two cards and then thought no more about it. Now I was sad that I hadn't said good-bye to them.

A map of the complex was glued on the glass door of the gatehouse. Under that was a list of emergency telephone numbers. The fire department, the police, the ambulance, and the number of the administrator. He'd written that he wished all his renters a Happy Holidays and a Happy New Year. The notice was decorated with a clipart picture: a Christmas tree branch and candle.

Formerly, hundreds of people had worked in this factory, but after production and, later, development were both outsourced overseas, the complex emptied until only the two gatekeepers remained. The business itself became a holdings company and moved into offices near the train station. The old brick buildings on the lakeshore stood empty for a long time before being rented out room by room. Artists, architects, and graphic designers now work in the development lab. In the weighing office, a former factory worker had opened a small bar where we would meet at noon for a sandwich or coffee. A violin maker and a cabinetmaker had set up shop in the production wing, and a few start-ups too, though no one really knew what they did. A number of rooms, briefly rented, were already empty again.

The complex had a spectacular location, being on the lake, and every few months there was talk in the newspapers of huge projects in the works, of luxury apartments, a casino, or a shopping center. But they never found the necessary investors. We all had short-term leases that were regularly renewed whenever one of these projects fell apart. The administrator still occasionally showed up with a group of men in dark suits, and we would see them standing around outside, leveling and re-building whole structures with flamboyant gestures. The gateman who was on duty at the time would follow the groups through the complex at a distance and only approach when there was a door to unlock. At first these tours had always led to wild speculation and rumors among us renters, but after a while no one seemed to believe that anything would ever change.

When I came to work in the morning, one of the gatemen would already be there. Biefer mostly sat in the gatehouse, glassed-in on three sides, smoking his pipe and reading the paper. Sandoz would stand outside even in extreme cold, his hands in his coat pockets.

In the early days, the two would hand out the mail, but after we got our own mailboxes, they only received the occasional large package or told a bicycle courier how to find our studios. They took down the numbers of improperly parked vehicles, and sometimes you'd see them walking around the complex, a massive key ring in one hand and a stick for picking up trash from the disused tracks in the other. Still, they were mostly stationed at the gate, which was now always left open, observing silently who entered the complex and who left.

You never saw Biefer and Sandoz together. One relieved the other around noontime and they seemed to be careful not to run into each other. At first I couldn't tell them apart, though they couldn't have been any more different. They were only physically similar, both being short and stocky with thinning hair. They both wore a blue uniform. When the weather was bad Sandoz would also wear a black coat and hat made out of synthetic leather. He originally came from French Switzerland, and though he'd already worked here for more than thirty years, he spoke with a strong accent. He was moody: some days he would talk nonstop, but then he would hardly say a word the next, and, when you greeted him, he would act as if he didn't know you. Biefer, on the other hand, who was local, was almost too friendly. Whenever I ran into him he inquired about my children, whom he'd seen once or twice. We would talk about the weather, about soccer, about local politics. He rarely spoke about himself or his family. He occasionally mentioned his wife in some passing remark. Only once did he tell me about his sons, who lived abroad.

On a cold, foggy morning maybe two months ago, Biefer stopped me. From a distance I had only seen his dark silhouette next to the gatehouse and I'd assumed it was Sandoz. It took until I was very near for me to recognize Biefer. I was waving to him when he raised his hand like a police officer. I stopped my bike next to him, and he asked if I could help with something. I asked what he needed help with. "Not here," he said in a conspiratorial tone, turning around.

I'd never been in the gatehouse before. In spite of the big, inward-leaning window, the room had a cozy feel. The little oil heater gave off a dry heat, and it smelled sweetly like pipe smoke. Biefer sat down at his console and opened a drawer. He took out a beat-up briefcase and laid it in front of himself without opening it. Then he stood up abruptly and poured two cups of watery coffee without first asking if I wanted any. He handed me a cup and pointed to a plate with rolls on it in front of him.

"Honey cakes," he said, "if you like those."

There was only one chair. Biefer had sat down, so I stood behind him in the shadows and looked down at his wide head, at the stringy gray hairs between which the rosy skin of his scalp could be seen. He filled his pipe but didn't light it. He seemed not to know where to begin. More than once he started speaking, got muddled, coughed. In between he would wave to the people driving into the complex. He said he'd originally been a baker but had had to give up the profession because of an allergy to flour. He always loved to travel. Sports, on the other hand, didn't interest him. Outside of soccer, of course. He said he'd married young. At the time that was the custom. He didn't regret anything. He said that several times. He didn't regret anything.

After a few minutes of talking like this, I finally understood what it was all about. At the end of the year, when he retired, Biefer wanted to emigrate to Canada and open a bed-and-breakfast there. I asked, why Canada, of all places?, but Biefer didn't reply. He talked about the visa application he'd sent in months ago, about a points system: in addition to education and knowledge of French and English, age and financial assets played a role. Not long ago he'd received a letter from the Canadian embassy in Paris that he didn't understand. He said that he hadn't spoken any French since school, and that was fifty years ago now. He'd been taking English courses for a few months, but he was just too old to learn yet another language. He opened the light brown briefcase, took out the topmost sheet, then closed the briefcase again. He handed me the letter. In complicated French legalese, the applicant was requested, further to the completion of his dossier, to send an up-to-date list of all his assets as well as the appropriate documentation, which would all have to be sent on the same date. When I explained what it meant to Biefer, he seemed relieved. He asked me not to tell anyone about his plans, least of all Sandoz.

I had nearly forgotten about it when Biefer stopped me again a few weeks later. He made a conspiratorial face and motioned for me to follow him into the gatehouse. It was shortly before Christmas and on the console was a sparse arrangement of Christmas tree branches, two silver ornaments, and a thick, unlit candle. Next to this was the light brown briefcase. Biefer opened it, took out a sheet, and handed it to me, beaming. His visa application had been accepted. He thanked me for my help. I said that it really wasn't worth mentioning. He hesitated and then opened the briefcase once more and left it lying open in front of us. Inside was a red envelope from a photo lab. Biefer took out a stack of pictures and laid them slowly and carefully next to each other on the desk. The photographs hardly differed from one another. A forest could be seen in all of them, short trees and scrub, and sometimes a gravel road in the foreground. Biefer's hands hovered over the photos, making him look like a fortune-teller trying to read the future from cards. That was his land, he finally said, in Nova Scotia. He took some papers from the briefcase and spread them out in front of us—a deed of purchase, a passport, a plane ticket, a tourism brochure, and some post cards. At the bottom of the briefcase was a land survey on which an irregularly formed lake and a few tracts of land were plotted, all covered over with handwritten notes. One of the tracts had been circled carefully in red marker. In the middle of the property two rectangles had been drawn on in pencil, under which I saw the traces of previously erased attempts. He would build his house there, Biefer said, a cabin with ten guest rooms and a large lounge, with his apartment on the floor above. The small rectangle would be the garage.

Though I was standing next to him, I couldn't see his face while he explained the project to me, but his voice sounded enthusiastic and full of energy. He said he'd bought the property years ago: ten thousand square meters for thirty thousand Canadian dollars. True, he wouldn't have direct access to the lake, but the property was on the main road, which would be good for business. At the end of the year he'd fly to Halifax. From there it'd be two hours by car. He'd already been there a year ago. The area was absolutely beautiful: sure, a little secluded, but there was a lot of potential. A paradise for hunters and fishermen.

I couldn't imagine Biefer in the Canadian forests. He was pale, his face was bloated, and he didn't seem very healthy. But he kept going on and on about his land and about Nova Scotia. The area was as far south as Genoa, he said. In the summer it could get warmer than thirty degrees Celsius. The winters, however, were cold and snowy. He said that building permits were easy to come by, and gas cost only half of what we paid for it here.

I asked him why he wanted to move away in the middle of winter, whether it wasn't cold enough for him here. He said it was because he wanted enough time to prepare everything for the tourist season in the summer. Of course the forest would have to be cleared first thing and then the house would have to be built. There was a lot to do. He said that the moving company was coming after the holidays. The contents of his entire house would be loaded in boxes and shipped off. Until the new house was built he would have to store the stuff. I asked him where he would live until his departure. He looked at me as if he'd never thought about that. "And your wife?" I asked. What did she think of these plans? He said that they weren't plans, they were done deals. Before I left, he asked me again not to tell anyone.

As I exited the gatehouse, I saw Jana, a young artist who had her studio on the same floor as me. She rode her bike over, braking at the last moment and coming to a stop a few centimeters in front of me. She grinned at me and asked if I was playing gateman now. Why not, I said. It wouldn't be the worst job. "Not stressful. And you get a fixed income."

"I'm really going to miss those two," she said. "Especially Erwin."

She got off her bike and walked with me to the entrance of the old development building. She said she'd been one of the first ones in the complex. Back then nothing worked. The heat would shut off for a while and sometimes the power too. She'd had a lot to do with the two gatemen at the time. Erwin had helped her a lot. He was an unbelievably nice guy.

The empty gatehouse was depressing. I didn't miss Biefer or Sandoz, but I had always been happy that there was somebody there when I came to work in the morning, someone who unlocked the door and turned on the lights, someone who began the day. Now the place seemed dead. The façades of the old buildings seemed even more uninviting than usual and there were no lights in any of the windows. Sooner or later it would all be cleared away. We were only guests there: our days were numbered, even if we acted as if we owned the place.

The violin maker parked his car. I waited for him at the entrance and we chatted a bit. He asked whether I liked it here, and I said it was just a temporary setup for me. At some point I was sure to leave this city. He said he'd stay as long as he could. He'd never find such a suitable studio again. While we were talking, Jana arrived, as did a journalist who had moved into the floor below us a few weeks before. We got to talking about Biefer and Sandoz. The journalist said he'd never been able to tell them apart. I asked what we'd ended up buying them as a going-away present. No one knew.

I had made a lunch appointment with a client. It was with regard to the construction of a double garage, my first job in months. We ate in a restaurant in the city. When I came back to the complex at two, the fog had finally begun to lift. I went down to the shore of the lake and looked out over the smooth, clear water. I was suddenly quite sure that I would never get away from here, that I would have to remain here until the end of my days, building garages and little one-family houses, or, if I had some luck, a kindergarten or a multiple-family house. We would all stay here, the violin maker, the journalist, Jana, and the others. Biefer was the only one who would manage to get away. Jana sat alone in the old weighing office bar and read the newspaper. I grabbed a coffee and sat with her. She thumbed back a few pages, folded the newspaper in the middle, and handed it to me over the table.

"Have you read this?" she asked and pointed to an obituary.

"Gertrud Biefer," I real aloud: "After a serious illness, which she bore with great patience, our beloved wife, mother, and grandmother passed away on December 27th. A memorial was held for the family and close friends."

"That must be Erwin's wife," said Jana. "His name's written there. And those two below it, they must be his sons."

She said it was crazy. Now that he finally had time to enjoy life. He'd often talked about trips he wanted to take after his retirement.

"He's made plans to emigrate to Canada," I said. Jana said she couldn't imagine that, since his wife was so sick.

"I'm sure of it," I said. "I helped him with the papers. He showed me the letter from the embassy and pictures of his property in Nova Scotia."

Jana said again that she couldn't believe it. I said she should call him up if she didn't believe me, but she said it wasn't really any of our business.

"Do you know where he lives?"

Jana shook her head. She said she'd look it up in the telephone book and send him a sympathy card.

The next morning the weather was so unfriendly that I went to work on foot. The fog was as thick as nearly every morning this time of year, but even from a distance I could see that there was light in the gatehouse. The blinds were up, and at the console sat Erwin Biefer in his blue uniform. He looked the same as ever, only he wasn't smoking, and he wasn't reading the paper. I moved closer and waved at him. He looked straight ahead as if he hadn't noticed me. I knocked on the glass, but he still didn't react. His eyes were half closed and the corners of his mouth were raised. He looked as if he were smirking, or beginning to cry. I waved again. When he still didn't react, I moved on. Maybe an hour later someone knocked at the door to my office. It was Jana. She asked if I'd seen Erwin.

"I knocked on the glass," I said. "It was like he didn't see me."

Jana thought we should notify someone, a doctor or the police or at least the administration. I said that I thought it'd be better to wait it out. "He lost his wife. I can understand why he doesn't want to sit around the house."

In the old weighing office that afternoon, Biefer was the only topic of conversation. Everyone had seen him and were now discussing what was to be done. The room was filled with smoke. When somebody came or went a gush of cold winter air rushed in. The man who ran the bar turned the music down and joined the discussion. He'd known Biefer the longest. He said he'd tried to open the door to the gatehouse, but it was locked. It would have to be broken down, if it came to that. I didn't say anything about Biefer's plans to emigrate, and when Jana wanted to mention it, I made a gesture and shook my head. Suddenly someone called, "There he is!" and pointed out the window. Outside, Biefer shuffled past, looking straight ahead. He was only wearing his blue uniform, and his face was white from the cold. We were silent for a moment. Then the journalist suggested someone go out and try to speak with him. Who knew him best? We all looked at each other. Finally Jana said she'd try it.

We stood at the window and watched how she walked alongside Biefer and talked to him. He didn't say anything back, just looked forward and kept going. After a while, Jana came back. She said it didn't make any sense. Erwin seemed not to have noticed her at all. The journalist doubted there was much we could do. Biefer was a free man. No one could force him to speak with us if he didn't want to. Someone could tell the administration if we decided that was necessary. But everyone agreed this was a bad idea. We decided to wait and see. A little meekly, we returned to work.

From then on, Biefer was there every day. He sat at his accustomed place most of the time, wandering through the complex only occasionally. Jana tried to speak with him a few more times. Finally she gave up. She told me her sympathy card had been sent back to her in the mail with a note that the addressee had moved without giving a forwarding address. We decided to spend one of the next evenings in the violin maker's studio, which had the best view of the gatehouse. We wanted to watch Biefer and see where he went.

The violin maker opened a bottle of wine and drank a glass with us. At seven he gave us the key and told us he was heading home. Jana and I sat down at the window, drank the wine, and looked over at the gatehouse. We had turned off the light to be able to see better and in order not to be seen in turn. Although we'd known each other a long time, we'd never exchanged more than a few words. Now Jana began to talk about her childhood in a mountain village and how she'd left at sixteen to take her oral exams. Since then she'd barely had any contact with her family. She would drive to their town once a year at most. Her parents couldn't understand her art, and she'd never said a word to them about her living with a woman. She could imagine how they'd react. I asked what kind of art she did anyway. She said it was hard to explain, but she'd be happy for me to visit her in her studio. Then she'd show me the stuff she made. We were already pretty tipsy and Jana laughed and said we should invite Erwin to have a glass of wine with us. Then we were quiet and looked out the window. The moon had risen, almost as full and light as the snow. Its light outshone every one of the floodlights that lit the abandoned site. In the snow was a complicated pattern of foot and car tracks. Over there, in the window of the gatehouse, the little lamp was still burning.

"Have you noticed the look in his eyes?" Jana asked. "Like he's far away."

"I wonder why he wanted to go to Canada of all places," I said.

"The main thing is having a goal," Jana said.

At eleven, Biefer stood up and turned off the light. Then nothing else happened. We waited a bit, but when he didn't come out, we finally went home.

January was unusually cold that year. Ice formed at the lakeshore, though the waves broke it up again. The wind pushed the chunks over one another, forming odd landscapes that were strikingly beautiful. The snow, which had fallen shortly after Christmas, remained on the ground, becoming tightly packed and dirty. In some places in the complex, it had frozen into a thick sheet of ice. On the rare occasions Biefer would leave the gatehouse at all, he would move very slowly, almost without lifting his feet from the ground.

Then, one day toward the end of the month, he disappeared. When I came to work in the morning, there was no light in the gatehouse, though the blinds were raised. The door was unlocked. I opened it cautiously and went in. It still smelled like pipe smoke, but the heater was cold. It took some time before I found the light switch. The door to the back room wasn't locked either. It was tiny. There was a thin rubber foam mattress on the floor. Otherwise there were no signs that anyone might have been living here. I went back to the front room, started the oil heater, and sat down at the console. I waited. I didn't know what for. When a car drove into the complex I instinctively raised my hand and greeted the driver. It got warmer. Dawn came, but the sky was still gray and solid. Around ten, Jana arrived. I waved to her, and she put her bike away and came inside to meet me.

"Has he left?" she asked.

"I was waiting for you," I said.

She stood behind me, as I had stood behind Erwin Biefer a month before. She laid a hand on my shoulder. I turned to her and she nodded at me. Now, for the first time, as if I'd been waiting on a witness, I opened the drawer. I was not surprised to find the light brown briefcase in it.

TRANSLATED FROM GERMAN BY DUSTIN LOVETT

DEBORAH LEVY

FROM Swimming Home

We realized my friend and I
That the little car had driven us into a new era
And although we were both already mature men
We had just been born

[GUILLAUME APOLLINAIRE]

A MOUNTAIN ROAD. MIDNIGHT.

When Kitty Finch took her hand off the steering wheel and told him she loved him, he no longer knew if she was threatening him or having a conversation.

She was driving too fast. He dared not look down at the waterfalls roaring against the rocks or the uprooted shrubs that clung to the sides of the mountain. Sex had brought them to the edge of something. His tongue tasted of her. Her hipbones had gored into him. Her silk dress was falling off her shoulders as she bent over the steering wheel.

He smoothed down his hair and glanced at his watch. A rabbit ran across the road and the car swerved.

He heard himself say, "Why don't you pack a rucksack and see China like you said you wanted to?"

"Yes," she said.

He could smell petrol. Her hands swooped over the steering wheel like the seagulls they had counted from their hotel room two hours ago.

She asked him to open his window so she could hear the insects calling to each other.

He wound down the window and told her, gently, to keep her eyes on the road.

"Yes," she said again, her eyes now back on the road.

He leaned his head out of the window and felt the cold air sting his lips. Early humans had once lived in this mountain forest. They knew the past lived inside their bodies and in rocks and trees and they knew desire made them awkward, bad, mysterious. This was the road they were on, cut from these ancient memories. Was having sex with Kitty Finch a transgression or a mistake? When he was fifteen he had very lightly grazed his left wrist with a razor blade. Nothing serious. Just an experiment. The blade was cool and sharp. His wrist was warm and soft. They were not supposed to be paired together. It was a teenage game of Snap. He had snapped. Like the razor blade and his wrist, sex with Kitty Finch had been a perverse pleasure and a pain, but most of all a mistake. He stared miserably at his watch again and asked her to please drive him safely home to his wife and daughter.

"Yes," she said, and thumped her foot on the accelerator. "Life is only worth living because we hope it will get better and we'll all get home safely."

Deborah Levy **339**

■ ■ ■

The swimming pool on the grounds of the tourist villa was more like a pond than the languid blue pools in holiday brochures. A pond in the shape of a rectangle, carved from stone by a family of Italian stonecutters living in Antibes.

The body was floating near the deep end where a line of pine trees kept the water cool in their shade.

"Is it a bear?" Jonathan Mines waved his hand vaguely in the direction of the water. He could feel the sun burning into the shirt his Hindu tailor had made for him from a roll of raw silk. The silk was too raw. His back was on fire. Even the roads were melting in the July heat wave.

His daughter Nina Mines, thirteen years old, standing at the edge of the pool in her new cherry-print bikini, glanced anxiously at her mother. Rachel Mines was unbuckling her watch as if she was about to dive in. From the corner of her eye she could see Mitchell and Laura, the two family friends sharing the villa with them for the summer, put down their bags and walk towards the stone steps that lead to the shallow end.

Laura, a slender giantess at six foot three, kicked off her sandals and waded in up to her knees. A battered yellow inflatable mattress knocked against the mossy sides, scattering the bees that were in various stages of dying in the water.

"What do you think it is Rachel?"

Nina could see from where she was standing that it was a woman swimming naked under the water. She was on her stomach, both arms stretched out like a starfish, her long hair floating like seaweed at the sides of her body.

"Jonathan thinks it's a bear," Rachel Mines replied in a detached war-correspondent voice.

"If it's a bear I'm going to have to shoot it." Mitchell had recently purchased two antique Persian handguns at the flea market in Nice and shooting things was on his mind.

Yesterday they had all been discussing a newspaper article about a sixty-four kilo bear that had walked down from the mountains in Los Angeles and taken a dip in a Hollywood actor's pool. The actor had called the authorities, the bear was shot with a dart and then released in the nearby mountains. Jonathan Mines had wondered out loud what it was like to be tranquillised and then have to stumble home? Did it ever get home?

Nina watched her mother dive into the murky green water and swim towards the woman. Saving the lives of bloated floating bodies in rivers was probably the sort of thing her journalist mother did all the time. She disappeared to Northern Ireland and Lebanon and Afghanistan and then she came back as if she'd just nipped down the road to buy a pint of milk. Her hand, magnified under the water, was about to clasp the ankle of whomever it was floating in the pool. A sudden violent splash made her run to her father who grasped her sunburnt shoulder, making her scream out loud.

When a head emerged from the water, its mouth open and gasping for breath, for one panicked second, Nina thought it was roaring like a bear.

A woman with dripping waist-length hair climbed out of the pool and ran to one of the plastic recliners. She looked like she might be in her early twenties, but it was hard to tell because she was frantically skipping from one chair to another searching for her dress. It had fallen onto the paving stones but no one helped her because they were staring at her naked body.

Nina felt light-headed in the fierce heat. The bitter sweet smell of lavender drifted towards her, suffocating her as the sound of the woman's panting breath mingled with the drone of the bees in the wilting flowers. It occurred to her she might be sun-sick because she felt as if she was going to faint. In a blur she could see the woman's breasts were surprisingly full and round for someone all made from bones. Her thighs were joined to the jutting hinges of her hips like the dead legs of the dolls she used to bend and twist as a child. The only thing that seemed real about the woman was the triangle of golden pubic hair glinting in the sun. It was somehow an obscene intervention in the design of her. A suggestion that she could be explored and entered, a thought that made Nina fold her arms across her chest and hunch her back in an effort to make her own body disappear.

"Your dress is over there." Jonathan Mines pointed to the pile of crumpled blue cotton lying under the recliner.
They had all been staring at her for an embarrassingly long time.
The woman grabbed it and deftly slipped the flimsy dress over her head.
"Thanks. I'm Kah ... Kah ... Kitty Finch by the way."
She stumbled on her name as if she was trying to remember it.

Nina realised her mother was still in the pool. When she climbed up the stone steps, her wet swimming costume was covered in pine needles.
"I'm Rachel Mines. My husband thought you were a bear."
Jonathan Mines dragged his hands through his hair and glared at his wife.
"Of course I didn't think she was a bear."

■

Kitty Finch twisted her lips in what might have been an effort not to laugh. Her eyes were grey like the tinted windows of Mitchell's hired car, a Mercedes, parked on the gravel at the front of the villa.

"I hope you don't mind me using the pool. I've just arrived and it's sooo hot. There's been a mistake with the rental dates."

"What sort of mistake?" Laura glared at the young woman as if she had just been handed a parking ticket.

"Well, I thought I was staying here from this Saturday for a fortnight. But the caretaker . . ."

"If you can call Jean Paul a caretaker," Laura interrupted with disgust.

"Yeah. Jean Paul says I've got the dates all wrong and now I'm going to lose my deposit."

Mitchell wagged his finger at her.

"There are worse things than losing your deposit. We were about to have you sedated and driven up to the mountains."

Kitty Finch lifted up the sole of her left foot and slowly pulled out a thorn.

"It won't be the first time I've been sedated."

Her grey eyes searched for Nina who was still hiding behind her father. And then she smiled.

"I like your bikini."

Her front teeth were crooked, snarled into each other and her hair was drying into copper coloured curls.

"What's your name?"

"Nina."

"Do you think I look like a bear, Nina?" She clenched her right hand as if it was a paw and jabbed it at the cloudless blue sky.

Her fingernails were painted dark green.

■

Nina shook her head and then swallowed her spit the wrong way and started to cough. Everyone sat down. Mitchell on the ugly blue chair because he was the fattest and it was the biggest, Laura on the pink wicker chair, Rachel and Jonathan on the two white plastic recliners, Nina perched on the edge of her father's chair, avoiding his long toenails. They all had a place in the shade except Kitty Finch who was crouching awkwardly on the burning paving stones.

Rachel wrung the ends of her wet black hair.

"You haven't anywhere to sit. I'll find you a chair."

"Oh don't bother. Please. I'm just waiting for Jean Paul to come back with the name of a hotel for me and I'll be off."

"Of course you must sit down."

Laura, puzzled and uneasy, watched Rachel lug a heavy wooden chair covered in dust and cobwebs towards the pool. There were things in the way. A red bucket. A broken plant pot. Two canvas umbrellas wedged into lumps of concrete. She was making a place for Kitty Finch. Rearranging the space that had been claimed for the last two weeks by all of them. She was actually placing the wooden chair between her recliner and her husband's.

"Thank you." Kitty wiped it down with the skirt of her dress and sat down.

Laura folded her hands in her lap.

"Have you been here before?"

"Yes I've been coming here for years."

"Do you work?" Jonathan spat an olive pip into a bowl.

"Yes, I sort of work. I'm a botanist."

"Ah. There are some nice peculiar words in your profession."

He stroked the small shaving cut on his chin and smiled at her.

■

"Jonathan likes pe-cu-li-ar words because he's a poet." Mitchell said "peculiar" as if imitating an aristocrat in a stupor.

"So, Kitty Finch." Jonathan stroked his upper lip as if deep in thought. "Perhaps you could tell us what you know about co-tyl-e-dons?"

"Right." Her right eye winked at Nina when she said "right." "Those are the first leaves on a seedling."

"Correct. And now for my favourite word . . . how would you describe a leaf?"

"Leaves are the flat green parts of the plant at the end of a stem that contain chlorophyll. "

"Yes." Jonathan smiled and Kitty stopped winking.

Nina noticed that her mother was drifting off, her eyes half shut, the untouched glass of water in her left hand about to fall on the paving stones.

"And finally," Jonathan Mines absentmindedly stroked his daughter's sunburnt shoulder, making her flinch, "your prize will be a small glass of golden nectar . . . what is a rhizome?"

"Kitty," Laura interrupted sternly. "There are lots of hotels so you'd better go and find one."

When Jean Paul finally made his way through the gate, his long silver hair hanging in rats tails down his back, he told them every hotel in the village was full until Wednesday.

"Then you must stay until Wednesday," Rachel announced in her numb, flat voice. "There's a spare room at the back of the house."

Kitty frowned and leaned back in her new chair.

"Is that okay with everyone? Please say if you mind?"

She was whispering and stuttering. Almost pleading. It seemed to Nina that she was asking them to mind. Kitty Finch was blushing and clenching her toes at the same time. Nina felt her own heart racing. It had gone hysterical, thumping in her chest. She glanced at Laura and saw the giantess was actually wringing her hands.

Laura was about to say she did mind. She and Mitchell had shut their shop in Euston for the entire summer knowing the windows that had been smashed by thieves and drug addicts at least nine times that year would be smashed again when their holiday was over. They had come to the Alpes-Maritimes, the land between the coast and the Alps to escape from the futility of mending broken glass. She found herself struggling for words. The young woman was a window waiting to be climbed through. A window that she intuited was a little broken anyway. She couldn't be sure of this but it seemed to her that Jonathan Mines had already wedged his foot into the crack and his wife had helped him. She cleared her throat and was about to speak her mind but what was on her mind was so unutterable, the hippy caretaker got there first.

"So, Kitty Kat, shall I carry your valises to your room?" Everyone looked to where Jean Paul was pointing with his nicotine-stained finger.

Two blue canvas bags lay to the right of the French doors of the villa.

"Thanks, Jean Paul." Kitty dismissed him as if he was her personal valet. He bent down and picked up the bags.

"What are the weeds?" He lifted up a tangle of flowering plants that had been stuffed into the second blue bag.

"Oh, I found those in the churchyard next to Claude's café."

Jonathan looked impressed. "You'll have to call them the KittyKat plant. Early plant hunters often named plants after themselves."

Rachel stood up and walked to the edge of the pool. The old Polish woman who lived next door was waving from her balcony. As she dived into the green water, her arms stretched out in front of her head, her eyes closed, a voice inside her head gave her some information she did not understand.

When her fingertips touched the warm stone edge of the pool she flipped over and swam another length.

The voice continued, Rachel's voice speaking to Rachel under the water.

She has arrived so I can leave.

ALASDAIR GRAY

The Ballad of Ann Bonny

Blind and a beggar sir, also a sot that
tells tall tales. Who'd buy me drink did I not?
Don't sit too near—I stink but crave brandy
though won't refuse beer. Thanks! Long life to us both.
How I became thus, you will hear.

A woman caused it, Ann Bonny by name,
a little tough sailor, same as me then
but twenty years older. Dressed as a man
she'd swab decks, climb masts, reef sails, swear like the
rest of us dodging land, law, family.
She had pluck. Shame that her name did not fit her face
but young men will fuck holes in planks. Those who sought
swings in Ann's hammock drove her mad.
She broke my nose, being keen on a lad
of fourteen who thought her a joke.

Queer how shy Ann was with him near,
unable to speak or look at him straight

yet mending his breeks and scaring off
buggars after his bum. On yardarms, she
was the chum who steadied him—he'd a poor head
for heights. He cried at night like me years before,
when I joined ship and was whipped. I aint shed tears since.
Who'd whip the young Prince (we called him that)
must thrash Ann Bonny first.
Nobody durst.

It was bad for the lad, being loved
like a cub by a tigress. No rumpy-pumpy!
Ann's motherly rage cut that out, but boys
past the age of ten need men to teach them
men's ways. Aye, you wink sir, think me a sod.
More beer and I'll explain your mistake. My thanks.
Hard lives don't make all men brutes.
At sea we survive by helping each other.
Had the Prince been ugly he could still have
trusted me like a brother.

His looks showed he know'd he'd fare better
if Ann pulled out her hooks. When she was not nigh
some would cry, "How's your wife the Princess today?"
or, "No beard this morning sir? I suppose, the Queen
Mother shaved you before you arose?"
If he sneezed, "Wrap up well! If you catch cold
the royal nurse'll give us all hell."
He'd go white, would yell, "That aint fair!
I don't need, don't want, don't like that old woman!"—
when Ann was not there.

At last I said, "Stow that gab!," thrashed Abe the Yid
who joshed him most, declared the next who did
would feel my fist. The Prince looked up to me then,
Ann too. Since I commanded the main topsail
Ann got the first mate to let the Prince and she
serve under me. On their first day Abe cries,
"See aloft on the crosstree! A Sacred Family!
The Pa, Ma and Holy Little One all complete
and up in the air! How sweet!"
I blacked his eyes.

So before her last breath Ann did not know
I wanted her death, which I did not plan.
A stiff breeze struck sudden and hard
while we put about on a starboard tack.
We reefed in smart and Ann, not quite secure,
thrust out her hand, sure of my aid.
I just gazed back till her amazed face filled with fear
as her other hand lost hold. Clawing, clawing air she fell
eighty feet or more, smack onto the deck
without a yell.

That kind of end aint uncommon at sea
but was, near me. The Prince alone knew
what I'd failed to do so was no more my friend.
That I'd failed Ann to make him a man he
could not see. Others also grew strange to me.
I changed too—no longer sprang lightly aloft
but had to force myself up. I'd lost my pluck
which is most of a seaman's luck.

In a few days I became the glum numb dumb
Jonah of the crew.

Before the next part of my tale I need
fortified by brandy, not ale. My thanks sir.
When mending rigging an iron fork
is a handy tool, the space between prongs
wide as eyes in a face. One night I woke in
dreadful pain and dark and never saw light again.
I lay below deck like a log for weeks,
wishing those prongs had pierced my brain. Who
had blinded me I neither cared
nor knew.

But my old mates grew kind, me being blind,
fed me grub and grog. The Prince was now topmast king
and sometimes bathed what were once my eyes,
not saying much, but I knew his touch.
Abe, a Scotch Jew, so doubly weird, sat by me
talking of God who he called "Needcessity."
When I asked once, slightly curious, "Did you blind me Abe?"
He said sternly, "That question is spurious!
The past is unquestionable. Your job is
embracing NOW, anyhow.

"Forget your eyes. Days before losing them
you stopped rightly using them.
We all miss Ann but are glad *you* aint dead.
Two murders on one trip is bad for a ship."
Great gladness filled me then

and stays to this day. Confessing my vileness
is pleasant, I admit. This punishment justifies it.
Since coming ashore I begs from door to door,
pub to pub, enjoying life how I can,
a harmless old man.

This dismal tale may not seem worth
the price of the liquor you bought, sir.
I disagree, and you need not believe it,
unlike me.

PENNY SIMPSON

Indigo's Mermaid

Nell lay in the fishmonger's window, recognisable even though she sported an acrylic peroxide wig and a long mermaid's tail. The tail was made out of emerald velvet and studded with milk-bottle tops. Sebastian caught sight of her through the crowd of Christmas shoppers. She reclined on one elbow like Velasquez's Venus, the ridiculous wig almost submerging her pale face. Nell's ocean bed was more magnificent, consisting as it did of the shop's original ceramic tiles, decorated with bouquets of fantastical lobsters and fish. She was a temporary replacement for the shop's more usual fare; a one-off gesture to encourage new customers to Cliffe High Street, alongside reams of traditional paper chains, holly wreaths and the penetrating odour of roasted chestnuts.

Sebastian edged forwards until he stood directly opposite Nell. He was certain she would catch his eye, but what then? What gesture could they possibly exchange, the false mermaid and the grieving father? What was common to them both, he knew, was silence and distance. Nell started to yawn, causing amusement amongst the onlookers.

"Better than the zoo, innit?" said the man in front of Sebastian.

Sebastian gave what he hoped was a smile, but in truth he could no longer work those particular facial muscles. He slipped away and headed towards Malling Street. As he walked, he saw Nell yawning all over again, head thrown back, her collarbones arching outwards like small strongbows. His son Indigo's first (and last) girlfriend; the one who had been with him when he slipped down a wall, a stab wound delivered to his heart.

Accidents happened and that was how Indigo's death had been described in court over eighteen months ago. Stabbed accidentally, because someone else had held a knife out like a warning, but Indigo hadn't seen it coming. In court, Nell had spoken with surprising eloquence about the warmth of her boyfriend's body, pressed in against her bare skin at the fatal moment, but knowing simultaneously that his heart had stopped as suddenly as a watch plunged into water. She had screamed and screamed until a policewoman placed two fingers on her lips and said: "Enough." Not unkindly, the policewoman explained when giving evidence later, but what else could she say to a naked teenager terrified out of her mind?

What indeed, Sebastian reflected, opening up his studio and rushing inside to avoid a bitter squall of rain. He hadn't been able to bring himself to speak to Nell during the trial. The defendant was a man unknown to either Indigo or his girlfriend, a vague associate of someone called Herman who still ran the squat in a rundown Georgian town house, just metres away from Sebastian's studio. It was here that the fight had broken out, which started no one knew how, but that particular evening had ended so memorably.

And now Nell was back posing as a mermaid for Christmas shoppers. Sebastian believed she might have moved away after the court case, because what was keeping her in Lewes with Indigo dead? She had never been welcomed into his immediate family; Sebastian had even boycotted the bakery over the road where she once worked to supplement her college grant.

He pulled a chair up to his small escritoire and started to write out an invoice by hand. Some thought it was an affectation, but he was proud of his copper-plate handwriting. He liked to do things slowly, and it was the same with his carvings. He never felt inclined to stack up old car tyres, or fill milk bottles with paint and imagine he was challenging anyone's perception of the world. What you see is what you get, he always told his clients, a stone block carved into the marvellous intricacy of a bonsai tree, or a woman's elongated torso, ribs sticking out like coat hooks.

A loud knock at the studio door broke into his reflections. The raised fist he saw when he opened up convinced him that he was about to be mugged. A second later, he realised the fist belonged to Nell. She had changed into a heavy white wool coat. She didn't ask to come in, nor did she offer seasonal greetings, just brushed past him and made her way over to the studio fireplace. She seemed put-out to find there was no fire burning in the grate. She hovered for a while, as if hoping the flames would start up magically, like in a storybook. "You're still here then."

"And you've lost your tail."

Nell's feet were encased in a pair of black suede zip-up boots. They both looked down at the floor. Her hair was cropped in close to her skull and Sebastian saw the nape of her neck as she bent forwards. Her coat collar fell away when she put out her hands and steadied them against a block of stone. Her hands literally shook with the cold.

"I don't know what to say," she said, addressing the bare floorboards.

He flinched, remembering how he had ignored her at the trial.

"I can't help you," he replied, but the sight of her trembling hands stalled him.

Nell let go of the sculpture and faced him head on. "You never came for his stuff."

She had barely asked the question, before she slipped down onto the floor and began sobbing hysterically. Sebastian stood rigid with shock. He was guilty as charged, but more shocking than that, he resented Nell for what she had just done. She had a heart, if he did not. If he had a heart, surely he would have stuffed his house full of Indigo's every last drawing and sculpture? He didn't even have one of his schoolboy sketches pinned up on the fridge door. Nell's question prompted more vicious undercurrents: had he resisted asking for keepsakes, because he had been jealous of his son? That's what his partner Maura had hinted at, before helping him with college application forms. She had even bought him an impressive moleskin portfolio.

"You're not his mother," he'd remonstrated. "Why do this?"

"Because you won't."

Sebastian knelt down on his studio floor, his hands held stiffly by his sides. He couldn't think of a single word of comfort to offer, but maybe that wasn't what was needed just yet? He found a use for his hands eventually, pressing his palms down gently on top of Nell's shoulders. "I didn't know what to do."

"And you think I did?"

Nell took the opportunity of wiping her eyes on the loose cuff of his shirt (he never wore cufflinks), before delving in her coat pockets. She produced a scrap of paper and handed it over. "That's my address. I want you to come and look at Indigo's things."

Sebastian studied the address: 8 Enys Road, Eastbourne. Nell left without saying another word, and he slowly got to his feet. He went back to the escritoire and made a note of the address in his little leather address book. As he wrote, he acknowledged how he had never written down the address of the squat, because he believed that would have legitimised what his son had done. He had moved away and started a life that Sebastian had always held to be his life—the one he had before his three children were born and he'd had to support them teaching at the local secondary school. A life where every choice had been made for an objective in hand and not left hanging because of a child's cry.

"Talk to him," Maura had urged. "He's your son. You should be proud of him."

She had been Indigo's ally, as his divorce dragged on. Maura had known the minute she first saw his carvings that they were a kind of miracle. She cried when she found an early stone cross abandoned near the rhubarb patch, such a tour de force of carving for someone barely out of childhood, but Indigo claimed it was a failure and wouldn't take it back in. Maybe that's when they had first become competitors, Sebastian reflected, brushing down his jeans and hunting for his studio keys.

"You must go," Maura had insisted when he told her about his unexpected reunion at the studio. "Think what she must have been through."

"I was a bastard," he admitted.

"You were out of your mind," she corrected him. "We all were."

He caught the train to Eastbourne and asked at the ticket desk for directions to Enys Road. It was only a short distance from the station, so he decided to walk. He found Nell on the second floor of a large, shared Edwardian house. She took him on a haphazard tour through a dozen rooms filled with heavy 1930s furniture. The original fireplaces had all been displaced by ugly, imitation coal fires, whilst the ornate ceiling medallions were submerged under ugly '70s light fittings. The incongruity of so many clashing period styles blinded Sebastian at first from seeing that his son's sculptures were to be found in most of the rooms. Next, he became aware of the many drawings mounted in clip frames on the walls, all signed by Indigo. Nell disappeared into the basement kitchen to make a pot of tea, which she served with shortcake biscuits still in their wrapping.

They drank their tea in her bedroom, squatting on the bed. Above their heads, a unique objet trouvé made out of the glass doors of an antique cupboard pressed down on a cluttered montage of sepia photographs. Sebastian wondered if it was an alternative family photograph album, but there were no pictures of Indigo inside the frame, nor of anyone else who might have lived beyond 1940.

"I buy them in junk shops," Nell explained. "I change it round whenever I find someone new I like the look of."

Sebastian was stunned.

"What about your real family?"

Nell shrugged.

"And no Indigo either."

"I thought if I put him up there, it would all go wrong. Like a jinx . . ." Her reply petered out. Then she started up again. "You know, one minute, it was just like any other day. The next, his blood was running over my blue pumps. I loved those shoes . . ."

"And my son?" he broke in, unable to help himself.

But of course she'd loved him. He only had to think of the strangers in the photos masquerading as family. Nell had seemingly lost more than her lover in her short life. Why had he not understood before that someone else could love his son as much as he had, and why had he never let Indigo tell him about Nell's history? He imagined all sorts as he picked up a short-cake biscuit and dunked it in his mug of tea. Nell followed suit. He reached out and squeezed her hand.

"It can be like that with families sometimes," he tried reassuring her. "Hell in a handbasket. I mean, look at me: you'd never have imagined me here once upon a time, would you?"

Once upon a time, his son had thrown down a challenge and he had erupted like a storybook ogre. He'd huffed and puffed—and blown it.

"Is there anything that takes your fancy?" Nell asked, changing the subject abruptly. "Maybe a sundial. They were his speciality."

Sebastian was reminded of the botched sculpture abandoned in the rhubarb patch. He'd rescued it, but then slung it behind the organic compost bin in a rage when Indigo won his place at the very same art college which had rejected him over twenty years earlier. He'd been the child, he realised that now. Nell let her biscuit sink down into her tea. He saw tears on her cheeks, but knew he couldn't comfort her.

"It's not right, is it?" she barely whispered. "Indigo dying before you?"

He hunched over his cup, trying to warm his hands on his mug. The room was cold now that the late winter sun had disappeared behind the roofs of the houses opposite. Sebastian put his mug down by the side of the bed and then stretched himself out over Nell's lime green quilt.

"I haven't slept since Indigo died," he confessed.

"Try now," Nell said.

He looked over at her, rather bewildered. She sat cross-legged next to him, like an overgrown doll. Her cable-knit cardigan was too small for her, and she wore her Aztec-patterned gloves round her neck, secured on a piece of elastic. She wasn't looking at him, but concentrating on her disintegrating biscuit. Sebastian put his arms behind his head and closed his eyes. He was conscious of his breathing and Nell's too; somewhere in the far depths of the house a Hoover whined. He felt a hundred years old. He heard Nell shift about on top of the quilt and then everything went still. The quilt warmed his back and he began to relax. He pinched his eyes tight shut, so tight he could see colours buzz against the back of his eyelids; acid green, harsh yellow, pink and orange, all the colours on Nell's gloves. A dance of colour which he watched like a play.

"Sebastian?"

His name was a label peeling away from his skin. He wasn't concerned about it anymore. Who was Sebastian anyway? Someone repeated his name. A voice he had trouble identifying, until he let his eyes snap open. A woman in a white wool coat bobbed around on his sightline. It was Nell. He pulled himself up, but was disorientated by the squashy quilt. "You're going out?"

"Yeah." She rammed a black beret down over her cropped hair. "And you still haven't chosen anything. You must choose something, before I get back."

She left the bedroom, carefully closing the door behind her, as if he were still sleeping. Sebastian lay back on the quilt. He was exhausted, but he couldn't fall asleep again. He checked his watch. It was already seven o'-clock and he needed to catch a train back to Lewes. He levered himself slowly off the bed. Reaching down for his boots, he found one of Indigo's Celtic style crosses caught up in the voluminous folds of the quilt. In its centre, a small disc carrying a tiny portrait of Nell. He licked his fingers and scrubbed away the dust that had filled in the contours of her face. Indigo had captured his lover's expression in just a few confident incisions.

Sebastian propped the cross up against the wall and returned to bed. He wrapped himself in the quilt and lay on his side studying the cross. He must have slept again, because when he woke it was morning, snow was falling and the cross was wrapped up in brown parcel paper and string. A label was sellotaped to the parcel. The message on it read: "*Happy Christmas.*" Sebastian got up and tidied the quilt, before taking the mugs down to the kitchen. Then he slipped out of the front door and began his journey home, Indigo's mermaid tucked safely under his arm.

Author Biographies and
Personal Statements

INGA ĀBELE, novelist, playwright, short story writer and poet, was born in Riga, Latvia in 1972, and studied in the Department of Film and Drama at the Latvian Academy of Culture. Abele first achieved international fame as a playwright. Her play *Tumsie Briezi* (The Dark Deer) was staged by the Stuttgart State Theater in 2002, and *Dzelzszale* (The Iron Weed) has been produced by amateur companies in both Finland and Denmark. Her short stories have been included in Italian and French anthologies, and in 2005, a short story collection entitled *Nature morte à la grenade* (Still Life with a Pomegranate) was published in France. Her collection of poetry *Nakts pragmatike* (Night Pragmatist) appeared in 2000, and her first novel *Uguns nemodina* (Fire Will Not Wake You) in 2001; her most recent collection of poetry is *Atgāzenes stacijas zirgi* (The Horses of Atgazene Station), 2006. Her second novel *Paisums* (Flow) was published in 2008, and her latest play, *Sala* (Island), will be staged in 2009 at the New Drama Theater in Riga.

NAJA MARIE AIDT was born and raised in Greenland. Her family moved to Copenhagen when she was seven years old. She made her debut as a writer in 1991 with her poetry collection *Så længe jeg er ung* (As Long as I'm Young). Since then she has published eight additional collections of poetry and three collections of short stories. She has also written several plays, children's books, song lyrics, and the screenplay for the feature film *Strings* (2005).

All of Naja Marie Aidt's short stories have been translated into German, and her collection *Bavian* (Baboon) has also been published in Sweden, Norway, Germany, France, Canada, Latvia, and the Czech Republic. In 2008, *Bavian* received the most prestigious literary prize awarded in the Nordic countries—the Nordic Council's Literature Prize. As the jury wrote, her work contains "a graceful and ominous realism that draws out undertones of reality, allowing the reader to become aware that everyday life is resting on a mycelium of potential disasters."

"Bulbjerg," the short story included in this book, is the opening story of *Bavian*.

Naja Marie Aidt cites many inspirations and influences from European and, especially, Scandinavian literature, with the Danish poet and novelist Inger Christensen and the Norwegian novelist Per Petterson—both of whom have been published in English translation—among her favorites. Thomas Mann, Franz Kafka, Marguerite Duras, and Charles Baudelaire are all classic authors to whom she keeps returning, and among newer writers she has been most influenced by the Italian writer Niccolò Ammaniti and the Rumanian/French Agota Kristof.

As far as American literature, she feels closest to such authors as Faulkner, Cormac McCarthy, Paula Fox, Joe Brainard, Lyn Hejinian, John Ashbery and Gary Shteyngart.

Naja Marie Aidt is currently living and writing in Brooklyn, New York.

DAVID ALBAHARI was born in Peć, Serbia in 1948.

He writes in Serbian and has published ten collections of short stories, including *Opis smrti* (Description of Death, 1982), *Jednostavnost* (Simplicity, 1988), *Drugi jezik* (A Second Language, 2003), *Senke* (Shadows, 2007) and *Svake noći u drugom gradu* (Each Night in a Different City, 2008).

He has published twelve novels, among which are *Snežni čovek* (1995; *Snow Man*, 2005), *Mamac* (1996; *Bait*, 2001), *Gec i Majer* (1998; *Götz and Meyer*, 2005), *Pijavice* (Leeches, 2005) and *Ludvig* (2007).

His books have been translated into eighteen languages. *Bait, Snow Man, Götz and Meyer,* and *Tsing* have all appeared in English translation, as has *Words Are Something Else,* a selection of his short stories.

He has been living in Calgary, Canada since October, 1994.

Albahari writes, "As a writer of short stories, I have always felt a greater affinity for the American tradition than that of Europe. Although I have been most influenced as a writer by three Europeans—Samuel Beckett, Thomas Bernhard, and Peter Handke—it's always been the American short story writers who have most shaped my work in the form, particularly authors of 'metafiction,' such as Donald Barthelme, John Barth, and, most of all, Robert Coover. There have been periods, however, when the stories of John Updike, Isaac Bashevis Singer, and, of course, Raymond Carver, have influenced me as well. Generally speaking, there are many American writers in the period between William Faulkner and Carver, through J. D. Salinger, S. Bellow and T. Pynchon, who have influenced me in one way or another. After Carver that influence no longer exists, or rather, the American short story no longer works its 'magic' on me. Perhaps this is a sign that I have found my own narrative voice, but it also may mean that, at least for me, current American literature does not have story writers as exciting and innovative as their predecessors."

TRANSLATED FROM SERBIAN BY ELLEN ELIAS-BURSAĆ

ANDREJ BLATNIK was born on May 22nd, 1963, in Ljubljana, Slovenija, where he studied Comparative Literature and the Sociology of Culture and got his master's in American Literature and PhD in Communication Studies. He started his artistic career playing bass guitar in a punk band, was a freelance writer for five years, and now works as an editor for the Cankarjeva publishing house, teaches creative writing, and has been on the editorial board of *Literatura* since 1984. He is currently the president of the jury for the Vilenica Prize.

So far, he has published three novels, *Plamenice in solze* (Torches and Tears, 1987), *Tao ljubezni* (Closer to Love, 1996) and *Spremeni me* (Change Me, 2008), as well as four collections of short stories: *Šopki za Adama venijo* (Bouquets for Adam Fade, 1983), *Biografije brezimenih* (Biographies of the Nameless, 1989), *Menjave ko* (1990; *Skinswaps*, 1998) and *Zakon želje* (Law of Desire, 2000). In addition to this, he has published a collection of essays on contemporary American literature, especially metafiction, entitled *Labirinti iz papirja* (Paper Labyrinths, 1994), a collection of cultural criticism entitled *Gledanje čez ramo* (Looking Over the Shoulder, 1996) and *Neonski pečati* (Neon Seals, 2005), a collection of essays about literature in the digital age.

He has written for television and radio, and translated several books from English, including Sylvia Plath's *The Bell Jar* and Paul Bowles's *The Sheltering Sky*. He has won numerous major Slovenian literary awards, and his short stories have been translated and published in magazines and anthologies in over twenty languages.

STEINAR BRAGI was born on August 15, 1975, in Reykjavík, Iceland. He does not hold a BA in Comparative Literature and Philosophy from the University of Iceland. He has published five books of poetry, *Svarthol* (Black Hole) in 1998, *Augnkúluvökvi* (Eyeball-liquid) in 1999, *Ljúgðu gosi, ljúgðu* (Lie Pinocchio, Lie) in 2001, *Útgönguleiðir* (Exits) in 2005, and *Litli kall strikes again* (Little Guy Strikes Again). His first novel, *Turninn* (The Tower), appeared in 2000, followed by *Áhyggjudúkkur* (Worrydolls) in 2002, *Sólskinsfólkið* (The Sunshine People) in 2004, and *Hið stórfenglega leyndarmál Heimsins* (The Magnificent Secret of the World) in 2006—all published by Bjartur. In 2008 he published the novel *Konur* (Women) with Nýhil Publishing, and later with Forlagid. Steinar Bragi lives in New York.

Asked to speak a little about his influences and his place in European literature, Mr. Bragi responded with the following essay:

THOMAS MANN'S BOWELS

In literature you don't choose your own influences—in fact, the opposite seems to apply. At least for me. I was a practically a baby when I first read Thomas Mann—*Death in Venice*—and since then I've been stuck with him, which in a sense feels kind of uninspired; he's too well known, too much of a given. Soon, with terrible results, I'd made Tonio Kröger, the character, with his unstable mix of sensitivity and arrogance, into an ideal for my personal life. And *The Magic Mountain* is still my favorite book, which is pathetic—there's nothing in the least bit personal about it, and not in my reading of it either. But that's how it is.

In his book *Written Lives*, the Spanish author Javier Marías writes about the lives of a few well-known authors. Among them is Thomas Mann. Right away it becomes clear that he has a few bones to pick with Mann, and so he pits everyone's all-time favorite, the Coca-Cola of literature, none other than Charles Dickens, against him. Marías refers to Mann's criticism of Dickens, wherein he said that Dickens was too humorous, but lacking in irony, and soon Marías has admitted that he laughs at Dickens's books "on almost every other page," but less so—though how much less isn't clearly specified—when it comes to Mann. Finally he states his point, which is that Mann—as a person, at least in how he's represented in his diaries and letters—is boring and "dreadfully serious."

Unlike Marías, when it comes to Dickens, I weep with boredom over every single page he's written; with time I've even begun to weep just seeing his books on a shelf. For those who haven't read him, I would still suggest you do have a look, just so you can make up your own mind—I'm not a fascist! But don't spend too much time on it; really, it's easy to make a quick survey: the first paragraph—of any of his books—is exactly like the rest of the book, and each of his books is exactly like the others. Nothing in Dickens will ever manage to surprise you. And if you want those characters, if you've really got a craving for those "Dickensian characters," just go to a wax museum. It's faster.

So, I say Dickens is all the same. Am I thereby making surprise into an aesthetic criterion? Do I have to be surprised, do a writer's words have to shoot right up my ass on every page? —No. But I demand a certain tension from literature, preferably unresolved, that demonstrates, in some way, how an author struggled with life, reality, the world, or whatever you want to call it. I want a duel, I want to feel the author's sickness—as I do on almost every single page of Mann (and I laugh as well—probably not on every single page, but often . . . let's say often enough). I want to smell the author's bowels.

On this point, Marías and I will have to disagree. In *Written Lives*, in fact, Marías is indignant over how often Mann's diaries—which, by the way, I sunk my teeth into at twenty, right after *Tonio Kröger*—talk about his bowels: if they're moving, at what times, and how important he considers this to be. *As if it really mattered? As if anybody cared?*

My opinion on Marías as a writer is that he's okay. But as a person—at least as he's represented in *Written Lives*—I feel he's a bit naive, even something of a populist. Is he venting a repressed middle-class sensibility? Does he want everyone to "be good"—that is, to mask their failures and demons the same way everyone else does, and to act and talk exactly the same way as everyone else? To stage their lives with Dickensian sentimentalism and humor? Does he really think that the lives of authors—especially great authors—can ever be anything less than unusual, despicable even, antihumanist, filled with arrogance, narcissistic?

I'm just asking. I'm not trying to put words in Marías's mouth. But my own opinion on the above is this: You can't write European literature—at least not the sort that becomes a frame of reference, a classic—without embodying the sickness of the continent in some way, its split heart: on the one hand its optimism and audacity, its flight for the stars (or down the toilets of nineteenth-century Paris), the rhetoric that pretends both to reinvent reality and describe it "as is"; and, on the other hand, its skepticism, its suspicion that all of this is just a childish game, an oversimplification, its shame over its numerous unacceptable desires (homosexuality in Mann's case), its neurotic inability to comprehend matter and the body (as defined by Europe), its concurrent failure to learn how to control matter and body—and, of course, death (as defined by Europe). That's why, at least when it comes to literature, I can't think of anything more important than Thomas Mann's bowels.

And if I was fifty years younger or so, and if Mann's diaries were still accessible by the public, I'd be waiting in front of the library—or wherever they were kept—or in an apartment close by, leafing through his novels; and though this isn't, perhaps, an enormous issue, after the doors were finally open, I know I'd find a great deal of the spirit of his novels in the bowels of Mann, the author, or to be more specific: in the attitude that his bowels were important and worth documenting.

All their movements.

JUHANI BRANDER writes: "Juhani Brander was born May 17, 1978, in Turku, Finland, into a middle-class family. His father was a lawyer and his mother an accountant. He spent his childhood with books, their distant and captivating worlds interesting him more than silly children's games.

The environment he grew up in was filled with story and myth. His father's family originated deep in the Finnish archipelago: plunging rocky cliffs and the merciless sea on all sides. Growing up, he heard stories of smuggling and moonshine, unsolved murders and village brawls. His mother's family was from Lapland, land of hill villages and the northern lights. Thence his interest in mysticism, gloomy forests, the wilderness, and nature deities.

School seemed leveling and childish to him. He won a few writing contests, his themes were read out loud to the class. Once his mother read her brother, his much-decorated war veteran uncle, a thirty-four-page piece he wrote in the fifth grade telling of the uncle's war experiences and severe wounding. When that grown man wept and hugged him, deeply moved, he understood the power of words.

In high school he decided school was a waste of time. He wouldn't find a mentality as leveling and narrow-minded, as destructive of personality, until he was in the army. He has since launched literary attacks on institutions, organizations, and closed communities that erode the individual's freedom.

After high school he did menial jobs to support his writing. He started reading intensively, a book or two a day. He entered writing contests whose winners were published in anthologies, and was one of the lucky ones: his first satirical writings and poems soon saw the light of day.

Two years later, in 2000, his first poetry collection, *Aninkaisten mainingit* (The Heights of Aninkaisten) was published, after Pablo Neruda's *Alturas de Macchu Picchu*.

In 2002, he published his collection of anti-army satires, *Lepo! harmaissa tai ilman* (At Ease! In and Out of Uniform). So many drunken officers made threatening calls to his landline that he gave it up and now only uses a cell phone.

In 2003, his poetry collection *Valveuni* (Waking Dream) was published.

In 2005, his poetry collection *Palavat kirjaimet* (Burning Letters) was published.

In 2007, his prose work *Lajien tuho* (Extinction) was published. In it he found his authentic voice, his language, his expressive power as a writer."

TRANSLATED FROM FINNISH BY DOUG ROBINSON

ORNA NÍ CHOILEÁIN was born in West Cork, Ireland, and is a creative writer of modern Irish stories. She writes, "While the Irish language lay dormant for a couple of generations within Orna's family, she is very proud to have had the opportunity to revive it and to grow up in a bilingual community circle. This enhanced the possibility of acquiring further linguistic skills. She now communicates in six European languages and has enjoyed working in the financial service centres of many of Europe's beautiful historical cities.

As an avid reader, Orna found that much of the Irish-language literature that she reads is based around the authors' own locality and often on themes such as home life or emigration.

She has won numerous prizes for creative prose, poetry, drama, and short stories in the Oireachtas, as well as other Irish festivals. Throughout 2007, her work was reviewed by award-winning bilingual dramatist and author Éilis Ní Dhuibhne, under the auspices of a writers' scheme organised by Forás na Gaeilge. Orna also enjoys writing in English and has been awarded the An Post National Penmanship prize. She writes reviews for the magazine *Feasta* and the newspaper *Saol*, and has had her own work reviewed on national radio, in the *Irish Times* and the Irish-language newspaper *Foinse*. She presented readings at the 2009 Dublin Book Festival and Leabhar Power events organised by the Irish Book Publishers' Association.

As well as writing, Orna has a passion for Irish music, plays the Irish harp and the fiddle, and loves traditional Irish singing in particular. She has performed solo and in the company of other artists at festival and embassy venues at a number of national and international locations, and has received numerous prizes for her singing.

As a recipient of the prestigious President's Gold Award, Gaisce, she was selected to represent Ireland at the International Gold Encounter in Canada and later again in Hong Kong. There she met delegates from all over the world, delighting in the invitation to exchange ideas, share experiences and appreciate the diversity of so many cultures."

Canary Wharf (2009), from which the story in this anthology was taken, is her first published collection of short stories in Irish. She is currently concentrating on works for younger readers.

STEPHAN ENTER's debut, a collection of short stories entitled *Winterhanden* (Chilblained Hands), published in 1999, was received well and was nominated for the Libris Literature Prize 2000. His first novel, *Lichtjaren* (Light Years), published in 2004, was also nominated for the Libris Prize. Both books were nominated for the Gerard Walschap Prize. Enter's second novel, *Spel* (Game), appeared in 2007. In March of this year, a German translation of this last book was published as *Spiel*.

He writes, "Am I a European writer? Absolutely; I feel European through and through, for instance because I have this fairly amusing view of my family history winding its erratic but clear way back through the World and Napoleonic Wars into the Dutch Golden Age (when my ancestors chose to become fervent protestants), and still further back into darker ages—right up till the short-tempered and probably illiterate crusader who gave my mother and the main character of my latest novel their family name. By using this ancestral aspect in an ironic way, and thus creating a devoted, sensitive, arrogant young snob as a hero, I think I might very well be called a typical (North) European writer.

However, my Europeanism—as far as literature is concerned—ends right here. Naturally, there are European writers whose work I like and admire and to whom I feel connected, such as Woolf, Proust, Mann. But I feel the same towards some Russians like Turgenev, Tolstoy, Nabokov. Or towards some great Americans such as Updike, Salinger, and Harold Brodkey.

I consider all writers, including myself, to be individuals. Certainly, we are part of the times and places into which we are born and in which we spend our lives. But I do not believe there are such things as literary 'directions' or 'currents' or 'influences.' Most of these seem to me artificial contraptions created by literary critics and academics, merely made up (and often frantically maintained) in an attempt to outline an order that makes it easier to write well-structured essays, but sacrificing the uniquenesses of the writer in the process. And more often than not they seem a poor excuse for not saying anything thorough and lucid about the things that really matter in a book, like style, the psychological profundity and consistency of its main characters, or the pattern and peregrinations of a plot.

It seems to me that any observation about these aspects—style, psychology, plot—can hardly be linked to a country, or a continent. They are, I guess, universal."

ANTONIO FIAN writes: "I came into the world in 1956 in Klagenfurt, the capital of Carinthia, Austria's southernmost province, and the place from which a few of the most important Austrian authors of the twentieth and twenty-first centuries originate—for example: Ingeborg Bachmann, Peter Handke, Gert Jonke, Josef Winkler. Like most of them, I left Carinthia after graduating high school and moved to the big city, to Vienna. I began studying National Economics and put out a literary magazine at the same time—*Fettfleck* (Grease Stain)—which continued until 1983. By 1980, however, I'd broken off my studies, and have worked as a freelance writer ever since.

But the road was still long to my first book. In 1987 it debuted on the list of Literaturverlag Droschl, in Graz (and Droschl has remained my publisher to this day): a collection of short stories, *Einöde. Außen, Tag* (Desert. Outside, Day). This was followed by two more short-story collections, a collection of essays, and finally, in 1992, my novel *Schratt*. I spent many years writing the one hundred and thirty-three pages of *Schratt*, with the majority of this work—and the most important—focused on editing. During this time, as a side project as well as a way to practice my editing skills, my first 'dramolettes' came into being, satirical mini-dramas reacting to current events, primarily printed in the local Viennese magazine *Falter* (Moth). These 'dramolettes' quickly became popular in Austria and have been making sporadic appearances in the daily newspaper *Der Standard* over the last few years. A selection of these texts is available in four volumes.

Dramatic satire in both short and long forms has a storied tradition in Austria. The comedy writer, actor, and theater-director Johann Nepomuk Nestroy might be singled out as the father of this tradition, and it continues in Karl Kraus and his epic *The Last Days of Mankind* (which you could just as easily see as a collection of mini-dramas held together by the historical arc of the First World War), in Helmut Qualtinger and Carl Merz's famous portrait of an Austrian opportunist, *Der Herr Karl*, and on into the work of Thomas Bernhard.

However, the popularity of my 'dramolettes' has its disadvantages. Since my name has, over the years, come to be associated with this particular literary form to the exclusion of all else, it's often overlooked that I've also been producing poems, essays, and prose every year. The poems are collected in the volumes *Üble Inhalte in niedrigen Formen* (Bad Content in Low Form) and *Fertige Gedichte* (Finished Poems). My essays have finally been collected in *Hölle, verlorenes Paradies* (Hell, Paradise Lost). And my latest prose work, *Im Schlaf* (While Sleeping), from which the texts in this anthology come, was released in the summer of 2009."

TRANSLATED FROM GERMAN BY DUSTIN LOVETT

JOSEP M. FONALLERAS was born in Girona, Catalonia, in 1959. He is a novelist, short-story writer, children's author, columnist, and translator. He has received numerous awards, including the Premi Just M. Casero (1983), Premi Ciutat d'Olot (1984), Premi Ciutat de Palma (1997), Premi Octavi Pellissa (2000), and Premi de la Crítica Serra d'Or (2006).

He is the author of two novels: *La millor guerra del món* (The World's Best War, 1998), and *August i Gustau* (August and Gustau, 2001). His short story collections include *El Rei del mambo* (King of the Mambo, 1985), *Botxenski i companyia*

(Botxenski and Company, 1988/2001), and *Un any de divorciat* (Year of the Divorced, 2007).

Fonalleras has translated his own work into Spanish and German, and has also translated J. D. Salinger's *The Catcher in the Rye* into Catalan, in collaboration with Ernest Riera. He works as a columnist for *El Periódico* and *El Punt i Sport.*

He writes, "To say what type of literary tradition defines you or that you think you are defined by is difficult. Literature, despite being the fruit of whatever tradition you might happen to be talking about, is also a cannibalistic and solitary practice, one that devours all comers and only responds to the savage power of the creative process itself.

The Catalan philosopher Eugeni d'Ors said that 'Real originality only exists in the womb of tradition; what is not a part of that tradition is plagiarism.' Seen as such, I would rather confess to my sources than be considered a plagiarist. We are indebted to ourselves for what we have read, what we have managed to understand and then copy and then project out again, somehow, from our own 'new' writing. One of the aims of a writer, according to Antoine Compagnon, is to leave language in a different state from which it was found.

In this sense, I have a particular fondness for Catalan poets such as Josep Carner, who have shown me an entire world made of my own language and have made me realize that the writer has a certain moral obligation to that world. I feel a similar fondness for some prose writers as well, such as Josep Pla. I feel very close to Italian writers like Giorgio Bassani and Pier Paolo Pasolini, and I also enjoy (and owe much to) novelists (or were they moralists?) such as Diderot and Sterne. Kafka, of course, is always there, as is, perhaps, the work of Giorgio Manganelli—from whose well they say I drank, despite the fact that, when I was at work, I hardly recall tasting a drop. That's tradition for you: sometimes you dive into it without even knowing that you have your scuba gear on.

Bit by bit I feel more like I am engaged in a poet's work, in the sense that I value every word so much that it makes it difficult for me to take the next step, for fear of getting everything all wrong, fear of getting tradition itself wrong, fear of not knowing how to carry that tradition (carry those traditions) safely to an island without plagiarists."

TRANSLATED FROM CATALAN BY ROWAN RICARDO PHILLIPS

JON FOSSE, called "the new Ibsen" in the German press, and heralded throughout Western Europe, is one of contemporary Norwegian literature's most important writers. He was born 1959 in Haugesund, grew up by the fjord in Hardanger, and has since lived in Bergen for many years. He studied Comparative Literature at university, as well as philosophy and sociology.

Fosse is a poet, novelist, and dramatist. He has published some fifty books, and written about thirty plays. His novels include *Raudt, svart* (Red, Black, 1983), *Stengd gitar* (Closed Guitar, 1985), *Naustet* (The Boat-house, 1989), *Melancholia I* (1995; *Melancholy*, 2006), and *Det er Ales* (This is Aliss, 2004). Fosse's work has been translated into around forty languages, and he has received many prizes, as well as a lifetime grant from the Norwegian state. Fosse is chevalier of the French Ordre national du Mérite, and he is Commander of the Royal Norwegian Order of St. Olav.

He writes, "Fosse is often called a minimalist, and not without reason: in his writing, a small and select number of words and phrases are often combined and recombined in various ways in order to make a complex and emotional picture of the fundamentals of the human condition. His writing is more archetypical than realistic, and more experimental than conventional. Still there is always a simplicity to it, and Fosse claims that he tries to write as simply as possible, but without sacrificing depth. He says that simple writing is easy, as is complex writing— the challenge is to do both at the same time.

Fosse writes in Nynorsk, or 'New Norwegian,' a version of the Norwegian language used by some ten percent of the population, and he feels very connected to both this language and to its literary tradition, for instance to the writing of the poet Olav H. Hauge. On the other hand, Fosse also feels like a typical European writer, who has learned much of what he knows from authors such as Georg Trakl, Franz Kafka, Marcel Proust, and—last but not least—Samuel Beckett, who Fosse feels is the figure his own writing is most trying to connect with.

For Fosse there is no real difference between writing poetry, prose, or drama. Every form just provides different possibilities, and opportunities, for his writing. And in all his writing he has tried—as he puts it—to 'make the silent voice speak.' To say what cannot be said."

GEORGI GOSPODINOV was born in the all-important year of 1968—though he insists that this year never took place in his native Bulgaria.

His first book of poetry was entitled *Lapidarium* (1992, National Debut Prize) followed by *Chereshata na edin narod* (The Cherry Tree of a People, 1996; Best Book of the Year Prize of the Bulgarian Writers' Union), *Pisma do Gaustin* (Letters to Gaustin, 2003) and *Baladi i razpadi* (Ballads and Maladies, 2007). He is the author of a natural novel entitled *Natural Novel (Estestven roman)*, first published in the last year of the 1990s, and then several times after that: the novel soon began to appear in other languages—fourteen so far, including English, from Dalkey Archive Press. His collection of short stories, *I drugi istorii* (2001), has been translated into French, German, Czech, and Italian. The English version (*And Other Stories*, 2007) was longlisted for the Frank O'Connor Award.

He writes, "Georgi Gospodinov published his first poem in a local newspaper when he was nine, and for this he received the then-incredible amount of 4.50 levs (around $3.00). He quickly figured out that twenty poems would be enough to buy him a Balkan bicycle (the only kind available at the time). Sadly, he didn't manage to work his way up to this amount.

He loves to write about things that haven't happened, and how they're more important than anything that actually has. His native land is full of things that have unhappened. Other favorite techniques: sometimes he uses a fly's point of view to radically undermine our raging anthropocentrism, which he finds highly anti-ecological. What would the history of the world be like if it was told by a fly? He also likes to focus on childhood, 'when for the last time we were loved without a reason, for the simple fact that we existed.' Other focuses: toilets, anything that's been suppressed, things without voices—since these all belong to the same story.

His favorite genre is the aforementioned 'natural novel,' which can mix—and in a single book—a Bible for flies, lists of things one enjoyed in the '70s, collections of classic novel openings, and various stories from the '90s. Favorite themes? Just one: how to find a miracle where miracles, principally, have been denied us—in our own everyday lives. Also: why in God's name are our lives so unfairly short?"

JULIAN GOUGH was born in London, to parents of an exquisite, almost excessive Irishness. When he was seven, the family returned to Tipperary. He was educated by the Christian Brothers, back when throwing a boy across the room was considered healthful exercise for both parties. At university in Galway, he began writing and singing with the underground literary rock band Toasted Heretic. They released four albums, and had a top ten hit in Ireland in 1991 with "Galway and Los Angeles," a song about not kissing Sinead O'Connor.

His first novel, *Juno & Juliet*, was published in 2001. In 2007, his second book, *Jude: Level 1*, was described by the *Sunday Tribune* as possibly "the finest comic novel since Flann O'Brien's *The Third Policeman*, and was shortlisted for the Everyman Wodehouse Prize for Comic Fiction. Will Self, controversially, won. Gough subsequently kidnapped Will Self's pig, and posted the ransom video on YouTube.

The self-contained story "The Orphan and the Mob" forms the prologue to *Jude: Level 1*. It won the BBC National Short Story Award (the world's largest annual prize for a single short story).

Gough writes, "The West suffers from an unexamined cultural cringe before the Greeks. We've also thoroughly misunderstood them. The Greeks themselves believed that tragedy is the merely human view of life: comedy is superior, being the Gods' view.

But our classical inheritance is lopsided. We have a rich range of tragedies, but of the comic writers, only Aristophanes survived. (Comedies laugh at the naked emperor; tragedies weep at the loss of his clothes. Emperors tend to prefer, and preserve, tragedies.) More importantly, Aristotle's work on tragedy survived; his work on comedy did not. Western literature has been off-centre ever since.

Of course Europe in the Middle Ages was peculiarly primed to rediscover tragedy: the one church spoke in one voice, drawn from one book, and that book was at heart tragic. The Bible, from apple to Armageddon, does not contain a single joke.

Post-Renaissance, secular writers still felt the need for a holy book to guide them. Aristotle's *Poetics* provided that. If you wanted to write tragedy or epic, here were the classical rules. The University seamlessly succeeded the Universal Church, but tragedy remained the dominant mode. As a result, comedy's potential still has not been fully explored.

My generation, and those younger, receive information not in long, coherent, self-contained units (a film, an album, a novel), but in short bursts, with wildly different tones. (Channel-hopping, surfing the Internet, while doing the iPod shuffle.) That changes the way we read fiction, and therefore must change the way we write it. This is not a catastrophe; it is an opportunity. We are free to do new things, which could not have been understood before now. The traditional story (retold ten thousand times), suffers from repetitive strain injury. Television and the Internet have responded to this crisis without losing their audience. Literary fiction has not.

Steal from the Simpsons, not Henry James."

ALASDAIR GRAY

A CHRONOLOGY AND LIST OF SELECTED PAST WORK

12/28/34 Born in Riddrie, a good east Glasgow Corporation housing scheme.

1957 Diploma in Mural Painting and Design, Glasgow School of Art.

1957-62 Part-time art teacher. Paints murals in Scottish-USSR Friendship Society; Greenhead Church of Scotland, Bridgeton; Bellaisle Street Synagogue.

1962-65 Theatre scene painter, social security scrounger, artist.

1964 A fifty-minute BBC television documentary about my paintings and poetry gave me the experience to write my first TV play, *The Fall of Kelvin Walker*. I became a self-employed artist and playwright.

1967-77 Five TV plays networked, six radio plays broadcast, one full-length and five one-act stage play performed.

1969-95 Murals: *Falls of Clyde* in Kirkfieldbank Tavern; *The Story of Ruth* in Fulton Transept, Greenbank Church of Scotland, Glasgow; *Oak Tree Ecological Cycle* in Palacerigg Nature Reserve; *Arcadia* in the Ubiquitous Chip restaurant, Glasgow; *The Thistle of Dunfermline History* in Abbot House Local History Museum, Dunfermline.

1974 Retrospective painting exhibition, University of Strathclyde, Glasgow.

1975 Around this time, for various reasons, I received no more commissions to write plays until 2004.

1977-78 Glasgow's Artist Recorder, painting 32 portraits and cityscapes for the People's Palace Local History Museum.

1977-79 Writer in Residence, University of Glasgow.

1981 Publication of *Lanark*, my first novel. This was planned as a prose epic—a Scottish petite bourgeois model of the universe, which university lecturers think my best work. From this time onward I became a designer of my own books and occasionally those of other authors.

1983-2008 Eight more novels published, four short-story collections, three political pamphlets, two books of verse, two books of plays, one short history of Scottish literature.

2000 *The Book of Prefaces*, anthology with essays and marginalia amounting to a history of English literature in four nations.

CURRENT WORK

In 2003 began a large scheme of mural decoration for the Oran Mor Art and Leisure Centre, Glasgow. The auditorium ceiling is completed; the walls are still being worked upon. Two books are also being worked upon: *A Gray Playbook* and *A Life in Pictures*, for 2009 and 2010.

PERSONAL STATEMENT

My imagination has been shaped by too many other authors and artists to name here, but I love the work of Hans Andersen, Lewis Carroll, William Blake, James Joyce, Kafka, Coleridge, and anonymous makers of Scottish ballads. I do not know how my work fits into any literary tradition—there are many of them if we include the Old Testament, the *Arabian Nights*, and the Chinese *Monkey*. I fear I have baked more literary cakes than readers will have time and appetite to digest. In 2007 I was filling a ledger with lines for my verse play *Fleck*, a modern version of Goethe's *Faust* (published by Two Ravens Press). Words by which a beggar introduces himself before telling the story of Ann Bonny started happening among these—I don't know why, though when working out one big idea my imagination sometimes relieves itself by seizing on something different. My seafaring knowledge comes from Stevenson's *Treasure Island*, Melville's *Moby Dick* and *White Jacket*, and the beggar derives a lot from Blind Pew. "The Ballad of Ann Bonny" is the only thing I have written that has been translated into Hebrew.

GEORGE KONRÁD was born in 1933, and grew up amid the horrors of fascism and the Second World War, narrowly escaping the Nazi concentration camps. He saw the Germans leave Budapest, only to be replaced by the Russians. He fought the Soviet tanks in the 1956 uprising, was imprisoned for his writing, which he then saw censored, and fled abroad a number of times—always returning to his homeland.

He has worked as a social worker, editor, and sociologist, and is considered Hungary's preeminent essayist and novelist. He is the author of numerous books, including *A látogató* (1969), translated into English as *The Case Worker* (1974), *A városalapító* (1977), translated into English as *The City Builder* (1977) and *A cinkos* (1978), translated into English as *The Loser* (1982), and *Elutazás és Hazatérés* (2001), translated into English as *A Guest in My Own Country* (2007). Konrád lives in Budapest.

As Konrád said during a recent interview with Thomas Ország-Land in *Hungarian Literature Online*, "I've been a Jewish Hungarian or a Hungarian Jew at various stages of my life . . . Today, I am a Jew when I hear that the Jews are mean and pushy. And I am a Hungarian when people say that the Hungarians are fascists."

Celebrated for his memoirs as well as his novels, Konrád had this to say on the division between autobiography and fiction, in a 2007 *Jewish Daily Forward* interview with Joshua Cohen: "There's not too much difference. I realized if I kept out fiction, what would remain was fiction, too. Speaking from a certain distance, everything that happens to us in our lives eventually becomes fictionalized, a fiction: Our minds fictionalize our memories, which are not as much chronological as they are geographical. It's as if what we remember are only islands of oil floating upon the surface of a sea of everything that has ever happened to us."

PETER KRIŠTÚFEK was born in 1973, in Bratislava, Slovakia. He is a writer as well as director for television and film. He is the author of three collections of short stories—*Nepresné miesto* (Inexact Place, 2002), *Voľným okom* (By the Eye, 2004), and *Mimo času* (Out of Time, 2009). In 2005, he brought out the conceptual novel *Hviezda vystrihnutého záberu* (The Star of the Cut-out Shot), and in 2008 he published his first "regular" novel, *Šepkár* (The Prompter), which was nominated for a European Book Prize, and from which the selection in this anthology was taken. He is a three-time finalist for the prestigious Slovak literary contest Poviedka (The Short Story), and his work has been published in many newspapers and magazines in Slovakia as well as foreign countries (Czech Republic, Poland, Bulgaria).

He is now working on a novel entitled *Dom hluchého* (The House of the Deaf), which is set in a small town during the years between 1934–1990, a time of many upheavals in Slovakian history.

He writes, "A great part of the tradition of European fiction is based on reflecting the complicated history of history. In my previous books (mostly short stories) I was concerned with the relationship between the individual and the society surrounding him or her, and often threatening him or her. The hero is—somehow—battling against the world, often trapped inside himself.

My novel *The Prompter* basically talks about the same things, but in a more overt and satirical way. The novel is situated in a nameless postcommunist country (since all of Central Europe seems to be in more or less the same boat), which has just started to learn about the "accomplishments of capitalism": the *dolce vita* of political superstars, parliamentary speeches that say nothing, important summits that are actually luxurious parties, ubiquitous media attention, children born after the fall of communism and acting in ways that baffle their parents, and so forth—the future, in other words. This is the new theater of the absurd that the prompter, Kritof, passes through . . .

My greatest influence as far as commenting on the historical context of a particular era is Günter Grass, and to some extent Peter Høeg as well. Europe is the great theme. And I've become more and more interested in Slovak history as well: the history of a small nation, often dependent on the larger ones—which very much resembles the helplessness of the individual in a hostile society. Anyway, I try to look at these things with wit and irony."

DEBORAH LEVY, a playwright, novelist and poet, was born in 1959 in South Africa. She moved to Britain with her family and studied theatre at Dartington College of Arts. She was a Creative Arts Fellow at Trinity College, Cambridge, between 1989 and 1991. Her novels include *Beautiful Mutants* (1989, shortlisted for the John Llewellyn Rhys Prize), *Swallowing Geography* (1993), *The Unloved* (1995), and *Billy and Girl* (1999). Her short story collections include *Pillow Talk in Europe and Other Places* (2003).

She writes, "When I was sixteen I wrote on paper napkins in a bus drivers' café, known in the UK as a 'greasy spoon.' I had a vague idea this was how writers were supposed to behave because I had read books about glamorous existentialists drinking coffee in French cafés while they wrote about how unhappy they were.

There were no cafés like that in the UK at the time and certainly not in the gray suburb I lived in. But I was convinced a café was an essential key to escaping from my life and began my impersonation of the European Writing Life while drinking tea with the bus drivers while Angie the cook fried bacon and everyone stared glumly at the rain.

It would be right to observe therefore, that some of the writers and artists that lifted me out of the British rain, the tangle of the British class system, and a solid tradition of literary realism—and then walked me back to all of the above to search for my own voice—were the Surrealists, Freud, and above all, French pre- and post-war writers such as Jean Genet, Marguerite Duras, and Robbe-Grillet . . . and later the novels *Whatever* by Michel Houellebecq and *The Butcher* by Alina Reyes. I throw in to this mix the American expatriates who found themselves in Paris for a while: Djuna Barnes, Hemingway, Gertrude Stein, Ezra Pound, not to mention Edmund White, whose biography of Genet I consider one of the finest books to honour my shelves.

The Austrian writer Elfriede Jelinek seems to me to not only belong to a European tradition, but to have made a whole new language on the way. The British writer who most interests me after Angela Carter is the late and much mourned J. G. Ballard, both of whom helped build a literary atmosphere I feel most at home in.

Yet it would also be true to declare that my major influences will always be the children anywhere in the world who learn to transgress their way out of conflicts with bullies in the school playground and become adults interested in how personal and societal power (and the lack thereof) can be rearranged, in both fiction and life. This then takes me to the novels of James Baldwin, to Mohamed Choukri (translated by Paul Bowles), Franz Fanon, and the writing of Edward Said. These days, all I know is that when I get nearer to an idea that has been interrupting my every day and begin to unfold it, to write it, I feel more alive. What else is there to do in life than feel more alive? In any tradition."

VALTER HUGO MÃE was born in Angola in 1971, grew up in Paços de Ferreira in the north of Portugal, and has lived in Vila do Conde since 1981. He has an undergraduate degree in law and a graduate degree in Modern and Contemporary Portuguese Literature. He has published seven books of poetry and three novels; edited anthologies of the poets Manoel de Barros, José Régio, and Adília Lopes, among others; and translated works from Italian and Spanish. He also dabbles in art: his first show, "the face of gregor samsa," took place in Porto in 2006.

valter hugo mãe's first literary efforts were in poetry. A collection of his complete poetic work will appear in 2008 with the title *folclore íntimo* (intimate folklore). His first work of fiction, *nosso reino* (our kingdom), came out in 2004. The *Diário de Notícias*, a very important daily newspaper, called it the best Portuguese novel published that year. valter hugo mãe was awarded the José Saramago Prize in 2007.

He writes, "it's hard to look at ourselves and realize exactly what our place is in life, including, and especially, as writers. i suppose i'm still a dreamer and write believing that books can make humankind better. they certainly made me—and hopefully keep on making me—a better and more conscientious person. i like to think that this effort of mine is easily understood by anyone who reads my novels, because they are always common people living through the heroic adventure of simply being alive.

i prefer to underline the weird and unexpected aspects of reality, because life is weird, after all, and reality, in fact, is merely personal, and is truly different for everyone. by sharing a particular point of view i hope to provoke a reader to decide what he or she needs to believe in. it's not that i want the reader to agree with me, or with some character, this is really for the reader to decide and, by deciding, to participate. this will bring a reader to some sense of right and wrong—at least about my book and its subjects.

since childhood i have been interested in reading whatever could interfere most with my life, the life of a person from a small and somehow forgotten country such as portugal. living away from the big cities, growing up was wandering freely in the fields, but all the while i was sculpting away at my self, my insides, getting to know me and thinking that, despite my isolation, i was, after all, a person like every other person in the world. so, despite living in this tiny place, where i've always lived, i know i can feel and feel accurately the anguish of kafka's gregor samsa, and am able to assume the same questioning sensibility as albert camus's stranger, and can imagine my country drifting in the sea, as josé saramago did, and can be a luxurious snob along with oscar wilde, reading the dramatic story of dorian gray. i have spent my life with vergílio ferreira, herberto helder, lobo antunes, borges, stig dagerman, isidore ducasse, but also with herzog, lynch, bergman, pedro costa, oliveira, hitchcock, and goya, bosch, cruzeiro seixas, lisa santos silva, isabel lhano, and bach, billie holiday, amália, josé afonso, coltrane, patty waters, joão gilberto, caetano veloso, sonic youth, current 93, the cocteau twins, dead can dance, mão morta, radiohead, xiu xiu, sigur ros, antony and the johnsons, devendra banhart, and oh-my-nonexistent-god so many beautiful people i beg please forgive me not mentioning."

COSMIN MANOLACHE was born in the town of Mizil, in Walachia, Romania, on January 16, 1973. He graduated from the A. I. Cuza Police Academy in 1995 and was subsequently posted to the Danube Delta as an officer of the Romanian Frontier Guard. Since 1998, he has worked as a curator at the Museum of the Romanian Peasant. His work has been widely anthologized, and his first collection of short stories, *Ce fată cumplită am* (What a Frightful Face I Have), was published by Polirom in 2004. His forthcoming semi-autobiographical novel, *Aether*, is set in the Danube Delta.

He writes, "I didn't start reading literature seriously until around the age of twenty. Up till then, books were just something that got forced on us at school, and which I used to go out of my way to avoid, substituting books about football whenever possible. When reading these, I always felt as though I were deep in the roar of the stadium, supporting my team ... in other words, I was passionate. It was also around this time that a classmate and I came up with the idea of collaborating on some adventure stories, but because we each wanted our name to come first on the cover, we quickly gave up the idea. Something else I read willingly in those days—even passionately—were almanacs, and I think these have had a real influence on me; the fact that almanacs contain writing on many subjects, and combine both images and text, fascinated me, and led me to want to emulate this structure in my fiction. My own writing borrows from the almanac form, which has always seemed to me like a building with many windows, each opening onto a very different landscape. Subsequently, as a museum curator, I've also had the opportunity to work on oral-history projects, and to immerse myself in the stories of 'ordinary people.' Leafing through their diaries, I found that they'd been composing unintentionally intertextual work—and rediscovered Borges in them. To Borges I soon added Nabokov, Beckett, Claude Simon, W. G. Sebald, Calvino, Esterházy, Leonid Tsypkin, Vladimir Sorokin, and the two Erofeyevs, Victor and Venedikt—but these are just a few of the ingredients that have made up my reading for the last fifteen years. I like authors with an overwhelming, extravagantly aestheticized style (Nabokov, Esterházy), but also those who double their texts with rigorous documentation (Tsypkin, Sebald)—not forgetting the American experimentalists, particularly Donald Barthelme. The writers closest to my heart, however, are Raymond Carver and Julio Cortázar, whom I can still read without the least interference from my own critical pretensions, as someone who has, in turn, devoted himself to writing. My literary influences and preferences do not relate to ideologies or movements, but rather to individual people and their stories."

CHRISTINE MONTALBETTI is a novelist, critic, and playwright. She was born in Le Havre, France, in 1965 and lives in Paris. She has published three novels— *Sa fable achevée, Simon sort dans la bruine* (His tale concluded, Simon walks into the drizzle, 2001), *L'Origine de l'homme* (The Origin of Man, 2002), and *Western* (2005)—a short narrative entitled *Expérience de la campagne* (Experience of the Country, 2005), and two books of short stories, one fictional—*Nouvelles sur le sentiment amoureux* (Novellas on Love, 2007)—and the other (mostly) nonfiction: *Petits déjeuners avec quelques écrivains célèbres* (Breakfasts with a Few Famous Writers, 2008), from which the story in this anthology was excerpted. Another novel, a road novel that takes place in Oklahoma and Colorado, will be published in October by POL Editeur.

She is also a professor of French Literature and creative writing at the University of Paris VIII.

She writes, "I'm concerned with the moment, with the swarm of emotions passing through it, with the contradictory sensations that innervate it and lead to all sorts of miniature battles, of which a narrative work can take advantage.

I am concerned with all the possible microscopic sagas residing in the perception of a moment, and which themselves concern everything surrounding us: the insects passing by, to whom I readily attribute monologues, or the various objects, which I like to bring to life . . . each of these has a story. Its own method, let's say, of spinning out new details.

Hence my taste for digression. Digression—for its inherent dynamism, for the extent to which it constitutes the driving force behind all writing, but especially because it is, in effect, right at the heart of our experience, whose structure is itself dreamy and digressive.

It's also a way of using humor to keep melancholy at bay, a way that also involves continuously calling upon the reader to confirm his presence, to remind him that it's really for his sake that all this is being done. A reader with whom I try to form a connection based on the commonality of our experience—on whatever he, and then the main character, and then I myself might have in common. Thus, in this way, the novel or short story in question, though speaking of fictional characters, and sometimes including a perhaps openly autobiographical reflection on an event from my own existence, describes nothing, in fact, if not *your* own particular story."

GIULIO MOZZI has published twenty-one books—as editor, fiction writer, and poet—with such prestigious Italian publishers as Theoria, Einaudi, and Mondadori. His first collection, *Questo è il giardino* (This is the Garden, 1993) won the Premio Mondello; the story "L'apprendista" (The Apprentice), from that collection, appears in Mondadori's anthology of the top Italian stories of the twentieth century, *I racconti italiani del novecento* (2001). The story "Carlo Doesn't Know How to Read," included in this anthology, was originally attributed to **CARLO DALCIELO**, a fictional artist and author created by Giulio Mozzi and artist Bruno Lorini; the piece is a part of a Mozzi/Lorini project entitled, *Il pittore e il pesce: una poesia di Raymond Carver, un opera di Carlo Dalcielo* (The Painter and the Fish: a poem by Raymond Carver, a work by Carlo Dalcielo), which reflects on the notion of authorship. In this art exhibit and book (2008), Carlo has responded to the translated Raymond Carver poem "The Painter and the Fish" with a storyboard; the various frames of the storyboard were then interpreted by a number of Italian artists whose pieces, taken together, make up Carlo's exhibit (ilpittoreeilpesce.wordpress.com). Dalcielo's published work includes *Diario dei sogni* (Dream Diary, 2003), and he also makes an appearance in Mozzi's book *Fiction* (2001).

MATHIAS OSPELT lives in Vaduz, Liechtenstein, where he was born in 1963. He writes short stories and plays (mainly Liechtenstein related). As well as creating his own texts he has run his own (one-man) business over the last twelve years, writing on commission (ghostwriting, books of general interest, translations, columns, musical libretti, etc.). He also performs as a comedian (Kabarett), mainly in the venue he founded with a group of friends in 2003. He is the Secretary of PEN Club Liechtenstein and head of the Writers in Prison Committee Liechtenstein.

VICTOR PELEVIN was born in Moscow in 1962. Before studying at Moscow's Gorky Institute of Literature, he worked in a number of jobs, including as an engineer on a project to protect MiG fighter planes from insect interference in tropical conditions. He is one of the few writers today who writes seriously about what is happening in contemporary Russia, but with a style of ironic detachment characteristic of his generation—one which never had time to absorb the ideologies accepted, or rejected, by its predecessors.

He is the author of (in English translation) *Omon Ra* (1996), *The Yellow Arrow* (1996), *The Blue Lantern* (1997), a collection of short stories that won the Russian "Little Booker" Prize, *A Werewolf Problem in Central Russia and Other Stories* (1998), and *The Life of Insects* (1998). The translation of his novel *Buddha's Little Finger* (2000) was shortlisted for the International IMPAC Dublin Literary Award. He was named by *The New Yorker* as one of the best European writers under thirty-five, and by *The Observer* as one of "twenty-one writers to watch for the 21st century." His most recent novel is *The Sacred Book of the Werewolf* (2008). Pelevin's work has been translated into fifteen languages.

When asked to contribute a personal statement for this anthology, Pelevin replied, "Can I offer a piece of my inner silence? That's my only true statement, the rest will not be quite as sincere."

GIEDRA RADVILAVIČIŪTĖ was born in 1960. She graduated from Vilnius University with a degree in Lithuanian philology in 1983, working as a teacher in the provinces for the next three years. At present she lives in Vilnius and is involved in organizing the international literature festival Šiaurės vasara (Summer of the North).

Radvilavičiūtė made her debut in 1985 with a book of short stories, but it was in 1999 that she became truly involved in Lithuanian literature by publishing her essays in the cultural press. In 2004 Radvilavičiūtė published her essay collection, *Suplanuotos akimirkos* (Planned Moments).

She writes, "Ending up in an anthology of European short fiction is just as strange as living in a virtual house.

I believe that European literature—insofar as being a category with unique, identifying traits (and I don't mean such superficial indicators as place names, surnames, historical events, social realities, etc.)—doesn't exist.

Basically, there aren't any geographically specific literatures: not from North America or South America, not from Africa, not from Australia.

Nor does literature fall into categories: postcolonial literature, Soviet literature, queer literature, fireman's literature, text-message literature.

Literature is good or bad.

Its only country of origin—its only identity—is in what it evokes.

Someone like the South African-born John Maxwell Coetzee is considerably closer to me, as far as "bloodtype," than any Lithuanian author I might bump into on the street, not least because his biography is almost identical to my own.

I don't know why.

Perhaps he's my kind of writer because, as one of his former colleagues said—someone who worked with him for many years—Coetzee, a Nobel laureate, laughs maybe once every decade.

My writing has been described as resembling short fiction. But there's no such thing as a pure genre, these days.

There's almost nothing left in the world that is natural, ecologically speaking.

The only genre my narratives really belong to is that of the mongrel, the centaur.

They differ from pure essays primarily in my use of a protagonist, a narrator—a conscious creation.

She is single, shy, and not particularly attractive. She suffers from insomnia and various phobias, and she exhibits a tentative kind of impertinence. She tries to use humor to cover up her sensitive nature and her complexes. And she lives with a beautiful cat.

My narratives also differ from authentic essays because they contain a large dollop of imagination; because there is a distance, in them, from the events depicted; and because they try to make readers wonder about the above elements, not just become submerged, emotionally, in the story (though that too is important).

One of the best Czech (European? World?) writers of all time, Bohumil Hrabal, said: 'If I could write, I'd write a book about man's greatest joys and greatest misfortunes.'

So, even this genial Czech, who—more often than not—looked at the world through a mug of amber-colored beer, believed that books were, sadly, beyond his reach.

So what could a woman like me—a single, not particularly attractive woman who lives with a beautiful cat, a woman who suffers from insomnia and various phobias, covering up her complexes and her sensitive nature with humor, who exhibits a tentative kind of impertinence, and who's taken a liking (for instance, in this text) to pretending to be her own narrator—have to say?"

JULIÁN RÍOS is Spain's foremost postmodernist writer. His first two books were coauthored with Octavio Paz. Since that time he has written a number of novels, including *Larva: Babel de una Noche de San Juan* (1983; *Larva: Midsummer Night's Babel*, 1990), *Poundemónium: Homenaje a Ezra Pound* (1986; *Poundemonium*, 1997), *Amores que atan* (1995; *Loves That Bind*, 1998), *Monstruario* (1999; *Monstruary*, 2002). He divides his time between Paris and Madrid.

Asked about his influences, in a 2005 interview with Mark Thwaite, Ríos replied, "Their names are legion, a multitude, but the important thing to me is to distinguish among the parade my own tribe, my ancestors and relatives: an old lineage whose founders are Rabelais (in the beginning was the word of words), Cervantes (in the beginning was the book of books), and Sterne (in the beginning was the page, for short), a trinity for eternity, because their books are endless. Joyce and his fellow countryman Flann O'Brien, and many others before, such as Flaubert and the Brazilian Machado de Assis, belong to the same tradition. I always have presented Joyce as an example of integrity, exactness and permanent creativity."

PENNY SIMPSON studied at Brighton Art College and Essex University. A former journalist and reviewer, she was awarded the inaugural Theatre Management Associations's Theatre Critic of the Year Award in 1991. Her debut collection of short fiction *DOGdays* was published in 2003. Two consecutive bursary awards from the Arts Council of Wales assisted in the research and completion of her first novel *The Banquet of Esther Rosenbaum* (2008). Her second novel, set in Croatia just after the 1990s war, is being completed with the help of a 2009 Hawthornden Fellowship. In 2007, she won the Rhys Davies Short Story Competition with "Eagle in the Maze," later broadcast on BBC Radio. Her short fiction has been included in anthologies from Bloomsbury, Virago and Tindal Street Press. She combines writing with her work as Head of Media for Welsh National Opera.

She writes, "I've always been interested in novels and short stories that project a sense of another world, maybe that of an outsider, but one that is nevertheless still rooted in a real place, possibly through a specific location, or by a strong evocation of the senses. Patrick Süskind's *Perfume* and *The Tin Drum* by Günter Grass are two novels that have been influential in shaping the approach to my novel *The Banquet of Esther Rosenbaum*. My central character is a seven-foot tall giantess and celebrity chef, who uses recipes as a means of recording stories about her life in 1920s Berlin.

I studied literature from the Enlightenment at university and loved the experiment and range of fiction from that period—a range that surprised me for its ambiguity, irony, wordplay, and different writing styles. To name but three that surprised, intrigued, and delighted: Laurence Sterne's *The Life and Opinions of Tristram Shandy*, Voltaire's *Candide* and Jonathan Swift's *Gulliver's Travels*."

GOCE SMILEVSKI was born in 1975 in Skopje, Macedonia. He was educated at University of Sts. Cyril and Methodius in Skopje, Charles University in Prague, and Central European University in Budapest. He is the author of several novels, including *Razgovori so Spinoza* (2002; *Conversation with Spinoza*, 2006) and *Sestrata na Zigmund Frojd* (Sigmund Freud's Sister, 2006), from which the story in this collection is excerpted. *Conversation with Spinoza*—which has been translated into several languages, including English—brought him the Macedonian Novel of the Year Award.

He writes, "The question of belonging and the attempt to situate oneself in a literary context have a rather numbing effect on a Macedonian writer. A decade or so ago, we were part of Eastern Europe, and so we were considered a part of the European context. Now, however, the concept of a Europe divided into East and West has disappeared: after the creation of the European Union, one either lives in the EU, or they're thrown into 'the other' Europe—beyond the borders of the Union.

When I meet with writers and publishers from abroad and when they hear the title of one of my novels, the most common question I get is: 'Why did you write about Spinoza?' Behind the general politeness of this question, I can't help but notice their strong emphasis on the words *why*, *you*, and *Spinoza*. It always makes me feel as though I somehow have no right to write about someone who belongs to 'them,' to their Western European context (and now let's call it their

'European Union context'), and not to mine. This discourages me to the extent that I give up explaining that I've dreamed of writing about Spinoza ever since I first heard of Spinoza—in grammar school, in a philosophy class (yes, unlike in the European Union, philosophy is a mandatory course in Macedonian high schools). So, in the end, I always answer by referring to a larger context—I say that I was interested in writing about someone who felt his only allegiance was to his own high ideals, not to a group of people defined by their religion, language, or geographic borders. The title of my latest novel, *Sigmund Freud's Sisters*, provokes a similar question. The explanation I offer is that I wanted to mirror Sigmund Freud's relationship to his sisters with the relationship of Gustav Klimt to his sister Klara—who was Freud's patient—and likewise with Franz Kafka's to his sister Ottla, who became a close friend of Freud's sisters during the last months of their lives in the Theresienstadt concentration camp. But: I feel as though my answers to the question of 'why I write' always sound like apologies. At the same time, regardless of the tone of the question, I must say I always feel honored when I receive questions about my writing because the authors of 'the Other Europe' rarely have a chance to talk about their literature—questions directed at us almost always concern our current politics. As writers, we are neither far away enough (so we can't be 'exotic') nor close enough (to be 'real Europeans'): we're somewhere in between, in a place where we can barely be noticed and thus are easily and so often forgotten. Our place on the margin evokes two different feelings at the same time: one of inferiority, and then one of freedom. Our inferiority complex makes us feel that we are nothing but intruders in the European context, but the freedom that our 'marginal lives' allows us gives us the ability to choose only the best of the European tradition to help us move forward."

PETER STAMM was born in 1963 in Weinfelden, Switzerland. After a few semesters spent studying English, Psychology, and Psychopathology, he took up a career as a freelance author and journalist, writing for the *Neue Zürcher Zeitung*, *Weltwoche*, *Tages-Anzeiger* and the satirical magazine *Nebelspalter*. His fiction includes *Agnes* (1998; 2000), *In fremden Gärten* (2003; *In Strange Gardens*, 2006) *Ungefähre Landschaft* (2001; *Unformed Landscape*, 2004), *An einem Tag wie diesem* (2006; *On a Day Like This*, 2008). He has lived in Paris, New York, and Scandinavia, and is now based outside of Zurich.

He writes, "The first texts that I read as literature and not merely as a diversion or for school were the short stories of Edgar Allan Poe and the plays of Henrik

Ibsen. I was maybe sixteen at the time. Later I distanced myself from both authors and discovered the French—Flaubert, Camus, Henry de Montherlant —and the Americans—Hemingway, Fitzgerald—and above all the English and Irish—Joseph Conrad, James Joyce. National literatures have never interested me. Europe is so varied and Switzerland is so small that the foreign author is more banal than the domestic. That I read most of this foreign literature in its original language and not in my own, and that we Swiss don't speak the same language that we write, may have led to my never finding wordplay that important. Literature for me was always what came to be in the mind of the reader, the effect of the words, not the words themselves. And so, besides writers, visual artists, filmmakers, and even architects also appear among my important influences. Art, and literature especially, still has a high value in Europe. It is not a product, its quality is not measured by success on the market, but rather by the power of innovation. Creative writing as a college subject is not very common. Being an author is a profession unlike any other. Literary writing cannot be learned in the conventional sense. In the culture section of the newspaper a clear distinction is made as well between serious literature and literature for entertainment. Writing has remained—in the best sense of the word—elite. German and Swiss literatures are not particularly difficult, but they see their assignment not so much in the reassurance as in the unsettling of a reader, in the firm belief that beauty and truth are not consumable but instead must be—in the sense of a catharsis—cultivated and experienced."

IGOR ŠTIKS was born in 1977 in Sarajevo, Bosnia and Herzegovina. His fiction, literary criticism, poetry, and essays have appeared widely in journals and reviews of the former Yugoslavia. His novel *A Castle in Romagna* received the Slavic Award for Best First Book in 2000. To date it has been translated into German, English, and Spanish. The American edition of this novel was nominated for the prestigious International IMPAC Dublin Literary Award (2006). His second novel, *Elijahova stolica* (Elijah's Chair), published in 2006, received both the Gjalski and Kiklop Awards for Best Fiction Book of the Year. This novel has been translated into a dozen European languages. Igor Štiks holds a PhD from Institut d'Etudes Politiques de Paris (Sciences Po) and Northwestern University (Chicago). He is a postdoctoral research fellow at the University of Edinburgh, UK.

Štiks writes, "I've tended to see my childhood in Sarajevo as a 'golden age' in my life; but, as with every golden age, it needed to end—and mine ended in catastrophe, when the war in what used to be Yugoslavia culminated in the brutal siege of my hometown. This catastrophe—as it is often the case in mythological narratives—was followed by exile. My personal exile took me first to Zagreb (Croatia) where I started my literary career, and then to Paris, Chicago, and, lately, Edinburgh. My fiction is influenced both by the fact that I come from the Balkans —a tumultuous history (and present day), to say the least—but also by the fact that I have spent a considerable—and intellectually formative—time abroad, in France and the U.S. In my first novel, *A Castle in Romagna*, written in my early twenties, I tried to avoid dealing directly with the war . . . My idea at the time was that absence of recent events in my narrative would be more 'eloquent' than their explicit description. I wanted to 'write' about the war in Bosnia and the former Yugoslavia through historically and geographically separated (but inter-connected) stories. However, in my second novel *Elijah's Chair*—"At the Sarajevo Market" is an excerpt from this novel, which I mostly wrote in Paris, sick of Balkan nationalisms—I couldn't escape it anymore. As If somebody had whispered in my ear, there on the streets of Paris, that I wouldn't be able to move on until I'd dealt with the war, creatively, in fiction. But I was immediately faced with certain dilemmas: what right did I have to write about the war and Sarajevo since I hadn't lived through the siege (being lucky enough to escape)? And: If I was finally going to write about it, what voice should I use? I found the answer in my main character, an Austrian novelist named Richard Richter, whose life brings together the Second World War, the Holocaust, leftist engagement in the 1960s and the 1970s, and the siege of Sarajevo . . . At the beginning of *Elijah's Chair* readers only know that he is writing a 'report' about what's happened to him since coming to Sarajevo to reconstruct his own family history. They are also aware that he has a loaded gun. They suspect that he might use it once he finishes the manuscript. It is writing that keeps him alive. But, as we should know by now, writing is a losing game . . ."

PETER TERRIN was born in 1960. In 1996, he won a short story competition. He collected the prize-winning story and others in *De code* (The Code, 1998). His first novel *Kras* (Crass) appeared in 2001, followed in 2003 by *Blanco*, and in 2004 by *Vrouwen en kinderen eerst* (Women and Children First), which was shortlisted for the BNG Literary Prize in 2005. His most recent book is *De bijeneters* (The Bee Eaters), published in 2006. This collection of seven shorter pieces—from which "The Murderer" was excerpted—was longlisted for the AKO Literature Prize, and won the Provincial Prize of West Flanders. His latest novel, *De bewaker* (The Guard), will appear in 2009.

Terrin writes, "In 1991, in a London hotel room, unable to sleep because worrying about what to do with my life, I read a book, the first one I'd read since being in school. It was a very special book, by a writer I now regard as the greatest in my language. A young account executive in despair, reading one of the best novels around: *The Darkroom of Damocles*, by W. F. Hermans. I can only blame my youth, but after that long, exhilarating night of suspense and tragedy and recognition, I found myself thinking that I myself—Peter Terrin—might one day be able to write something that other people would actually want to read. But that's exactly what happened. The universe of Hermans had become my universe, and when morning came, I called my boss in Belgium to inform him that I would no longer be selling his marble products to London architects. Young and stupid. Thank God. My life changed, and I wrote—for many years without anyone noticing. I discovered plenty of excellent teachers. Carver, Flannery O'Connor, Malamud. But the biggest influence came from European masters, such as Franz Kafka, Dino Buzzati, and Albert Camus. Writers of exciting stories that reveal the complexity of truth—a mystery fascinating as a brilliant diamond."

JEAN-PHILIPPE TOUSSAINT, writer and film director, was born in 1957 in Brussels, Belgium. He is the author of nine novels, including *La Salle de bain* (1985; *The Bathroom*, 1990), *Monsieur* (1986; 1991), *L'Appareil-photo* (1989; *Camera*, 2008), *La Réticence* (1991), *La Télévision* (1997; *Television*, 2004), and *Fuir* (2005; *Running Away*, 2009).

Below is an excerpt from an interview with the author included in the Chinese edition of *Zidane's Melancholy*:

Why did you choose Zidane as a subject?

I think that an author has a responsibility to examine the contemporary world. And, in today's world, football has acquired enormous significance . . . I think it's a writer's duty to take an interest in things that influence the contemporary world. Certain topics aren't less interesting than others; all subjects are interesting, especially if they're in tune with the times. Football is right at the core of our society; therefore it's quite normal to take an interest in it. And then, in taking a topic that is not, apparently, literary,

I'm turning Zidane into a sort of modern icon. To my mind it's something akin to Andy Warhol's approach thirty years ago, when he created pictures of Mao Zedong, Marilyn Monroe, or Jackie Kennedy: he'd take some photos, cut them, repaint them, and turn them into icons of modernity . . . and when you want to evoke the '60s or '70s, those images are the ones which perfectly represent that time. Similarly, the moment I take Zidane as a literary subject, he becomes a kind of contemporary icon.

Do you think only artists understand Zidane's melancholy?

Artists are on familiar terms with melancholy. More, almost, than making it a writer's book, I tried to make [*Zidane's Melancholy*] . . . well . . . an artist's book. I think there are many registers in this book, and simultaneously there is the desire to write a kind of novel, a very short novel, but one with Zidane as a character. There is also a psychoanalytic approach . . . there's a text by Freud called *Leonardo da Vinci and a Memory of his Childhood*, which interested me greatly—in it, Freud analyzes Leonardo da Vinci's childhood. You don't actually know if what Freud is saying has anything to do with reality or truth, but that's not important. What's interesting is how Freud himself appropriates, or invents, Leonardo da Vinci. And, in my case, I invented Zidane, I appropriated Zidane, and what does it matter if that's connected to reality or not? There are many different genres in the text: in one place you've got a novel, in another you've got literary criticism—because I go back over my novel *The Bathroom*. There's also psychoanalysis and, lastly, poetry, because at times there are expressions like "the black card of melancholy," which refers to the "black sun of melancholy"—one of Nerval's very well known poetic figures:

> My sole star *is dead,—and my constellated lute*
> Bears the black sun *of* Melancholia.

TRANSLATED FROM FRENCH BY URSULA MEANY SCOTT

NEVEN UŠUMOVIĆ was born in 1972 in Zagreb, Croatia, and grew up in Subotica, Serbia. He received a degree in Philosophy, Comparative Literature, and Hungarian Studies from the Faculty of Philosophy, University of Zagreb. He won critical acclaim for two collections of short stories *7 mladih* (7 Youngsters,

1997) and *Makovo zrno* (Poppy Seed, 2009), and a "short-winded novel" *Ekskur-zija* (Excursion, 2001). He has translated the works of Béla Hamvas, Ferenc Mol-nár, Péter Esterházy, and Ádám Bodor into Croatian. Together with Stjepan Lukač and Jolán Mann, he edited an anthology of contemporary Hungarian short sto-ries entitled *Zastrašivanje strašila* (Methods of Intimidation, 2001). Since 2002 he has worked as a librarian in Umag.

He writes, "My first literary attempts, in the late eighties, were adolescent at-tempts at uncovering the life and history of the town where I grew up—Subot-ica (Hungarian: Szabadka). Subotica is a town with a complex Austro-Hungarian history; today it is in Serbia, with a Hungarian majority as well as a significant population of Croatians; formerly there were significant contributions from Jew-ish as well as German culture; and it was there that four writers were born who have been my constant inspirations: Géza Csáth (1887–1919), Dezső Kosztolányi (1885–1936), Danilo Kiš (1935–1989), and Radomir Konstantinović (1928–). The ravages of the war in Yugoslavia during the '90s directed my creativity—in a trau-matic way—towards the violent tentativeness of our national language and ter-ritory, and encouraged a postmodern sensibility (imbued with the poetics of Danilo Kiš, or, for example, David Albahari, but at the same time intoxicated with the noisy versatility of musical trailblazers such as Sonic Youth, John Zorn, or Einstürzende Neubauten), politicizing me and directing me not only towards tex-tuality in general, but also towards a new poetics of the Pannonian area. My writ-ing moves in starts and stops, defying the smooth rhythm of speech, just like the language of Marina Tsvetaeva, Miloš Crnjanski, or Ádám Bodor; and whatever basic poetic interest I have in the landscape is anything but romantic: I'm inter-ested in the consequences of industrialization, in all the aspects of environmen-tal destruction—I draw inspiration for my grotesque, symbolic scenes from the world around me, looking for the single point of stillness in this increasingly pre-cipitous globalist carnival . . . a point of reversal and reflection."

TRANSLATED FROM CROATIAN BY DINKO TELECAN

ELO VIIDING was born in 1974. Viiding comes from an impressive literary dy-nasty: her grandfather Paul Viiding (1904–1962) was a short-story writer. Her grandmother Linda Viiding (1906–2003) was a translator of Finnish literature. Her father was the major Estonian poet Juhan Viiding (1948–1995).

Elo Viiding's poetry is often zany, with strange jumps of association. Nevertheless, the subject matter of her poetry is commitment to society and its changes. She is often tongue-in-cheek, introducing a healthy dose of humor into her work.

Elo Viiding's debut under the pseudonym "Elo Vee" occurred in 1991, when she published her first collection of poetry, the chapbook *Telg* (The Axis). Her next two collections of poetry, *Laeka lähedus* (The Nearness of the Casket, 1993) and *Võlavalgel* (Under the Light of Debt, 1995), and the collection of short stories *Ingelheim* (1995) were also published under the same pseudonym. After the death of her father, she abandoned the pseudonym and she has published her recent collections of poetry under her real name: *V* (1998), *Esimene tahe* (The First Will, 2002) and *Teatud erandid* (Certain Exceptions, 2003).

ORNELA VORPSI was born in Tirana in 1968 and studied there at the Academy of Fine Arts. In 1991 she emigrated to Milan and in 1997 moved on to Paris where she works as a photographer, painter, and video artist. Vorpsi's first novel, *The Country Where No One Ever Dies*, from which her piece in this anthology was excerpted, was originally written in Italian, not in Albanian. It was initially published in French as *Le pays où l'on ne meurt jamais* (2004), and has since appeared in Italian, German, and Spanish. Vorpsi is also the author of *Nothing Obvious* (2001), *Buvez du cacao Van Houten!* (Drink Van Houten Cocoa!, 2005), *Vetri rosa* (Pink Glass, 2006), and *La mano che non mordi* (The Hand that Does Not Touch, 2007).

She writes: "I never wanted to be a writer, or at least I never wanted to write a book filled with words. My greatest dream was to be a painter, to create images without words. Even now, I still have a strained relationship with stories and the written word, because what I'm primarily interested in, I think, are the thoughts that come out of silence, out of images. I didn't choose to write, let's just say that writing chose me, and I've learned to accept this, day after day, while nonetheless resenting the likelihood of giving up on the visual arts—since I can hardly dedicate myself to both mediums at once, when each demands everything of an artist. Still, there is no single activity that's ever obsessed me as much as reading. My mother used to catch me spending all my days and nights reading; she'd ask me if I thought I was Rockefeller's daughter. I'm made of Russian and French literature. I'm talking about the classics, of course. And even though I write in an adopted language—writing meant having to abandon my mother tongue—I am entirely an Albanian writer."

TRANSLATED FROM FRENCH BY AUDE JEANSON

MICHAŁ WITKOWSKI was born in 1975 in Wrocław and now lives in Warsaw. He studied Polish philology at the University of Wrocław and he has published five books: *Copyright* (2001), *Lubiewo* (2005; *Lovetown*, 2010), *Fototapeta* (Photomural, 2006), *Barbara Radziwiłłówna z Jaworzna-Szczakowej* (Barbara Radziwill of Jaworzno-Szczakowa, 2007), and *Margot* (2009). *Lubiewo* shot Witkowski to the heights of literary celebrity in Poland, winning him both the Literary Prize of the City of Gdynia and the Polish Booksellers Association Prize. He was twice a finalist for the prestigious N I K E award (in 2006 for *Lubiewo*, and 2007 for *Barbara Radziwiłłówna*), and his works have enjoyed success in adaptation for the theater as well.

Lubiewo—from which the story in this anthology was excerpted—has been translated widely and published in over a dozen countries, including England, where it appears as *Lovetown*. The original title refers to a seaside hamlet on the Baltic Sea that lends its name to a gay beach there; and the subtle resonance of the place name with words like *lubić* ("to like" in Polish; "to love" in Russian) and *lubieżny* (lascivious) is just one indication of the poetic complexity of Witkowski's writing. The book, which is fragmentary and many-voiced, takes place for the most part in two locales and times: at Lubiewo in the present day, and in the Silesian capital city of Wrocław between the seventies and early nineties—as mediated through the recollections of a number of "old queens," nostalgic holdovers from the Communist era.

On the subject of *Lovetown*, Witkowski writes, "I fear that if this book is taken up in the press or on TV, the media will have to remake it in their own fashion. That which is private and unique will be silenced, and instead the book will be mined for things that aren't even in it ... They'll link it to the 'struggle for equality'; they'll make a 'manifesto' out of it, 'the first Polish gay novel,' etc. Just as long as it's the first of something, like 'first serious attempt at ...' or 'first queer novel in ...' But really it's simply the first (and last) of my books to deal not just with homosexuals, but with a particular subgroup called 'queens' or 'faggots,' and with their customs, which are exotic for many readers, and were formed by their environment over the years. I'm interested, among other things, in which models of femininity were adopted, why certain ones and not others.

It's not gays from the middle class that interest me, but precisely those 'repulsive, filthy, and naughty' ones, because all that's left to them is telling stories, language, making things up—and that has to suffice for an entire world. Middle-class gays have their long-term relationships, their little houses and gardens and lawnmowers, but the other ones—they don't have a thing. Theirs is a double disenfranchisement: it's not enough that they're gay, there's that criminalized stratum of theirs as well: thieves, prostitutes, floozies. If they even have a job, then all they have to do at it is sit. They sit. And as they sit there on their night shift, as wardens in a prison or wherever, they dream and fantasize about the most extraordinary things: which is what makes them so attractive as literary figures. Reality, no matter how hideous it is, doesn't affect them in the least, because they live in their own unreal world. Even when they gossip, all they're doing is satisfying a need for narration unmet in others. This faggot *bohème* escapes madness by turning to the theater, camp, surrealism. They rebel against social hierarchies —that which is hideous to others is not so for them—and they apprehend the middle-class world in all its rose-colored futility. So they cannot but relativize 'generally accepted' standards of taste, 'universally respected' moral principles . . . They're a slap in the face to whatever is totalitarian, general, universally binding, and sanctified . . ."

Translator Biographies

TIMOTHY BEWES is Associate Professor of English and Director of Graduate Studies at Brown University. He has authored two books, *Cynicism and Postmodernity* and *Reification, or the Anxiety of Late Capitalism*. His articles have appeared in such journals as *New Left Review, New Literary History, Parallax, Genre, Cultural Critique, Twentieth-Century Literature,* and *Differences*.

ALISTAIR IAN BLYTH's translations from Romanian include the novel *Little Fingers,* by Flip Florian, *An Intellectual History of Cannibalism,* by Cătălin Avramescu, and *Our Circus Presents,* by Lucian Dan Teodorovici.

CHRISTOPHER BURAWA is a poet and translator. His book of poems, *The Small Mystery of Lapses,* was published by Cleveland State University Press in 2006, his translations of contemporary Icelandic poet Jóhann Hjálmarsson won the 2005 Toad Press International Chapbook Competition, and his translation *Flying Night Train: Selected Poems of Jóhann Hjálmarsson* will be published by Green Integer Books in 2009. He is the Director of the Center of Excellence for the Creative Arts at Austin Peay State University in Clarksville, Tennessee.

IMOGEN COHEN teaches translation, creative writing, and linguistics at the University of Amsterdam. She has translated for radio, television and theatre, and works now as a literary translator in association with the Foundation for the Production and Translation of Dutch Literature. Imogen lives in Amsterdam with her husband and two children.

ERIC DICKENS is a translator and reviewer of Estonian and Finnish-Swedish literature. He is currently translating work by the novelists Toomas Vint and Hannele Mikaela Taivassalo.

ELLEN ELIAS-BURSAĆ has been translating novels and non-fiction by Bosnian, Croatian and Serbian writers for the last twenty years. Her translation of David Albahari's novel *Gotz and Meyer* was awarded the National Translation Award by the American Literary Translators Association in 2006. She has coauthored a textbook for the study of Bosnian, Croatian and Serbian with Ronelle Alexander and has written a study on poet Tin Ujević and his work as a literary translator.

ROBERT ELSIE is the author of fifty books on Albania and its culture, including numerous literary translations from Albanian.

ELIZABETH HARRIS is an Associate Professor of Creative Writing at the University of North Dakota. She is currently translating Giulio Mozzi's collection *Questo e' il giardino* (This is the Garden). Her translations of Mozzi's stories appear in various journals, including *The Literary Review, The Missouri Review,* and *The Kenyon Review.*

CELIA HAWKESWORTH was Senior Lecturer in Serbian and Croatian at the School of Slavonic and East European Studies, University College, London until her retirement. She has published numerous articles and several books on Serbian, Croatian, and Bosnian literature, including a study entitled *Ivo Andric: Bridge between East and West,* and *Voices in the Shadows: Women and Verbal Art in Serbia and Bosnia.* She has also published numerous translations, including several works by Ivo Andric and Dubravka Ugresic.

ANASTASIA LAKHTIKOVA is a native of Ukraine. She is a Lecturer in the School of Literatures, Cultures, and Linguistics at the University of Illinois, Urbana-Champaign, where she teaches courses in literary translation.

DUSTIN LOVETT has studied translation at the University of Illinois at Urbana-Champaign and the University of Vienna, Austria. He is focused on the translation of German-language literature, and is currently working on translations of the Austrian satirist Werner Kofler and the Swiss writer Daniel Zahno.

ANA LUCIC translated Svetislav Basara's *Chinese Letter* for Dalkey Archive Press, where she works as Foreign Language Editor.

ANNE METTE LUNDTOFTE is a Danish writer and has worked for various Danish and American publications. She has a PhD in Comparative Literature from New York University and has translated numerous Danish writers into English. Her book, *New York, New York,* will be published by Gyldendal in the fall.

W. MARTIN is a PhD candidate in Comparative Literature at the University of Chicago, and Literature Programmer at the Polish Cultural Institute in New York. Published translations (from Polish and German) include Natasza Goerke's *Farewells to Plasma,* selected essays in *The Günter Grass Reader,* and

Erich Kästner's *Emil and the Detectives*. From 1999 to 2004 he was Fiction Editor of the literary journal *Chicago Review*, for which he also edited the "New Polish Writing" issue (2000) and co-edited the "New Writing in German" issue (2002). He has taught in the MA Program in the Humanities and in the College at the University of Chicago, and is a 2008 recipient of an NEA Award for Translation.

JANICE MATHIE-HECK is a poet, translator, editor, and literary critic. Most recently, her essay on the poetry of Visar Zhiti appeared in *Mehr Licht!*

ABIGAIL MITCHELL lives in Zurich, Switzerland, where she is currently pursuing a doctorate in mathematics.

EVGENIA PANCHEVA is Associate Professor of Renaissance Literature at Sofia University. She is the author of *Dispersing Semblances: an Essay on Renaissance Culture*, co-author of *Literary Theory: from Plato to Postmodernism*, and co-editor of *Renaissance Refractions*. Her major translations include Shakespeare's sonnets and poems, Marlowe's *The Jew of Malta* and *Hero and Leander*, and poems by Byron, Poe and N. Vaptsarov.

ROWAN RICARDO PHILLIPS received his BA from Swarthmore College and his PhD from Brown University. His fields of interests are the writing and practice of poetry, poetics and translation. His poems have appeared in *Callaloo, Chelsea, The C. L. R. James Journal, Harvard Review, The Iowa Review, The Kenyon Review, The New Republic, The New Yorker, No: A Journal of the Arts,* and *Seneca Review*, among others. He has also published translations of Dante and of the Catalan poets Josep Carner, Tomàs Garcés, Joan Maragall, and Melcion Mateu.

KERRI A. PIERCE is a translator focusing on German, Danish, Dutch, Portuguese, Spanish, Norwegian, and Swedish.

THANGAM RAVINDRANATHAN is Assistant Professor of French Studies at Brown University. Her articles and fiction have appeared in *L'Express, Symposium, New Formations,* and *Muse India*.

DOUG ROBINSON is professor of English at the University of Mississippi and author of *Pentinpeijaiset* (Avain 2007), the Finnish translation of his novel about Pentti Saarikoski, as well as ten scholarly monographs in the fields of translation studies, language theory, and American literature and culture.

DARIUS JAMES ROSS is a Canadian transplant to Vilnius who, over the course of the past decade, has written and reported extensively on Lithuania for local and international English-language news media and leisure publications. He has translated many texts and excerpts of Lithuanian literary prose for the Vilnius Review, as well as for other publications.

IVAN SANDERS teaches literature at Columbia University, and has translated novels by George Konrád, Milán Füst, and Péter Nádas.

URSULA MEANY SCOTT is a Fellow in Applied Translation at Dalkey Archive Press, focusing on French and Spanish. She holds an M.Phil from Trinity College, Dublin.

TAMARA M. SOBAN was born in Ljubljana, Slovenia, in 1962, and received her BA in English from the University of Ljubljana. Among other works, she is the translator of Andrej Blatnik's *Skinswaps*, a collection of short stories (Northwestern University Press, 1998). Since 2002 she has worked as a translator and editor for the Moderna galerija/Museum of Modern Art in Ljubljana.

HEATHER TREBATICKÁ (née King) was born in London in 1942. She graduated in English language and literature at Manchester University. Since her marriage in 1967, she has lived in Bratislava, teaching English at Comenius University and translating mostly in the field of literature and culture.

SEVINC TURKKAN is completing her PhD in Comparative Literature at the University of Illinois, Urbana-Champaign.

LAURIS VANAGS is the translator of numerous texts from Latvian for the Latvian Literature Centre and other organizations.

ANDREW WACHTEL is Bertha and Max Dressler Professor of the Humanities, Dean of The Graduate School, and Director of the Roberta Buffett Center for International and Comparative Studies at Northwestern University. He serves as Editor of the "Writings from an Unbound Europe" series at Northwestern University Press, and is a renowned critic, historian, and translator.

Online Resources for
Countries Appearing in
Best European Fiction 2010

*Sites applicable to more than one country
are included in all appropriate sections.*

ALBANIA

Albanian Literature in Translation: www.albanianliterature.net

AUSTRIA

Austrian Academy Corpus: complete run of Karl Kraus's periodical *Die Fackel*
   (registration required): www.corpus1.aac.ac.at/fackel (German only)
Austrian Cultural Forum New York: www.acfny.org
Austrian Literature Online: www.literature.at
DIMENSION2 (contemporary German-language literature): www.dimension2
   .org
Literaturhaus: www.literaturhaus.at
Modern Austrian Literature & Culture Association: www.malca.org

BELGIUM

AMVC-Letterenhuis: www.amvc.be
Behoud de Begeerte, Center for the Literary Arts: www.begeerte.be (Dutch only)

De Papieren Man: www.papierenman.blogspot.com (Dutch only)

Flemish Literature Fund: www.buitenland.vfl.be/en/o

Flemish PEN: www.penvlaanderen.be (Dutch only)

Het Beschrijf: www.beschrijf.be

NOK: www.nok.be (Dutch only)

Ons Erfdeel: www.onserfdeel.be

The Low Countries: www.thelowcountries.blogspot.com

Recensieweb: www.recensieweb.nl (Dutch only)

Royal Academy of Dutch Language and Literature: www.kantl.be (Dutch only)

BOSNIA

Bosnian Institute literature site: www.bosnia.org.uk/bosnia/literature.cfm

ODJEK review: www.odjek.ba

Spirit of Bosnia: www.spiritofbosnia.org

BULGARIA

American Foundation for Bulgaria: www.en.afbulgaria.org

Athenaeum, LitClub: www.litclub.bg (Bulgarian only)

Bulgarian Society of Publishers in the Humanities: www.bsph.org (Bulgarian only)

Cult: www.cult.bg (Bulgarian only)

Elizabeth Kostova Foundation: www.ekf.bg/en

FAKEL: www.fakelexpress.com (Bulgarian only)

GrosniPelikani, Literature and Culture: www.grosnipelikani.net (Bulgarian only)

Republic of Bulgaria Institute for Culture: www.sic.mfa.government.bg

I Read: www.azcheta.com (Bulgarian only)

KULTURA: www.kultura.bg (Bulgarian only)

LiterNet: www.liternet.bg (Bulgarian only)

National Culture Fund: www.ncf.bg

Next Page Foundation: www.npage.org/en

The Red House, Centre for Culture and Debate: www.redhouse-sofia.org

Translator's Union: www.bgtranslators.org

CROATIA

Books about Croatia: www.books-croatia.com

Council of Europe site on Croatian Art and Literature: www.ecml.at/html/croatian/html/art.html

Croatian Literature in English: main.acmt.hr/~mario/

DENMARK

Ars Baltica: www.ars-baltica.net

Bogens World (Paper World): www.bogensverden.dk (Danish only)

Danish Arts Agency Literature Centre: www.danishliterature.info

Danish Literary Magazine: www.danishliterarymagazine.info

Naja Marie Aidt's website: www.najamarieaidt.com

Nordic Voices in Translation: www.nordicvoices.blogspot.com

ESTONIA

Ars Baltica: www.ars-baltica.net

, ET: www.teataja.ee/et (Estonian only)

Bahama Press: www.bahamapress.org (Estonian only)

Elo Viiding's blog: eloviiding.blogspot.com

Estonian Institute: www.einst.ee

Estonian Literary Magazine: www.einst.ee/literary

Estonian Literary Museum: www.kirmus.ee

Estonian Literature Centre: www.estlit.ee

Estonian National Cultural Foundation: www.erkf.ee (Estonian only)

Estonian Writers Union: www.ekl.ee

Folklore (Electronic Journal of Estonian Folklore): www.haldjas.folklore.ee/folklore

Kirikiri: www.kirikiri.ee (Estonian only)

Kirjanike Kodu: www.kirjanikekodu.kongress.ee (Estonian only)

Kriteerium: www.kriteerium.ee (Estonian only)

Littérature estonienne: www.litterature-estonienne.com (French only)

Looming: www.looming.ee (Estonian only)

Ninniku: www.eki.ee/ninniku (Estonian only)

Nordic Voices in Translation: www.nordicvoices.blogspot.com

Poogen: www.poogen.ee (Estonian only)

Tuglas-seura: www.tuglas.fi (Estonian only)

Under and Tuglas Literature Centre: www.utkk.ee

Urdu: www.hot.ee/muku/urdu.html (Estonian only)

Värske Rõhk: www.va.ee (Estonian only)

Vihik: www.vihik.tfd.ee (Estonian only)

Vikerkaar: www.vikerkaar.ee (Estonian only)

FINLAND

Ars Baltica: www.ars-baltica.net

Books From Finland: www.booksfromfinland.fi

Electric Verses, Contemporary Finnish Poetry: www.electricverses.net

FILI—Finnish Literature Exchange: www.finlit.fi/fili/en

Finnish Literature Society: www.finlit.fi

Finnish Translations Database: www.dbgw.finlit.fi/kaannokset/index.php?lang
=ENG

Modern Finnish Writers: www.kirjailijat.kirjastot.fi

Nordic Voices in Translation: www.nordicvoices.blogspot.com

FRANCE
[ALL SITES FRENCH ONLY, EXCEPT AS LISTED]

Boojum, L'animal littéraire: www.boojum-mag.net

Cairn (electronic journal archive): www.cairn.info

Chaoid: www.chaoid.com

Chimères: www.revue-chimeres.fr

Chroniques de la Luxiotte: www.luxiotte.net

Evene (book section): www.evene.fr/livres

Fabula: www.fabula.org

French Book News: www.frenchbooknews.com (English only)

French Cultural Agency: www.frenchculture.org (English only)

Gallica (Bibliotheque nationale de France digital library): www.gallica.bnf.fr

L'Express (book section): www.livres.lexpress.fr

Lire: le magazine littéraire: www.lire.fr

La Femelle du Requin: www.lafemelledurequin.free.fr

La Feuille: www.lafeuille.homo-numericus.net

La Licorne: www.edel.univ-poitiers.fr/licorne

La Vie des idées: www.laviedesidees.fr (French and English)

Le Centre National du Livre: www.centrenationaldulivre.fr

Le Magazine Littéraire: www.magazine-litteraire.com

Le Matricule des anges: www.lmda.net

Le Monde (book section): www.lemonde.fr/web/sequence/0,2-3260,1-0,0.html

La République des Livres: www.passouline.blog.lemonde.fr

Le Monde Diplomatique (book section): www.monde-diplomatique.fr/index/sujet/litterature

Le Nouvel Observateur (book section): www.bibliobs.nouvelobs.com

Le Tiers Livre, littérature et Internet: www.tierslivre.net

English translation of François Bon's blog: www.tierslivre.net/engl

Léo Scheer: www.leoscheer.com/blog

Libération book section: www.liberation.fr/livres

Lettres Ouvertes: www.lettres.blogs.liberation.fr/sorin

Non-Fiction: www.nonfiction.fr

Palimpsestes: www.yves-lefevre.nuxit.net/palimpsestes (French and English)

Transfuge, literature et cinéma: www.transfuge.fr

Zazieweb: www.zazieweb.fr

Zone Littéraire: www.zone-litteraire.com

HUNGARY

Database of Translations of Hungarian Literary Works: www.translations.bookfinder.hu/indexa.htm

George Konrád's website: www.konradgyorgy.hu

Hungarian Literature Online: www.hlo.hu

Hungarian Book Foundation: www.hungarianbookfoundation.hu

Hungarian Translators' House: www.c3.hu/~bfordhaz

HUNLIT: www.hunlit.hu/index.d2

KonTextus: www.kontextus.hu (Hungarian only)

Könyves Blog: www.konyves.blog.hu (Hungarian only)

Litera: www.litera.hu (Hungarian only)

Literatura Hungara Online: www.lho.es (Spanish only)

The Hungarian Quarterly: www.hungarianquarterly.com

ICELAND

Bókmenntasjóður, the Icelandic Literature Fund: www.bok.is/english
Nordic Voices in Translation: www.nordicvoices.blogspot.com

IRELAND

Aosdána: www.aosdana.artscouncil.ie
Books Ireland: www.islandireland.com/booksireland
Cúirt International Festival of Literature: www.galwayartscentre.ie/cuirt.htm
Culture Ireland: www.cultureireland.gov.ie
Cyphers: www.cyphersmagazine.org
The Dublin Review: www.thedublinreview.com
Dublin Writers' Festival: www.dublinwritersfestival.com
Fortnight: www.fortnight.org
IMPAC Dublin Literary Award: www.impacdublinaward.ie
Ireland Literature Exchange: www.irelandliterature.com
Irish Book Publishers' Association: www.publishingireland.com
The Irish Book Review: www.theirishbookreview.com
Irish Translators' and Interpreters' Association: www.translatorsassociation.ie
Irish Writers' Centre: www.writerscentre.ie
The James Joyce Centre: www.jamesjoyce.ie
Julian Gough's website: www.juliangough.com
Poetry Ireland: www.poetryireland.ie
THE SHOp, a Magazine of Poetry: www.theshop-poetry-magazine.ie
The Stinging Fly: www.stingingfly.org
Verbal Magazine: www.verbalon.com/magazine

ITALY
[ALL SITES ITALIAN ONLY]

Il Club degli Autori: www.clubautori.it
Ellin Selae Associazione Letteraria: www.ellinselae.org
Giulio Mozzi's website: www.giuliomozzi.com
Griselda Online: www.griseldaonline.it
The Ministry for Cultural Heritage and Activities: www.beniculturali.it
Il Primo Amore: www.ilprimoamore.com

Romanzieri: www.romanzieri.com

Vibrisse, bolletino: www.vibrisse.wordpress.com

LATVIA

Ars Baltica: www.ars-baltica.net

American Latvian Association: www.alausa.org

International Writers' and Translators' House: www.ventspilshouse.lv

Karogs: www.ekarogs.lv (Latvian only)

Kultūras Forums: www.tvnet.lv/izklaide/avize

Latvian Authors and Their Work: www.autornet.lv (Latvian only)

Latvian Culture Portal: www.culture.lv

The Latvian Institute: www.li.lv

Latvian Literature Center: www.literature.lv

Portal for Literature and Philosophy: www.satori.lv (Latvian only)

LIECHTENSTEIN

ArGe Liechtensteiner Literaturtage (literary festival, co-organized by Mathias Ospelt): www.lielit.li (German only)

Digital Liechtenstein: www.liechtenstein.li/en

Liechtenstein PEN: www.pen-club.li (German only)

Literaturhaus Liechtenstein: www.literaturhaus.li (German only)

National Library: www.landesbibliothek.li (German only)

Schichtwechsel, action-space for new art and communications: www.schicht-
wechsel.li (German only)

LITHUANIA

Ars Baltica: www.ars-baltica.net

ArtNews: www.artnews.lt (Lithuanian only)

Books from Lithuania: www.booksfromlithuania.lt

Cultural News: www.g-taskas.lt (Lithuanian only)

Kulturpolis: www.kulturpolis.lt (Lithuanian only)

Vilnius, European Capital of Culture 2009: www.culturelive.lt/en

MACEDONIA

Identities, Journal for Politics, Gender, and Culture: www.identities.org.mk
Macedonian PEN: www.pen.org.mk
Republic of Macedonia cultural site: www.culture.in.mk

NETHERLANDS

Digital Library of Dutch Literature: www.dbnl.org (Dutch only)
Dutch Language Union: http://taalunieversum.org (Dutch only)
Foundation for the Production and Translation of Dutch Literature: www.nlpvf.nl
National Library of the Netherlands: www.kb.nl/index-en.html
De Papieren Man: www.papierenman.blogspot.com (Dutch only)
Radio Netherlands Worldwide literature section: www.rnw.nl/category/tags-english/dutch-literature

NORWAY

Ars Baltica: www.ars-baltica.net
NORLA (Norwegian Literature Abroad): www.norla.no
Bok & Samfunn: www.bokogsamfunn.no
Nordic Voices in Translation (multicultural blog): nordicvoices.blogspot.com

POLAND

Ars Baltica: www.ars-baltica.net
Bacacay, The Polish Literature Weblog: www.bacacay.wordpress.com
Michał Witkowski's website: www.free.art.pl/michal.witkowski (Polish only)
Polish Book Institute: www.bookinstitute.pl
Polish Cultural Institute in London: www.polishculture.org.uk
Polish Culture Institute in New York: www.polishculture-nyc.org
Polish Institute of Arts and Sciences in America: www.piasa.org
Polish Writing: www.polishwriting.net

PORTUGAL

[ALL SITES PORTUGUESE ONLY EXCEPT AS LISTED]

Blogue de Letras, Artes e Ideias: www.bloguedeletras.blogspot.com

General Directorate for Book and Libraries: www.dglb.pt (English and Portuguese)

Instituto Camoes: www.instituto-camoes.pt

Ler: www.ler.blogs.sapo.pt

Librairie Portugaise in Paris: www.librairie-portugaise.com (French only)

Nova Cultura: www.novacultura.de

Os meus livros: www.oml.com.pt

Portuguese Literature Portal: www.portaldaliteratura.com

Projecto Vercial: www.alfarrabio.di.uminho.pt/vercial

Portuguese Author's Society: www.spautores.pt

Storm Magazine: www.storm-magazine.com

valter hugo mãe's website: www.valterhugomae.com

ROMANIA

BookBlog: www.bookblog.ro (Romanian only)

Contemporary Romanian Writers: www.romanianwriters.ro

Observator Cultural: www.observatorcultural.ro (Romanian only)

The Observer Translation Project: www.translations.observatorcultural.ro

Romanian Cultural Institute: www.icr.ro

Romanian Cultural Institute New York: www.icrny.org

Terorism de Cititoare: www.terorista.ro (Romanian only)

The National Book Centre: www.cennac.ro/en

RUSSIA

Ars Baltica: www.ars-baltica.net

Culture of Russia: www.russianculture.ru

О чем говорят: www.resheto.ru/speaking (Russian only)

Russian journal and magazine portal: www.magazines.russ.ru (Russian only)

Victor Pelevin's website: www.pelevin.nov.ru (Russian only)

SERBIA

B92: www.b92.net/kultura/knjige/vesti.php (Serbian only)

David Albahari's website: www.davidalbahari.com

Knjizara: www.knjizara.com (Serbian only)

Project Rastko: www.rastko.rs

Serbian Unity Congress literature page: www.serbianunity.net/culture/literature

SLOVAKIA
[ALL SITES SLOVAK ONLY EXCEPT AS LISTED]

Amnezia: www.amnezia.sk

Archa: www.archa.muaddib.info/index/tvorba.php?sekcia=knihy

Beo.sk: www.beo.sk/recenzie

Center for Information on Literature: www.litcentrum.sk (English, French, German, Russian)

Slovak Literary Review: www.litcentrum.sk/45410 (English, German, Italian, French)

Čítame: www.citame.sk

Euforion: www.literatura.euforion.sk

Izurnal: www.izurnal.sk

Knihy a spoločnosť: www.fan.sk/kas

Laco Remeň: www.remen.blog.sme.sk

Miro Veselý's blog: www.vesely.blog.sme.sk/r/1213/Recenzie-knih.html

Slovak Review: www.slovakreview.sav.sk

Stránka pre knihomilov: www.aladin.elf.stuba.sk/~kustvan

SLOVENIA

Airbeletrina: www.airbeletrina.si (Slovene only)

Center for Slovenian Literature: www.ljudmila.org/litcenter

Association of Slovenian Writers: www.drustvo-dsp.si (Slovene only)

KUD Logos: www.kud-logos.si (Slovene only)

Locutio: www.locutio.si (Slovene only)

Nova Beseda: www.bos.zrc-sazu.si/nova_beseda.html

Studies in Slovenian Literature: www.lit.ijs.si/literat.html

Trubarjev sklad (Support for publishers of Slovenian literature in translation): www.drustvo-dsp.si/si/drustvo_slovenskih_pisateljev/dejavnosti/567/detail.html

Ventilator besed: www.ventilatorbesed.com

SPAIN

CASTILIAN [ALL SITES CASTILIAN ONLY]

Barcarola, Revista de Creación Literaria: www.barcaroladigital.com

Delibros, La Revista del Libro: www.delibros.com

El Ojo Fisgón: elojofisgon.blogspot.com

Eñe, Revista Para Leer: www.revistaparaleer.com

Insula, Revista de Letras y Ciencias Humanas: www.insula.es

La Página Ediciones: www.telefonica.net/web2/lapaginaed/index.html

Leer, Revista Decana de Libros y Cultura: www.revistaleer.com

Litoral, Revista de Poesia, Arte y Pensiamento: www.edicioneslitoral.com

Moleskine Literario: notasmoleskine.blogspot.com

Quimera, Revista de Literatura: www.revistaquimera.com

CATALAN

800 years of Catalan Literature: www.cultura.gencat.net/ilc/literaturacatalana-800/index.html

Association of Catalan Language Writers: www.escriptors.cat

Blocs de Lletres (literary blog portal): www.blocsdelletres.com (Catalan only)

Catalan drama database: www.catalandrama.cat

Catalan PEN: www.pencatala.cat

Translation and Language Rights Committee: www.pencatala.cat/ctdl

Institut Ramon Llull: www.llull.cat

Lletra, Catalan Literature Online: www.lletra.net

SWITZERLAND

Art-TV literature site: www.art-tv.ch/17-0-literatur.html (German only)

Swiss Authors: www.a-d-s.ch

Bloc Notes Review on Italo-Swiss literature: www.culturactif.ch/revues/blocnotes (Italian only)

Das Literatur Café: www.literaturcafe.de (German only)

DIMENSION2, contemporary German-language literature: www.dimension2 .org (English only)

Entwurfe: www.entwuerfe.ch (German only)

Gazzetta, Prolitteris's magazine www.prolitteris.ch/set.asp?go=/wis/gaz/gaz .asp

Peter Stamm's website: www.peterstamm.ch (German only)

Pro Helvetia, the Arts Council of Switzerland: www.pro-helvetia.ch

Radio Sheherazade, online radio for Swiss literature: www.sheherazade.ch

Solothurner Literaturtage: www.literatur.ch (French, German, Italian)

UNITED KINGDOM
ENGLAND [ALL SITES ENGLISH ONLY]

Arts Council England: www.artscouncil.org.uk

Booktrust: www.booktrust.org.uk

Booktrust Translated Fiction: www.translatedfiction.org.uk

British Centre for Literary Translation: www.uea.ac.uk/bclt

Deborah Levy's website: www.deborahlevy.co.uk

English PEN: www.englishpen.org

Exiled Writers Ink: www.exiledwriters.co.uk

Literature Matters, the British Council's literary e-zine: www.britishcouncil.org/ arts-literature-literature-matters.htm

London Review of Books: www.lrb.co.uk

New Statesman: www.newstatesman.com/books

Orange Prize: www.orangeprize.co.uk

Ready Steady Book: www.readysteadybook.com

Royal Society of Literature: www.rslit.blogspot.com

Stand Magazine: www.standmagazine.org

The *Drawbridge* magazine: www.thedrawbridge.org.uk

The *Guardian*'s Books Blog: www.guardian.co.uk/books/booksblog

The *Guardian* Review: www.guardian.co.uk/theguardian/guardianreview

The *Independent* (Book Section): www.independent.co.uk/arts-entertainment/ books

The Interview Online: www.theinterviewonline.co.uk

The Man Booker Prize: www.themanbookerprize.com

The *Observer*: www.observer.guardian.co.uk

The Short Story Website: www.theshortstory.org.uk

The *Spectator* Bookclub: www.spectator.co.uk/books

The *Telegraph* (Book Section): www.telegraph.co.uk/culture/books

This Space: www.this-space.blogspot.com

Times Literary Supplement: entertainment.timesonline.co.uk/tol/arts_and_entertainment/the_tls

SCOTLAND [ALL SITES ENGLISH ONLY]

Alasdair Gray's website: www.alasdairgray.co.uk

Books from Scotland: www.booksfromscotland.com

The Scottish Review of Books: www.booksfromscotland.com/Books/Scottish-Review-of-Books

Chapman magazine and publisher: www.chapman-pub.co.uk

Edinburgh Review: www.edinburghreview.org.uk

Lallans, Journal of Scots Arts and Letters: www.lallans.co.uk

Markings: www.markings.org.uk

Product: www.productmagazine.co.uk

Textualities: www.textualities.net

The Bottle Imp: www.thebottleimp.org.uk

The Dark Horse, The Scottish-American Poetry Magazine: www.project.star.ac.uk/darkhorse.html

The Ranfurly Review: www.ranfurly-review.co.uk

Variant: www.variant.org.uk

WALES

A470: www.academi.org/a470_e

Academi: www.academi.org

Books from Wales: www.gwales.com

Cambria: www.cambriamagazine.com

Envoi: www.cinnamonpress.com/envoi

Library of Wales classics series: www.libraryofwales.org

National Library of Wales: www.llgc.org.uk

National Writers' Centre for Wales: www.tynewydd.org

New Welsh Review: www.newwelshreview.com

Penny Simpson's website: www.pennysimpson.com

Planet arts quarterly: www.planetmagazine.org.uk

Taliesin (Welsh-language literary periodical): www.academi.org/academi-publications/taliesin

Welsh Book Council: www.cllc.org.uk

Welsh Literature Exchange: www.walesliterature.org

Acknowledgments

The publication of this first volume of the *Best European Fiction* series was made possible by primary support from Arts Council England, with generous additional support from the following cultural agencies and embassies:

Books from Lithuania

Cultural Services of the French Embassy

Cyngor Llyfrau Cymru—Welsh Books Council

DGLB—General Directorate for Books and Libraries / Portugal

Embassy of the Principality of Liechtenstein, Washington, D.C.

Embassy of the Republic of Macedonia in Washington, D.C.

Embassy of Spain in Washington, D.C.

Estonian Literature Centre

FILI—Finnish Literature Exchange

Hungarian Book Foundation

Icelandic Literature Fund

Institut Ramon Llull, Catalan Language and Culture

Latvian Literature Centre

Literárne informaäné centrum (The Center for Information on Literature)
Bratislava, Slovakia

NORLA (Norwegian Literature Abroad)

Pro Helvetia, Swiss Arts Council

Romanian Cultural Institute

Royal Netherlands Embassy in Washington, D.C.

Vlaams Fonds voor de Letteren (The Flemish
Literature Fund—www.fondsvoordeletteren.be)

Dalkey Archive Press would like to thank the following individuals for their kind assistance in assembling this anthology:

MITJA ČANDER

NATAŠA DUROVICOVÁ

ERIC GIRAUD

RASMUS GRAFF

MIKHAIL IOSSEL

ELIZABETH KOSTOVA

MAURICE LEE

KELLY LENOX

ANTONIA LLOYD-JONES

NIKOLA MADZIROV

BENJAMIN PALOFF

RICHARD POWERS

ROMAN SIMIC

MÄRT VÄLJATAGA

TIM WILKINSON

Rights and Permissions

Alasdair Gray: "The Ballad of Ann Bonny" © 2009 by Alasdair Gray.

George Konrád: "Jeremiah's Terrible Tale" © 2009 by George Konrád. Translation © 2009 by Ivan Sanders.

Peter Krištúfek: excerpt from *Šepkár* (The Prompter) © 2008 by Peter Krištúfek. Translation © 2009 by Heather Trebatická.

Deborah Levy: excerpt from *Swimming Home* © 2009 by Deborah Levy.

valter hugo mãe: "dona malva and senhor josé ferreiro" © 2009 by valter hugo mãe. Translation © 2009 by Kerri A. Pierce.

Cosmin Manolache: "Three Hundred Cups" © 2009 by Cosmin Manolache. Translation © 2009 by Alistair Ian Blythe.

Christine Montalbetti: "Hotel Komaba Eminence (with Haruki Murakami)," excerpt from *Petits déjeuners avec quelques écrivains célèbres* © 2008 by P.O.L. éditeur. Translation © 2009 by Ursula Meany Scott.

Giulio Mozzi: "Carlo Doesn't Know How to Read" © 2008 by Giulio Mozzi. Translation © 2009 by Elizabeth Harris.

Mathias Ospelt: "Deep in the Snow" © 2004 by Mathias Ospelt. Translation © 2009 by Sevinc Turkkan.

Victor Pelevin: "Friedmann Space" © 2009 by Victor Pelevin. Translation © 2009 by Anastasia Lakhtikova.

Giedra Radvilavičiūtė: "The Allure of the Text" © 2009 by Giedra Radvilavičiūtė. Translation © 2009 by Darius James Ross.

Julián Ríos: "Revelation on the Boulevard of Crime," excerpt from *Puente de Alma* © 2009 by Julián Ríos. Translation © 2009 by Kerri A. Pierce.

Penny Simpson: "Indigo's Mermaid" © 2009 by Penny Simpson.

Goce Smilevski: "Fourteen Little Gustavs," excerpt from *Sestrata na Zigmund Frojd* (Sigmund Freud's Sister) © 2009 by Goce Smilevski. Translation © 2009 by Ana Lucic.

Peter Stamm: "Ice Moon" © 2009 by Peter Stamm. Translation © 2009 by Dustin Lovett.

Igor Štiks: "At the Sarajevo Market," excerpt from *Elijahova stolica* (Elijah's Chair) © 2006 by Igor Štiks. Translation © 2009 by Andrew Wachtel.

Peter Terrin: excerpt from "The Murderer," from *De Bijeneters* © 2006 by De Arbeiderspers. Translation © 2009 by Kerri A. Pierce.

Jean-Philippe Toussaint: Original French text © 2006 by Les Éditions de Minuit. Published by permission of Georges Borchardt, Inc., on behalf of Les Éditions de Minuit. Translation © 2007 by Thangam Ravindranathan and Timothy Bewes.

⬓ SELECTED DALKEY ARCHIVE PAPERBACKS

For a full list of publications, visit: www.dalkeyarchive.com

SELECTED DALKEY ARCHIVE PAPERBACKS ▣

For a full list of publications, visit: www.dalkeyarchive.com

◳ SELECTED DALKEY ARCHIVE PAPERBACKS

For a full list of publications, visit: www.dalkeyarchive.com

SELECTED DALKEY ARCHIVE PAPERBACKS

For a full list of publications, visit: www.dalkeyarchive.com

▣ SELECTED DALKEY ARCHIVE PAPERBACKS

JAN X X 2010 .